KISS ME, COWBOY

Books by Diana Palmer

CHRISTMAS WITH MY COWBOY
The Snow Man*

MARRYING MY COWBOY
The Rancher's Wedding*

CHRISTMAS KISSES WITH MY COWBOY
Mistletoe Cowboy*

LONE WOLF
COLORADO COWBOY*

*(Part of the continuing series by Diana Palmer,
COLORADO COUNTRY)

AMELIA
(available as an e-book)

Published by Kensington Publishing Corp.

KISS ME, COWBOY

DIANA PALMER

ZEBRA BOOKS
KENSINGTON PUBLISHING CORP.
www.kensingtonbooks.com

ZEBRA BOOKS are published by

Kensington Publishing Corp.
119 West 40th Street
New York, NY 10018

The Rancher's Wedding originally appeared in MARRYING MY COWBOY, published by Zebra Books in April 2019.
Colorado Cowboy originally appeared in LONE WOLF, published by Zebra Books in May 2021.

First Printing: April 2022
ISBN-13: 978-1-4201-5557-0
ISBN-13: 978-1-4201-5558-7 (eBook)

10 9 8 7 6 5 4 3 2 1

Printed in the United States of America

Contents

The Rancher's Wedding

To my friend Tara Gavin,
who has been with me through many adventures.
And to her lovely daughters,
Emma Grace and Mary Margaret,
who seem like part of my family, too.

Dear Reader:

I started this story with little more than the opening scene, which is how many of my stories begin. I see something in my mind, a tableau of two characters, and the book builds from there. In this case, I saw a poor, thin, straggly girl standing in the rain alone with a placard. There was a ranch nearby. That was all I saw. The rest developed from that one little thing.

Writing has always fascinated me. I sit down at the computer and I never know what's going to appear on the page. It is a magical process that never loses its mystery or its delight. Every story I craft is like the first one I ever wrote, and I enjoy them all.

I am so happy to be working with Tara, my Kensington editor, once more. I love writing about Colorado, and I feel privileged to be included in these anthologies with such talented other writers. I hope you enjoy JL and Cassie's story. I truly adore these characters.

Love,
Diana Palmer

Chapter One

Cassie Reed wondered why none of the other protesters had shown up at this ranch, where they were supposed to be picketing. At the restaurant where she was a waitress, one of the customers who flirted with her had told her horror stories about this place.

This rancher had three big chicken houses, the cowboy said, and he kept lights on all night so that the poor chickens would be forced to lay over and over again, without rest. It was just sad, he said. So he and some of the other men who worked on ranches near Benton, Colorado, were going to form a picket line and show Big Jack Denton that he couldn't get away with animal cruelty in this small community.

Cassie, who'd recently moved to Benton from a house north of Atlanta, on a huge lake, was shocked that such a thing would be tolerated. Couldn't the cowboy just call the local animal control people? He'd replied that they didn't have one. There was a county shelter, but it was hard to get people to go against Big Jack, who had a reputation locally for his hot temper. So if they picketed, maybe some newspaper or television station would come and do a story and put him out of business. The thought of newspaper coverage gave her pause, but after all, this was Colorado. Neither Cassie nor her father were known here. That was a blessing, after the tragedy they'd sustained.

Her customer, whose name was Cary, said that she could join them, if she liked; they were protesting on Saturday morning. She'd agreed that she'd love to help. Her father had been skeptical, but she'd convinced him to drop her off at the entrance to the ranch. There would be lots of people, she assured him, and she'd phone him when he needed to come and get her. He was off on Saturday from his job at the local farm supply store, where he sold heavy equipment like harvesters and irrigation equipment. He'd gotten the job through an acquaintance. He couldn't go on living in New York City after the scandal. He wanted a change. He'd lost his wife, Cassie's mother, as well as a fabulous, well-paying job. The scandal had cost him. The stigma was so great that he and his daughter had moved across the country in the hope that they wouldn't be hounded by reporters anymore.

His full name was Lanier Roger Reed, but a lot of people would recognize that first name, with the story so fresh. So he used his middle name instead, hoping that in a small town like Benton, he would go unnoticed.

Colorado seemed like a nice place, and her father got along well with Bill Clay, the man who owned the agricultural equipment business. Cassie and her father had found a house and she'd lucked out finding an open job at the town's only restaurant, the Gray Dove, waitressing. It wasn't her true profession, but she had to take what she could get for the time being.

So here she was, several weeks after starting her new job, and she wondered if she'd left her mind back in Georgia. It was insane to be standing out here all alone in the driving rain. Because it was raining. Not only raining, sleeting. Her father had left her reluctantly. She had a coat, but it was better suited for Georgia's warmer climate, not freezing Colorado weather. Winter here was harsher than she'd expected, and her light coat wasn't doing much good. Her fingers were freezing as she carried the homemade sign that read CHICKENS SHOULDN'T BE MISTREATED! Her feet were freezing, too. What had seemed like a good idea in the warm restaurant was looking like foolhardiness in the face of icy winter.

She shivered. Surely the other picketers would eventually show up! Nobody was anywhere around. There wasn't even any traffic on this back road. There was a sign that read DENTON BAR D RANCH, and an odd-looking symbol that was probably his registered cattle brand. No cowboys were in sight, either. Maybe they were gathering eggs in those warm chicken houses.

She paced and marched some more, unaware of a security camera that was recording her every move.

Minutes later, a big burgundy luxury SUV pulled up at the gate and the engine died. The door opened.

A big man in denim and a shepherd's coat with a black Stetson slanted over one eye and big boots peering out from under thick denim jeans stood looking at her incredulously.

"Do you . . . work here?" she asked, her teeth chattering as she shivered.

"Sort of. What are you doing?" he asked in a deep, amused voice.

"Picketing! The man . . . who owns this place . . . oppresses poor chickens!"

He blinked. "Chickens?"

"In his chicken houses," she explained. She pulled her

useless coat closer. She didn't even have a cap on her long reddish-gold hair. Her blue eyes met his shaded ones. She wondered idly what color his eyes were, because they weren't visible under the brim of his hat. "He tortures chickens," she continued. "He keeps the lights on all the time so the poor creatures will lay eggs! It's an abomination!"

He pursed sensuous lips and cocked his head at her. "Chicken houses," he said, nodding.

"That's right."

"Who sent you?"

She blinked. "Nobody sent me. This cowboy in the restaurant where I work said a whole group was coming to picket and he invited me, too. He's nice. His name is Cary."

"Cary." Now he looked very amused. "Tall guy, black hair, scar on his lip . . . ?"

"Well, yes," she said.

He chuckled. "He's my cousin. I gave him the scar on his lip."

Her eyebrows raised. "Your cousin?"

"Yes. And he's known for practical jokes. Although this one is low, even for him," he added, studying her. "Come with me. You'll freeze to death in this weather." He looked around. "You didn't drive here?"

"My dad brought me. Can I see the chicken houses, if I go with you?" she asked, trying to sound belligerent.

He smiled. "Sure. Come on."

She put her sign in the back seat—the letters on it were faded because it was cardboard. She got in beside the man and automatically fastened her seat belt. It was a nice vehicle. Big and fancy, with heated seats and powered windows and a CD player built into the dash.

"This is great," she remarked.

"It's functional," he replied. He wheeled the vehicle

around and headed it down the ranch road. "You got a name?" he asked.

"Oh. I'm Cassie," she said. "Cassie Reed." She studied him. He had a handsome face, if a little rugged. Sensuous mouth. Long nose. Square jaw. "Who are you?"

"You can call me JL," he offered.

"This is a big place," she remarked as he sped down the road.

"Thousands of acres," he agreed. "Plus a lot of leased government land for grazing. It takes a lot of cowboys to keep it going."

"Does Cary work for you?"

He laughed. "He does his best not to work at all," he said. "Mostly he goofs off and lies to people."

"Lies to people?"

He slowed as they approached a sprawling brick house sitting in the middle of other widely spaced buildings, including a barn, a stable, a silo, and a metal equipment shed far bigger than the house Cassie and her father lived in.

She looked around, frowning. "Where are the chicken houses?" she asked, surprised.

He chuckled as he pulled up the drive toward the house. "I don't keep chickens," he said. "I run purebred Black Angus cattle."

"But Cary said—" she began.

"Cary was pulling your leg," he assured her.

"How do you know that?"

"Because this is my ranch," he replied. "I'm JL Denton."

She ground her teeth together. She was embarrassed. "Why?" she asked miserably, pushing back a scrap of drenched red hair. "Why would he do that to me?"

"Cary likes a practical joke," he said. He was recalling another of his cousin's jokes, even less funny than this one was. Cary would spill his guts for enough drinks, and an unscrupulous woman had plied him with alcohol to find out enough about JL to come on to him in a big way.

JL had thought he'd found the perfect woman. She seemed to be exactly like him in attitude and politics, likes and dislikes, everything. She had taken him almost to the brink of marriage, in fact, until he heard what she'd said to someone on her cell phone when she hadn't known his cousin Cary was listening.

Cary was heartbroken to tell him about it. He said she was telling a friend that she'd found this reclusive rich rancher, and he was dumb enough to accept her pretense as fact. She'd learned enough about him to mirror his thoughts, and now he was going to marry her and she'd have everything she wanted. She wouldn't stay on this dumpy ranch for long, she added; once the ceremony was over she'd go out to Beverly Hills and get a nice apartment in some fancy building and shop, shop, shop.

It had seemed to surprise her, Cary added, when she turned around and found him standing right behind her. She'd stammered an excuse, and begged him not to tell JL. He'd refused. It was a rotten, low-down, dirty thing to do, he'd said indignantly. And he'd marched right back to JL's ranch to tell him all about it.

JL had been livid. She'd come home that night and he'd met her at the door with her things neatly packed by his housekeeper into two suitcases. He'd asked for the engagement ring back and told her that he wanted nothing else to do with her.

She'd stared at him blankly, as if she feared for his sanity. Why was he doing this, she asked.

Because he knew what sort of woman she was, and Cary had told him what he'd overheard her saying on her cell phone.

She'd countered that she knew what he thought of her family, and she should have broken the engagement when he made that remark about her father.

He couldn't remember saying anything about her father, whom he'd met and instantly disliked, but he'd passed over it. He never wanted to see her again, he added. Cary had also mentioned her opinion of him as a lover, which put his pride in the dirt. He didn't tell her about that. It still hurt too much.

She wanted to talk it out, but he knew he'd cave in and take her back, and she'd stab him in the back. He'd closed the door in her face and she'd left. He hadn't heard anything else from her. Cary had mentioned that he heard she'd gone to Europe to take a job at some winery as a receptionist. JL hadn't paid that remark much attention. It didn't occur to him to wonder how Cary knew it.

The whole experience had warped him. He'd have staked his life on her honesty, but she'd sold him out. He'd never trust another woman. He'd had three months of absolute bliss until Cary told him the truth about his perfect fiancée. Now he was distraught. He drank too much, brooded too much. He'd let the ranch slide, endangering his livelihood. He didn't blame Cary, exactly, but he associated the man with his misfortune, and it was painful to have him around.

And here sat a victim of his cousin's warped sense of humor. She looked absolutely crushed.

"Don't take it so hard," he said. "Cary can fool most people when he tries." He glanced at her as they approached the huge, one-story brick ranch house. "Why did you think I kept chickens on a ranch?"

"I'm from Atlanta," she said, and then flushed because she hadn't wanted to admit that. "Well, north of us a lot of people have chicken houses. I'd heard stories about how they were kept, but Cary said . . ." She stopped, swallowed. "I guess Cary knew about them somehow. I'm sorry I picketed you," she added miserably.

He was surprised at how much he liked her. She was vulnerable in a way that most women today weren't, especially in his circle of acquaintances. She had a sensitivity that was rare. "What do you do?"

"I'm a waitress at the Gray Dove restaurant in Benton. Cary comes in there a lot," she added reluctantly.

A waitress. Well, he hadn't expected a debutante, he thought sarcastically. "Cary runs his mouth too much," he murmured.

"Yes, he does," she agreed.

"That coat is too thin for a Colorado winter," he remarked.

She winced. "I guess so. We don't get a lot of really cold temperatures in Atlanta," she added.

He chuckled. "I wouldn't expect it to be that cold in the Deep South," he agreed. He liked her accent. It was a soft, sweet drawl.

"Yes, well, we don't get much snow, either, only very rarely. And then the whole city shuts down," she added with a soft laugh.

He grinned. "I can imagine. We get used to snow because we have so much of it."

He pulled up in front of the ranch house. "Come on in," he said as he swung down out of the SUV.

She hesitated. She'd never gone to a man's house or apartment in her life. Her father and mother had sheltered her. She was an only child and she'd had a lot of health problems through her youth. She'd dated very rarely, and mostly double dates with her best friend, Ellen. She grimaced. She missed Ellen.

"It's all right," he assured her as he opened the door for her. "I don't bite."

She flushed. "Sorry. I'm not . . . well, I'm not used to men. Not much."

Both thick eyebrows went up over silvery eyes.

She cleared her throat. She unbuckled her seat belt and held on to the handle above the door so that she didn't fall out. It was a very tall vehicle.

"Shrimp," he mused.

She laughed self-consciously. "I'm five foot seven inches," she protested. But she had to look up, way up, to see his amused smile.

"I'm six foot two. To me, you're a shrimp," he added.

He went ahead of her to open the door. She hesitated, but just for a minute. She was really cold and her clothes were drenched.

"Bathroom's that way," he said, indicating the hallway. The floors were wood with throw rugs in Native American patterns. The furniture in the living room was cushy and comfortable. There was a huge television on one wall and a fireplace on the other. It was very modern.

"Thanks," she said belatedly when she realized she was staring around her.

"I'll see what I can scare up in the way of dry clothes."

"We're not the same size," she protested, measuring him.

He chuckled. "No, we're not. But my housekeeper's daughter left some things behind when she came to visit her mom. You're just about her size."

He walked off toward the other end of the house.

She darted into the huge bathroom and took off her

coat. She looked like a drenched chicken, she thought miserably. At least the bathroom was warm.

She heard heavy footsteps coming back, and a quick rap on the door. She opened it.

"Here." He handed her some jeans and a shirt.

"Thanks," she said.

He shrugged. "Come out when you're ready. We'll throw your wet things into the dryer."

"Okay."

She had to put the jeans and shirt over her underwear, which was damp, but she wasn't about to take it off and put it in a dryer in front of a man she didn't know. She was painfully shy.

She came out of the bathroom. He called to her from a distant room. She followed the sound of his voice to a sprawling kitchen.

"Drink coffee?" he asked.

"Oh, yes!" she agreed.

"Give me those." He held out his hand for her clothes. "I'll stick them in the dryer."

"Thanks."

He gave them a cursory look, pursed his lips amusedly at the lack of underthings, and took them to the dryer in still another room. She heard it kick off.

He came back in and poured coffee into two thick white mugs. "Cream, sugar?"

"No," she replied, seating herself at the small table against the window. Outside, cattle were milling around a feed trough. "I always drink it black and strong. It helps keep me awake when I'm working. . . ." She stopped suddenly. Waitresses didn't work at night in Benton.

He raised an eyebrow, but he didn't question the odd comment.

She sipped coffee and sighed. "This is very good."

"It's Colombian," he replied. "I'm partial to it."

"So am I."

He sipped his coffee and stared at his odd houseguest. He wondered how old she was. She had that radiant, perfect complexion that was common in young women, but she didn't look like a teenager, despite her slender figure.

She lifted both eyebrows at his obvious appraisal.

"I was wondering how old you were," he said, smiling.

"Oh. I'm twenty-four."

He cocked his head. "You look younger."

She smiled. Her blue eyes almost radiated warmth. "Everybody says that."

She wondered how old he was. His hair was black and thick, conventionally cut. His face was strong, with an imposing nose and chiseled mouth and high cheekbones. His skin had a faint olive tone.

He chuckled. "Sizing me up, too? I have Comanche ancestors."

"I thought Comanches lived in Texas and Oklahoma," she began.

"They do. I was born south of Fort Worth, Texas. That's where my mother was from. My folks moved back here when I was ten. The ranch was started by my great-grandfather. My grandfather and my father had some sort of blowup and Dad and Mom left when I was on the way. I never knew what happened. Dad lived on the ranch, but he didn't own it. My grandfather held the purse strings until he died, and even then, he left the ranch to me instead of my dad."

"That must have been hard on your father."

"It was. They never got along." He smiled. "I missed Texas when we came here. It's very different."

"I love Texas," she confessed. "Especially up around Dallas. There's a place called Dinosaur Valley. . . ."

"With thousands of bones," he added with a glimmer in his eyes. "Yes. I've been there. My father was trained as a paleontologist. He taught at a college in Dallas."

She caught her breath. "I'd love to study that," she said. She laughed self-consciously. "I only had two years of college," she confessed. "I minored in Spanish. We have a large Hispanic population in Georgia. I thought of teaching. But I couldn't decide, so I just took core courses."

"I majored in business," he said. "You need to know economics to run a ranch profitably." He didn't add that the ranch wasn't his main source of income. His fortune was the result of an inheritance from his grandfather that included several million dollars plus thousands of acres here near Benton, Colorado, and a thriving Black Angus purebred ranch. He'd parlayed that fortune into a much larger fortune by investing in oil stocks and buying up failing exploration companies and refineries. His inheritance plus his business sense had made him a multimillionaire.

It didn't show that he was rich. Right now, he was glad. This little violet was good company. He had a feeling that she'd have run right out the door if he'd shown up in a stretch limo wearing designer clothes and a Rolex—all of which he had.

"I've never been around ranches," she confessed, staring out the window. "We have big farms in Georgia, but not so many ranches, especially not in the Atlanta suburbs. We're very metropolitan."

"But you know about chicken farms," he teased.

She laughed self-consciously. "Well, yes. I love animals."

"So do I," he added. "We use old-timey methods around here. The livestock are treated like part of the family. They're all purebred. We breed for certain traits that they'll pass down to their progeny. We don't run beef cattle," he added when she looked perplexed.

"You don't?" she asked, surprised.

He shrugged. "Hard to kill something you raised from a baby," he said. "I'm partial to fish and chicken. I don't eat a lot of beef."

She was fascinated. It showed.

He laughed. "Not that I mind a well-cooked steak," he added. "As long as it's not one of my prize Angus."

"There are always pictures in the local cattle journal of cattle sales."

"We have a production sale here in February," he told her. "It's a big deal. We entertain a lot of out-of-state buyers. We feed them great barbecue and hope they'll spend plenty of money."

"You sell off the little cows, then?" she asked.

He chuckled at her terminology. "Yearlings, mostly," he said. "Some open heifers, some pregnant ones, a few bulls."

She was out of her depth. "It sounds very complicated."

"Only to an Eastern tenderfoot," he teased gently.

She smiled back, a little shyly, and sipped her coffee.

"I like your house," she said after a brief and vaguely uncomfortable silence. "It looks just like I'd expect a western ranch house to look."

He frowned slightly. "Never been out west?"

She shook her head. "No. Mom and Dad lived in New York and I went up to visit a lot, but I've only seen the states back in the East."

"Does your father still live there?"

"No." She sipped coffee, wincing at her blunt reply. "He came out here because he had a cousin who worked at the local equipment store," she added hurriedly. "His cousin had already moved on, but he gave him a good reference.

Daddy's worked there for about a month. Like I have, at the restaurant."

"Big-city people," he mused, studying her. "The culture shock must be extreme."

She flushed and fumbled with her coffee cup. "It is, a little, I guess. I got used to traffic noises and sirens in Atlanta. The small house Dad and I rent is close to a railroad, so that's nice at night." She laughed. "It's like home." She didn't add that she'd moved into a luxurious house on the lake north of Atlanta, to get away from those traffic noises. She missed the lake.

"What did you do in Atlanta? Another waitressing job?"

She couldn't tell him that. It might lead to embarrassing questions about why she'd left such a lucrative position to get a minimum wage job out in Colorado. "I did feature stories for a newspaper," she said finally. It wasn't so far from the truth. She'd started out as a newspaper reporter after college, working her way up to news editor before her father introduced her to some people in New York. She'd ended up doing screenplays, a much more profitable career. Gone now. It was gone, like the life she'd had.

He wondered why she looked so stricken. "Newspaper jobs must be thin on the ground these days," he remarked. "Almost everything is digital now. I get my news fix on the Internet."

She smiled. "So do I. But the local paper is very nice. I like the features about old-fashioned ranch work, and the recipe page."

He smiled back. "Do you cook?"

"Oh, yes," she replied. "I'm partial to French cuisine, because of the sauces, but I like Tex-Mex, too. Anything spicy." She sighed. "I used to have a gourmet herb patch that I babied all year. I had raised beds, so I had herbs at

Christmas to add to my recipes." Her face was sad as she recalled the past. Those had been good days, when her mother was still alive. Before the fame and then the tragedy that had taken her mother's life and sent Cassie and her father running far away from the notoriety.

"I have an herb patch of my own, but it's in a glassed greenhouse," he remarked. "Hard to keep little things alive out here in the winter. It can be brutal in the mountains."

"I've heard that," she replied. "They said one year you had a foot of snow."

He chuckled. "Most years we have a foot of snow," he mused. "Sometimes six feet."

She gasped. "But how do you drive in that?"

"You don't," he said. "Not until the snowplows come, at least. On the ranch, we have heavy equipment that we can use to clear a path to the road." He shook his head. "It's hard on the cattle. It's a lot of work to keep them alive. We have lean-tos in the pastures and a big barn and corrals where we can bring the pregnant cows and heifers up to get out of the worst of the weather."

She liked that. She smiled. "I never thought of ranchers being kind to cattle," she said. "I mean, we hear about slaughterhouses and—"

"We don't eat purebreds," he interrupted, and his eyes twinkled. "Too expensive."

She laughed. "I guess so." She searched his face. "Do you have pets?"

He sighed. "Too many," he replied. "We have cattle dogs—border collies—that help with roundup. They're not really pets, but I keep a couple of Siberian huskies and we have cats in the barn. They keep the rodent population down."

"The cats, you mean?"

He grinned. "The huskies, mostly," he corrected. "Best

mousers on the place. The cats, I'm told, are jealous of that ability."

"You talk to cats," she teased.

"All the time. I talk to myself, mostly," he added with a chuckle. "Bad habit."

"Only if you answer yourself," she replied.

He sighed and leaned back in the chair with his coffee cup. "I was engaged," he said after a minute. "Until someone overheard her bragging to her friends about how she'd marry me and then go live in a city and get away from this run-down wreck of a ranch."

She winced. "I'm so sorry," she said. "That must have hurt your pride."

He was surprised at her compassion. He was also suspicious. Marge had been very sympathetic at first, too, but it was all an act. A means to an end. He was warier now than he'd been before.

"It is a little run-down, I guess," he conceded after a minute. He grimaced. "I've spent a lot of time drinking. Too much." He didn't add why. He also didn't add that he'd let the ranch and the business slide while he got over the tragedies in his life that had dumped him in Marge's lap. Marge had been a newer, worse tragedy, if that was even possible. He was usually a better judge of character, but he'd been lonely and Marge had played him. That was on Cary, whose sense of mischief was getting old. He'd introduced JL to Marge, and the mutual attraction had been immediate. He'd missed Marge. It took a lot of getting over, and not only because she'd left him.

"My dad drank for a while," she said unexpectedly, staring into her coffee cup. "It was hard to convince him to stop."

He frowned. "Why did he drink?" he asked bluntly.

She sighed. "My mother died," she said, wrapping up an anguished time into three quiet words.

"I see. Had they been married long?"

"Thirty years," she replied. "They'd given up hope that they'd have kids when I came along," she added with a sad smile. "I wasn't born until five years after they married."

"Marriage." He made a face. "Not a future I've ever seen for myself." And it hadn't been, until Marge caught him in a weak moment. As a rule, women came and went in his life. For years, they'd been permissible hors d'oeuvres. Now, after Marge, he'd lost interest. He never wanted another painful experience like the one he'd had with her.

"Don't you like children?" she asked innocently.

His face closed up. There was something dark and disturbing in his expression for a few seconds. He got up. "If you're ready, I'll run you into town."

"Oh, but, I can call my father," she began, flushing. "I've been too much trouble already."

"Not so much." He picked up her empty cup and put it, with his, into the sink. He picked up his keys. "Let's go."

She followed him out to the SUV. Only then did she notice that the ranch house needed a coat of paint and repairs on the front walk. The fences looked as if they'd once been white, but the paint was peeling off them now. The rain seemed to emphasize the neglect around her. She wondered why he hadn't made repairs, and decided that he probably didn't have the money. The SUV he drove was nice, but it wasn't the newest model and he was probably making payments on it. Certainly, his clothes—a shirt with a frayed collar and jeans that were torn where they draped over scuffed, worn cowboy boots—didn't reflect any great wealth.

"Your ranch is nice," she said as they drove away. She

wondered once again how a poor rancher could afford to run purebred livestock. Perhaps he had a partner somewhere who contributed money.

"It keeps me running," he said with an absent smile.

They rode in a companionable silence. Cassie was surprised at the comfort she felt, sitting beside him. It was an odd thing to feel. He was handsome, in his way, and she liked his deep, velvety voice. But he wasn't the sort of man she was used to at all. Her male friends back east, and there had never been a serious one, were obsessed with the gym and proper diet and they preferred an evening at the theater or the symphony orchestra. None of them would have considered life on a cattle ranch.

"Where?" he asked when they reached Benton.

She caught her breath. "Sorry, I was lost in thought. It's on Third Street, just off Main, about a block from the Quick Stop."

He chuckled. "The old Barrett place," he replied. "Yes, I know it. Jed Barrett lived there all his life. When he died, there was no family, so the house went on the market to pay his funeral expenses. A local businessman owns it. He didn't want to sell it because of the property it sits on, so he rented it out while he decided what to put on the acreage."

"You mean, like a ranch?"

"I mean, like a subdivision," he mused. "Or apartment houses."

"Oh, dear," she said with a long sigh. "I loved it because it was so remote," she confessed. "Lots of room to walk and think, and there's a little creek out back. . . ."

He grimaced. He liked lonely places to walk, too. "It will take him some time to work that out," he added comfortingly. "He's overseas right now, taking care of some business in Australia. He owns a huge cattle station there."

"He's Australian?" she asked, surprised.

He chuckled. "His father was. Rance was born here in Colorado, but his father had properties all over Australia and South America. Rance has managers for all of them, but he likes the hands-on approach. He says it keeps his employees on their toes if he walks in unexpectedly from time to time."

"I see," she replied.

"He's a nice enough guy," he said easily. "A little abrasive, but it's understandable. He's had some issues over the years." He glanced at her. "You didn't meet him, when you rented the house?"

"Dad did," she said. "I was at work. We'd been living in the local motel." She said that because there was only one motel in Benton. It was nice enough, but paying for two rooms indefinitely had threatened to wipe out their combined savings. Her father had heard about the place at work and called Rance Barkley at just the right time to obtain it as a rental.

"Expensive, living in motels," he remarked.

She nodded. "Very."

"Why Benton?" he asked curiously as he pulled onto her street.

"Because Dad's cousin lived here," she sighed. "It seemed as good a place as any to start over."

"I guess the city got too much for you," he teased.

She smiled back. "Yes. It did. For both of us. Honestly, we wanted to live someplace where we didn't have so many memories of my mother. Besides, Benton is nice."

"Nice, if you don't like nightlife," he chuckled. "They roll up the sidewalks every night at six sharp."

"That doesn't bother me," she replied. "I like the peace

and quiet." She didn't add that she'd gotten used to it on the lake.

He laughed. "Good thing. We don't have much excitement around here."

"That suits me very well."

He pulled into the long driveway and pulled up next to an old pickup truck sitting in front of the little white frame house. The property was surrounded by pastureland that ran to the horizon in the shadow of the mountains.

"I always liked this place," he remarked.

"It's very pretty," she agreed. She grimaced. "Look, I'm sorry about the picket sign. . . ."

"I'll tear a strip off Cary and we'll be even. Don't worry about it."

"Thanks. And thanks for the coffee and the ride." She opened the door and jumped down, pausing to get her wet, faded sign off the floorboard in the back seat.

"Stay warm," he said.

She smiled. "Drive safely," she replied, and closed the passenger door before she saw his bemused expression.

He waved and drove off.

She propped her sign against the wall and opened the door.

Her father, tall and thin and graying, looked up from the sofa, where he was reading a book. "Back so soon?"

She grimaced. "He doesn't have a single chicken house," she said with a long sigh.

His eyebrows rose. "Then why were you picketing him?"

"It's a long story," she replied, shedding her wet coat. She hung it up and plopped down into the easy chair across from the sofa. "He owns this run-down ranch," she began.

Chapter Two

"A run-down ranch, an owner who drinks, and purebred cattle?" he mused. "I think he was having you on, Cassie," he chuckled. "A poor man can't afford to run purebreds. They cost thousands of dollars. A good herd bull alone sometimes goes for half a million."

"Oh. I see. Well, he was nice about it, anyway. He gave me coffee and dried my jeans and . . . Oh, my gosh, my clothes are still there!" she exclaimed. "I forgot all about them!"

He was watching her with wide, stunned eyes.

"These clothes belonged to his housekeeper's daughter," she explained. "He handed them to me in the bathroom. I put them on and he put my things in the dryer. My outer things," she added. "I wasn't about to take off my underthings in a strange man's house."

He smiled gently. "You're so like your mother," he said with a sad smile. "She was straitlaced, too, very Victorian in her attitudes. I guess we didn't do you any favors, giving you such an old-fashioned upbringing when the rest of the world is so permissive."

"I like me just the way I am, thanks," she laughed. "I

like being out of step with the world. I stay healthier, for one thing," she added, tongue-in-cheek.

He sighed. "Yes, but you don't date anybody."

"I dated Jackson Hill," she pointed out.

"Sweetheart, Jackson Hill was gay," he reminded her.

"He was great company, too," she replied, smiling reminiscently. "His parents were so conventional, and he loved them so much, that he didn't want them to know. We went out together so we could both hide. I didn't want a loose relationship with some career-minded man, and he didn't want notoriety. We suited each other." She sighed. "I miss him. He was so much fun!"

He nodded. "Well, I guess we settle for what we can get in life. I would have liked grandchildren, though," he added with a smile.

She had a sudden picture of the reclusive rancher with a baby in his arms and swatted it away. "Maybe someday," she said. "Right now, I'm busy learning how to balance a plateful of food on a tray without dropping it while I set up the tripod."

He laughed out loud. "And I'm busy learning how to persuade ranchers to buy equipment they may not know they need."

"I daresay we'll both do well, once we learn the ropes," she replied.

He sighed. "I keep hoping. I miss my crew."

She knew it was hard for him. To be such a celebrity, with his own television show, loved by millions. And with one unfounded accusation by a vengeful woman, it was all gone and he was in hiding. The damage had been far-reaching. His attorneys had done their best, but social media had destroyed him. It was suggested that if he got away for a few months, things might calm down and they could reassess his position. The fact that he was innocent seemed to count for nothing. The woman who accused him, however, now had her own television show—his former one—and she was raking in cash and ratings, thanks to several special interest groups that had funded her. His attorneys knew this and they'd hired one of the best investigators in the business to do some discreet snooping. There was still hope.

"I miss my job, too, although it wasn't a patch on yours," she said with a wistful sigh. "The series is still on TV, and there were some terrific other writers on staff. But I liked to interject humor and they didn't."

"Maybe one day, we can both go back to what we love," he replied sadly. "But for the time being, we're in camouflage, pretending to be normal middle-class Americans. That's not a bad thing, either," he added. "You can get too addicted to five-star restaurants and expensive quarters. You can lose sight of the things that are really important."

"Yes, like no reporters trying to knock down the doors, hiding in the trees, parachuting onto the roof . . ."

He chuckled. "It wasn't quite that bad, although I couldn't eat out or be seen in public. I was too recognizable." He shook his head. "Growing a beard and wearing glasses does seem to have put them off, for the time being."

"Yes. You look quite judicial," she teased.

He smiled. "At least you didn't have to modify your looks. Writers aren't quite as noticeable as television personalities with weekly shows."

"That was my good luck," she agreed. She stretched. "I'm using muscles I didn't even know I had. I got lazy. I spent my life at a keyboard, living in a fantasy world. I'm looking at the world in a totally new way."

"So am I," he said. He drew in a long breath. "And I

hope we're far enough away that they won't come looking for us here."

"Who would?" she mused. "Honestly, working in equipment sales has to be the last place reporters would expect to find you!"

"We can hope," he said. He shook his head and his face tautened. "That woman," he bit off. "Stabbed in the back by my own executive producer, accused of sexual harassment and assault, the media flooded with lies and opinions and gossip. Journalism in this country has sunk to a whole new low."

"The major media outlets are owned by a handful of people with agendas," she said simply.

"Well, there's nothing we can do about that," he told her. "Millionaires make policy, and corporations own everything of worth. It will take a disaster of some kind to provide a reset. And I hope I'm long gone when it happens."

"You're practically immortal," she teased. "And we don't need a reset. We just need people to demand objective reporting. If enough do, things will change."

"Optimist." Her father put down his book. "Speaking of news, which we never watched anyway until my sudden notoriety, I suppose we should buy a television set."

"What for?" she asked. "We hardly watched TV even when we had one."

"I was thinking about all the movies we had on the Cloud," he replied.

"Now, that, I wouldn't mind at all!" she agreed, laughing. "How about we buy one tomorrow? Something cheap."

"A used gaming system would be nice, too, so you can play those games you've also got on the Cloud," he teased. Her gaming habit amused him. She loved console games on XBox One and had several that were her hobby.

"I miss my games," she confessed. She frowned. "But I'd better play off the Internet for now. A few people knew my gamer tag," she added. "Best not to advertise that I'm still around."

He nodded solemnly. "I'll keep on my attorneys," he said. "If their investigator turns up something on Trudy Blaise, things may start to look up."

"They may. But meantime, I have a nice job and I'm happy to get a check every two weeks," she said. "We could have landed in a worse place."

"Yes, we could." He frowned as she sneezed. "You need to push your friend Cary into a thorny bush. You're sneezing. It was cold and wet, and you have bad lungs. . . ."

She shook her head. "I'm fine," she said firmly. "Nothing to worry about. I've been much better with the new inhaler."

He sighed. "If you say so."

She got up, smiling. "I'll start some rolls rising, so we can have them for supper," she said. "How about *coq au vin*?"

He gave her a droll look. "How about chicken and mashed potatoes?" he countered.

She sighed. "Ah, poverty," she laughed. "I guess it will be good for our characters."

"Everybody has hard times, sweetheart," he said softly. "Everybody gets through them."

She just smiled on her way to the kitchen.

JL pulled up in front of his house and studied it with a frown. He hadn't noticed how dilapidated it was getting. Honestly, since he'd broken his engagement, things hadn't mattered much to him. Not even the ranch, which was his pride and joy.

But now it was falling apart. He'd been having a whiskey after dinner every night. Sometimes, it was two whiskeys. He hated what his life had become. He was alone and tired of his own company. His big romance had turned into a disaster. He was afraid to trust another woman, because of what his "fiancée" had done to him. The experience had turned him inside out. He was so depressed that he paid no attention to broken fences, to equipment that stopped working, to employees who pleaded for money to repair infrastructure. Now, it was all catching up with him.

He walked out to the big barn where his foreman, Isaiah Drummond, was staring under the hood of the truck they used to haul feed to the cattle in the near pastures. He had the physique of a range rider, much as JL himself did, but Drum, as most people called him, was a few years younger and had a temper that the cowboys tried to avoid. He looked up as the boss approached, his black eyes flashing in a lean, tanned face under a thick head of black hair.

"Damned thing's on the blink again," he muttered. "And the Bobcat has a flat tire."

"Horrors and wonders, the world's ending," JL drawled sarcastically.

Drum's chiseled mouth pulled down on one side. "It will, if you don't get on the ball, boss," he said curtly. "If things go downhill fast enough, you could end up with a wheat farm instead of a ranch."

JL shrugged. "Not likely. Beef's at a premium since all the flooding down in Texas last summer."

"Yes, well, growing cattle need food, and to have food, you need working equipment to plant things with."

JL sighed. "Okay, call that repairman from the equipment company and let him come out here and fix it."

Drum managed a smile. “Okay.”

“Any other little headaches . . . ?”

Drum pushed back the beat-up old black Stetson he wore. “I hear you’ve taken up chicken farming.”

JL’s eyes widened. “Huh?”

Drum grinned. “You had a picketer out front, accusing you of abusing hens.”

“Oh, that.” He smiled reminiscently. “Cary told her I had chicken houses. She was soaking wet and sneezing. Funny little thing. Red-gold hair. Blue eyes. Thin as a rail. Repressed as all hell. Works as a waitress in town. I drove her home.”

Drum waited, curious.

JL gave him a droll look. “I don’t have any inclination to let a woman back in my life. Not in the near future. Maybe never.” His face darkened. “I’ve got enough trouble as it is.”

“I can understand your viewpoint,” came the reply. “But you have to understand that some women are as mercenary as some men. They have ways of hiding it. You have to look deeper than surface things, like beauty.”

“You ever been married?”

“Never. I came close once.” Drum shook his head. “She didn’t want to live with a man who worked around cattle and smelled like fertilizer, she said.” He shrugged. “Wasn’t much of a sacrifice, at that. She couldn’t cook and she wanted a life of leisure. I told her she’d have to look for a richer man than me. So she found one.” He laughed. “I saw her once, when I took that trip to Denver to check out some cattle at auction for you. She said she wished she could go back in time and make a different choice. I guess she was paying a price for that wealth.”

"People mostly do," JL sighed. "I don't understand greed."

"Me, neither," Drum replied. "Well, I'll go call that equipment repairman and see when he can get out here."

"The chicken picketer's father works there, she said."

"That must be the new fellow." He shook his head. "Owner says he sits and reads equipment manuals all the time so he can understand what he sells." He frowned. "Odd man. New York accent, and he doesn't have the hands of a man who does any sort of physical labor. I'd have pegged him as a businessman. He seems out of place."

"Curious."

"It is. But it's not my business."

"Nor mine," JL told him. "I've been taking a look around the place. We have lots of things that need to be repaired and painted. I've been living in a blue funk, whatever that is. Time I snapped out of it and got some things done. And don't agree with me," he said suddenly when Drum opened his mouth. "I'll call a contractor first thing in the morning and get the ball rolling. Another thing, the chicken picketer left her clothes here. I put them in the dryer, but she went home wearing Bessie's daughter's jeans and shirt. I guess I'll have to make time to take them to her."

"Is she pretty—the chicken picketer?" Drum teased.

JL chuckled. "She was pretty bedraggled while she was here. Not much to look at, but a tender heart and plenty of compassion. I used to think looks were the most important thing. Now I'm convinced that a good heart's better."

"I'll take pretty, thanks," came the amused reply.

"You're welcome to all the pretty women you can find. I'm off women for life," he added. "I'm never being taken for a ride again."

"Where have I heard that before?"

"Never you mind. Get busy. I'm going to ride out to the line cabin and see how Parker's doing with the new horses."

"Why won't you let him work them here, close to the house?"

JL raised both eyebrows. "You ever heard him cuss?"

"Oh."

"I'm not having him around when visitors come to look at our new crop of cattle. He'll put everybody's back up and I'll have to sell my calves at a loss."

"We could rope him, tie him to a post, and gag him."

JL pursed his lips and chuckled. "What a thought. But, no, it's just as well to leave him where he is. If I have to call him down about his behavior, he'll quit, and he's the best man with horses I've ever had."

"I'll echo that. The man has a gift."

"It's that Crow in him," JL replied. "He said his people have a way with animals that runs all the way back through his lineage, all the way to his great-grandfather. He can gentle horses without any rough treatment. Horses love him. I mean they really love him. They follow him around the fence when he's outside."

"Imagine a guy with a talent like that," Drum said. He made a face. "And a mouth like that."

"He was in the military. He said he learned to cuss dodging bullets in Iraq." He shook his head. "I've dodged my share, but I'm not his equal in a cussing contest," he added, chuckling. "I guess we all have a few rough edges."

"His are sharper than knives. But he is good with the horses."

"Yes. Okay, you call the equipment people, I'll go talk to Parker."

"Sure thing, boss."

* * *

The line cabin was about a mile from the main ranch house, set back in the lodgepole pines, with majestic mountains making an exquisite backdrop for the long, open pasture, cross-fenced, that stretched to the horizon. The cabin was efficient, but small. With its rustic timbers, it looked like part of the landscape.

JL dismounted at the front porch and tied his horse to the rail. There was nobody around. He rapped on the door, but there was no answer. Odd, he thought. Parker was certainly here, somewhere. He wondered what was going on.

He opened the door and walked in. There was a fire in the fireplace. A hot, fresh pot of coffee sat on the counter with an empty cup by it. Wherever Parker was, he must not have expected to be gone long.

JL went back outside and looked around. "Hey, Parker!" he called.

No answer. He walked around the house and saw hoofprints headed down the road. He got back in the saddle and followed them.

He hadn't gone far when he heard a rifle shot. Heart racing, he turned his horse in the direction of the shot and urged him forward.

"Nothing to worry about, Hardy," he told the horse, patting him gently on the mane to calm him. The horse was nervous enough without loud noises. "Come on, fellow. Just a little way to go."

The horse moved forward, but not quickly. In the distance, JL caught sight of a red plaid shirt. Closer, he could tell that it was Parker by his tall, lean body and the white Stetson he wore. But he could tell better by the language that was audible even this far away. Parker was eloquent.

He rode down to the pasture. Parker had left his horse on this side of the fence. He was on the other side, standing over the carcass of a calf.

He looked up at JL with narrowed blue eyes in a face as hard as stone. "Wolf," he said angrily. He indicated the calf.

JL grimaced. The calf had been savaged, while it was still alive, from the look of it. Parker had obviously put it out of its misery.

"I wish all those damned bleeding-heart liberals living in apartments in cities could come out here and see what we have to deal with because of their blankety-blank legislation!" Parker said angrily. "In fact, I wish we could shove a few starving wolves into the apartments with them. My, my, what a change of heart the survivors would have!"

"Bad cowboy," JL said, shaking a finger at him.

Parker sighed. "Yeah, I know. I just get tired of seeing little things like this in such agony."

"Was it Two Toes?" JL asked, referring to an old and wily wolf who was known to the ranchers locally. The wolf was past his prime and couldn't find a pack that would let him join, so he went hunting for game he could catch. That meant helpless calves that wandered too far from the herd.

"I think so. Didn't really have time to count toes," Parker added, "or see his face to identify him. But he was snow white and limping and he looked like ten miles of rough road. That limp pretty much identifies him as Two Toes."

"We need to adopt him, lock him up, and feed him canned chicken," JL said whimsically. "He'd be a threat to nobody, then."

"Or find a wildlife rehabilitator who could be bribed or threatened to take him on and feed him canned chicken."

JL chuckled. "That's really not a bad idea," he said. "I'll

talk to Butch Matthews and see if I can sell him on the idea. He's always talking about wolves. He loves them."

"I don't mind them in a pack. Mostly they avoid ranches. Two Toes is a separate and individual case. You can't scare him, you can't intimidate him, he just does what he wants to and lopes off when he gets a scent of you."

"We'll be old and toothless and hungry one day."

Parker gave him a dirty look. "Well, I won't be eating poor little calves who get lost," he returned.

"If you were starving, you just might."

That earned him another nasty look.

JL sighed. "Well, I'll go back home. I'll let you know when I talk to Butch. We may have to take a few men and hunt Two Toes, in that case."

"Don't mind hunting him if he'll be leaving here," Parker replied. He pursed his lips. "I have been wondering if wolf stew tasted any good."

"You'd have to parboil that old devil for a week to get him tender, and he's too stringy to do much for your taste buds," JL pointed out.

Parker chuckled. "Point taken."

Cassie was back at work at the Gray Dove two days later. At least, she thought, she'd learned to carry a tray without dumping half the drinks on it. Her boss, Mary Dodd, had been very kind and patient. It made Cassie work even harder. So few people these days were patient at all.

"You're doing very well," Mary told her.

"Except for the coffee," Cassie said, grimacing. "I'm so sorry."

"You've only dropped a cup one time this whole week," Mary said, trying to find a bright note. "And we allow for ceramic breakage in the budget, you know." She leaned forward. "When I used to work here, years before I bought the place, I turned three plates of spaghetti on a tray into the lap of a vacationing millionaire from DC."

Cassie's lips fell open. "What did you do?" she exclaimed.

"I bawled and apologized and bawled some more."

"What did he do?" she persisted.

Mary smiled. "He married me."

Cassie chuckled. "I begin to see the light."

"He gave me the money to buy the restaurant, with the idea that I might never improve enough to be able to hold down a job in it. So I hired people who were less clumsy than I am."

"Not so much," Cassie began.

Mary patted her on the back. "You're doing fine. Really you are. Don't worry. Life is an adventure. Every day is a gift. You have to live an hour at a time, kid. It's what keeps you going."

Cassie smiled. "Thanks. I really mean that."

"You're welcome. Back to work."

"Yes, ma'am!"

It had been several days since Cassie had gone haring off to JL Denton's ranch. The rancher had been very kind to her, despite her antagonism when they first met. She still hadn't called him about getting her clothing back. She was too shy. Besides, she had plenty of other clothes. She wouldn't have to go naked.

Secretly, she wished she had the nerve to call him. There was an odd vulnerability about him. He loved animals. He had a kind heart. That was far more important to Cassie than wealth. Not that JL was rich. The peeling paint on the house and fences testified to that. If he'd had money, he'd have kept the ranch up better than he did.

But he had told her that he ran purebred cattle, which her father said only a rich rancher could afford to do. Still, he might have inherited them from a wealthy relative. Cassie always tried to make allowances for people. Most people. It was hard to make allowances for the woman who'd ruined her father's life and driven her poor mother to a desperate act after the scandal broke.

She cleaned tables and filled orders. It was getting easier as she went along. Mary had known that Cassie had never waited tables in her life. But she was getting the hang of it, and she worked hard.

That Friday, she had a familiar customer at her table. She glared at him.

Cary held both hands up. "I'm sorry," he said before she could go on the attack. "I'm really sorry. Cousin JL read me the riot act. I swear, I'll never tell another lie. Well, not to anybody he knows, at least," he added with a charming smile.

"That was a really nasty thing to do," she pointed out.

He shrugged. "Life gets boring. I like to liven things up."

She sighed. He wasn't getting it at all. She pulled out her pad. "What would you like to eat?"

"What's good?"

"The beef stew and the lemon pie."

"Fine. I'll have that, with black coffee. You off tomorrow?"

She gave him a cold, hostile look.

"No more games," he promised. "I'm not planning any more nonexistent picketing parties." He pursed his lips. The scar on the lower one was blatant. She could picture a furious JL slugging him.

"Why did your cousin slug you?" she blurted out before she thought it through.

He grimaced. "Sorry. Best not to drag up painful memories."

"I shouldn't have asked," she said quickly. "Stew and lemon pie. Be right out."

She turned to go.

"There's a bowling alley in downtown Benton," he said before she walked off. "I wondered if you might like to try it out with me. It's brand-new."

She was disconcerted. She gnawed her lower lip. She didn't quite trust him after he'd played that practical joke on her. She didn't know him, either. JL had been disparaging about him. Those things added up to a distrust she was too polite to admit. She forced a smile. "Thanks, but I promised Dad I'd help him with a project this weekend."

He just smiled, seemingly not offended at all. "No problem. Maybe I'll ask you again sometime."

She didn't reply. She went to get his order. His narrow eyes watched her go and there was a calculating expression that she couldn't see.

Nobody told her, but Cary held grudges, especially when women gave him the cold shoulder. The woman who'd messed up JL's life had started out as Cary's girl. JL thought that when she'd seen the size of his ranch, and knew he was rich, she tossed Cary out of her life and wormed her way into JL's affections. It wasn't true, but Cary had told JL all about it when he succeeded in prying Marge out of his cousin's life.

Cary had been shattered when Marge walked right over him to get to his cousin. She'd been really in love, but Cary felt that she belonged to him. They'd dated for several weeks before he introduced her to JL. He'd wanted her for keeps, but she'd gone running to his cousin.

Well, it had turned out badly, especially when he told JL a few things that caused him to throw her out of his life. JL had started drinking shortly thereafter and he wanted nothing to do with Cary. His cousin had never admitted to being the serpent in paradise, but JL was suspicious these days. It had soured their relationship. Cary was sorry about it, from time to time, but she'd been his girl first. He'd been upset about losing her to a richer man, even if the man was his cousin.

He'd sent the red-haired waitress out to picket the ranch as a joke, but he'd found Cassie interesting and he wanted to take her out. She was cool with him, which made her a challenge. He liked a woman he had to chase. Now it was just a matter of finding a way to get close to her. And keep her out of his cousin's sight. He wasn't going to lose another woman to JL.

Cassie, blissfully ignorant of her customer's thoughts, brought out his meal and dessert, along with the strong black coffee he'd ordered.

"Bowling is fun," he remarked as she wrote out the ticket. "You really ought to put off your father's project and come with me."

She just smiled. "Sorry. No can do."

He shrugged. "Your loss." He tossed her a flirty smile. "I don't have any trouble getting women to go out with me."

"How nice for you," she said with a careless smile.

He glowered at her. "Look, I'm sorry I tricked you into picketing JL's ranch," he said reluctantly. He didn't like apologizing; it made him feel weak.

She laid the ticket beside his plate. "No problem."

He slid a hand around her waist and smiled. "You might give me a chance to make it up to you. . . ." he began, and his hand slipped lower, whether accidentally or not.

She turned her hand, bent his the wrong way, pulled him out of his seat, and put him on the floor.

He lay there, looking up at her with wide eyes and a bruised arm.

"You touch me like that again," she said very softly, "and I'll cripple you, before I sue you for sexual harassment."

Mary Dodd had seen what went on. She moved to the table and stood over Cary. "And that's called just deserts," she told him coldly.

"My hand slipped!" he said, wincing as he dragged himself to his feet. "I swear!" He turned to Cassie. "I'm really sorry. It truly was an accident! I'd never treat a decent woman that way on purpose!"

He looked so pitiful that Cassie believed him. "Never again," she cautioned him.

He put his hand over his heart. "I'll just sit here and eat my stew and pie, and not make another accidental move!"

"If you do," Mary said softly, "it will be the last time you eat here. Is that clear? Nobody harasses my waitresses," she added.

"I'm really sorry," he repeated. He grinned. "No more slippy hands. Honest!"

He was incorrigible. Mary rolled her eyes. She walked off, shaking her head.

Cassie laughed. He did look so miserable.

"Am I forgiven?" he persisted.

"This once," she replied.

He crossed his heart. "I'm turning over a new leaf right now, ma'am," he said, and grinned. "Honest."

He sat down and dug into his stew.

Several people had amused smiles on their faces as Cassie went on to the next table and the next order.

"You okay?" Mary asked Cassie a little later, after Cary had left and the customers had thinned out a little.

Cassie smiled. "I'm fine," she said. She was uneasy. Confrontations unsettled her, especially after what she and her father had suffered publicly only a short time ago. "I'm sorry I caused a scene."

"Nonsense," Mary said. "Just as well to let that man see his limits. He's not mean, but he can get overbearing. He won't again. Not with you," she chuckled.

Cassie smiled. "I almost felt sorry for him," she confessed.

"How did you do that, if you don't mind saying?" she asked.

"I'm a black belt in tae kwon do," she said simply. "I've taken lessons for five years. I used to compete," she added sadly. She smiled. "I can't do it anymore."

"That's a shame. It was a sight to see," Mary told her.

Cassie grinned. "I truly enjoyed the look on his face. And maybe his hand did slip."

"Maybe it didn't," came the amused reply. "But that's Cary. He's been no end of trouble to JL, his cousin," she added in a lowered voice as they walked back behind the counter. "In fact, he was responsible for his cousin's broken engagement."

"He was?"

"He carried tales to both of them. It was a shame what he did to JL. He really loved the woman," she said. "Gossip was that she fell hard for JL, too. Cary put a stop to that with a few whispers in her ear and JL's. There's no excuse for the way Cary treated her. He was jealous, you see, because she was his girl first and she threw him over for JL."

"He was trying to get me to go bowling with him. I don't like going out with men I don't know," she added softly.

"Wise woman," Mary said. "In Cary's case, very wise. He drinks to excess. JL just goes to bed when he's had too much liquor. Cary gets in fights. Or he used to." Her eyes twinkled. "Not so much since the last one. Anyway, JL can handle him when he's drunk, if he has to. When JL's sober, that is," she added.

"When he's sober . . . ?" Cassie probed.

"Best not to carry tales," Mary replied. "Sorry."

"No, it's my fault. I shouldn't have asked. It's just that Cary set me up picketing Mr. Denton's ranch because Cary said he was torturing chickens in his henhouses." She made a face. "I must be far more naïve than I thought I was. I went out there alone and stood in the freezing cold and rain until Mr. Denton drove up and found me. He took me to the ranch house and let me dry my stuff. He even made me coffee." She sighed. "He's very nice. I felt so bad about what I'd done."

Mary grinned. "Trust me, JL will dine out on that story in a few weeks. Chicken houses." She shook her head. "Eastern tenderfoot," she chided affectionately.

Cassie laughed. "That's what he called me. I guess I am. I'll get back to work. Thanks for standing up for me," she added softly.

"Nobody messes with my employees," Mary said simply. And she smiled.

Chapter Three

Cassie didn't tell her father about the unpleasantness in the restaurant with Cary. He had enough on his mind without having to worry about her. She fixed supper for him and they watched a movie on the little television set he'd bought from a coworker. She didn't let on that she had a care in the world.

The next morning, she was surprised to find JL Denton occupying a booth in the restaurant where she worked. He'd dropped his white Stetson onto the seat beside him. He had thick black hair with a faint wave, and he was wearing a western-cut shirt with jeans and boots. Cassie's heart skipped when he looked up at her as she came to take his order. But he wasn't smiling.

"What did Cary do to you yesterday?" he asked quietly, and there was a look in his dark eyes that made her faintly nervous.

She hesitated. She didn't like carrying tales. Gossip was what had cost her father his job, and the ensuing notoriety put Cassie on the run as well.

"Come on," he said, his deep voice dropping softly. "Tell me what happened."

She took a breath and glanced around. The boss was

in the kitchen and there was only old Mr. Bailey in the restaurant this early and he couldn't hear a cannon go off.

"He wanted me to go out with him," she said, lowering her voice. "I didn't want to. He kept trying to coax me and then he slid his hand over my, well, my bottom"—she fought a blush—"and I put him on the floor."

"You . . . ?" he asked, spellbound.

"I put him on the floor," she said simply. "I'm a black belt in tae kwon do."

"Did Cary know that?"

She pursed her lips and her blue eyes twinkled. "I think he might suspect it, now. He was very apologetic. The boss saw what happened from the kitchen. She told him if he ever did that again, he'd never get back in here. He apologized for three minutes straight. He said his hand slipped," she added. She drew in a breath. "I'm so sorry for making a scene. . . ."

"Why?" he asked, searching her eyes. "That's what should have happened. No man has the right to harass a woman on the job. I've fired cowboys who got fresh with my housekeeper's daughter."

She was impressed. "I thought you might be mad," she said. "He's your cousin. . . ."

"By marriage, not by blood," he said shortly.

She didn't mention what she'd heard about Cary and JL's fiancée, but it ran through her mind.

"If he starts giving you any trouble, you call Todd Blakely. He's the police chief here in town, and a friend of mine. Tell him I told you to call. He'll take care of Cary, and he'll enjoy it," he added. "It was Todd who put Cary in jail for assault. Cary's girlfriend slapped him. He called the law on her." He smothered a grin at Cassie's expression.

"He called the police because his girlfriend slapped

him?" Cassie asked, wide-eyed. "But you said he went to jail for assault," she added, confused.

He pursed his chiseled lips. "Well, see, when Todd got there, Cary swung on him. Our chief's a martial artist, too. Cary had lots of bruises. But assault on a police officer is a felony and Cary couldn't talk Todd out of the charge. So he spent a couple of weeks behind bars before his attorney pulled a few strings and got him out." He shook his head. "Whatever he is, Cary's still part of one of the founding families of Benton. That reputation goes a long way around here. And Cary had been drinking, which he almost never used to do."

"I heard about him going to jail," she said. "I thought it was because he was dangerous."

"No, he's not dangerous and he doesn't want to go back," he assured her. "So he'll be more careful. But don't trust him. I don't mean that he's dangerous. He's mostly mischievous. He's like old Two Toes; he's a sneak."

"Two Toes?"

"Our resident bad boy. He's an old wolf. He preys on our calves because he can't get a pack to take him on, apparently, and he sneaks around my ranch looking for helpless little strays."

"Oh, how awful," she said softly.

He smiled. He liked her nurturing attitude. She reminded him of his mother, long ago, when he was small. She'd been like this, all heart.

"We're hoping we can talk the local wildlife rehabilitator to take him on. I don't want to kill him, but we have to stop him."

"Do they let people keep wolves as pets?" she asked.

He laughed. "Not so much. You have to have training for that sort of work. Most of the rehabilitators are overworked. All of them around here specialize. We have one for raptors, one for small mammals, one for large mammals, that sort of thing."

"What a wonderful job," she sighed.

"You wouldn't think so if your phone rang off the hook all hours with people needing help."

"I don't know," she replied. "It sounds like a worthwhile occupation." She glanced toward the kitchen. Her boss was just coming out of it. Cassie's worried expression told him a lot.

"Two eggs, scrambled, with bacon and toast and grape jelly," he said at once. "Strong black coffee to go with it."

She smiled and her eyes mirrored her gratitude as she jotted down the order. "I haven't spilled anybody's coffee so far today," she said.

"I spill mine half the time," he said easily. "I trip over my own feet. I catch pot holders on fire." He shrugged. "I won't mind if you spill the coffee."

She laughed. "Okay. Thanks."

"No problem."

She went at once to get his order. Mary gave her a secretive smile and a hidden thumbs-up. Cassie flushed. Mary laughed as her newest employee dashed to the counter and gave the order to the cook.

Cassie managed to get the coffee to JL in one piece, without dropping the cup. She let out a sigh of relief when she had it on the table before him, along with a napkin and silverware.

"Not bad," he remarked. "You know, your clothes are still at the house."

"Oh, gosh, I keep forgetting about them!" she exclaimed apologetically.

"It wasn't a complaint," he replied. "But I thought you might like to come over and get them Saturday. You can see the calves."

Her eyes lit up. "You have calves?"

"Lots of them. Even a pair of twins," he added. "We have our cows drop calves in the early spring, when the young grass is just coming up and most of the snow and sleet is done with." He sighed heavily. "Not that it's quite spring just yet," he added, shaking his head. "We've got our hands full with this latest snowfall."

"I love snow," she said softly. "It's so beautiful."

"Not when you're trying to shovel it out of cattle pens and feeders."

She laughed. "Yes, but I don't have to do those things."

"Don't they have snow where you come from?"

She made a face. "One or two days a year."

"Heaven," he retorted.

"It's a matter of perspective," she pointed out. "What we don't have often becomes a joy."

"I can think of several inappropriate replies to that," he said with a wicked smile. "The main one being raging indigestion."

"Oh, boy, can I sympathize with that!" she said. "I have heartburn so bad! I have to take medicine for it."

"Acid reflux?" he asked.

She laughed. "Yes."

"I have it, too." He shook his head. "The sad part is that I love spicy food, preferably Tex-Mex with lots of salsa and peppers. Can't eat it very often."

"I like spicy Asian food," she confessed. "Especially Chinese."

He laughed. "Kindred spirits. So," he added. "Saturday morning, about ten? I'll come and get you."

Her face colored. She was shy and it was difficult for her to be herself with a man. But she was excited and happy, and that showed as well. "I would like that," she said, trying to rein in her enthusiasm.

"So would I. Cassie, isn't it?"

She nodded. "Cassie."

"Is it a nickname or your actual name?"

She sighed. "My actual name is Cassandra," she confessed. "My mother was reading a romance novel just before I was born, and she loved the heroine's name. So Cassandra I became. But everybody just calls me Cassie."

"I like it," he said softly.

She smiled. He smiled back. They exchanged a look that made her toes curl inside her shoes. "Oh! Your order . . . !" She laughed self-consciously and retreated to the counter to pick up his breakfast.

"Aren't you lucky that we're not crowded?" the cook, Agatha, asked with a wicked grin. "He's a dish, isn't he?"

Cassie went red from her forehead down. "Oh, Agatha . . . !"

"Never mind me. I always wanted a little bow and an arrow and a cherubic face. . . ."

Cassie wrinkled her nose at the older woman and carried the plate and the saucer containing the toast on a tray to the table where JL had cleared a path in between his coffee cup and his utensils for them.

She eased the plate down and almost lost the saucer, but she recovered it just in time. "Oops. Nearly a disaster. Sorry."

He chuckled. "Nice reflexes. I'll bet you're a terror on the tennis court."

"I don't play tennis," she said.

"I do. I'll teach you."

She laughed. “I’d trip over my feet and go headfirst into the net.”

“Okay. How about horseback riding?”

“I’ve only ever been on a horse once or twice, but I really liked it,” she replied.

“Fine. We’ll forget tennis and go riding.”

“I’d love that.”

“Me too.”

She picked up the empty tray and held it under her arm. “Ten o’clock Saturday.”

He nodded. He smiled. “I’ll look forward to it.”

She hated her helpless blush. “Me too.” She went back to the counter and put up the tray quickly, because a party of four just walked in the door. The morning rush had started.

JL paid the bill at the counter, because Cassie was in over her head trying to cover three tables at once.

“She’s shaping up nicely here,” Mary told him as she returned his change, indicating Cassie. “She’d never waited tables, but she’s honest and quick to learn, and she works hard.”

“Nice character traits,” JL replied.

“She’s pretty green. . . .” She said it hesitantly, not wanting to interfere.

“I noticed that, too,” he said softly, and he smiled. “Another very rare trait, in these overly modern times.”

She laughed. “It is.”

“Tell Agatha the eggs were perfect. Nobody cooks them like she does.”

“I’ll tell her. She’ll swoon,” she teased. “She thinks you’re the dishiest man since Sean Connery.”

"My God, what an image to have to live up to," he returned with a grin. "I'll have to grow a beard and practice my Scots accent."

"Then she'll really swoon," Mary assured him.

He turned and caught Cassie's eye and waved. She tried to wave back, dropped her order pad, and then scrambled to pick it up again. She was as red as a beet.

He chuckled with pure pleasure and waved again as he walked out the door.

"You're very unsettled tonight," her father remarked when they were eating supper.

"It's been an odd couple of days," she replied.

"Cary hasn't been back, has he?" he asked with some irritation.

She just stared at him. "Cary?" she asked softly, fishing for how much he knew.

"Small towns run on gossip," he reminded her. He chuckled. "What I heard was that Cary got fresh with you and you put him down. One of my coworkers said he wished his wife had that kind of spunk."

She laughed. "I wasn't going to tell you," she confessed. "You've had so much worry lately. . . ."

"This doesn't worry me. Actually, it was nice to have something to laugh about. People say Cary's bad to drink with and he gets aggressive. I was afraid he might come back and say something to you."

"No," she told him. "That's not what happened at all. He swore that his hand slipped, and he apologized profusely. But JL Denton heard about what happened, too, and he came for breakfast to ask me about it."

"Protecting his cousin?"

"No. Protecting me, actually," she said. "He doesn't like his cousin."

"A lot of people don't like Cary, from what I've heard."

"Mr. Denton asked me if I'd like to go horseback riding with him on Saturday."

"Well!"

"He's got lots of calves," she added.

He chuckled. "Say no more. I can drive you over there and pick you up later."

"He's coming to get me," she returned.

"A gentleman."

"I hope so." She finished her meat loaf and mashed potatoes and put the plate to one side. "I don't really know him."

"Everybody in town knows him," he replied. "He's respected and well liked. People are still sorry for him about his fiancée walking out; something his cousin provoked, they say."

"That's what he says, too."

"You should be safe enough. You can always call me if you run out of defensive techniques."

She laughed. "I don't plan to throw Mr. Denton around, Dad."

"He was in the military," he said surprisingly. "And he was a master trainer in hand-to-hand combat, they say. I expect you'd have your work cut out to put him down the way you did his cousin."

"Well!" she said with a quick breath.

"He does drink, like his cousin," he told her. "So be careful."

"I will."

"Make sure you keep your cell phone charged, so you can call me if you get into a situation you can't handle.

And make sure you don't leave without your meds," he added firmly.

"I will. Worrywart," she teased.

He grinned.

She didn't sleep that night, thinking about JL. She didn't know much about men, despite working around them for several years. Most of them were businessmen or entertainers, and they wore nice suits or expensive leisure wear, not denim and cowboy boots. JL Denton was completely out of her experience. He was very attractive. She hoped she could keep her head. She didn't want to become a notch on his bedpost.

On the other hand, he seemed like a gentleman. Her mother always said that a man treated a woman the way she signaled that she wanted to be treated. If she acted like a lady, that's how she'd be treated.

Her mother would have been taken aback if she'd seen Cary in the restaurant putting his hand on her daughter's bottom.

Accident or not, that had been offensive and it made Cassie angry. No man had the right to be that forward with any woman. It was condescending and crude.

She was glad that JL was angry about it, too. It made her feel better. In all the years since she'd graduated from high school and then college, she'd never had a man treat her that way. She'd never worked for the public, though, especially in a job like waitressing. And she'd been sheltered, mainly because she'd been sick so often. When she was a reporter, almost every man she knew treated her like one of the guys. Only one man had asked her out in all those years, but she'd turned him down. He worked for the same paper she did. She didn't want to risk a workplace romance. She smiled, remembering what her mother had said about the fellow reporter. Her mother had been very protective.

It hurt her to remember her mother, shamed and flooded with e-mails and nasty notes on social media. Neither Cassie nor her father had known about them until they checked her computer and found them after she died. Several had invited her to kill herself because she was married to a nasty and obscene lecher.

Cassie's father had never been a lecher. He was a perfect gentleman, and he was completely faithful to his wife, a rarity in the circles he moved in. Her mother had snapped under the unrelenting pressure of crusading newsmen and newswomen ceaselessly pointing fingers at her father for being one of those overbearing animals that preyed on women who were subordinate to him at work. The tragedy was something that Cassie and her father still couldn't talk about. The wound was too new, too fresh.

The only good that had come out of it, and it was small consolation, was that the media backed off after the tragedy. One newscaster was angry enough to castigate his colleagues on the air for being so aggressive and unfeeling that they cost a human life. But it was like closing the gate after the horse was gone. It didn't bring back Cassie's sweet mother.

She rolled over in bed and fluffed up her pillow. She had to stop looking back. Life was sweet again. It was a new start. She could live in Colorado for the rest of her life in total obscurity. No reporters would come here to harass her and her father. They'd left no trail that could be followed, even by an aggressive reporter. This little town was like shelter in a storm, and Cassie looked forward to making a new life here with her dad.

It might be a pipe dream, she thought as she closed her eyes. But dreams were sweet, when you had little else to cling to. She smiled, thinking of JL and Saturday, as she drifted off to sleep.

Saturday morning, she was up at seven o'clock. She made breakfast, cleared away the dishes, and then spent two hours trying on clothes to see what looked best on her. She didn't have a large wardrobe; she and her father had packed the bare minimum to come out here, putting everything they owned in storage for the time being. Back home in Atlanta, she had nice clothes, even a few designer ones, especially things for evening. But she didn't want to wear anything fancy around JL. It would be stupid and cruel to wear designer clothes around a cowboy who lived in a house with peeling paint, on a ranch with broken fences. She wasn't going to do a number on his pride. So she wore simple off-the-rack jeans with a pullover yellow sweater and ankle boots. She left her hair long, curling around her face and shoulders, and she used a bare minimum of makeup and cologne.

"You look nice," her father remarked as she folded the clothes she'd borrowed, which she'd washed and dried, to give back to JL.

"Thanks," she told him. "I didn't want to look too dressy."

"Nice manners," he said softly. His face saddened. "Like your mother."

She bit her lower lip. "Oh, how I wish we could go back there and punch those reporters!"

"Life pays us out in our own coin," he reminded her.

"God gets even with people who hurt us. They'll find that out one day, in this life or the next," he added. "You can't dwell on wrongdoing, even things that make you miserable. Hating only hurts you. It never hurts the person you hate."

"I guess not," she conceded.

"Got your rescue inhaler?"

"Yes," she said, smiling.

"Okay. EpiPen, too?"

"Right here." She patted the small purse where she carried her necessary medicines. "But we're not too likely to run into stinging insects in the snow," she pointed out.

"There are still venomous spiders about."

"I hope they have overcoats, so they don't freeze," she said, tongue in cheek.

He laughed. "All right. I'll stop being overprotective. Where's your coat?"

"Oops. Forgot."

She went back to the closet and pulled out her swing corduroy coat. It was tan and matched her ankle boots. She drew it on.

He frowned. "Is that going to be warm enough?"

"Surely it will," she said. "I'm layered."

"I'm used to cold weather, but you aren't, sweetheart," he replied softly. "Colorado is very different, especially here in the mountains."

"I'll be fine," she assured him. She listened and heard the loud purr of a truck approaching. She dashed to the window and her heart raced.

"It's him!"

"Well, have fun," her father said.

"I will. See you later. Love you, Dad."

"Love you back."

She opened the door and ran outside just as JL was climbing down out of the cab of the big SUV.

He looked surprised to see her running toward him. He laughed with pure delight and went around to open the door for her.

"Handhold's just inside, above," he said.

"Thanks! It's a long way up," she laughed as she got inside.

"For a shrimp like you, it is," he teased, closing the door on her mock-indignant reply.

He climbed in beside her and put on his seat belt, glancing at her to make sure hers was in place as well before he started the big vehicle and turned it around, heading it down the driveway.

He was wearing a shepherd's coat over a red-and-black flannel shirt, with jeans and big boots and that creamy Stetson. He looked like a man who lived on the land.

There was patchy snow on the side of the road. She glanced over the rolling landscape to the snow-peaked mountains beyond. "It's so beautiful here," she murmured.

He smiled. "I think so."

"Were you born here?" she asked.

He smiled. "No. Near Dallas, remember?"

She ground her teeth together. "No, sorry."

"No problem. My father was born here. So was his father, and his grandfather, and so on."

"It must be lonely, with your parents gone," she said delicately.

He nodded. "It's hard to lose both parents within a few months. Dad was never the same after she died. They were married for a long time, and they loved each other desperately. I had an older brother. I lost him overseas, in the last Gulf war." He sighed. "It's lonely when you don't have anybody. Well, except for Cary, and I'd give him away to anybody who wanted a bent and broken relative to keep. He's not even a blood relative, at that."

She grinned.

He laughed at her expression. "I told him to keep his hands to himself, but it wasn't necessary. He said he was getting into a tub of liniment and he hoped you'd understand if he went searching in another direction for company."

She laughed, too. "Oh, I understand perfectly. No problem."

He pulled up in front of the sprawling ranch house. There were men working everywhere, including on the front porch.

"This is why I said we'd go riding," he said under his breath. "They seem to multiply every time I leave home."

"What are they doing?"

"Upkeep and maintenance," he said as he got out of the SUV and went around to help her down. He held her just in front of him for a long moment, savoring the closeness. "Something I should have been doing all along. Now it's piled up and it takes a lot of manpower to set things right. Your eyes are the oddest shade of blue," he added, searching them in the long silence broken only by hammering nearby. "They're china blue."

"Like my mother's," she said with a sad smile. "But her hair was black. I inherited mine from her grandfather. I'm the only redhead in the family right now—well, what there is left of it. I have an uncle in Grand Rapids, Michigan, and a grandfather somewhere in Canada. He roams."

"I had a great-uncle who lived in a cabin up in Alberta with a black bear." He shook his head. "No accounting for taste, I guess."

"The bear didn't eat him?" she asked.

"Not that we know of. He died slumped over a poker hand at his weekly game. He'd won the pot, too."

"That's a shame," she said.

"Not so much. He was always happy, always smiling. We figured he went the way he would have wanted to go. Quick and easy, no long stay in a hospital or a nursing home. There's a lot to be said for that."

"I totally agree," she said.

She reached back into the SUV for the bag she'd put the clothes in. "I almost forgot to give these back. Thanks so much for the loan," she added, handing it to him.

"I'll put these," he indicated the bag, "in the house and bring yours out. Bessie washed and dried them for you."

"Bessie?"

"My housekeeper. The clothes I loaned you were her daughter's."

"Oh." She smiled. "Thank her for me."

"She wouldn't mind. Nita works for a bank down in Denver. She's sweet."

"I see."

He cocked his head and smiled at her. "No, you don't. I'm not carrying a torch for her. She's sweet, but she's outlived three husbands already. She's on number four now. And she's only thirty-one."

"My goodness!"

He sighed. "I guess some people have a hard time with marriage."

"I guess."

He led the way to the front door. "Want a cup of coffee before we go?" he asked.

"That would be nice."

"And warming," he added, noting her slight discomfort

in the way she hugged her arms around herself. "You're not used to Colorado weather yet, I see."

She raised her eyebrows in a question.

"This is fur coat country. Or shearling coat country. Lightweight jackets won't cut it out here."

"I'm not really cold," she lied. "I just had a chill."

"Uh-huh," he murmured.

He led the way into the kitchen.

She remembered it from the last time she'd been here. It was roomy, spotless, with appliances like the ones she had in storage, that she'd cooked on when she lived in Atlanta.

"I love your kitchen," she said with a sigh. "You must have every gourmet tool they make."

"Bessie does," he said, smiling. "She can cook anything. Food's great, too."

"I'll bet."

"Do you cook?" he asked.

She nodded. "I can't do haute cuisine, but I can do most any food there's a recipe for. And I can make any kind of homemade bread and rolls. I do those for Dad. He loves fresh yeast rolls," she laughed.

"Bessie doesn't do breads. I'd love to try those rolls sometime," he added, pouring the brewed coffee into two cups.

"I'll make you a pan of them, if you like."

His dark eyes searched hers and he smiled. "Yes. I'd like that."

She flushed a little from the intent gaze she was getting.

He put her coffee in front of her and sat down next to her at the table. "Do I make you nervous?" he asked.

She drew in a breath. "A little."

"In a bad way?" he asked, without looking at her.

"N . . . No. Not . . . in a bad way." She was floundering

like a child in school facing an oral book report for a book she hadn't read.

He turned and stared at her quietly, his dark eyes intense. "I speak pretty bluntly sometimes. But it's best to set boundaries, don't you think?"

She swallowed. "Yes."

He leaned back in the chair and sipped coffee. "Okay. It's like this. I'm still getting over a failed engagement. I'm pretty raw and I'm still not quite myself. So suppose we begin as good friends and let it go at that. For the time being."

She let out a sigh. "I'd like that."

His thick eyebrows arched. "You look relieved."

She bit her lower lip. "Look, my mother was overprotective. A lot. I wasn't allowed to date until I was in my late teens, and then only double dates. I don't know much about men, I've never had an affair, and I've tried to avoid men who were aggressive because I'm not . . . well, modern." She felt as if she'd rambled, but he only smiled.

"In other words, you don't sleep around."

"That's it."

"No problem. Even if I were over my ex-fiancée, you'd have nothing to fear from me," he said softly. "I don't amuse myself with innocents."

She laughed. "Thanks."

He drew in a long, heavy breath. "I'm glad we got that out of the way. I didn't want to give you the idea that I was in the market for a serious relationship."

"I'm not, either," she confessed. "Dad and I have had a traumatic time just lately. Neither of us is quite ourselves, either."

"Oh? What happened?"

"My mother killed herself."

Chapter Four

"I'm sorry," she said at once. "I didn't mean to blurt it out like that!"

He winced. "God, you poor kid!"

She linked her hands around her coffee cup. "It's hard, getting over it."

"Was she always depressed?"

"Never," she said softly. "She wasn't a selfish person. She always put all of us before herself, in everything. She would never have put such sorrow and guilt and heartache on us if she hadn't been half out of her mind . . . !" She stopped, fearful of saying too much.

He tugged one of her hands loose and linked it with his. It felt good, that big, calloused hand so tender as it curved around her own. "What happened to her?"

She hesitated, trying to find a way to put it that wouldn't make him suspicious. Even out here, they'd probably heard of the scandal. She looked at his clean, flat nails instead of his face. "She was harassed on social media, constantly," she said finally. "She had . . . enemies. She never hurt anybody in her life, but something happened to someone she loved, and she became a target." She closed her eyes and shuddered. "She walked out onto the balcony of her twentieth-floor apartment and . . . jumped."

"Dear God." His hand tightened.

"Dad had to identify her at the morgue," she said. She bit her lower lip. "We had a closed casket. Even morticians can't fix some things. She'd have hated having people stare at her. Not that there was a crowd at the memorial service. It was just me and Dad."

"Didn't you have family, friends?"

Their friends had deserted them and their family, sparse as it was, ran from them, fearful of being connected to the scandal.

"They were too far away to come," she said, forcing a smile. "It was very sudden."

"What about the culprits who harassed her?" he asked. "Did you file suit against them? Surely there are laws that apply in a case like that."

Of course there were laws, but if you were a public figure, as her father was, you had no right to privacy. Especially if you were the biggest story in the headlines. But she couldn't say that.

"Dad isn't the type to sue people," she said finally. "Neither was my mother. We used to say that she could find one nice thing to say about the devil."

He smiled. "My mother was like that, too. She never moved with the times. She was a founding member of our local Baptist church."

"I'm Methodist," she said softly. "Or I was."

His fingers closed around hers for a minute and then let go. She felt cold and empty and alone, all of a sudden, and smiled to hide it.

"I hope you have a horse who likes people for me to

ride," she said. "The last one I was on tried to scrape me off against a tree. Maybe it was the soap I used," she confided.

He chuckled. "Not likely. If you're afraid, horses can sense it."

"I'm not afraid of most of them. Just the ones that try to scrape me off against trees," she said, grinning at him.

"I'll make sure we don't give you one of those," he promised. He finished his last swallow of lukewarm coffee and got up. "Ready to go?"

"You bet!"

He laughed. "Are you always so enthusiastic about things?"

"I've never been on a real ranch in my life," she said. "I'm looking forward to seeing the calves."

"We've got a nice crop of them this year. We've only lost two, and that's very few considering the size of the herd."

"What happened to them?" she wondered aloud.

"Two Toes," he said curtly. "But not for long. We're going to track him and trap him and give him to that wildlife rehabilitator I told you about. He can eat soft food and lay by the fire in his old age."

She laughed at the picture that popped into her mind. "Just make sure you don't dress him in a granny gown and put a frilly cap on him. And don't let little girls wearing red hoods into the house where he lives."

He stared at her pointedly.

"I don't have a red hood," she said quickly.

He chuckled. "Come on."

He had a cowboy saddle two horses. The one he gave her was called Buck, and it was a very gentle gelding.

"Why is he called Buck?" she wanted to know as they

rode lazily down the trail that led around the stables toward sprawling pastures dotted with black-coated cattle.

"In his younger days, there wasn't a cowboy on the place who could stay on him."

She looked worried.

"He's twenty years old," he added when he saw her concern. "And Parker tamed him seven years ago. He's converted."

"Parker?"

"Man who works for me," he said. "He's part Crow. He has a way with horses. I've never seen one, however wild, that he couldn't calm just by talking softly to it. He's the best wrangler we've ever had."

"Was he the man who saddled the horses back there?"

"Oh, no," he said. "We keep Parker out at the line cabin."

"Should I ask why?" she teased.

He chuckled. "He was in the military. He's got a mouth that ten bars of soap wouldn't wash clean, so we keep him away from the house. Great with horses. With people, not so much."

"He sounds fascinating."

"A couple of single women felt that way, too, until they talked to him for five minutes. One developed a sudden headache, the other had a hair appointment she'd forgotten. Neither of them ever came back."

"Maybe he likes being alone," she pointed out.

"That's exactly my take on it," he agreed.

"Does he say why he cusses so much?"

"He said he learned how while dodging bullets in Iraq," he sighed. "I know how he feels. I learned a few bad words of my own, doing the same thing."

"It's rough for soldiers over there," she said, recalling a

friend who'd helped her with research for a screenplay she was writing; one that later was made into a TV movie.

He glanced at her. "And you'd know this, how?"

"I had an acquaintance who was in spec ops over in the Middle East," she said. "He told me a lot of things that civilians don't usually get to hear."

"Civilians?"

She took a breath. "I started out as a newspaper reporter," she confessed. "Newbies get to do the police beat. Things you have to see, you don't share with people who don't have a connection to news or emergency services. I loved it," she laughed. "I got to know all the local law enforcement, the EMTs, the dispatchers, the politicians. It was hard to leave it."

"Where did you work?"

"A small town outside Atlanta," she replied. "I got a better job, but I missed reporting. I always knew where the bad guys were," she added with a grin.

He laughed. "It's like that here, too. We only read the paper to see who got caught. We already know everybody's business."

Not mine, she thought thankfully, *or my dad's.*

They came to a fence post that was leaning, with the wire attached to it bent down by a tree limb that had fallen. He swung out of the saddle, looped the reins over the horse's head, and let them drag, while he went to right it. She noted that he had thick gloves on those big hands. Muscles rippled in his powerful legs as he lifted the limb off the fence and then righted the fence post and straightened the wire. He pulled out his cell phone when he was finished and called out some numbers to someone and instructed them to get out and fix it before cattle poured out onto the road.

He came back and climbed into the saddle with the ease of long practice. "Can't afford to let cattle get out," he said as they rode forward. "Even on a spread this big, every head counts."

"Are they all Black Angus?" she asked.

"Every one. We sort them when we start branding. Those with good conformation go into one pen, the others are gelded and put into a separate pen. We feed out the yearlings for the sale lot, for breeding stock."

"And the others, the ones you don't breed?"

He glanced at her and pulled his wide-brimmed hat over one eye. "I think you can guess."

She made a face.

He laughed. "That's ranching," he said. "We can't keep them all. I sell the steers and keep the rest."

She frowned. "Why don't you keep them for beef?"

"I can't eat something I've raised," he said simply. "Some ranchers have gone into signature beef that they produce and slaughter and package and sell, right from their own ranches." He grimaced. "I'd never be able to do that. So I run purebreds."

She smiled. "I like that."

He glanced at her with warm brown eyes. "Tender heart."

"I can't help it. I take after my mother."

He drew in a long breath. "I guess I'm more like my dad," he said. "He was a third-generation rancher, but he was so educated that he never really took to the chores. I hated the ranch when I was in high school. There was a girl I liked, and she said she didn't like boys who smelled like manure." He shook his head. "I told my grandad that, and he hit the ceiling. He was good for thirty minutes about snooty city girls with stuck-up noses. They'd never get down in the dirt and work with you, if you had to grub for a living, he said. They lasted only as long as the money did. Better to find a woman who wanted to make a home and have a family, even if she didn't wear silk dresses and look like a magazine cover."

"Smart man," she murmured.

"Sometimes money would get tight and my grandfather would work for a mechanic in town, just part-time, you know, to tide us over." He didn't add that his father didn't offer any such thing. Not that there was a college in Benton where he could have taught. "That was when my brother and I were in grammar school." He didn't add that it was also before their grandfather died and left them a fortune. The ranch had never fallen on bad times since. "Dad was bad to drink after we lost Mom."

"What happened to him? If you don't mind telling me," she added quickly.

He shook his head. They rode down the long, wooded path toward the mountains. "We found him sitting up in a line cabin, stone dead." He grimaced. "It was one of the coldest nights of the year, snow piled up six feet deep. It looked to us like the fire went out in the fireplace after he dozed off. He just never woke up." He glanced at her. "Not a bad way to go, I guess, but Mom had died a few months earlier of a heart attack. We didn't even know she had a heart problem." He smiled sadly. "She wouldn't go to the doctor for what she thought was simple indigestion. It wasn't." He pushed his hat down over one eye. "My dad was never the same, after. He blamed himself because he didn't make her see a doctor."

"Sometimes things happen because they're meant to," she said simply. "It doesn't make sense to some people, but it does to me. I think we die when we're supposed to."

"Maybe we do."

"Was it a long time ago?"

"Six years," he said. "My older brother's unit had been called up three years before all that and he died over in the Middle East."

"I'm truly sorry. At least I still have my father."

"I miss my grandfather," he confessed. He'd missed his mother, but he and his father weren't close. They had very little in common until after JL went to college and then his father found him interesting. His dad missed teaching. It was the only thing he ever talked about.

They rode along in a peaceful silence for a few minutes, with only the creaking of saddle leather and the pleasant rhythm of the horses' hooves on hard ground making a noise.

Snow was just starting to fall. She lifted her face to it and smiled. The wind picked up and she shivered slightly.

"Cold?" he asked, reining in.

"Just a little chill," she lied. "I love snow."

"Nobody who ranches out here loves it, I can promise you," he chuckled. He glanced out over the landscape. The mountains were topped with snow. The ground was getting lightly covered with white.

"I hope we get enough to make a snowman," she said, laughing.

He glanced at her, fascinated with the way she looked when she laughed. She was pretty, in her way. He liked her all too well.

"We'd better get moving before we turn into snowmen," he teased.

"I guess so."

They rode on down the trail when a sudden blur of movement stopped them in their tracks. Wolves!

There were several of them. Cassie's heart almost stopped as one of them halted just a few yards away and growled. Her horse neighed and reared.

"Don't jerk on the reins," JL said suddenly. "Just sit still. They aren't after us."

She shivered, and not from the cold. She'd never really seen a wolf up close. They were huge! She hadn't realized how big they were, or how dangerous they could look when they snarled.

Out of the corner of her eye she saw JL pull a long rifle out of a scabbard on his saddle. He shouldered it and looked down the sights, controlling the uneasy motion of his horse with his legs.

The wolf obviously thought he meant business, because it turned its head toward the others and loped away without a backward glance.

Cassie let out the breath she'd been holding. Or she tried to. She couldn't get the air out, which was the major problem with people who had asthma. Getting air in was easy. Getting it back out could be an issue.

She needed her rescue inhaler, but it was under her buttoned coat, in her purse. She swung down out of the saddle, a little unsteadily, and moved away from the horse, fighting to breathe.

"Here, now, it was just a wolf or two," he said, faintly irritated by her reaction. He put the rifle back in its scabbard. "Nothing to get so upset about."

She couldn't talk to tell him what was wrong. She was fumbling with her jacket, trying to get to her inhaler. She panted like a winded runner.

JL's dark eyes narrowed as he swung down out of his saddle gracefully and moved toward her. His ex-fiancée had overreacted like that anytime she was upset. It was a painful reminder of what he'd lost, and it made him irritable. "Hell," he said with a scowl. "Don't be so melodramatic. You were in no danger!"

When she felt better, she thought dimly, she was going to kick him in the knee. Meanwhile, it was an ordeal just to get half a breath of air.

She finally worked her way into the purse under her light jacket and dragged out the rescue inhaler. She sat down on the ground, shivering, and held it up to her mouth. She took a puff and waited for the soothing spray to ease down into her tortured lungs and reduce the spasms.

He suddenly seemed to realize what had happened. He went down on one knee. "Here, are you all right?" he asked with belated concern.

She didn't answer him. She couldn't. One puff wasn't enough, and she had to wait a minute or two before she took another. It was frightening to smother like this. The cold air, the chill, the unexpected wolf sighting, all had combined to bring on an attack. She hadn't been using the preventative her doctor had prescribed. It was hard enough to afford the rescue inhaler. The other medicine was expensive, and she'd tried to do without it. Not a good idea, apparently.

He watched while she took a second puff and held it in. Slowly, the spasm turned loose, and she was able to get her lungs to work again. She leaned forward with her forehead on her knees.

He felt two inches high. He grimaced. "Can you ride?"

She nodded. She got to her feet, still breathing heavily, and let him help her into the saddle.

He turned his horse, watching her worriedly as she followed suit. They rode back to the stable in a tense silence. She was glad that she couldn't breathe properly, because she was really angry. So much for that kind attitude that he didn't really have. Apparently, it was all just an act. At least she knew now what sort of person he really was, even if it was a bad way to have to learn it.

"Would you like some coffee?" he asked.

She shook her head. "I need to go home," she said in a hoarse voice.

"Is your father there?"

She nodded.

He opened the door of the SUV, noting that she got in all by herself and fastened her seat belt without a word.

They drove in silence to the house she and her father rented.

"I'm sorry," he bit off when he pulled up at her door.

She forced a smile, although she didn't quite meet his eyes. "It's okay," she managed.

She got out before he could reach the door to open it for her.

"We forgot your clothes," he said, for something to break the tense silence.

She smiled again and just shook her head. "It doesn't matter. Thanks for the ride," she said, and turned away, walking slowly to the front porch.

He watched her go, feeling empty and guilty, and angry that he hadn't realized something was physically wrong with her. He'd made a mess of everything. He hoped he'd have the chance to make it up to her, when she had time to get over his clumsy accusation.

He climbed back into the vehicle and drove, reluctantly, away.

Her father knew something more than an asthma attack was wrong with her, but he didn't pry. She seemed uncomfortable talking about it. She pulled out her nebulizer and turned it on. It gave her something to do while she got over the misery of the afternoon.

She was going to cook supper, but her father insisted on making sandwiches instead. He sent her to bed early, worried about the sudden rattle in her chest. She'd gotten chilled, and her lungs were weak even on good days.

"You should have a heavier coat," he said worriedly. "I should have made arrangements to have our winter things sent out here."

"Too big a risk right now," she said. Their winter things were expensive clothing, stuff they wouldn't want anybody local to see. In retrospect, she thought, they should have put the furs and designer gowns into a consignment shop and they'd have had more money for incidentals.

Her voice was hoarse. She hated what she knew was coming. She'd had too many problems not to know what lay ahead. "I should never have gone riding in the snow."

"I should have noticed," he began.

"My fault, not yours," she said firmly. She patted his hand. "I'll be okay. Honest."

He didn't look convinced.

"Honest," she repeated. "I'll have a good night's sleep, and I'll be fine in the morning," she added brightly.

He wasn't smiling as he went out and closed the door behind him.

She wasn't better in the morning, but at least she wasn't any worse. She got dressed and went to work, shoving yesterday into the back of her mind so she wouldn't have to think about it.

In the meantime, at work, her father had two men walk onto the lot and peer at a huge new combine parked there.

One man was dressed like a working cowboy in denims and worn boots and hat and a denim jacket. His SUV was parked in front. The other customer was wearing a nice suit and had driven up in a fairly new luxury car.

Roger Reed went straight to the man in the suit, bypassing the cowboy, and asked the man if he needed help.

The cowboy gave him an amused glance and walked back into the office.

"Hey, JL," the owner, Bill Clay, called to him as he walked in with a cup of coffee and a sweet roll from the town's only coffee shop. "I should have brought more coffee!"

"Mine's still out in the truck," JL Denton chuckled.

"What can I do for you?"

"I came to replace my combine," he said, glancing out the window. "I guess I should have worn a suit. Your other customer attracted your salesman."

Bill's face hardened. "Don Terrell. He never buys a damned thing. He comes over to see the new equipment so he can tell his grandson what to buy him. At a dealership down in Denver, at that."

"I guess your new salesman didn't know that."

"He'll find it out. Sorry about that."

"Who is he?" JL asked as he dropped into a chair in front of Bill's desk.

"Roger Reed. He's from back east somewhere. His cousin worked here until recently. I hired him as a replacement." He shook his head while JL wondered at the familiarity of that last name. "He's good with schematics, knows everything about the equipment so he can fill the customer in about its advantages. Not so good at deciding which customers to help first."

JL shrugged. "No problem. How about writing it up for me in between sips of coffee and I'll sign in the appropriate place," he added with a grin.

"Happy to!"

* * *

Outside, Cassie's harassed father was feeling less intelligent by the minute. He'd gone over all the pertinent information with his potential customer, but all he'd received in reply was a series of grunts. God knew what that meant.

Finally the man nodded. "Okay, I'm sold," he said. He grinned. "It sounds like a great piece of equipment." He pulled out a notepad and asked for the particulars. He wrote down the item number, the price, and the exact name. He snapped the notepad shut and slipped it back into his pocket.

"Can I write it up for you?" Roger asked the customer politely.

"Write it . . . ? Oh! No, sorry, I'm not buying it here," he replied. "My grandson buys all my ranch equipment for me. He works for an equipment company down in Denver. I just decide what I want and tell him." He grinned. "He gets an employee discount, you see. Sure helps my budget! Well, thanks again." He shook hands and walked off the lot, back to his expensive car.

Cassie's father stood there, blank-faced, watching his potential customer reverse his expensive car and pull out into the highway.

The man in denims was just coming out of Bill Clay's office when he walked back inside the building.

"Glad to help," Bill was saying. "I'll have it delivered tomorrow morning."

"Fine, fine," JL said. "No rush. We aren't going to be harvesting anything in the near future," he added with a laugh. He shook hands. "Thanks again, Bill."

He walked out, ignoring the salesman who'd ignored him.

Roger Reed just gaped after him. The cowboy he hadn't thought was worth a dime had apparently just purchased one of the most expensive pieces of equipment on the place.

"Missed a hell of a commission there," Bill told Reed quietly. "I would quote the old axiom about not judging a book by its cover, but I think you get the idea, don't you?"

The older man grimaced. "Do I ever," he said heavily.

"Old Don Terrell never buys anything here," Bill told him. "His grandson works for an equipment company down in Denver. Don comes over here to look at our new stock and pick out what he wants, then he calls his grandson with the information. He's never spent a dime here. On the other hand," he added amusedly, "JL Denton could buy this place and everything on the lot out of petty cash, if he wanted it."

Roger felt the blood going out of his face. "Denton?"

Bill nodded. "He owns a big Black Angus stud ranch outside town. It's more of a hobby for him than anything else. He's a multi-generation rancher here. His money's mostly in oil and mining. He has a fortune in oil stocks that his grandfather left him."

And Roger had told his daughter that only a rich man could afford purebred cattle. He'd judged the man on old working clothes. What a lack of foresight. Lately it seemed to be his chief asset.

"I'm truly sorry," he said.

"We live and learn," Bill replied. "You're new here. It will take time for you to get used to the populace. No harm done."

Except there was. He'd made an enemy of the man his daughter was interested in, and he'd lost a huge sale. Neither thought made him particularly happy. He did still wonder what had happened the day before to bring his daughter home with an asthma attack and that aching sadness in her eyes. If he hadn't been such an idiot, he might have found out from JL while he was selling him a piece of equipment. But by slighting the rancher, he'd done himself no good.

He went back to work with a heavy heart.

Cassie was drooping. She had a cough that was productive and the sputum was colored, not a good combination, especially when added to what was most likely a fever. She kept going anyway. She couldn't afford to lose a day's pay.

Mary noticed that her newest hire wasn't feeling well. "You need to go home," she told Cassie early in the afternoon. She waved away the girl's protests. "I won't fire you for getting sick, for heaven's sake! I'll call Sarah and she'll come in and work the rest of your shift." She gave Cassie another long look. "I'm going to tell her to take over for you tomorrow as well. You need to see a doctor and go to bed!" she added firmly. "You're sick!"

Cassie drew in a painful breath. "I'm so sorry."

"Everybody gets sick once in a while," she said, her voice gentle. "It's not a big deal. You're a wonderful little worker. I'm happy to have you here. Now go home! And if you need anything, you call me, okay? I can send meals over for you and your dad if you can't cook supper."

Tears rolled down Cassie's cheek. "That's so kind. . . ." She choked up.

"Don't do that, or you'll have me bawling, too," Mary teased. "Go home. I'll call and check on you in the morning."

"Thanks," she said.

* * *

She called her father at work. He had to ask Bill to let him off long enough to get his sick daughter and take her home.

"I knew you shouldn't have gone out in that lightweight coat," he said heavily when he saw how ill Cassie was.

"We all do dumb things," she told him.

"Funny you should mention that," he murmured as he helped her inside the house. "I lost a huge sale this morning. I had to choose between a customer in blue jeans and one in a suit. I chose the wrong one."

Cassie's eyebrows rose.

"The man in the suit was just looking," he said with a wry smile. "The man in blue jeans bought a brand-new combine from my boss while I was going over all the advantages of the equipment to a man who had no intention of buying it from me."

"Oh, dear," she said.

"It gets worse. The man I slighted was JL Denton."

Cassie's heart jumped. She bit her lower lip.

"Pity I didn't ask him to bring you inside when he dropped you off here yesterday, or I'd have known who he was," her father said sadly. "He didn't even look at me when he went out the door. I've made an enemy there."

"Just as well," she said, averting her eyes. "I'm not too keen on him, either."

"Care to tell me what happened yesterday?" he probed gently.

"There was a pack of wolves," she said. "I was already chilled. One of the wolves stopped and growled at my horse, who reared and unsettled me. JL had his rifle out and the wolf saw it and took off. But it brought on the asthma attack."

"I'm so sorry," he began.

"It gets worse," she interrupted. "He thought I was being melodramatic when I gasped for breath. It wasn't until I managed to get out my rescue inhaler that he stopped being sarcastic."

"No wonder you were upset."

"Just one of those things," she said. "But I don't care if I never see JL Denton again as long as I live."

He could see the pain in her eyes, in her face. She'd never cared enough about a man to be so angry at one. That alone told her father that she'd felt something for the rancher.

"Life hurts," he said.

"Tell me about it. You should go back to work before Mr. Clay fires you," she said, trying to smile.

"If he was going to fire me, he'd have done it already. At least he saved the sale I lost."

"I'm going to bed."

"I can bring home something for supper."

"Nonsense," she replied. "I can cook. I'm just going to lie down for a few minutes and use my nebulizer. I'll take some of that leftover cough syrup and I'll be fine."

"We can afford a doctor visit," he replied.

She made a face. "Sure we can. I'll do that, while they're filling up our yacht with diesel."

He laughed softly. "Okay. But I'd rather make payments on a doctor visit than lose my only child. Just saying."

"I love you, Dad."

"I love you, too."

She smiled and walked off toward her bedroom.

Chapter Five

JL was half out of sorts after being ignored by Bill Clay's salesman. He realized that the man wasn't likely to know much about local people since he'd just started at the concern. But it hurt to be ignored, as if he was of less worth because he dressed in working clothes.

He was curious about the newcomer. Hadn't Cassie said that her father was working for an equipment company? There was only one in town, and he'd just come from it.

He frowned. What if that had been her father? It made sense now that he'd have ignored the man who'd made fun of his daughter's asthma attack.

It shamed JL that he'd done that. He hadn't realized she'd had a health issue. He'd thought she was being overly dramatic about the wolf. In fact, his ex-fiancée had done the same thing over a similar incident. It had brought back painful memories. Of course, he hadn't said anything to the other woman about overreacting. He'd been kind and solicitous to his ex-fiancée, because he'd fancied himself in love with her.

He wished he'd been kinder to Cassie. No wonder she was mad at him. He didn't blame her, or her father. It hadn't been until she'd pulled out what looked like an inhaler that he realized she wasn't putting on an act.

He walked out to the barn to tell Drum about the new purchase and give him a time frame about delivery the next day.

"You look preoccupied," Drum noted.

"I did a stupid thing yesterday. I thought Cassie Reed was being overdramatic because a wolf growled at her mount and made it restless. She had an inhaler in her pocket, one of those things people with asthma use," he added. He sighed. "She was already chilled. Eastern tenderfeet don't know about Colorado winters, and she's from Georgia. She was wearing a lightweight coat. I guess she got chilled enough to bring on an attack."

"My mother had asthma," Drum replied. "She got pneumonia a lot. All she had to do was be around somebody with a cold and she'd get sick. It would always go right into her chest. We spent a lot of time in the hospital with her."

JL frowned. He hadn't thought that Cassie might get sick from being chilled. He felt even more guilty.

"She was barely speaking to me when I got her home," he murmured. "I hardly even had time to apologize." He scowled. "I made a worse mistake this morning. I think her father is Bill Clay's new employee. I snubbed him going out of the office. He'd passed me over for a man in a suit when I was looking at the combine I bought."

"In your favor, you didn't know," Drum pointed out.

He made a face. "That won't do much to help me." He pursed his lips. "I think I'll stop by the restaurant and see how much damage I did," he added. "It's getting on suppertime, anyway, and I'm hungry."

"Not me. I had a big lunch. Cook made pork chops and potatoes and onions. Not to mention, homemade rolls."

"I'm not living right," JL sighed. "I should have a cook full-time, instead of pleading with my housekeeper to do it three nights a week. This isn't one of those nights, and I'm sick of my own cooking."

"Your bunkhouse cook is awesome. You should come eat with us." Drum's eyes twinkled. "Of course, I do understand that it would work a hardship on you, eating with the peons . . . watch it!" Drum added, having just sidestepped a swat from that big hand.

"You watch it. I'm not a bad man."

"You sure about that?" Drum asked. "I haven't checked the FBI's most wanted list in a while. . . ."

"I'm going to town. Be back later."

"Good luck."

JL sighed. He was going to need some of that.

He sat down in a booth and waited for Cassie to come out. But she didn't. Sarah, a buxom middle-aged woman, came out instead.

"Hey, JL," she said pleasantly. "What can I get for you?"

"Where's Cassie?" he asked.

"Had to go home," she replied. "She was sick. Coughing her head off. Well, Mary made her go home," she amended. "She didn't want to. Mary promised she wouldn't fire her. She called her dad to come get her."

He was more concerned now than before. He glanced at the clock. "How about making me up three plates to go?" he asked, and chose the special.

"You going to take supper to her? That's nice," she said gently.

"I owe her a supper," he said. "She got sick riding around in the cold with me yesterday. She didn't have a proper coat."

"I told her that a week ago," Sarah said with a sigh. "She said she couldn't afford anything better right now. Proud, that one."

"Yes," he said, feeling small. His conscience was killing him. "Very proud."

"I'll get this ready as soon as I can. Want coffee while you wait?"

He nodded. "Please."

Cassie felt even worse as the afternoon wore on. She was going to have to try to get up and fix something for her father to eat, but she was too sick to stand at the stove and cook.

She dragged herself out of bed, wrapped in a pretty embroidered chenille housecoat that fell to her ankles. It was something from the old life that she'd brought along. It had been her mother's.

She held on to the wall as she wobbled toward the kitchen and prayed that she could make it that far. As it was, she had to stop halfway down the hall to pant for breath.

She heard a vehicle drive up and the engine cut off. She glanced at the clock. It was ten to five. Her father wasn't due home for at least thirty minutes. She grimaced. She didn't have dinner ready. . . .

There was a knock at the door. Surely that wasn't her father, she thought as she went to the door very slowly and opened it.

Her lips parted as she saw JL standing there with a big white bag in his hand.

He made a face. "You look like death warmed over."

"I'm not feeling up to company," she rasped.

"Good Lord," he said softly. He moved in past her. "I'll just put these in the fridge."

He opened the refrigerator door and grimaced at the lack of food in it. He slid the diner meals inside and closed it.

"What was that?" she asked from the doorway.

"Food," he said. "I brought supper. But you aren't eating anything until you've seen the doctor."

Her face flushed. "I don't need . . . !"

He picked her up gently and walked out the front door, pausing to pull it closed behind them with Cassie balanced on one powerful, raised thigh. "We can argue later."

She fought tears. She didn't want to tell him that she couldn't afford a doctor. She had health insurance, but she was afraid to use it. And it didn't cover office visits, even if she'd been willing to risk it. An enterprising reporter would be looking for things like insurance claims. Any good skip tracer would jump on the charges like a duck on a june bug.

"I can't afford—" she began.

He kissed her forehead. She felt feverish. "Just hush," he said gently.

She couldn't hold back the tears. He was being so kind!

He put her into the cab of his ranch truck and closed the door. He handed her his cell phone as he got in beside her and started it, checking to see that her seat belt was on before he fastened his. "Call your father and tell him where we're going," he added softly.

She wiped away the tears. She punched in numbers. "Dad? JL's kidnapped me," she rasped, "and he's taking me to a doctor." She frowned. "Turncoat," she accused. "Yes. Yes. All right. He brought supper, too, it's in the fridge." She gave JL an accusing look, which he ignored. "Okay, Dad. Yes, I'll tell him. Good-bye." She hung up and passed the phone back to her companion. “He said to thank you and that he’s sorry about this morning.”

“It doesn’t matter. Not his fault if he didn’t know who I was,” he replied, sticking the phone in his coat pocket.

She wrapped up closer in her robe. “I should have changed first.”

“You’re sick, and we’re going in the back door, anyway,” he replied.

“The back door?”

He nodded. “The doctor’s a good friend.”

“Oh.”

He pulled up to the back of a one-story building with a big parking lot, pulled out his cell phone, and made a call.

He explained the situation. “Yes. I’ll bring her right in. Thanks, Sandra,” he added, a smile in his voice. He hung up.

“Lorna’s receptionist said I could bring you in the back. The nurse will wait for us.”

“Thanks,” she managed weakly as he lifted her out of the truck and bumped the door shut with his hip.

“You look terrible,” he remarked, searching over her pale face.

She laid her cheek against his coat. It was cold from the wind and it felt good against her fevered skin. “I feel terrible,” she said in a hoarse tone.

“You’ll be better soon,” he promised.

He carried her in the back way. An elderly nurse was waiting for them with a gentle smile. She led them into a cubicle and went out to get the doctor.

JL deposited Cassie on the examination table and dropped into one of two chairs against the wall.

Before he could speak, a young woman with thick chestnut hair and dark eyes came into the room. She was wearing a white lab coat and there was a stethoscope draped around her neck.

She glanced at JL curiously and then at the redhead on the table. "I'm Dr. Lorna Blake," she introduced herself.

"Cassie Reed," came the hoarse reply. "Thanks for seeing me."

The doctor frowned. She put the stethoscope against Cassie's chest and had her breathe and cough while she listened. She looped it back around her neck, took Cassie's temperature, and asked questions, a lot of them.

"I'm pretty sure it's bronchitis," she said. "I need to send you over to the hospital for a chest X-ray. . . ."

"No. Please." Cassie's eyes were troubled. There was no way she could afford that.

The doctor sighed. "All right. I'll send you home with antibiotics and instructions, but if you're not better in two days, I want you back here and you'll definitely get an X-ray then," she added firmly.

"Okay," Cassie said.

The doctor filled out a prescription and handed it not to Cassie, but to JL. "Go to bed," she added to Cassie. "Plenty of fluids. Take the antibiotic. Got cough syrup?"

Cassie nodded.

"Acetaminophen for the fever," the doctor added.

"Okay," Cassie agreed.

"Thanks, Lorna," JL said as he lifted Cassie from the table into his arms.

She grinned. "You're welcome."

He sighed. He knew what was coming later. He'd never brought a woman to his high school friend as a patient, not even that she-shrew he'd been engaged to. It was unusual to see JL so concerned about anyone's health. He was sure Lorna sensed a romance.

JL gave her a speaking glance as he walked out the back door with his patient. Lorna was still grinning when she shut the door behind them.

JL stopped by a pharmacy on the way home, leaving the engine running so that the heater would stay on, and Cassie wouldn't get chilled while he coaxed her prescription out of an amused pharmacist inside. He didn't have to wait. The pharmacist was dating Lorna, so they'd have plenty to talk about on their next evening out, JL was sure.

He drove Cassie home. By then, her father's car was parked at the door. Roger Reed opened it for them as JL carried her inside, straight to her bedroom. He deposited her gently on the bed.

"I heated up supper. You're staying for it, right?" Roger said pointedly.

JL hesitated.

"I made strong coffee," Roger added.

JL glanced at Cassie. "Okay," he said.

She smiled, her eyes bright with fever and delight.

"You can have yours in bed," her dad told the patient.

"Okay, Dad. Thanks."

He just smiled.

He punched the microwave, where the first of three plates was waiting to be heated. When it was done, he added utensils and a napkin and gave them to JL to take to Cassie on a tray he'd found earlier under the cabinet.

"Can you manage this?" JL asked her as he propped the tray on her legs.

"Yes, it's fine," she said.

He paused to read the directions on the antibiotic and shake a capsule out into her hand. She took it and he gave her a spoon and the cough syrup. She knew it was useless to argue. She took that, too.

He smiled. "You'll be better in no time."

"Thanks. For everything."

He brushed back her wild reddish-gold hair. "I'm sorry, about what I said," he told her with genuine regret. "I'm not good with people."

She managed a smile. "Me neither."

He stood up, searching for more words, but he couldn't find any. He smiled, turned, and went out to the dining room, where her father had two plates sitting on the table, along with two mugs of steaming, strong black coffee.

"I didn't know who you were," Roger told him in an apologetic tone as JL sat down. "I'm truly sorry. I'm not really good at working with the public. It's pretty much a life-changing experience," he added with a soft chuckle.

JL just nodded. The man had a very cultured voice, like that of a radio announcer. It sounded oddly familiar.

"Not your fault," JL said after he'd sipped coffee. "I never came inside and introduced myself when I took Cassie out to the ranch." He grimaced. "I should have realized she was getting too chilled. I didn't know about the asthma, either. I chided her for being melodramatic when she gasped for breath." He ground his teeth together. "I'll have hell living with that on my conscience, let me tell you," he added curtly.

"We all make mistakes," his companion said quietly. "God knows, I've made my share."

"Well, a friend of mine said that's why they put erasers on pencils," JL replied.

"I'd need a very big eraser," the other man commented.

They ate in a pleasant silence. The food was good. Mary had one of the best cooks in the county in the kitchen at her restaurant.

"This is really good food," Roger commented.

"Nobody cooks like Mary," JL replied. "We all know each other pretty well around here. Benton's only got a population of about two thousand souls. Only a few people ever leave, mostly kids who want more excitement."

"I've had all the excitement in my life that I care for," Roger said quietly. "The peace and quiet is comforting."

"I heard about what happened to you," JL said.

Roger felt the blood drain out of his face. "Oh?" he asked, trying to sound indifferent when he was churning with fear inside.

"Yes. From Cassie. It must have been very difficult, losing your wife in such a way."

Roger swallowed, hard, and felt relief at the same time. "It was traumatic, for Cassie and me," he said. "We were all close."

"You should sue the people who drove her to it," JL said firmly.

"I'm not that sort of person," Roger replied with a sad smile. "Besides all that, there would be too many to summon to court." He sighed. "Far too many."

JL frowned. It was an odd comment.

Roger realized that, just in time. "She had a page on Facebook," he added. "I hate social media."

"I know what you mean. Say one thing that offends somebody, and the world camps on your doorstep," JL chuckled. "Happened to my foreman a couple of years back. He's very political. Doesn't pay to advertise what party you support. Somebody's always waiting with smart remarks and threats."

"Tell me about it. We're too connected, I think sometimes. Cassie and I have a small TV set, but we don't watch it much. We get our news from the Internet."

"Me too," JL confessed. "I don't like getting news from a handful of people who own all the media in the country. They decide what's news and what's not."

"Too true. Back when I was young, news reporters were required to be objective and even-handed. Now, it's just a handful of executives pushing their own agendas and calling it news."

JL chuckled. "We think alike."

"On that issue, of a certainty."

"I'm sorry I let her get chilled," JL said, nodding toward the bedroom and lowering his voice. "I knew that coat was too thin. I should have made her wear a heavier one."

Roger couldn't bring himself to mention that she didn't have a heavier one here. Actually, she did have one in storage back home; a very expensive one, but they didn't dare wear any couture stuff out here. It would stand out like a sore thumb.

JL noted the pained look on his companion's face and translated it as wounded pride. "You do the best you can when you're living on a budget," he said after a minute. "When I was a kid before we moved back here, my dad worked as a paleontologist and taught at a college in Texas. Times were hard, because my mother was fragile and couldn't hold down a job. It wasn't until my grandfather asked Dad to come back that we were able to afford good clothes and warm coats." He frowned because it sounded odd even to him that his father's salary didn't cover such essentials. "Funny," he said, almost to himself, "I never looked at it that way."

"Budgeting is new to me, and I'm not very good at it,"

Roger confessed. "But I'll get the hang of it. I want to get Cassie a gaming system for her birthday next month. She misses playing online."

JL's eyebrows raised. "She games?"

He laughed. "She games. She loves this space game called *Destiny 2*. She played it all the time when she lived in Georgia."

"I thought Cassie said you lived in New York?"

"We all did, when Cassie was small. She went to Georgia State University in Atlanta and liked it so well that she stayed."

"Yes, she worked as a reporter, she told me."

"She was a good one. She worked for a weekly paper." He laughed. "She found the most unusual people to do feature stories about. Her columns were often picked up by major dailies."

"She might get on with our local paper," JL said thoughtfully.

"She gave it up," Roger replied. "The stress made her asthma worse."

"Oh. I see." He grimaced. "I'll have to be a lot more careful with her, when I take her out," he added, thinking ahead. "I'll make sure she's bundled up properly, even if I have to roll her up in one of my rugs."

Roger laughed at the picture that made in his mind. "She's a black belt," he reminded his companion.

JL grinned. "So am I."

"I heard about that."

"I'll take care of her, just the same. She's got a bagful of medicine. Make sure she takes it. And don't let her go to work tomorrow. Mary already tried to get her to go home today and she argued about it."

"I'll get a strong chain with a lock," Roger agreed, grinning.

"I can pick locks!" came a hoarse voice from the bedroom.

Her father just laughed. So did JL.

Cassie was flushed with excitement and joy when JL came in to say good-bye.

"You get better," he instructed.

"I'll work on it every day," she said in a hoarse tone, and smiled.

"Next time we go riding, I'll get you one of the old coats Nita left when she moved to Denver."

Her lips parted. She searched his dark eyes and felt warm inside, as if a fire had been kindled there.

He was feeling something similar. He reached out and brushed back her disheveled red-gold hair. It had been a very long time since he'd been needed by anyone. His mother was often ill, and he'd been attentive when she was. His father was never sick; his older brother had never even had a cold. But here was this little newcomer who needed nurturing and he felt a bond with her already.

He drew in a breath. He recalled what he'd told her, that he wasn't ready for a relationship. He was feeling surprisingly comfortable with her. "I don't think I've ever been around a redhead in my life," he teased softly.

"We're rare," she had to admit. She smiled. "It comes with freckles."

He chuckled. "I like freckles."

She drew in a rasping breath. "I don't, but it isn't as if I get a choice about having them," she laughed.

"You need to sleep," he said gently, getting to his feet.

"I'll check on you in the morning. You can call me if you need anything."

She looked at him with wonder. "I can?"

"Where's your cell?"

"In my housecoat pocket, there," she said, pointing to the robe she'd draped around the back of a chair.

He lifted it, admiring the intricate embroidery. It looked very expensive. Definitely not something off the rack.

She could see the wheels turning in his mind. He was suspicious.

"It was my mother's," she said, noting the intent look he gave the robe as he searched for the phone. "It's one of the few things I have left of her. Dad gave her the robe three Christmases ago. She fussed because he splurged for it," she added quickly.

"Oh. I see," he said, smiling easily. His suspicions retreated. He opened her contact list and put his phone number into it. He put the phone on the table by the bed. "In case you need it," he said.

"Thanks," she said softly.

He grinned. "You're welcome. If you can't get your dad, and you need anything, you call me, okay?"

"Okay."

"I'll see you tomorrow, sprout."

She grinned. "Okay. Thanks for getting me to the doctor," she added. "I'll pay you back. . . ."

"Over my dead body," he said with a laugh. "This was my treat."

She bit her lower lip and fought tears. "It was so kind . . . !"

"Don't you start," he said, waving a finger at her. "You start bawling and your dad's going to go looking for a shotgun."

"Not likely," her dad said from the doorway, chuckling.

"Figure of speech," JL replied. He smiled at both of them. "I'll see you tomorrow."

"Thanks for all you did," Roger told him. "For supper, and for taking care of Cassie."

"My pleasure." He went out without another word or a backward glance, closing the door behind him.

Outside, he lifted his face to the cold wind and sighed. He was getting in over his head here, and he didn't know how to stop. Her vulnerability appealed to him as other feminine traits never had. His ex-fiancée had been a kind person, or seemed to be, until Cary told him the truth about her. He'd been badly taken in. He didn't trust his own responses. What if Cassie was playing a game? What if she wasn't what she seemed to be?

He dismissed the thought. She was as honest as the day was long, and why would she pretend to be poor, anyway? It was obvious that she and her father had very little money. She'd worried excessively about paying the doctor. She was proud, too, offering to pay him back when he knew she didn't have the money.

No, she seemed like the genuine article. But he'd do well to put on the brakes. He had enough to take care of at the ranch, with the improvements he was finally making. He'd keep close to home for a bit. But he'd check on her in the morning, because he'd promised.

He knocked on her door midmorning. She opened it with a big smile. She was wearing the housecoat, but her color was better.

"Those antibiotics work very fast," she said. "I can feel the difference already." She paused to cough into a tissue.

"Well, I'm still coughing, but it's not as bad as it was. Come on in. Would you like coffee?"

"You shouldn't be up," he fussed.

"Yes, I should," she replied. "My doctor back home told me that it's never a good idea to stay in bed completely with a chest infection. You have to keep moving so that you're more likely to cough up the bad stuff. I've been in the kitchen."

He followed her in. On the counter was a baking sheet with several rolls just rising. They were covered with a sheet of plastic wrap.

"I made those for you," she said gently. "Let them rise for another hour or so, then bake them at three hundred fifty degrees Fahrenheit for about sixteen minutes. If they're not brown, put them back in the oven for another couple of minutes."

"I'll enjoy them," he said. "Thanks."

She grinned. "I love to cook. But I especially like to make breads. I love the feel of dough. It's almost alive."

"My mother could make bread," he said. "But it's been a long time since I've had any fresh from the oven. This was nice of you."

"Payback," she teased. "For your kindness yesterday."

"It's not hard to be kind to someone as sweet as you are," he said, and he wasn't teasing.

She searched his eyes and felt her stomach drop. It was new, the feelings she had with him.

He saw that and grimaced. Everything she felt was plain on her face. "Listen," he began worriedly.

"I can't get married this morning," she broke in, embarrassed by what he'd likely noticed, and desperate to change the mood.

He stared at her. "Excuse me?"

"I can't get married this morning," she said firmly. "Or this afternoon. Not even this year. And that's final. I'm sorry, but I have my heart set on climbing Mount Everest. I'll need an oxygen tank, of course, and the right clothing, and I'll have to save up. But I should have enough in about twenty years, so you can check back with me then."

It took him a minute to realize that she was teasing. He chuckled, deep in his throat. "Just when I think I've got you figured out, you throw me another curve."

"I'm quick, I am," she joked. "Sit down and have some coffee, if you've got time."

"I've got time." He tossed his hat into a spare chair and sat down at the table.

She poured coffee and sat down beside him. "I love coffee first thing in the morning."

"So do I," he said, sipping his. "Nice. I like strong coffee."

"Dad and I do, too," she said.

"I noticed. He makes good coffee as well."

"I forgot to offer you cream and sugar," she said suddenly.

"I don't take either. When you serve in the military, you get used to life without the frills," he chuckled.

"Reporters learn that early," she told him. "I was always on the run. It's a hectic sort of life."

"Your dad said the excitement made your asthma worse."

She nodded. "It did. I missed it, though."

"So, what did you do for a living before you moved out here?" he asked.

She just stared at him. That was the one question she hadn't anticipated, and there was no way she could tell him the truth.

Chapter Six

JL scowled. She looked guilty, and he wondered why.

She thought for a minute. "I had a job as an assistant to a producer at a television station north of Atlanta," she said finally. It wasn't quite the truth. But it sounded better than confessing she'd been a top writer for one of the most successful network weekly shows in the country. She didn't dare admit that, because he might have heard about the scandal that involved her family.

"Assistant producer?" he asked.

"It's like being a research assistant," she continued. "I had all sorts of assignments and I didn't have to sit at a desk all day. Once I got to do a feature story all by myself with just a cameraman and a sound man with me in the van."

One of her friends had such a job, and she was able to recall what the other woman had told her about the assignments she got. It was like being a reporter, but with television cameras instead of a pad and pen—or, more recently, a notebook computer.

"It sounds complicated."

She laughed. "It's not. I covered news stories occasionally, too, but it was mostly feature stuff."

"We have a weekly paper here in Benton," he said. "In fact, the editor used to work in New York City."

Her heart stopped beating. She just sat and stared at JL, vaguely horrified. "Oh?" she asked. "Recently?"

"No," he said, wondering at the sudden paleness of her face. "About ten years ago. Are you okay? You look wan."

"I'm still weak," she said. She smiled. Ten years ago was a relief. The weekly editor wouldn't know about her father.

"I guess you are. I still feel bad that I let you get chilled like that."

"You made up for it," she told him. "It's okay."

He sipped more coffee. "What I was getting at, is that maybe you'd be happier working on the newspaper than waiting tables," he said hesitantly.

"I couldn't go back to it," she replied. "The stress would be too much."

"It's just a weekly paper. Not a daily," he teased.

"You don't understand. The stress on a weekly is much worse than on a daily paper. On a weekly, you're expected to do all sorts of things besides just report. On a daily, you just write your copy and turn it in to the city editor or the state news editor."

"Oh."

"Besides, I like being a waitress," she said, grinning.

"Almost anybody can be a waitress, with the right training. But it takes more than just training to be a reporter."

"Thanks," she said softly, searching his dark eyes.

"You're wasted, is what I meant."

She sighed. "It's not stressful, what I do now, and I love the people I work with," she said. "Besides, I don't have to sleep with a pistol under my pillow at night."

"What?" he exclaimed.

"Back when I worked for the newspaper, we had this reporter, Barney. He did a story about corruption in the county commission and ticked off members of one commissioner's family. He got death threats. He slept with a pistol under his pillow. He was run off the road one night and hit a telephone pole. The perp was never caught, and Barney decided he'd like to work in a happier place, so he got a job as a telephone lineman." She chuckled. "He said that it was a lot less stressful."

He laughed, too. "I guess so. I never thought of reporting as dangerous."

"It can be, depending on who you tick off," she replied.

"Did you ever get a death threat?" he asked easily.

She felt that question to the soles of her feet. She looked hunted suddenly, haunted. "Yes," she confessed. "Once or twice." It had been a lot more than once or twice. She and her parents all had death threats from people who supported the conniving woman who'd wanted her father's job. Social media had hounded them to the point of madness, cost her mother her life. It was unreal, how much damage people could do with just words.

He frowned as he saw how upset she'd become. His big hand slid over her cold one and curled around it. "Sorry," he said gently. "You were thinking about your mother, weren't you?"

He was amazingly perceptive. She took a deep breath and had to fight a cough. "Yes, I was," she confessed. "Sorry."

"I didn't think," he said apologetically. "I know it must be a hard thing to get over. Losing a parent is painful."

"Something we both know," she agreed. Her fingers curled around his. "It's still fresh."

"Life goes on," he replied softly. "It has to."

She nodded. She felt choked inside.

He squeezed her fingers and then let go. "I've got to go," he said. "We've got storm warnings for tonight. The boys and I have to bring the few remaining expectant mothers up to the shelters near the house. Calves are hard on heifers that are bred for the first time."

"I can imagine. I never did get to see the calves," she added suddenly.

"Next time," he said softly, and he smiled.

She smiled back, her heart in her throat. "Next time," she agreed.

"Just friends," he added firmly, even though he was feeling something that was definitely stronger than friendship.

"Just friends," she agreed pertly. "I've already told you that I have to climb Mount Everest before I can even think about marrying anybody."

He chuckled. "I'll remember that." He stood up and put on his hat. "You stay warm. I'm still on call if you need me. Don't go to work if there's ice on the road. Call Mary and tell her you can't get out. She has two other workers who live in town who can fill in if they have to."

His protective attitude made her feel warm inside. "Okay," she said softly.

"And don't go out unless the house catches on fire," he said firmly.

She laughed. "I won't."

He tilted his hat over one eye. "I'll be back by tomorrow. Just to check in."

"Okay. I'll have coffee ready. Oh, wait . . . !" she called as he started out the door.

She handed him the pan of rolls. "Three fifty, sixteen minutes," she repeated.

He smiled slowly. "I won't forget. I'll see you later."

"See you."

She watched him walk out the door with new emotions boiling over inside of her. He said they'd just be friends, but there had been a look in his dark eyes that made her giddy even in memory. They were building to something wonderful.

Her face fell. Something false. Because he didn't know the truth about her and her father. What would he feel, if he found out? Would he believe the lies people had told about her dad? Would he even listen if she tried to explain?

She bit her lower lip, hard. She didn't know what to do. In fact, there was nothing she could do, unless she wanted to tell him the truth right now. That was unwise. If he wasn't sympathetic and he told anybody, the media might be able to find them out here and start the persecution all over again. There would be no place left to go except maybe overseas, and they didn't have enough money for that anymore.

She poured herself another cup of coffee and turned off the pot, her face drawn with worry. Life had seemed so simple when she and her dad moved here. It was a small community, they'd blend in, nobody would know them. It would be fine.

Except that life was never static. You met new people and got involved with them, even superficially. Then you were hostages to fate. Anybody might suddenly see a news item on television and connect it with the new man at the equipment store, or the waitress at the restaurant. It wasn't likely, but it was possible that her father could be recognized, even out here.

Then what would they do? She drew in a long, painful breath. Life was becoming more complicated all the time. She wanted to get closer to JL, but he didn't want a serious relationship. And even if he did, how would she tell him the truth?

She sipped coffee and put the worry to the back of her mind. She had to live one day at a time. It was no good anticipating trouble. That only made things worse. One day at a time, she told herself firmly.

JL went home, with snow falling softly on the back roads, on the tall sharp peaks of the surrounding mountains. He grimaced as he thought what a time they were going to have if the snow amounted to more than an inch or two. He was short-handed. Two of his cowboys had quit for no apparent reason. He was still trying to replace them, and not having much luck. It put more strain on the other workers, trying to absorb the overflow of routine tasks.

Pregnant cows, especially purebred ones, required a lot of work. No rancher could afford to lose many calves in this economy. It meant checking on the herd several times a day to make sure they were sheltered and fed and watered, and safe from predators.

He thought about Two Toes and grimaced. That old wolf would be lounging in the tree line, waiting for his chance at another little lost calf. Just the thought of it made him irritated.

He parked the truck at his front door, went inside, and pulled out his cell phone. He had Butch Matthews, the wildlife rehabilitator, on the phone seconds later.

There was a long pause while he outlined his problems with the resident bad boy of the wolf variety.

"Only two toes?" Butch mused.

"Only two. Well, on one foot, that is. We can tell that much by tracking him through the snow. He limps. He's also old and he must be missing some teeth, because all he wants to bring down are little calves."

"I may be able to do something about that," Butch began.

"I don't want him killed," JL said at once.

There was deep laughter. "Neither do I. I have a special regard for them. A wolf saved my life once."

JL frowned. "You're kidding."

"I'm not," Butch replied. "I fell off my horse and rolled down into a ravine. Broke my leg. Somewhere along the line, my cell phone was torn out of its carrier and I had no way to get help. I heard howling close by. A big white wolf wandered up. It was old and grizzled and looked hungry. I thought my number was up. It wasn't. The animal came close, sniffed my leg, looked at me, and lumbered off. A couple of hours later, the wolf came back, sniffed my leg again, huffed, and trotted off. Not long after that, two men on horseback rode down the ravine to where I was. They made a makeshift travois of lodgepole pine trunks lashed together with rope and topped with a spare rain slicker. They got me back to their ranch, called an ambulance on the way there. I was barely conscious and in a lot of pain, but I remember calling it a miracle that they found me before I was buried in the snow. One of them laughed and said the damned wolf led them to me. They were riding along fence lines to check on pregnant heifers when the wolf came up to them and just sat down and stared at them. They moved toward him and he moved off a little distance. He sat right back down and stared at them some more. They finally got the idea that he wanted them to follow him. They did, and found me." He laughed. "That happened eight years ago, and people still tell that story. In retrospect, it really was something of a miracle."

"I guess so. I don't guess you ever saw the wolf again?" JL asked curiously.

"Not yet. But I might. The wolf that saved my life had a track the men followed. A unique track. The front left paw only had two toes."

"Son of a gun!" JL exclaimed. "I'm getting cold chills down my spine," he chuckled.

"Me too. So no worries about how we'll cope with the old fellow. He can come and live with me. I'll feed him venison and turkey and let him watch television with me."

"I'll buy him a doggy bed," JL promised. "It would be great not to find any more savaged calves."

"There are other predators," he was reminded. "And it's still mostly winter here."

"I know. But most predators aren't quite as smart as that old wolf."

"So it would seem. I'll be around tomorrow after lunch, if that's okay. I'll bring a live trap with me."

"Good job. I'll expect you. And thanks."

"My pleasure."

JL hung up the phone. Well, that was a story he'd enjoy telling Parker and Drum. And maybe Cassie as well.

A few days later, he drove out to town and picked up Cassie after work to show her the growing calf crop.

"How about your wolf?" she asked curiously.

"Now, there's a story and a half," he chuckled, and related the story that Butch Matthews had told him.

"But you're going to lure him into a trap?" she asked, aghast.

"A live trap."

She just stared at him.

"It's called a humane trap. You put bait in it and wait for

the animal to walk in. There's a spring that closes the gate and traps him inside, unharmed."

"Oh." She hesitated. "But what if you don't go back to check the trap and he starves to death?"

He shook his head with an affectionate smile. "Oh, tender heart," he teased.

She sighed. "I guess I am."

"It wasn't a complaint. Butch checks the trap every few hours," he added. "He's staying with us until Two Toes cooperates."

"What is he going to do with the old wolf when he traps him?" she asked worriedly.

"Take him home and feed him venison stew."

"Don't tease," she said gently.

"I'm not. He's going to take him home and feed him venison stew. Butch is the wildlife rehabilitator I told you about. He loves wolves. He had another one that was injured and couldn't be released into the wild. It lived with him for six years. He grieved for a long time after. Two Toes will be good for him."

"I see. That's not what I expected," she confessed, and laughed self-consciously.

"Not what I expected, either," he laughed. "We usually trap animals like that and take them far up into the mountains and release them. We can't do that to Two Toes because he'd starve."

"He hasn't caught him yet?"

He shook his head. "Two Toes is wily. He's hard to fool."

"I can see why. He sounds very intelligent."

"Like some dogs," JL agreed. "We had a shepherd dog here a few years back, as a guard dog. He understood most of what you told him, and whole sentences, not just random words. You could tell him to go into another room, get a particular toy, and bring it back, and he'd do it." He sighed. "Never had another dog that smart."

"What happened to him?" she asked.

"He belonged to Drum, my foreman. Drum's girlfriend loved the dog to death and phoned every day to find out how he was when they broke up. In the end, Drum gave him to her. He said she'd grieve herself to death if he didn't."

"Poor Drum," she said.

"The dog was happy with her," he replied. "She took him everywhere with her. In fact, her next boyfriend didn't like him, so she got rid of the boyfriend." He laughed. "Tickled Drum to death."

"Think she might come back to him?"

"Anything's possible. But he's had several girlfriends. Women love him. He's just not easily lassoed. He likes being by himself. He doesn't mix well with other people. His girlfriend was making long-term plans, and it spooked him. He said he wasn't ready for all that."

"All that?" she wondered.

"Picket fences, kids, dinner at home, no more poker on Friday night with the boys. That sort of thing."

"Maybe it's just as well," she said. "I think it takes a lot of work to keep a couple together. My mom and dad loved each other very much, but even they had arguments and threatened to split up every so often. They compromised."

"So did my parents. Besides that, both of them were kind-natured. They never went out of their way to hurt each other, like some couples do today. I think compromise and tolerance are key parts of a good relationship."

"I do, too."

He glanced at her, a little concerned.

"I haven't climbed Mount Everest yet," she said abruptly and without looking at him.

He burst out laughing as he got the reference about when she planned to get married. "Stop reading my mind."

"Stop thinking absurd things," she shot right back.

He just shook his head.

They had a pasta salad and fruit for lunch, courtesy of JL's housekeeper, Bessie. The older woman was overweight and abrupt, but she had kind eyes and she seemed to approve of Cassie on sight.

"Heard you got sick?" she said as she poured hot coffee into their mugs as they sat at the table.

"Chest infection," Cassie replied. "I have asthma, so I'm prone to them."

"Had a grandma who was like that," the housekeeper said. She put the coffeepot up. "Back in a sec," she said, and ambled down the hall.

"This is wonderful coffee," Cassie mentioned to JL.

"Bessie likes it strong. So do I," he said.

Bessie was back in a minute with a long, heavy wool coat. She draped it over the back of an empty chair beside Cassie. "That belongs to my daughter," she told Cassie. "You wear that when you go out into the cold with him," she said, indicating JL. "Colorado is no place for a lightweight coat," she added with a kind smile.

Cassie's pride throbbed but she bit her tongue. "Thanks," she said huskily. "Thanks so much."

Bessie patted her gently on the back. "It's no problem, taking care of nice folks," she replied.

Cassie was fighting tears. The woman had a big heart.

JL saw those glistening eyes and he smiled tenderly. "That's what we're both doing," he added. "Taking care of nice folks."

"Thanks," she said softly.

"Eat up," he said. "A full belly makes traveling easier."

"Are we traveling, then?" she asked as she blinked away the tears and dug into her pasta salad.

"We are. To see the calves."

"Oh, boy!" she enthused.

He laughed out loud at her enthusiasm. "We've got a good crop this year," he told her. "Lucky for us that we only had an inch or two of snow. The spring grass will pop up, soon, just in time to feed the new babies."

"I can't wait to—"

The ringing of his phone interrupted her. It was playing the theme song of a popular new movie. She grinned as she recognized it.

He winked at her as he answered it. "Yes? Oh, hi, Butch," he added. "How's it going? Yes, I remember. Yes." His eyebrows arched. "You did? When?" He paused. "Sure, I can send Drum. I'll come myself. The three of us should be able to get him into the truck without any issues. We can go home with you, if you think . . . Okay. Well, you know wolves better than any of us. Sure. About ten minutes? We'll meet you there." He hung up.

"He got Two Toes," he told Cassie and Bessie, who were both waiting to hear what was said.

"Hooray," Bessie broke out. "Peace and quiet at last!"

"We hope," JL chuckled.

"Are you going to see him? Can I come?" Cassie asked at once.

He scowled, a little concerned.

"Please?" she added, and her blue eyes pinned his and pleaded with him.

He drew in a breath. "It might be risky. . . ."

"It won't be," she said with certainty. "I'll stay back and do what I'm told. Please?"

He was remembering how she'd panicked when the wolves had crossed their paths, the day she got sick.

"It was because they came up so suddenly," she said, puzzling Bessie, who didn't know what had happened that day. "It wasn't the wolves. Honest."

"Okay then. But, got your rescue inhaler with you?"

She pulled it out of her pocket and showed it to him.

"All right. You can come."

She grinned and grabbed the coat Bessie had brought out for her.

Butch Matthews was waiting for them at the edge of a section of lodgepole pines, with the snow-covered peaks of the mountains for a backdrop. A tall, lanky man, he was leaning up against the truck with his arms folded.

That was when Cassie, bundled up in Bessie's daughter's warm, wool coat, noticed that one of his arms was artificial. That would explain why he couldn't lift the wolf into the truck by himself. She noticed something else when she looked past him at the trap. That wolf was twice the size of a large dog. He was huge. He was prone in the cage, just looking at the approaching humans without howling or making a noise of any kind.

"Has he been like that all this time?" JL asked, puzzled, as they approached the cage.

"Yep," Butch Matthews said with a grin. "Never tried to bite me, even when I gave him some jerky and a little water. I think he remembers me," he added, and took a minute to explain the remark to Cassie, who was fascinated by the story he told.

JL was staring intensely at the huge wolf. "I never get tired of looking at them," he said quietly. "They're magnificent creatures. I hate losing calves to them, but it isn't malicious, what they do. They're hungry and when they find food, they eat it."

"Except when they're old and their teeth are rotten and they can't half see."

"What?" JL asked.

"This old pet is just about blind, JL," Butch said, indicating Two Toes. "His eyes are milky, as if he's got cataracts. I'm going to get one of the wildlife service people over to look at him, to make sure. But I don't think he can see much. He must have been going on smell alone to find even a calf."

"What a shame," JL said. "Left in the wild, he'd die."

"He would. He could easily fall off the side of a sheer cliff, without being able to see where he's going. Starvation would probably be a better bet. I don't anticipate much argument over getting to keep him." He grinned. "Except he might have to just listen to TV instead of watching it with me."

"He's so pretty," Cassie said involuntarily. "I never realized wolves were so big."

"Most people don't, if they've never seen one in person. Native Americans have all sorts of legends about them."

"I've read some of those," she confessed.

"She was a newspaper reporter," JL told his friend.

"Really?" Butch asked. "That must be a high-pressure job."

"It was," she said. "I don't do it anymore. But if I did, what a feature story Two Toes would make," she added with a sigh.

"Feel free to interview me, anytime you like," Butch said with a twinkle in his eyes. "I can tell plenty of stories about wildlife that you'll never read in a book."

"I might take you up on that sometime," she said, but not with any great enthusiasm. In fact, she moved just a little closer to JL, although she still smiled at Butch.

JL felt oddly protective when she did that. His arm slid

over her shoulder and drew her close. He smiled down at her. "She's softhearted," he said gently. "She was afraid we were going to kill Two Toes."

"We'd never do that," Butch laughed. "He's so well-known around these mountains that they'd probably ride us out of town on a rail if we even talked about it."

"People know about him?" she exclaimed.

"Sure they do," JL answered. "Benton's so small and thrives on gossip. Two Toes is a great conversation starter. People have spotted him all around town on government land and private land. He's recognizable."

"But they can't see from a distance that he has just two toes on one foot, can they?" she began.

They both laughed.

"That's not why. Come over here," Butch invited, and positioned himself right in front of the wolf.

She joined him, with JL, and caught her breath. "Well, for heaven's sake!" she exclaimed.

The big wolf was snow white except for a dark gray ruff around his head. But that was where he was most distinctive. His dark gray head had several white streaks through it, as if he'd had his fur dyed in a unique pattern.

"As you see," Butch continued, "he isn't hard to recognize, even at a distance. There isn't another wolf anywhere around with his particular coloring."

"He really is unique," Cassie said softly, staring at the big animal.

It turned its head and looked at her. It made an odd woofing sound and then whined. It cocked its head at her and sniffed.

She was fascinated. Without asking, she went closer to the cage, very slowly, and dropped down to one knee beside it.

"Pretty boy," she said softly. "Sweet old wolf."

He whined again and lowered his head to look up at her with big pale milky brown eyes.

She reached into the cage, slowly, and rubbed her fingers over his head, between his eyes. He whined again and sighed, making no move to bite or snap at her.

"Animals like you, miss," Butch remarked.

She laughed softly. "I've always had dogs," she said. "Well, until the past few months," she added sadly. "My last dog was very old. He developed cancer and we had to put him down."

"They can treat that, but it's massively expensive," Butch said.

"Massively," she agreed, not adding that she'd had the dog given chemotherapy in a hopeless effort to prolong his life. Finally, her father had convinced her that she was only adding to the animal's suffering. There was no hope of recovery. She gave in. Even the vet said that it was the kindest thing to do. "I still miss him," she added gently.

"What sort of dog was he?" JL asked.

She smiled. "A malamute," she replied.

"In Georgia?!" JL exclaimed.

She laughed. "Well, we had air-conditioning, you know. Although one day I came home from work and found him sitting inside the refrigerator. He'd opened the door after the air conditioner apparently failed." She shook her head. "It was a mess to clean up. He just laughed," she added, recalling the dog's happy expression.

"I had a malamute, and a Siberian husky once," JL said. "They're great pets. Lousy watchdogs."

"I know!" She laughed out loud. "If you were ever robbed, they'd follow the burglars around, show them the best stuff, and help them carry it outside to their getaway car. At least, Ranger would have," she added.

"But they're great company."

"Yes," she agreed. "Ranger would sit outside with me on nights when we had meteor showers, and just lie down and be quiet the whole time, sometimes for hours."

"You like meteor showers?" JL asked.

"I love them."

"So do I."

She got to her feet. "Good luck, old fellow," she told Two Toes.

"He won't need luck. He's got Matthews," JL chuckled.

"Well, if you'll help me get him loaded up," Butch began.

A pickup truck pulled off the road and parked next to JL's SUV. A tall, powerfully built man with long black hair and a somber face joined them. "Caught him, I hear?" he asked.

"Caught him. Hey, Parker," Butch greeted, shaking the newcomer's hand. "I could use a little help. . . ."

"No problem." Parker walked over to the cage, knelt beside it, and passed something into the cage for the wolf. He patted it on the head and said something else. Then he got to his feet and, without asking for assistance, picked up the cage and slid it onto the bed of the pickup truck all by himself. He put up the tailgate and secured it in place.

"I didn't see that," Butch said.

"I didn't see that, either," JL added.

"I lift weights," Parker said, glaring at them. "You could do it, too, if either of you ever went to a gym!"

"Wouldn't do me much good," Butch sighed, indicating his mechanical arm, but smiling, as if making light of his disability.

"Wouldn't now," Parker agreed. "But you couldn't have lifted him before you lost that arm, Matthews," he added with a grin.

"I guess not. I hate gyms. Nasty, smelly places," Butch said, making a face.

"Well, he won't build me a gym," Parker said, jerking a thumb at JL, "so I don't have much choice, do I?"

"Why should I build you a gym?" he asked the tall man.

"Because I can break horses like nobody else who works for you. And mostly, so I wouldn't have to go to town where there are nasty, smelly gyms and wandering gangs of panting women."

Cassie blinked. "Excuse me?"

"Panting women," Parker said, turning his twinkling black eyes and his infectious grin on her. "Every time I take off my shirt to work out, I have to fend them off with shields. A man with my assets gets harassed all the time by women."

"You should sue," JL said with a straight face.

"Absolutely," Butch agreed. "Or, at least, take me with you to the gym so that I can get the overflow."

Parker chuckled. "I might take you up on that."

"Thanks for the help," Butch said.

"No problem, Sarge," he replied. "I still owe you for that last deployment in Iraq."

"Yeah, well, I owe you a couple of favors, too," came the reply.

Cassie sensed the affection between the two men and wondered at it.

Parker threw up his hand and went back to his own truck. Butch thanked JL again, got into his truck, and drove away, leaving Cassie and JL alone.

"Why did he call Mr. Matthews 'Sarge'?" she asked.

"That's a long story," he replied. "I'll tell it to you, on the way to see the calves."

Chapter Seven

"Isn't Mr. Parker the man you said you had to keep away from people because he cussed so much?" she asked.

"He is."

"But he didn't cuss a single time," she pointed out.

"Must have a fever or something," he teased.

"Really?" She just laughed. "Were he and Mr. Matthews both in Iraq?"

"They were. Butch was his sergeant. They got into a firefight with insurgents and Butch was badly wounded. Parker dodged through a hail of gunfire to get to him, threw him over his shoulder, and dodged back behind our own lines. He was hit twice before he got there."

"A brave man," she said solemnly.

"Very brave. Butch lost his arm, but kept his life. Later on, he returned the favor by taking out an insurgent who'd sneaked into camp and had an automatic trained on Parker. Butch shot the man and saved Parker's life."

"I begin to understand," she said.

He nodded. "Combat makes fast friends of strangers."

She searched his hard face. "You were over there, too," she recalled.

He nodded. "I was in a different outfit than Butch and Parker were in, but in the same general vicinity."

She recalled that he never talked about it, so she didn't push.

He noticed that. He loved it about her. Most women would have tried to pry it out of him, become insistent. She didn't. She just accepted people the way they were.

He did wonder at Parker. The man was notorious for his blistering and politically incorrect vocabulary, yet he'd said not one bad word in Cassie's company. He was going to ask about that later. It was a real mystery.

Meanwhile, he took Cassie to the barn and walked her down the wide, paved aisle to the stalls where three calves were kept.

"These little ones have been sick," he told her. "So we brought them in here." He didn't add that taking her out in the pasture to see the calves could get dangerous. He didn't run polled, or dehorned, cattle, and mother cows could be dangerous if they perceived a threat from human intruders. He'd seen one cow actually attack one of his cowboys for petting a calf on the head. That particular cow had been culled. It wasn't wise to keep an aggressive animal around his cowboys. But sometimes you didn't know a cow was aggressive until you found it out the hard way. He wasn't risking Cassie.

Polled cattle were less dangerous around cowboys and equipment, but in an area with predators, like JL's ranch, it was more profitable to leave the horns on, so that the cattle could defend themselves, especially when big snows made it difficult for workers to get to them.

"They're so pretty," Cassie remarked, leaning on the fence to smile over it at the calves. "Black as coal."

He nodded.

"Will they get better?"

He laughed. "Sure, they will. Then they'll go back to the herd with their mothers."

"I read that some mothers reject their calves. Then what do you do?"

"They become bottle calves," he said simply. "We bring them into the barn and keep them here until they're weaned. We always have a few of them."

"That's sad."

"That's life," he replied easily. "Sometimes mothers don't know what to do with their calves, especially first-time mothers. They walk away and can't find them again, or they just walk away, period. We check the herds several times a day during calving, so we'll find them if they're by themselves. Usually. Sometimes we have problems, like old Two Toes raiding our pastures."

"I like your Mr. Matthews," she said. "He's nice."

He chuckled. He liked it, the way she described his friend. He'd found over the years that women who thought men were nice didn't feel much attraction to them, except as substitute brothers. It pleased him that Matthews hadn't made an impression. Not that he was interested in her that way. Of course he wasn't!

On the other hand, Parker had been very interested in her. He'd never seen the man so animated.

"Mr. Parker lifted that whole cage into the truck by himself," she added worriedly. "I hope he didn't hurt himself. I imagine Two Toes is very heavy. He's a big wolf."

"Parker frequently amazes us," he replied. "We don't know a lot about his background. He never speaks of it. We only know about Iraq because Matthews was in his unit."

"Mr. Parker looks sort of different," she replied.

He laughed. "He's part Crow."

She nodded. "Yes. One of Custer's scouts was part Lakota; Mitch Bouyer, who died with him at the Little Bighorn. His best friend was Thomas Leforge, who wrote a book entitled *Memoirs of a White Crow Indian*. He lived with the Crow people. It was a fascinating book!"

He knew his jaw had dropped.

She glanced at him. She laughed. "I love that period of history," she explained. "I've read everything I could find on the Battle of the Little Bighorn, including eyewitness accounts by the Native Americans who fought there. Isn't it amazing," she added, "that people of the period said there were no eyewitnesses left alive, when there were literally hundreds of Native Americans of many tribes who fought in the battle?"

"I know what you mean," he said. "It was a particularly sad period in our history."

She nodded. "It's painful to look too deeply into those fights. But I had a history professor who told me that we should never judge the past by the morality of the present. You have to judge by the morality of the time period. That's never easy."

"We learn as we grow," he agreed. "Our time period isn't perfect, but we're a hell of a lot better than we were a century ago."

She smiled. "I think that, too."

"I always loved history," he remarked. "I studied it in the military. Dad wanted me to go to law school, but I needed business courses to keep the companies operating in the black. I majored in business, minored in economics and marketing."

Cassie had majored in history, but she wasn't going to mention it. He might wonder why a woman who'd gone to college was waiting tables. “Dad said you deal more in oil than you do in cattle,” she said.

“That’s true. I inherited the cattle. But I made a fortune in oil by speculating and taking chances,” he replied, chuckling.

“I’ve never taken a chance in my life,” she murmured. Actually, she had—coming out west incognito with her dad.

“I never used to. Then I went into the Army.” He sighed and shook his head. “My dad and I fought it out, because he wanted me to go to college first. I wanted experience.” He glanced at her. “I got my way. Wished I hadn’t, too. I’d heard all these stories about combat, about how noble it was.” He laughed. It had a hollow sound. “I had a buddy, Rick. We went through basic training together and ended up in the same company. We both came from rural backgrounds and we pretty much agreed on life and politics, so we spent our liberties together.” His eyes had a faraway look as he stared over the fence at the little calves, as if he wasn’t really seeing them. “We shipped out to Iraq. We were slated for an incursion into enemy territory, to take care of some insurgents who were standing off and taking potshots at us.” He drew in a long breath. “It wasn’t until we closed on them that I noticed one man was drawing back to throw something. Before I could say a word, Rick went up in the air, as if he’d been tossed by a giant hand. He died instantly.”

“Oh, my gosh,” she said softly.

“The insurgents moved up behind their grenade-tossing front man. We had to call in reinforcements before we could recover our casualties.” He winced. “There wasn’t a lot of Rick left. . . .”

She slid her hand over his where it rested on the gate. His fingers curled around it. She could feel the tension in him. “So that was my introduction to the ‘noble’ art of war.

There's nothing noble about it. There's fear and terror and grief and blood." He smoothed his hand over hers. "I took a round in the shoulder, fortunately not a fatal one, and got sent home because I was so close to being discharged. So Dad finally got his way after almost four years. I did go to college, after all."

She laughed softly. "I'm sure your dad was happy about that."

"Until I fought overseas, I wasn't sure I wanted to keep the ranch," he said, surprising her. "But when I came home, and settled back in, the very peace of it was comforting. Animals and people depending on me, needing me." He shrugged. "It was a new concept. I got used to it."

"I used to take care of Mama when she was sick," she said. "She never asked me to. She was always trying to convince me that she could take care of herself, even when she couldn't. She was a sweet, kind person. It wasn't right, what happened to her."

"I still think you have a potential lawsuit there," he remarked.

"It's like my father said, we aren't that sort of people," she said, heading off trouble. There was no way she could bring a lawsuit without going back east and blowing her cover. It would bring the weight of the media right back down on them all over again.

He looked at her with affection. "You feel things deeply, don't you?"

She nodded. "My dad always said I was too sensitive to live in the real world. I take things hard."

"Like ignorant men making fun of you for being overly dramatic, when you were gasping for breath," he said with a wry smile.

"Oh, I didn't blame you," she said, looking up into soft brown eyes. "I'm sure it looked like I was overreacting."

"I should have known better," he replied. He brushed back her disheveled red-gold hair with a gloved hand. "You hold things inside."

"I never wanted to worry Mama, so I had to. She was even more sensitive than I am." She sighed. "I miss her."

"You've still got your dad."

"Yes. My biggest blessing."

"He has a very cultured voice," he said abruptly. "I don't think I've ever heard one quite like it, except for radio announcers. I don't guess he ever worked for a radio station?"

She laughed and tried to make it sound natural. "No. I've always thought he had the voice for it, too."

"What did he do, before he came out here?"

"He was a businessman," she said. "He worked for a corporation that marketed commodities." Well, it had, she rationalized, it marketed entertainment.

"And here he is in Benton, Colorado, selling farm and ranch equipment," he observed.

"It's an honest living," she told him. "At least he isn't holding up convenience stores to swipe chicken burritos." She recalled that last item from a movie she'd loved—*Battleship*—and she burst out laughing.

He looked down at her with howling amusement. "There was this movie . . ."

"Yes!" she laughed. "They ended up fighting aliens in a World War Two battleship, aided by the former crew!"

"It's one of my favorites," he confessed.

"Mine too, and nobody in my whole family was ever in the Navy. My people were Army all the way, through all the wars."

He laughed. "My family was strictly Marines."

"I won't hold it against you," she said with a wicked grin.

He sighed and shook his head. "I knew you'd be one of those, the first time I saw you," he mused.

"One of those?"

"Madcap people," he explained. "Outrageous and funny."

"Thanks. I think."

"Oh, it's a compliment," he said, turning back toward the aisle. "I tend to like outrageous people."

"So do I," she said, as she fell into step beside him. "Do you like superhero movies?"

"Love them."

"How about cartoon movies?"

He stopped halfway down the aisle and turned to her. "Cartoon movies?"

"*Moana*," she said. "*Lilo and Stitch. How to Train Your Dragon. Despicable Me*."

"Oh, those." He chuckled. "I don't watch many of them. I did watch *Moana*. We had a guy from New Zealand who worked here when it came out, a Maori. He dragged us all into the theater to see it. He was right. It was spectacular. Besides," he added, "it had The Rock."

"The what?"

"The Rock," he repeated. "Don't tell me. You've never watched wrestling."

"Dwayne Johnson!" she exclaimed. "That Rock!"

He grinned. "Yes. That Rock."

"Isn't he awesome?" she sighed. "He could stand on a stage and read the telephone directory, and I'd buy a ticket. He's gorgeous."

"Women do love him. Men admire him because he's so accomplished. An athlete and an actor, a very unusual combination."

"Dave Bautista's in *Guardians of the Galaxy*," she pointed out. "He was a wrestler, too, and he's a terrific actor."

"Nice, that we like the same ones," he returned. "Although,

we have to keep in mind that you haven't climbed Mount Everest."

"Oh, I always keep that in mind," she agreed. "Do you have more calves?"

"Lots, but they're out in the pastures and I don't run polled cattle."

She stopped and looked up at him with wide, curious blue eyes.

"They all have horns," he explained.

"So?"

"So," he said, taking her gently by the shoulders, "mama cows are very protective of their babies, and some of them can be aggressive. We don't take chances our guests will get hurt."

"I see."

"But there's still the bottle calves," he added.

Her eyes lit up.

"Not today," he said, smiling. "I have a business meeting in Dallas on Monday, and I have to get to the airport early in the morning, so I'll have time to talk to some other investors over the weekend. How about next Saturday?"

"I'd love that," she said, her feelings spilling out of her like foam out of a latte.

"I would, too," he replied. He smiled. "I'll pick you up about noon and Bessie can fix us lunch."

She grimaced. "Saturday. I have to work!"

"Sunday," he amended.

She nodded. "Sunday's fine."

"I never mentioned how good those rolls were that you made me," he said. "Drum came in to ask a question, smelled the air, and promptly grabbed three and took them with him. They were delicious."

"I'm glad you liked them," she said, feeling warm inside.

"What would you like from Texas?" he asked.

"A longhorn?" she ventured.

He gave her a long-suffering look. "Something I can get on an airplane."

"Peanuts?"

That took him a minute. He burst out laughing. "Hell. I'll bring you something unexpected."

"Okay," she said, grinning up at him.

He was still laughing when he dropped her off at her home. He drove away feeling new, reborn. It was as if the past few months hadn't even happened. He was already looking forward to the next weekend.

"Did you have fun?" her father asked over supper.

"Lots," she replied. "They caught the wolf who's been bringing down their calves."

"Oh? Did they shoot it?"

"No. It's an old wolf, almost blind. There's a local wildlife rehabilitator who's going to adopt it."

"That's nice. Not what I expected from ranchers, I have to confess," he added.

"JL's not your average rancher," she said. "The rehabilitator only has one arm. He and this guy named Parker who works for JL were overseas in combat."

"So was JL, I hear."

She nodded. "He talked about it, just a little. He lost his best friend to a grenade."

"Damned shame, what young men and women have to go through when they join the military," he replied. "Not that I didn't try to join," he added ruefully and with a smile. "I had a bad heart valve. I tried more than once, but they wouldn't let me in." He grimaced. "The valve's still bad, and I've never had a minute's trouble from it. Go figure."

"Rules are rules."

"So they say."

"I'm going back over to the ranch for lunch next Sunday," she told him. "I'll make sure you've got something nice cooked before I go."

His eyebrows lifted. "Getting serious?"

"Trying not to," she said. "He isn't ready to get involved again, and I'm not sure I should. We've still got the scandal hanging over us. JL would think I'd been deceptive because I didn't level with him about why we're out here. But I can't risk telling him, in case he let it slip."

"I can feel your pain. I'm the same. I'm afraid to open my mouth."

"She's getting away with it all," she said angrily. "It's not right."

"I've got Jake working on things back in Manhattan," he said unexpectedly.

"Your attorney?" she asked, surprised.

He nodded. "He's asking questions. He thinks there may be a way to make her confess."

"That would take a miracle," she said.

"Don't ever discount miracles," he said affectionately. "Trudy Blaise has enemies. One of them used to be a television producer in Los Angeles. He got fired for harassment and she got his job."

"Why does that sound so familiar?" she asked with biting sarcasm.

"And it may not be the only instance of malfeasance. People who cause problems to get ahead generally use the same scheme over and over, because it works. But it can be a deal breaker if it gets found out."

"Oh, how I hope it gets found out!"

"Me too," he agreed. "At least, there's a little light at the end of the tunnel. All we have to do is be patient and wait for developments."

"Patience is hard," she said.

"I know. But we don't have much choice." He grimaced. "I'm so sorry that I didn't see it coming. I'll never stop blaming myself for what happened to your mother. If I'd just given in, at the very beginning . . . !"

"Don't do that," she told him firmly. "Neither of us realized what she might do. She never told us about the scathing things people were saying to her on social media. She took those comments to heart and let them eat at her. What she did was in a moment of depression and madness. It was an impulse that arose out of mental torment. We'd have stopped her if we'd known. But she never said a word."

"She was like that," he recalled sadly. "Always putting other people first, in everything. I just wish she'd told me."

"We can't go back," she replied. "We have to go ahead, however difficult it is."

"I know. It's just . . ."

"I miss her, too," she said softly.

He managed a smile. "Yes. So do I."

They watched the evening news on the little television set with no real enthusiasm. One particular news item caught their attention. It was just a quick note, running across the bottom of the screen on the scrolling news items. It said that one of the writers on the television program Cassie used to write for had met with a terrible accident on a snow-covered lane in Vermont, where he was spending a week with his wife. He'd died instantly.

"Oh, poor Frank," she said, her face reflecting her sadness. "He was one of the best writers we had. And poor

Essa, his wife. They didn't have children. All they had was each other." She sighed and lowered her eyes to the floor.

He patted her hand. "It's rough, what we're going through. But you know what your mother would say."

She nodded. "She'd say that God had a plan, that we were all part of it, and we'd realize one day why things happened the way they did. She was a fatalist."

"I'm sorry about Frank."

"Me too." She glanced at the screen again and noticed that the commentator was speaking about the writer's death. The producers were lamenting that their best writer, CN Reed, had given up "his" job. It was kept quiet, at least to the media, that CN Reed was, in fact, a woman. Everyone she worked with obviously knew she was female.

There was another news item about the *Warlocks and Warriors* weekly series—the one Cassie had written for—concerning its producer. He'd been accused of entertaining an underage girl at his apartment and executives with the network were discussing whether or not to fire him. Trudy Blaise, they added, had been discussed as coming on board at the show.

Gossip was that she might take a position, since the show she'd inherited from disgraced producer Roger Reed was failing in the ratings.

"Failing because she had a hand in it," Cassie said angrily. "She's like poison. She spoils everything she touches."

"Amen," he said quietly. "I'm sorry for your show," he added. "She'll send it to the scrap heap, if they give her that job. I can't understand why they would."

"It was an open secret that Matley Butler liked younger women," she said. "But he never entertained underage girls, and nobody ever accused him of anything. But Trudy could make a meal out of him. All she'd have to do is have someone trick him into a compromising situation and get photos of it and imply that his conquest was underage. The media would feed on the story and ignore anybody who tried to correct her lie, just like they did with you. She's sleeping with her attorney and he has an investigator who's known for dirty tricks," she added.

"So I've heard."

They listened again to the commentator. He was mentioning that a powerful network executive had stepped up to defend Mr. Reed and was adamant that he wasn't the sort of man to ever be indecent to any woman. He'd added an unflattering comment about Ms. Blaise, who seemed to inherit a lot of jobs from executives who were found in compromising situations.

"Kind of him," Roger said quietly. "But he's in the minority. Almost every executive on the network lined up to kick me out the door."

"They've mentioned both our names," Cassie said worriedly.

He drew in a breath. "We're safe out here," he assured her. "Nobody will connect us with the scandal. We're living in one of the smallest towns in Colorado. They won't look for us here."

"That's not what I meant," she said. "What if somebody local sees it on television and realizes it's us?"

"They only used your initials, like they used on the show's credits."

"Yes, but my last name is Reed and they gave your last name as well," she persisted.

He smiled sadly. "We'll have to hope we don't get connected with what happened in New York."

She bit her lower lip. "If JL sees it, he'll think I've been lying to him the whole time, about being poor and all."

"I don't think it would matter now," he replied. He smiled gently. "He's sweet on you. Maybe he doesn't want to be, but I don't think he'd walk away even if he knew the truth."

She grimaced. "I guess I can hope. Can't I?"

"Things will look up. I promise you they will," he said. "We just have to live one day at a time, sweetheart."

"You're right."

"We both have to stop trying to live in the past."

"That's harder."

"Of course it is."

She glanced at him. "Are you really happy out here, Dad?" she asked.

He shrugged. "It isn't as if I have a choice. Nobody in television in New York would touch me after what I've been accused of."

"That producer who defended you might."

"Hartman Spencer," he said, smiling. "He never believed Trudy in the first place. He called her a liar to her face. She just laughed."

"She'll get her comeuppance one of these days," she replied quietly. "You wait and see. Lies always get found out."

"Mostly."

"And that private detective may come up with something really nice to throw at her, especially if she's pulled that trick before."

He nodded.

"We should have made her take you to court," she said suddenly. "She'd have had to prove the charges and she couldn't. During the time she said you were assaulting her, you were in a meeting with the president of the film company and two of its directors."

"The president might be willing to testify to that, but I

promise you that the two directors would run for their lives. Nobody sane wants to be sucked into this mess."

"It's not right, that one person can make such an accusation and suddenly get a million people yelling for blood."

"I do agree," he said. He smiled. "We've seen our share of them, for sure."

"What we have to do is fight back," she replied, meeting his gaze. "I don't know how to do it, and we don't have any money . . ."

"My attorney got paid before I got fired," he said. "So he's got the capital to pursue the case. A very wise decision on my part, I must say, considering that I didn't know what was about to happen."

"I like your attorney. He reminds me of those old *Perry Mason* episodes I like to watch on YouTube."

"He does bear a certain resemblance to Raymond Burr," he chuckled.

"He has first editions, and even an illuminated manuscript."

"Yes," he said. "He could retire to Europe and live like a king on what he inherited, but he practices law. He's good at it, too. Mostly he takes cases that no other counselor will."

She smiled. "He's dishy, too," she teased.

"My secretary used to think so," he chuckled. "She said it was fortunate that she was married, because otherwise she'd lie down on the floor in his office and refuse to leave until he took her to dinner."

"She'd have a long wait, from what I heard," she replied. "He went through a bitter divorce. He said he'd never marry anybody again."

"He probably means it. He says that his investigator is hot on the track of some vital information. He wouldn't tell me what it was. I hope it's coming from his investigation of Trudy."

"So do I. I would really hate to see her get away with what she did. Mama would still be alive, but for her!"

"We don't know that," he said unexpectedly. "We're all living on borrowed time, if you think about it. We know that we're going to die eventually. We just don't know when and how. Maybe she was right, and there really is a plan that God has in store for all of us. We die when we're supposed to."

"It's a kind way of looking at it," she said. "I just wish—"

"Yes," he interrupted. "Me too."

Cassie didn't sleep much that night, remembering the horrible accusations Trudy Blaise had thrown at her father in the news media. She'd made friends with one lonely reporter who worked for a major news agency, and she'd fed him pitiful stories about what that lecher Roger Reed had done to her.

It was all an act, all for show. The woman pretended to cry, but there were no real tears, no red eyes, no sign of true misery. Trudy had lied and it had cost Cassie's mother her life. She wasn't ready to talk about forgiveness even if her father was. She wanted to nail the woman's reputation to a tree. She wanted revenge.

But then she thought about how she wasn't telling JL the truth about her past. She sighed, and worried about what he would think if he ever found out. She just prayed that he'd understand that it wasn't malicious that she had to hide the truth.

Chapter Eight

Cassie went to work the next morning, still a little weak from her bout of bronchitis, but feeling much better.

She was nervous as she hung up her coat and looked around at the customers. She was hoping against hope that nobody local had seen the news last night and made any connections.

She went to work, forcing a smile as she thanked Mary for letting her have the days off to get better.

"I'll work really hard to make up for my lost time," she promised her boss.

"You always work hard," Mary teased. "And it was no trouble at all. We have people who can fill in for you when you're sick. I've never fired anybody for having bronchitis," she added with a grin.

"I appreciate that."

She went to work her tables. Two people were sitting at one of the tables, obviously businessmen. They looked at the menu and barely glanced at Cassie as they gave her their orders. Their accents were definitely New York ones. They must be passing through. Odd, that they'd be in such a small place on a business trip.

As she was turning to leave, she overheard one of the men say that he'd heard some news last night about one of the writers for his favorite television show dying.

"Hell of a shame, he was really good," the man said. "Of course, I miss having CN Reed on the job. He was a hell of a storyteller. Nice sense of humor in what he wrote. The show hasn't been the same since he left."

Cassie wanted to wait and hear more, but she didn't dare. Eavesdropping could be deadly if the men grew curious about why a waitress was spying on them. She put their orders in and went to another table, where two senior ladies were sitting.

They gave her their orders and she took them down slowly so that she could hear more of what the traveling businessmen were saying. It relieved her that they thought the show's missing writer was a man. Cassie had always used just her initials, because she liked her privacy. Even in Georgia, fans of that show were resourceful enough to find out who she really was and where she lived. There had been a young man who actually stalked her, not for romantic purposes, but to try and wheedle the next month's developments in the show out of her. Fortunately, he'd been harmless and the local police had given him a nice talking to that resulted in no more midnight visits to Cassie's home.

The two men were now discussing a business associate. Cassie wished they'd had more to say about the scandal. They seemed to know a lot about the program she'd written for. But maybe they were just fans. A lot of people were. The series was very well-known.

She came back with their order. They hardly noticed her as they started to eat. She smiled and went back to the counter to get the elderly women's orders. As she walked to their table, she overheard one last remark from the businessmen.

"They say that Trudy Blaise may be replacing the producer who put *Warlocks and Warriors* on the air in the first place. Something about an underage woman he took home with him. She's also alluding to sexual harassment of some kind."

"I thought she was still spouting off about the Reed man . . . ?"

"No. He got fired, remember? She got all the news media involved, as well as several women's rights groups, acted the victim, and put it all out on social media. She got his job. Nobody knows where he went. After his wife's death, he just vanished. Poor guy. Now here's another poor sucker who's going to fall to Trudy Blaise's lies. It's a damned shame."

"Yes," the other man said heavily. "It is. She'll ruin that show. She has no experience at producing. Ratings are falling fast for the program she took over after Reed left. Nobody likes her. One of the stars has already said he's not renewing his contract if it means putting up with her. She interferes in every facet of production. Shame. It was a novel idea, having a weekly series built around a budding singing group's career rise. Not only that but setting it in the seventies with all the accompanying old songs that went with the era. Sheer genius."

"You can pin a rose on that. Reed was a man of vision. I hated seeing him go. I wish Blaise would get hers. I'd love to see it. I wish the media would eat her alive."

"Dream on," his companion said. "Pity about Matley Butler, the *Warlocks and Warriors* producer. She says he's got an underage lover."

"He ought to take her to court and make her prove it."

"Chance would be a fine thing. She's sleeping with one of the best lawyers in New York, and he's working pro bono for her. What a skunk."

"I can think of a better word," the other man replied.

Cassie, hovering, noticed one of the men glancing at her curiously. She smiled, grabbed the coffeepot, and moved beside them. "Can I warm up your coffee for you?" she asked pleasantly.

"Yes, thanks."

She poured hot coffee into their almost empty cups.

"Just passing through, are you?" she asked conversationally.

The older of the two chuckled. "I wish. We took a private plane to see a writer who lives up in Wyoming and it had mechanical failure. So we decided we'd hire a car and drive to the airport in Denver, where they have major airlines." He shook his head. "Give me New York any day! Sorry," he added.

"No offense taken," she said brightly. "Small towns aren't for everyone. A writer who lives near here?" she probed, worried that they might be looking for her.

The shorter man nodded. "Writes western novels. We work for the network that's producing a series based on them. Great writer." He named the man.

"Oh, I've read one of his books!" she exclaimed. "He's really good."

"We think so."

"Well, let me know when you're ready and I'll bring the check."

"Will do."

She smiled again and left them to talk. What an interesting story she was going to have to tell her father. And what an amazing coincidence, to find two New Yorkers involved in television production out here in the middle of nowhere.

"So now she's angling to take over the show you write for," her father said over supper. He shook his head. "She'll ruin it, too. My show has such low ratings that they'll probably never get them back up again."

"Your show was popular because you were the guiding force behind it," she replied. "You had a genius for hiring the best writers for the job, not on the basis of favorites."

"Thanks, sweetheart," he said. "But it was the writers who made the show. They were its heart."

"I'm so sorry about Frank," she said sadly. "I can't even send a card to his wife."

"I know." He made a face. "Not that we've got enough money between us to even send a small bouquet of flowers. When I think of how we used to live . . ."

"We still have each other, Dad," she reminded him. "And there's always hope. The men said that Trudy was probably going to get the executive producer spot on my show. She's got something on Matley. He's such a nice guy." She sighed. "I guess she'll micromanage things and my show will drop in the ratings like a rock, just like yours."

"Maybe we can do something about that in time," he said. "I need to call Jake and see what he's come up with. Think the budget will stand one phone call to New York?"

"Call him on Skype," she teased. "At least it's free."

"Got a point, kid. I'll do that."

She worried about their names being so prominent on a national news show, but except for the two businessmen—

obviously not from Benton but just passing through—nobody had made the connection.

Her father had phoned his attorney, who wouldn't tell him anything except plans were in the works to bring a happy resolution to the problem. They'd have to be patient and let things develop.

Meanwhile, Cassie's phone rang Friday night and she didn't recognize the number. She hesitated and searched her contacts list and almost dropped the phone when she saw the new contact number and realized whose it was.

She fumbled the answer button on. "Hello?" she asked breathlessly.

There was a deep chuckle on the other end of the line. "Didn't recognize the number, I gather?"

"No! And then I saw it on my new contacts list. . . ." She swallowed. "Sorry." She laughed with self-consciousness. "How are you?"

"Lonesome. How about you?"

"Oh, I'm not lonesome," she said. "I have two movie stars and a bagger from the local grocery store sitting on my front porch right now, pleading for company."

"Two movie stars?"

"Yes!" She paused. "One of them plays the hero's dog on that police show, and the other is the drug-sniffing dog from one of the SWAT reality shows."

He chuckled. "You nut."

"Actually, the bagger would like to take me out," she added. "His girlfriend threw him over last week and he wants to make her jealous, so she'll come back to him. I've been nominated because nobody else in Benton will date him."

He laughed louder. "Oh, the exciting life you lead."

"It's very hectic," she agreed. "I have to mark up calendars so I won't mix up my invitations."

"We still on for Sunday?"

"You bet!" she said.

"I'm looking forward to it. Not much going on here in the big city. Well, sirens, and loud music and whistles—the usual."

"I know," she laughed. She stopped suddenly. "Atlanta was like that," she added quickly when he paused.

"I'd forgotten you lived in a city," he said.

"Just while I worked for the newspaper," she replied. "I like the country sounds much better."

"Me too. I don't mind travel so much. I enjoy foreign places. But I'm always glad to get home."

"Are you still in Dallas?" she asked.

"Dallas? That was last weekend," he pointed out.

"Oh."

"I'm in Paris."

"Paris!" she exclaimed. She'd been there year before last with a girlfriend. They'd spent a week shopping and eating and enjoying the atmosphere. "It must be lovely," she added with a sigh.

"Most cities I visit all I do is end up in hotels and airports," he said wryly. "I did get to visit a vineyard, however, and they didn't even ask me to help stomp the grapes."

"I would love to have a vineyard," she sighed. "I don't even drink wine. I just love to watch grapes grow."

"Where did you see that in Georgia?" he asked, surprised.

"Up in the north Georgia mountains, there are vineyards," she replied. "The soil is really good for growing grapes. Some of the wines win prizes."

"We learn something new every day," he said.

"Yes, we do. Paris. You do get around."

"Business drives the money machine," he said. "I'm talking mergers with a man who lives here but owns refineries in Dallas. It's doing business the long way around," he laughed.

"I guess so."

"I miss you," he said suddenly.

She caught her breath. "I miss you, too," she said, and felt her heart jump.

"About that not getting involved thing," he began.

"But there's still Mount Everest," she interrupted.

He laughed. "Okay. We can talk about mountains when I get home. I'll see you Sunday."

"Be careful in foreign parts," she said. "You never know if you're having coffee next to a Russian spy."

"You watch too many old James Bond movies," he teased.

"No, no, it's the new ones, with Daniel Craig!"

"And they're espionage agents, not spies."

"Have it your way. Just don't get captured."

"We need to talk about spies."

"When you get home," she promised.

There was a lazy affection in his deep voice. "When I get home," he agreed. "I'll see you Sunday."

"Bye," she said.

"So long."

She hung up and caught her breath. She hadn't expected him to call her. It was a surprise, a very nice one. He missed her. She felt lighter than air, happier than she'd been in ages. Life was looking up. Way up!

* * *

She wished that she and her father could afford one of the nice cable packages that offered *Warlocks and Warriors*, so that she could keep up with the series she'd written for. She missed being part of it. She missed the other writers, the crew, the actors, she missed all of it.

She'd written for the show for three years. It had been quite a feather in her cap to become even an associate writer. Her father's contacts had given her a boost. Her writing skills had clinched the deal, of course. Even contacts would do nothing for a person with no literary ability. But her father's contacts had certainly helped.

She'd worked for a daily newspaper while she was in college in Atlanta. It had taught her a great deal about communities and how they worked. That insight also helped with her chosen craft. Even medieval communities had much in common with small towns, like the one she'd lived in while she was going to school. Human nature never changed, even if plenty of other things did.

It had been hard, giving up her work on *Warlocks and Warriors*. But the harassment wouldn't have stopped. Her father was leaving town. If she'd stayed, the brunt of the publicity would have shifted to her. It was a no-brainer, that she'd have to go with him. Waiting tables, she thought sadly, with two years of college and three years as a prestigious TV writer working on one of the top series on television. It was a comedown. But she had to be philosophical about it. At least she had a job, and a place to live, and food to eat. The necessities. It would be a learning experience, as much of life was.

She fixed a light supper for her father and herself Saturday night when they both got off work.

"My feet are throbbing," she laughed as they ate chili and corn bread. "I'm still not used to being on them all day."

"It's a comedown, I know," he said apologetically.

"Nobody made me come out here," she pointed out. "You're my dad. We're a matched set."

"Thanks, sweetheart." He finished his chili and sat back to drink coffee. "I wish we could afford satellite," he added wistfully.

She laughed. "I was just thinking how nice that would be," she confessed. "I miss seeing *Warlocks and Warriors*."

"You miss writing for it, too, I know," he said. He grimaced. "I miss being part of a hit TV show as well." He shook his head. "One mean-spirited woman and her lies, and look at the trail of misery she's left behind her."

"It sounds trite, but what goes around does come around," she pointed out. "She won't get away with it forever. Eventually, somebody's going to call her bluff."

"I wish I had," he said. "I could have produced witnesses, even if I'd had to have Jake browbeat them first into testifying. All she had for evidence was a big mouth and accusations."

"Mama always said that God never closed a door, but He opened a window. There's a benefit to anything, if you look for it."

"I'm short on benefits and long on misery," he laughed. "Sorry. It's been a long day. I missed another sale. This time, it wasn't my fault. The customer was willing to buy the machinery. But his bank informed us that he didn't have the price of a roll of paper towels." He sighed. "Just my luck. It would have been a very nice commission."

"There will be other ones," she said. "It's just now technically spring, even though we're still dealing in snow. People will need to replace equipment."

"I guess so."

"Don't get discouraged," she pleaded. "It's early days

yet. We'll get through this. No matter how rough it gets, it won't be as bad as what we've already lived through."

"Your grandmother had a saying about that. She said life rewards us in the same measure that it punishes us. Bad things happen, then good things do. It all evens out."

"I'm so ready for good things," she laughed.

"Me too." His eyes twinkled. "I do believe you have a good thing due tomorrow."

She looked blank for a moment until she remembered. "Tomorrow's Sunday. JL's coming to pick me up," she said, and laughed.

"Definitely, a good thing," he teased.

"Definitely!"

JL was ten minutes early. Which didn't matter, because Cassie had been ready for an hour.

He came to the door to get her, carrying a bag from an exclusive store. "I brought you some peanuts from the airplane," he said dryly.

Her eyes widened at the size of the sack.

"A lot of peanuts," he amended.

"Hi, JL," her father said. "Have a good trip?"

"A long one," he chuckled. "I'm always glad to get back home. Well, go on, open it," he prompted Cassie.

She dug into the bag and pulled out a beautiful fringed leather jacket, with beadwork in a colorful and intricate pattern. "Oh," she whispered, admiring it. "It's beautiful!"

"It's warm," he said dryly, and grinned. "No more bronchitis."

Tears stung her eyes. Once, she would have taken such a thing for granted. Now, in her impoverished circumstances, it was almost too much for her. "Oh, JL," she began, her voice breaking.

"You stop that," he said firmly. "You'll be standing here bawling and somebody will come by and next thing you know, the newspaper will have big headlines and I'll be the talk of Benton."

She stared at him. So did Roger.

He gave them a droll look. "They'll see you crying and think I did something to hurt your feelings. Then they'll interview my foreman, who'll tell them what a bad man I am, and it will all go downhill from there."

"Why would your foreman tell them you're a bad man?" she asked blankly.

"Oh, he's jealous," he said easily. "I'm way handsomer than he is, and one of his girlfriends brought me a homemade apple pie once. He's still looking for ways to get even." He gave her an angelic smile.

She and her father burst out laughing, finally getting the joke.

"That's better," JL said. "Put on the jacket and I'll drive you over to see the kittens."

"Kittens?!" she exclaimed. "You didn't say you had kittens!"

"I didn't have them until four days ago. Bessie's got them in the kitchen, where it's warm, along with their mother."

"I love kittens," she remarked.

"You can't have a kitten," her father said firmly. "You're allergic."

"I am not!"

"You are so," he returned.

"I'm allergic to rabbit fur," she countered. "Not cat fur.

That's why I was sneezing. It wasn't Ellen's cat, it was her coat."

"Oh." Her father looked perplexed. "Are you sure?"

"I'm sure." She slid into the jacket. "JL, this is the nicest thing anybody's done for me in a long time," she said softly. "I'll make you another pan of rolls!"

He grinned. "I was hoping you'd say that."

"Thanks," she said huskily, and flushed as she met his eyes.

"You're welcome. I'll have her home before midnight," he added to her dad, and chuckled. "But Bessie's working all day and everybody knows it. I'm not going to be the one to blemish Cassie's perfect reputation," he added, just to make the point.

"I appreciate that," Roger said quietly.

JL shrugged. "We should frame her," he mused. "Not many women with pristine reputations left in the world. Not these days."

"And you can pin a rose on that," Roger sighed.

"Stop it or I'm going to blush," Cassie chided.

"Okay," he said, but he was grinning.

"Have fun," Roger said as they were leaving.

"It will be. I'm going to teach her to play chess," JL said.

"Oh, but she . . ." Roger stopped abruptly. He laughed. "She plays checkers very well," he amended, having almost blown her cover. JL might wonder about a waitress who liked a cerebral game like chess.

"I've got a checkerboard," JL said. "We'll try a bit of both. See you later, Roger."

He herded her out to the truck and put her inside. She was admiring the jacket when he climbed in beside her.

She'd noticed that the beadwork wasn't machined. She flushed. This was a very expensive jacket. She'd thought at first that it was something off the rack. She almost remarked about the expense, but then he might wonder how she knew it was expensive. She bit her tongue.

"How was Paris?" she asked.

"Crowded," he sighed as he pulled out into the snow-lined road. "I'm not a social animal," he said. "I don't like high society. I hate brainy people with cocktail mentalities and city manners. You're a breath of fresh air," he added with a warm smile, missing the flush that flamed on her cheeks. "I can't remember the last time I was around a woman who didn't bathe in expensive perfume or wear couture."

She felt guilt all the way to her shoes. He was describing the real Cassie, not this pretender whom he thought he knew. "Not all brainy women wear couture," she said.

He laughed. "Care to bet?" He shook his head. "My ex-fiancée moved in those circles," he said with a cold smile. "She had to have the latest fashions, the most expensive purse. She paid hundreds of dollars to have her hair styled. She read all the popular novels. God, what a bore!"

"I see."

"You're nothing like her," he said, his eyes on the road. "You're a breath of spring. Unspoiled, natural. All I had to do was be around women in Paris at a cocktail party I attended to see the difference." He glanced at her with a warm smile. "I couldn't wait to get home."

"Thanks," she said, hating the guilt she felt.

"One of the attendees was a novelist." He made a face. "She'd just landed at the top of the *New York Times* best-seller list and readers gathered around her like flies around honey." He shook his head. "I don't mind a woman having a mind, I just hate women who think they have to flaunt how smart they are. I don't mean that in a bad way," he added quickly. "I know you worked as a reporter. But there's a world of difference between reporting news and swanning around in couture and preening because you can sell books."

"I like to read," she began.

"Me too. But I don't travel in those circles. I like living in the country, waking up to a rooster crowing, riding out early to see my cattle grazing in the pasture. Things like that. I guess what I'm trying to say is that sometimes rich, successful people live in an artificial world. They're removed from the simple things that make life worthwhile. They buy into a lifestyle that isn't real."

She'd never considered that. In a way, he was right. When she'd worked on *Warlocks and Warriors*, she was a world away from normal people. She'd associated with other writers, with business executives, with people who lived and worked in the city, in high social circles. Her whole family had lived like that.

It was only since she and her father had come to Benton, Colorado, that she realized how artificial that other world really was. She'd lost touch with everyday things, with normal people. And she hadn't even realized it.

"You're very quiet. Have I offended you?" he asked.

"Oh, no! No, of course not!" she said. "I was just thinking about what you said. I guess maybe people in those situations don't even realize how different the world is for those who have to struggle for a living."

"That's what I meant," he said. He laughed. "Nobody could accuse you and your father of being artificial. You live within your means and you don't put on airs. It's what I like best about both of you."

She smiled wanly. “Thanks.”

“You’re sure you’re not allergic to kittens?” he added as he pulled up into his own yard. “Your lungs still sound a bit twitchy.”

“I wasn’t kidding. It was fur, not cats. Honest. I love cats.”

He smiled. “Me too.”

They stared at each other for a long moment. Cassie felt her heartbeat skyrocket as his dark eyes fell to her mouth and lingered there. It was so quiet in the cab of the truck that she could hear her own heart beating.

“It’s been a long week,” he whispered. His big hand slid into the hair at the nape of her neck and tugged, very gently. “And I’m starving. . . .”

She felt his lips, cold from the wind, settle gently on hers, tenderly, so that he didn’t frighten her. He was slow, barely touching her as his mouth smoothed over her lips and began to part them.

Her fingers caught in the lapel of his jacket and tightened as he increased the pressure of his mouth. He heard her breath catch, felt her body stiffen, just a little. Then her lips softened under his and she shivered, just slightly.

He drew her completely against him and his mouth ground down into hers. She tasted him, drowned in him, as he explored her slowly warming lips in a silence that was static with feeling.

Finally, his mouth slid against her cheek and into the curve of her throat as he held her and rocked her in the silence.

“Maybe you should forget about climbing Mount Everest,” he whispered.

Her heart was beating her to death. “Maybe . . . I should,” she managed.

He laughed softly and drew away from her. He liked

that little flutter in her breath, the flush in her cheeks, the light that grew in her eyes. "How about coffee and pound cake?"

"I'd love that," she whispered.

He just nodded. There was an expression on his face that made her feel warm and protected and valued. She felt as if her feet didn't touch the ground as they went into the house.

"Oh, my goodness," she exclaimed as they entered the kitchen and she saw what was in the cloth-lined box against the far wall. "They're beautiful! They're all white!"

Bessie chuckled. "White, with blue eyes," she agreed. "We've had white cats here forever."

"They're precious," she said, picking up one of the tiny creatures and cradling it against her cheek.

"They're handy, too," JL remarked as he slid off his jacket and looped it around the back of a kitchen chair. "They keep the mice down in the barn. So you could say that they earn their keep," he chuckled.

"I haven't had a kitten since I was ten," she remarked. "We had a Siamese cat. He was beautiful and absolutely dangerous," she laughed. "He hated dogs. He'd sit outside our apartment when he could get past us and wait for the neighbor to come by with her little Pekingese. Then he'd chase it, and her."

"A vicious cat," he laughed.

"Very. We named him Lucifer. The name really suited him, too." She petted the mama cat, who just looked at her with soft blue eyes and purred. "What's her name?" she asked.

"Should we tell her?" Bessie wondered.

He shrugged. “We call her Lady Godiva.”

She frowned. “Why?”

“It should be obvious,” he remarked. He leaned closer and said in a stage whisper, “She doesn’t wear any clothes!”

Cassie burst out laughing. So did they. She’d never felt so much at home as she did here, in this bright kitchen with two of the nicest people she’d ever met. She thought about what JL had said, about artificial people, and she felt suddenly guilty. She was deceiving him. She hadn’t meant to become involved with him, but now that she was . . . how in the world was she ever going to tell him the truth without having him perceive her as the biggest liar in town?

Her face looked stricken as she processed the thought.

He stared at her, frowning. “What’s wrong?” he asked suddenly.

Chapter Nine

Cassie stared into his dark eyes and felt her cheeks flushing. She turned her attention back to the kitten. "I just had a sudden thought," she replied, and then tried to think of one that might divert him from her guilty expression.

"Something troubling?" he asked softly.

She drew in a breath. "Not really. We had a couple of New Yorkers in the restaurant recently," she added. "They were so glad to escape Benton. I felt sorry for them."

"I know what you mean," he said, relaxing back in his chair. "They can have big-city life, with my blessing. Come eat your cake and drink your coffee, before it gets cold."

"Okay." She put the kitten back with its mother and moved back to the table. "I love cats," she said. "I've always had them. But it wasn't until I went away to college that I was able to have a dog. Mama didn't really like them, but she agreed that I needed a watchdog. She was nervous about having me live off campus in a rented house."

"You didn't live in the dorm?" he asked curiously.

She sighed. "I was afraid I might get put in a coed dorm," she explained. "I guess I'm a throwback to Victorian times, but I don't think single men and women sharing a dorm is decent."

"I love you," Bessie said suddenly. "You can come and live with me and I'll feed you," she added with a grin.

Cassie laughed. "Thanks."

"So few women these days with that attitude," she sighed. She gave JL a speaking look. He gave her one back.

"I'm going to do the wash," Bessie said. "If you hear a big splash, come and pull me out."

"It's just a heavy-duty washer," JL repeated. "And it's not big enough that you can fall in."

"What do you know?" she retorted. "You've never seen it except from a distance. You're afraid of it," she accused with a grin. "Go on. Admit it."

"I don't do laundry," he said haughtily.

"Lucky you, that I do," she replied. "And lucky you, that you don't have to get grass stains and mud stains and cow poop stains out of your jeans!"

He gave her a long-suffering look. "I tell you how much I appreciate you, twice a day."

She shrugged. "I guess you do. Remember: big splash, come save me."

He waved a hand at her.

Cassie was laughing. "You two," she said with a tolerant look. "She's a treasure."

"I think so." He finished his coffee. "Want to see the bottle calves?"

"Oh, yes!"

"Finish up and we'll go."

The calves were big. She laughed as they bumped her and knocked her off-balance in their eagerness to get close to her.

"They're so sweet!" she exclaimed.

"They're pretty tame," he replied. "We all pet them."

She smoothed her hand over one's head. "I could learn to love cattle."

"Could you?" he asked with a secretive smile. "I'm going to have a party next weekend. Just a few friends, good food, dancing. Will you come?"

"Oh, yes," she agreed at once.

The smile widened. "I was hoping you'd say that."

"Were you? Why?" she asked absently, smoothing her hand over the muzzle of another calf.

"You'll find out," he said. "And I'm not telling."

Her eyes were a soft, curious blue. "It's a secret party?"

"Very much so."

"Special occasion?"

He pursed his lips. "I'm hoping it will be."

"Now I'm very curious!" she laughed.

"You'll have to wait and see."

She laughed. "Okay."

He drove her home after dark. They'd had fun, listening to music and finding that they had similar tastes in it, playing chess—although she pretended that she knew little about it. They even talked about television shows they liked, although his ran to old western movies, biographies, and nature specials. They had a lot in common. Even on tricky issues like politics and religion. She felt more and more at home with him. He didn't say much, but it was obvious that he was feeling something similar.

"I have to go to California for a meeting, and then to Dallas again, for another, and then to New Orleans," he said heavily. "I don't want to," he added gently, staring at her intently in the partial light from the house's porch light. "But business keeps the coffers full, so to speak."

"I understand," she said, not adding that she'd had to travel, too, while she was writing for *Warlocks and Warriors*.

He took her hand in his and drew the palm to his lips. "I didn't plan to get involved with you," he said softly.

"I didn't plan to get involved with you, either," she confessed. "There are reasons, good reasons, why. We need to talk about them."

"Okay. But not now," he chuckled. "I'm going to be running my legs off for a few days. We'll talk Saturday, all right? I'll pick you up about five." He frowned. "I told everybody semiformal. . . ."

"I have one good cocktail dress," she interrupted. "I got it from the thrift shop at the college earlier this year," she lied. "It's very nice."

He hesitated to say what he was thinking, that if his cousin Cary brought one of those sophisticated women he liked to date, the woman might savage Cassie for a cheap dress. But he didn't say it. She was proud. He'd have offered to buy her a dress, but he knew already that she'd never accept it. "Don't worry about it," he told her. "You'll look fine. My pretty girl," he whispered, and drew her close to kiss her softly, warmly. "I'll miss you."

"I'll miss you, too," she whispered back.

He kissed her again, not softly, with a passion that started fires inside her, that brought her arms hard around his neck, propelled her close, as close as she could get, and yet still not close enough. She moaned under his devouring mouth.

He came to his senses just as he was sliding his hand inside her jeans. This was not the time or place. He drew back, breathing hard. "We really have to talk, soon," he said huskily.

She nodded, her eyes wide and fascinated, her body throbbing.

"When I get back," he said.

"Yes."

He touched her cheek gently. "Five, Saturday."

"I'll be ready."

"He's throwing a party?" her father mused.

"Yes. He said it was a special occasion, but he wouldn't tell me what it was," she added.

He chuckled. "People in small towns talk. A lot. Sometimes you overhear things they wouldn't tell you."

"Oh? Like what?" she asked as she put dishes of food on the table.

"Such as the fact that a certain reclusive rancher walked into the local jewelry store and bought a diamond ring."

Her heart jumped. So did her hand. She almost upended the gravy boat. "Oh?" she repeated, and felt like a parrot. "For himself?"

He shook his head and grinned. "It was an engagement ring. Rumors are flying."

"Was it JL?" she asked.

He nodded.

She sat down, hard. "Wow."

"So I have a hunch about the reason for that party next Saturday."

Her heart lifted. Soared. Crashed. Her face was tragic. "He doesn't know about us," she said miserably.

"You need to tell him the truth," her father said gently. "I don't think it will matter. Really I don't. But he should hear it from you. And soon, just in case anybody local did connect that news broadcast with us."

"You haven't heard anything . . . ?"

"No. We're pretty isolated here, and we don't stick out as famous people. I'd know, if anybody suspected. People are honest and straightforward here. Somebody would say something."

She relaxed, just a little. "Okay. I'll tell him Saturday."

He smiled. "It will be all right. I know it will." He cocked his head. "Can you live in Benton, Colorado, you think?"

She laughed. "Oh, yes. Even if I went back to writing scripts, I could still go to New York when I need to. He's not a controlling sort of man. It will be a good life. What about you?" she added.

"I may go home and put up a fight," he said solemnly. "Something I should have done before. I was too distraught after your mother's death to do that." His face set in hard lines. "Trudy Blaise shouldn't be allowed to get away with what she's doing."

"Jake will help you expose her," she said firmly.

"We'll see how it works out. Your happiness is the most important thing to me. JL's a good man. He'll take care of you."

She smiled. "I'll take care of him, too."

She went to work, cooked, cleaned, talked to her father, and watched the days go by with maddening slowness. Time stood still, she thought, when you were anticipating something wonderful.

Her mind was on JL so much that he seemed to be with her all the time. He phoned her at least once a day, just to talk. Sometimes twice a day. She walked around feeling as if her feet weren't even touching the ground. She'd never really loved a man until now. It was overpowering with its intensity, its sweetness. The idea that she could live with JL, sleep in his arms every night, give him children, made her feel complete, as if she'd been only half a person before.

That Saturday, she fussed over her one good cocktail dress. Her father overheard her talking to herself and peeked in, chuckling. She had the dress on a hanger and she was picking it to pieces.

"He's inviting you over, not the dress," he emphasized. "If he'd wanted to concentrate on the dress alone, I'm certain that you wouldn't have been included in the invitation."

She laughed helplessly. "You're right. It's just, I want everything to be perfect. Mary even gave me the day off, and she had that same secret smile I saw on Agatha's face. It seems to be an open secret."

"I imagine it is," he replied. He glanced at the clock on the wall. "Two hours to go," he said.

She let out a sigh. "I've been grinding my teeth all week because time was so slow. Now I'm going to have to hurry to get dressed in time!"

"That's life," her father said dryly, and left her to it.

He smiled with pure delight when she came into the living room. The cocktail dress fit her nicely, but it was conservative and still in style. Her long red-gold hair was swept up in an exquisitely tricky hairdo that was held in place with jeweled hairpins. Her feet were in dainty black leather high heels with ankle straps. She wore a thick, black, wool crocheted shawl over it because she didn't have a good coat, and the beautiful fringed jacket JL had brought her wasn't quite dressy enough for this rig.

"Will I do?" she asked her father.

He chuckled. "You certainly will. You remind me so much of your mother's mother. She wasn't a redhead, but she had the same grace and poise that you do. Your mother would be proud tonight."

She smiled sadly. "I wish . . ."

He kissed her forehead. "Me too, sweetheart. I hope you have the time of your life tonight. And I won't expect you early!"

She laughed and kissed his cheek. "I'm so excited, I can hardly bear it!"

"I'd wish you luck, but you won't need it." He lifted his head and listened. "And I believe your enchanted carriage is coming up the driveway."

"Disguised as a pickup truck," she laughed wickedly.

He parted the curtains and whistled. "Apparently not."

She looked out over his shoulder and caught her breath. "Well!" she said.

"Unexpected. But not entirely," he replied, and grinned.

She walked out the door. JL was getting out the back door of a super-stretch black limousine, its liveried driver holding the door for him. He had a box in his hand. He was wearing evening clothes, no hat, and he looked devastatingly handsome.

He was doing some looking of his own. Cassie looked beautiful, and very sexy, in the nicest sort of way. He smiled and couldn't stop.

"Here," he said, handing her an orchid. "It's going to be an enchanted evening, however trite that may sound."

"Not trite at all," she assured him. She took the orchid out of its box and slid it onto her wrist. "I'll press it in a book, afterward," she said with breathless delight, and met his eyes. "I'll keep it forever."

His breath caught. She was so real, so innocent, so honest. He couldn't believe how perfect she was. And she was all his, if he wanted her. He did. He'd never wanted anyone so much, least of all his ex-fiancée.

"We can talk about that forever thing, after the party," he said softly. He brought her hand to his lips and kissed it lightly. "Shall we go?"

Her whole face smiled at him. "Let's."

It was the sort of gathering she was used to. She'd been to numerous cocktail parties in New York, and she was used to eating in five-star restaurants, sipping champagne, having the most expensive hors d'oeuvres. She mingled with his guests, most of them businessmen who were his friends, and she fit in effortlessly.

He saw that, and it disturbed him. She was too much at home here. How could a waitress from a small Georgia town feel so comfortable in what was an alien environment?

Cassie didn't notice his expression. She was meeting people, socializing as she was used to doing, drawing out people by asking them to talk about themselves. Authors were, by nature, introverts. But she'd had to learn to be outgoing when she started work for the weekly newspaper outside Atlanta. It had been a good preparation for what came afterward.

JL nursed a whiskey and soda and frowned as Cassie mingled with his guests. One was missing. He was still uncertain about inviting Cary, after the slight run-in his cousin had with Cassie, but he took the chance anyway. Cary was, after all, the only family he had left in the world.

It was fitting that he should be here when JL announced his engagement to Cassie. It would also be a way of letting Cary know that he held no grudges about Cary's part in breaking his former engagement.

He was growing certain that Cary wouldn't show up when the man walked in the door with, of all the damned people in the world, JL's ex-fiancée. He pushed away from the bar, where he'd been leaning, and glared at his cousin with flaming brown eyes. Damn the man!

Cary approached them with a nervous smile. What had seemed like a neat little stab in the heart to pay his cousin back for taking Cassie away was feeling more like Waterloo. JL glared at him. Cassie, unaware, at first, of who the sophisticated woman with Cary really was, smiled as she joined JL.

"Hi, Cuz," Cary said. "Marge was in town on business so I thought I'd bring her along." He smiled at Cassie. "This is Marge Bailey," he said. He pursed his lips with a faint glint in his eyes. "JL was engaged to her a few months ago."

Cassie felt all the joy and excitement drain out of her with the words. She knew the name. She recognized the woman, and not because she'd been JL's fiancée. Marge Bailey was in advertising. Cassie had been in a meeting with her and network executives about advertising for *Warlocks and Warriors*. She felt her stomach drop. So far, Marge hadn't recognized her. Hopefully, she wouldn't.

But even without that unexpected complication, she knew how hard it had been for JL to get over the woman. And here was Cary, throwing her in his face. What a dreadful thing to do! Why was he doing it?

"Hello, JL," Marge said with a tight smile, ignoring Cassie.

"You're here on business?" JL replied tersely.

"An advertising campaign for a new client. I was . . ." She stopped and stared at Cassie, recognizing her all at once. "My gosh, I know you! My company did the advertising for *Warlocks and Warriors*! It's my favorite show! You and I met at a meeting in New York," she said, stunned. "They were talking about you on a news show a few days ago. Well, it was about your father, of course, but they mentioned that you'd resigned as a writer for *Warlocks and Warriors*. Now that Frank's dead, they have to be missing you!"

JL seemed to turn to stone. His eyes slid around to Cassie. "Writer for *Warlocks and Warriors*?" he asked with a bite in his deep voice. Like most television viewers, he knew the show. It was in its sixth season, one of the most successful dramas in the history of cable.

Cassie felt her heart fall to her feet. The jig was up, it seemed. She glanced at Cary and saw the guilt in his face as he averted his eyes. The beautiful woman at his side was more surprised than guilty as she glanced from JL to Cassie. Cary had told her about JL's new friend and the engagement rumors before they arrived.

"Surely you knew?" she asked JL. When he didn't answer, she looked at Cassie. "I can't imagine how your father thought he'd outrun the scandal, even by coming all the way out here to a small town in Colorado. I read all about the case. He was charged with sexual harassment of several women, of trying to force himself on Trudy Blaise. . . ."

"He did nothing of the sort," Cassie said sharply. "Trudy Blaise has played that hand one time too many. After the accusations were made, my mother was hounded to death by the media, by so-called friends on social media as well. The pressure was too much for her. She committed suicide because of Trudy's lies. People who cause tragedies incur tragedies. Ms. Blaise's moment is coming," she added icily. "And it's coming soon! My father can prove his innocence. His attorney is already working on it."

"Your mother committed suicide?!" Marge's face closed up. "I knew that she died. I didn't know how. I honestly didn't know. I'm sorry."

"Well . . . this is awkward," Cary began slowly.

"Not so awkward for you, I'm sure," Cassie told him with heat in her tone. Her blue eyes were flashing like lightning in her pale face. "You planned it right down to the last detail, didn't you?"

Cary flushed. He tugged at his collar. "Listen, I never meant—"

"I wish we were in a less public place," Cassie said. "I'd put you on the floor and stomp on you!" Her lower lip trembled. "You worm. You despicable worm!"

JL's dark eyes were full of ice. "Cary isn't the one living a lie," he said to her. "I think it's time you went home, Ms. Reed."

Cassie wanted to argue, to plead, to explain. JL was so rigid that she knew it was hopeless. The light went out of her eyes. The evening that had begun with such promise had ended in tears.

"Okay," she said quietly.

He moved away and signaled the driver, who was sitting with a book in the corner.

The man came at once.

"Drive Ms. Reed home, if you please," JL told the man. He didn't look at Cassie. He didn't offer to go with her. He didn't say another word.

Music was playing and one couple was already on the makeshift dance floor. JL took Marge by the hand and led her out into a two-step. He smiled at Marge, his attention completely on her.

Cary drew in a breath. "I'm . . ." he began.

"Spare me," Cassie said coldly. "Someday you'll get what you deserve, Cary. I won't be around to see it, but your day's coming."

She turned on her heel and walked out the door, with the driver right behind her.

When she walked in the door, her father knew immediately that something terrible had happened.

"What is it?" he asked gently.

She fell against him, tears blinding her. "Cary brought JL's ex-fiancée to the party," she sobbed. "I know her. She works in advertising and her company did a campaign for *Warlocks and Warriors*. She told JL all about us."

"I should hire a hit man for JL's cousin," he muttered, patting her on the back. "I'm so sorry!"

She had to get through the tears to speak rationally. When she was calmer, she made coffee and they sat at the kitchen table together.

"We have to go back," he said after a minute. "I spoke to Jake just before you came home. He's got solid evidence that Trudy's done this before, and he has witnesses who'll testify. He's filing suit against her in my behalf for defamation of character and making malicious false allegations that cost me my job and held me up to public embarrassment. One of her victims is coming all the way from LA to testify." He smiled sadly. "The network has also been working behind the scenes to substantiate her allegations and their investigations have cleared me. It looks as if I'll go back to work. If that happens, you can also go back to work. With Frank gone, you'll be welcomed with open arms. I'm sure of it."

She thought of the restaurant where she'd worked, the nice people who'd been so good to her. She thought of JL and Bessie and the dreams that had made a silver web around her as she contemplated a beautiful future on that ranch with the man she loved. All of that would be left behind.

JL, of course, wouldn't miss her. He was hurt and angry and wouldn't even speak to her. He'd gone straight to Marge, probably to wound his cousin for bringing her. Maybe they'd end up back together after Cary's mischief. Maybe they'd be happy.

She hoped sincerely that someday Cary fell in love with a woman who tore him up like Marge had torn up JL. There had been too many lies. Too many false statements and cruel words.

None of that helped her situation. She couldn't stay here. Not now. Everybody would know the truth. It would be hard to live down in a small town. First her father had to prove his innocence, beyond a shadow of a doubt. When he did, and it was publicized, perhaps people here would think kindly of the strange Easterner and his daughter who'd lived among them for such a short time.

"I'm going back with you," Cassie said quietly. "There's nothing left for me here."

"JL might listen to you when he cools off."

She laughed hollowly. "He looked at me as if I were dirt, and then he made a beeline right back to his ex-fiancée, if only to put the knife in his cousin's ego. No," she added softly. "He'd never trust me again. He'll think I lied about everything deliberately. You can't build a life on lies. We've certainly found that out, and so will Trudy

Blaise. Besides," she said firmly, "it will be nice to get back to work, doing what I do. JL thought of me as a plain, no-frills country girl. I'm not. He never knew the person I am. It's just as well." She forced a smile. "If we can get Trudy Blaise in as much trouble as you were in, that will be worth giving up Benton, Colorado," she said with a cold laugh.

"That much, I think I can promise you." He grimaced. "I'm so sorry, Cassie."

She fought tears. "Me too. Life happens. Then we pick up the pieces and go on."

"Yes," he said. "We do."

After all the turmoil of the past few months, the solution to Cassie's and Roger's problems came quickly and all the furor died abruptly. Trudy Blaise was actually arrested on charges of embezzlement, of all things. She'd created a false vendor account, with the help of her attorney (who was facing disbarment), and pocketed assets to which she wasn't entitled. As it turned out, she'd done the same thing in LA, as her former boss testified to a grand jury. She hadn't been prosecuted for that crime, but she would face charges for it after an investigation had uncovered her illegal enterprise as producer of another program originating in LA.

Not only was she facing jail time for conversion of property, but she was also looking at defamation charges from both Roger and three other men. As part of a plea deal, she agreed to go on the air and refute her charges against Roger and her former boss, and make apologies on air as well as in all her social media accounts.

Roger was cleared in a firestorm of political activism.

At least one group made a public apology for its part in the death of Mrs. Reed. The others, of course, conceded only that occasionally, very occasionally, charges were made erroneously. It was politics as usual.

Cassie did return to work as a writer for *Warlocks and Warriors*, but she moved back to Atlanta, into an apartment complex where she'd lived before she bought the house that she'd put on the market when the scandal broke.

Sadly, she had to part with her dog, whom she'd left with a neighboring family once the scandal forced her to leave town. The apartment allowed only for dogs under thirty pounds, and hers had been a beautiful purebred neutered German shepherd named Josh who weighed over ninety pounds.

Happily, however, the family who adopted her pet promised to let her visit Josh when she wanted to.

She settled back into her job and watched spring become summer without any particular enthusiasm. She hadn't kept in touch with people in Benton because she didn't want to hear about JL and Marge. She was certain that they were back together now, if only to pay Cary back for his interference.

It had been such a sweet dream, thinking that she and JL would get married and live happily ever after on the ranch. A silly dream, as it turned out. She should have told him the truth in the very beginning. But they hadn't been headed for anything more than friendship when it started, and she was reluctant to clutter up their relationship with painful revelations about her father's past.

She was lonely. Lonelier, now, with memories of happier times stabbing her in the heart. She'd been so excited when her father told her about JL buying a diamond ring.

Marge was probably wearing the ring by now.

* * *

She had to go to New York for a writers' discussion about *Warlocks and Warriors*. She arranged to have lunch with her father at the Four Seasons near his office. He was back in charge of the hit show about a seventies singing group's rise to fame. He'd been completely exonerated of any charges relating to Trudy Blaise, who had plenty of problems of her own making, and he told Cassie that he wasn't even speaking to women on his staff unless it was work-related and in the company of coworkers. She thought how sad the world had become. Harassment was terrible. But so was creating an atmosphere of artificial coldness that denied any warm human feelings at all, in the effort to head off charges of misconduct. Lies and malice were toxic, and could ruin everything. She'd seen it with Trudy Blaise, with Cary lying to his cousin . . . and worst of all, she blamed herself for not being upfront with JL.

Cassie sat listening to her colleagues go over a necessary plot change because one of their actors had been injured in an accident. They'd have to write around him while he got through the aftermath of the mishap and into a cast for his broken leg. They solved the problem with a created injury in the series to compensate for his lack of mobility.

"And aren't we the creative geniuses?" Derry, a female coworker chuckled as they finalized the change.

"We're writers," Cassie said with a wicked grin. "It's who we are."

"Most of us," Ted, another writer, murmured dryly.

Angela, the live wire of the group, gave him a mock glare. "I am so a genius," she shot back. "In fact, I can prove it. Only this morning at a coffee shop, I instructed a barista in how to make change from a five without taking off her socks."

Everybody roared.

"And for that," Ted countered, "you could be sued for character assassination."

He realized belatedly that Cassie was in the group, and remembered what she and Roger had been through. "Sorry," he said at once, and grimaced.

"I am not politically correct," she assured him with a warm smile. "And I haven't ever sued anybody in my life. Yet."

He stood and bowed. "Thank you, my lady, for your kind regard."

She stood and curtsied. "My knight!"

Everybody groaned.

"Peasants," Cassie said huffily.

"And on that note," Angela, who now led the writers' room, said with a grin, "we'll adjourn to lunch. Cassie, coming with us?"

"I'm meeting Dad at Four Seasons," she replied. "But thanks! Rain check?"

"Next time you come to New York," Ted said. "Why don't you move up here? Hot as hell in Atlanta!"

"You get used to it," she said with a lazy smile. "Besides, we have a huge lake nearby. Sailing, hiking, picnic spots, fishing . . ."

"Fishing!" Angela groaned. "Who goes fishing, for God's sake?"

"Me," Cassie said, laughing. "Actually, it's great fun. Yellow flies, mosquitoes, water moccasins, copperheads, smelly worms . . ."

"Please," Angela said. "I'm headed for a restaurant!"

"And speaking of restaurants," Cassie said, "I'm going to have fish!"

"You can't reform misplaced New Yorkers," Ted said, shaking his head. "Fishing!" He rolled his eyes.

"To each his own," Cassie said with a flash of white teeth.

Chapter Ten

Four Seasons was crowded, but her father had reservations, so they went right in. Cassie was wearing navy blue slacks with a perky white-and-blue silk blouse and a white sweater. Her hair was up in a complicated hairdo, her small ears dripping gold earrings in a medieval design. She wore small stacked high heels, because everything in Manhattan was a long walk, even after riding around in a company-provided limo.

Roger Reed, in a blue business suit and patterned tie, looked every bit the producer as he rose to greet his daughter, smiling. She hugged him and sat down.

"How's it going?" he asked after they'd ordered.

She smiled. "Fine, fine. We're looking forward to the next season. Lots of twists and turns and surprises for the fans." She glanced at him. "How's your show going?"

He chuckled. "Better than ever. The staff was so happy to have me back that they bought a cake and party hats."

She smiled. "I could almost feel sorry for Trudy Blaise."

"I couldn't," he said flatly. "Her lies caused your mother's death and tainted the reputations of several of us. She'll get what's coming to her. In fact, she's already had to close down her social media accounts. The people who attacked us are now attacking her."

"Tit for tat," she said quietly. "But all the hate in the world won't bring Mama back."

He nodded, his face sad. "It's been an ordeal. I'm happy things are back to normal. Although, I have to confess that I do sort of miss Benton, Colorado."

Her fork slipped at the mention of the town where she'd left her heart. She picked it back up and didn't look at her father. "I miss Mary and Agatha," she said. "They were kind to me."

He nudged a perfectly cooked piece of steak with his fork before spearing it into his mouth. He sipped red wine before he spoke. "I had a phone call today."

"Did you?"

"From Colorado."

The fork jumped again, but this time she didn't drop it. "Oh."

"From Cary, of all people."

"Cary?" Disappointment welled up in her. Cary had called her father? "How would he have your number?"

"His friend, JL's former fiancée, gave it to him."

The mention of Marge Bailey closed her up like a sensitive plant. She didn't say a word. "What did he want?"

"To apologize."

She laughed shortly. "He's always sorry after he does something unspeakable."

"This time, he's really sorry. He's living in Denver. His cousin, who really is his last living relative even if not by blood, won't speak to him or have him on the ranch. He's lost his livelihood, his job, his prospects, pretty near everything he had."

"JL didn't seem that vindictive to me," she replied, surprised.

"It wasn't JL. It was the citizens of Benton."

She stopped eating and just stared at him.

"When the truth got out, about what Cary did to you and JL, the whole town turned against him. Nobody in Benton would sell him so much as a cup of coffee. He left in self-defense."

"Well!" She hesitated and lowered her eyes. "What about JL? Are he and Marge married now?"

"Marge is back in New York," he said. "She's still with the advertising agency, but your executive producer and the higher-ups at the network have switched their account to a rival agency."

Her lips parted on a shocked breath.

"You have friends in high places," he mused. "It wasn't Marge's fault, really, but they couldn't get to Cary."

"This gets stranger and stranger," she remarked, sipping wine. "Did JL come with her to New York?"

"He went off on an extended business trip to the Middle East, to talk to his partners in the oil business. At least one major newsmagazine has carried photos of him being entertained by some members of Arab royalty."

"I suppose he'll make even more money," was all she said.

"He phoned me, too."

She dropped the glass. It was unfortunate, because she was wearing a lacy white sweater over her silk blouse and it stained at once. She wiped at it and just gave up, when she saw the hopelessness of it all.

"He said he might come back to the States if he thought there was any chance that you could forgive him for the way he treated you," he continued, as if the accident hadn't happened. "He said it wasn't all Cary's fault. He should have realized that Cary was getting even. He should have spoken to you before he sent you home."

"Yes, he should have," she said with some heat.

"He did mention that if you hadn't kept secrets from him, none of it would have happened the way it did. I was forced to agree with him. I did suggest, if you remember, that it wasn't a good idea not to tell him."

"I was afraid to," she replied. "You know I was, and you know why."

"Yes, I do. But he didn't."

She drew in a long breath. She'd missed JL terribly in the time she'd been back at work. She was empty and cold and alone. She lived in Georgia, all by herself. She came to New York when she had to, for her job, which was why she was in the city right now. She came to see her father. But even writing, which she loved, was no substitute for the tall rancher who'd been a part of her life for such a short time.

"New York and Colorado aren't that far apart by plane," he said. "You could commute from there as easily as you can from Georgia. JL has a private jet, which would make the trip even easier."

She bit her lower lip.

"I'm not pushing," he said gently. "But JL is a fine man. He has wonderful qualities. He was shocked and upset by what Cary said and did that night. It doesn't excuse it, but it does explain it. Nobody's so perfect that they can't be allowed a second chance. That is, if you wanted to give him one."

She looked up, her eyes sad and quiet. "Maybe he

just wants to apologize and nothing else, you know," she ventured.

"He could do that in a letter. He wants to see you."

She drew in a long breath. It was a terrible chance to take. She might get over him, in time. She had her work. It was almost enough.

She looked down at her hands and thought how happy she'd been the day her father relayed the gossip that JL had bought a diamond ring for her. She thought about her finger being ringless for the rest of her life.

"You can always tell him to go home."

She looked up at his amused expression. "Yes. I guess I could."

"There's a nice symphony concert tomorrow night. They're playing Debussy. I understand that he likes Debussy very much, and that he has two tickets up front."

"Oh, he does, does he?"

"He only lacks the right partner for the event. And I believe you bought a new gown to wear to the opening of the arts center next month . . . ?"

She laughed, the first humor she'd felt in a long time. "Yes, I did."

"So he said that, if you were willing, he could pick you up at my apartment about six tomorrow evening? He mentioned supper at the Plaza. He has reservations for that, too. And he also mentioned that he was going to look really stupid with empty seats beside him at both those events. He'd be such an object of pity that he might never recover."

Her eyes grew bright with humor. "Well, I suppose I could listen to what he has to say."

"Exactly what I told him."

"Turncoat," she said, but she smiled affectionately when she said it.

"You've been miserable since we got back. So has he. Take a chance."

"I guess I'll have to. But if things don't work out . . ."

"You can have me paged at the airport."

"How would that pay you back?"

"You could tell people that I was a famous movie star traveling incognito, and have me mobbed for autographs," he chuckled.

"In that case, I'll do it."

"That's my girl!"

She tried several times to talk herself out of the date. But she couldn't help herself. She wanted to see JL so much that it was like a fire burning in the pit of her stomach. He was all she thought about, all she dreamed about, all she wanted in life. She pictured herself living on the ranch, traveling with him, rocking their children to sleep at night by a fire in the fireplace. She was miserable alone. Perhaps he was, too. There was only one way she was going to find out, and that was, as her father had said, by taking a chance.

She dressed in her new gown, a pretty beige couture one that fell in folds to the ankle straps of her leather pumps. Her red-gold hair was up again in a complicated coiffure, with her jeweled clips. She wore just enough makeup, without overdoing it. She wore pearls around her neck and in her ears. A gold designer watch was fastened around her wrist. She looked expensive and cultured, which she was. For once, she wasn't in disguise.

The phone rang. The clerk informed her that a gentleman awaited her in the lobby.

She picked up her purse, wished her father good night, and walked out the door.

JL was near the elevators, waiting. His first sight of her produced an expression of pride, of faint possession, of approval.

He smiled slowly. “The real Cassie,” he said softly as he approached her.

She smiled back, trying to contain her excitement. He was wearing designer clothing as well, evening clothes in which he looked debonair and very cultured. His thick black hair was uncovered. His face was tanned and handsome. His dark eyes ate her from head to toe. She had to fight to breathe normally.

“The real me,” she replied.

“If I start apologizing here,” he said softly as he escorted her toward the front door, “maybe by the time we get to the symphony, you’ll be in a forgiving mood.”

“It was my fault, too, you know,” she replied quietly. “I should have told you the truth. I was afraid to. It was so horrible here—”

“It’s all right,” he interrupted. “You don’t have to say a thing.”

He paused at a super-stretch black limo, whose driver was waiting with the back door open.

JL helped her inside, and followed her, the driver shutting them in before he went around to get in under the steering wheel.

“I hope you’re hungry,” he said, smiling. “I came straight here from Saudi Arabia.”

"I had a nice salad and light fish for lunch," she replied. "It's worn off."

He chuckled. "I had peanuts."

"You can get those on airplanes!" she exclaimed.

He glared at her.

She laughed. "Sorry."

He laughed softly. "I missed you."

"I missed you, too."

His hand slid over hers and curled into it. "It's going to be the best date we've ever had."

She caught her breath. "Yes."

His hand tightened. Hers tightened, too.

"Marge wasn't any happier with Cary than I was, when she knew who you were," he said. "She gave him the rough side of her tongue. So he turned around and called your bosses, to get even with her. He told them that she'd been rude and obnoxious to you."

"Is that why she lost the account?" she asked, shocked.

He nodded. "She wasn't even sorry about it. She felt guilty about what she let Cary talk her into. She called me and told me what happened. She said she felt even more guilty when she knew how your mother died. There have been too many lies, and mixed messages. Too many deceptions by both women and men. Trudy lied about your dad, Cary lied about Marge, and about you. But justice prevailed." He squeezed her hand. "Trudy is in jail, and Marge will be fine. Cary won't. He's living in Denver now, and nobody back home will speak to him. Especially me."

"He's done a lot of damage," she said quietly.

"More than you know. It's about time he faced the music. I'm not letting him back on the ranch again, ever. He almost separated us for good out of jealousy."

"Who was he jealous of?"

"You and Marge, because you both ended up with me and he felt jilted," he replied. "He's got some real ego issues. Maybe he can deal with them. Whether he can or not, it's not my business anymore. I've had enough of his mischief."

"I can see why." She shook her head. "Maybe I'm lucky that I don't have any extended family living nearby!"

He laughed. "Maybe you are, honey."

She felt her heart expand at the endearment. She felt warm and protected. She looked up at him with her heart in her eyes and found him staring back at her hungrily. It was a moment out of time, when everything was perfect. Just perfect.

All too soon, they arrived at the exclusive restaurant. When they were seated, poring over the menu, he glanced at her.

He smiled. "I suppose French dishes on a menu aren't intimidating to you."

She laughed. "I speak it and read it. My grandmother was French."

"My great-grandmother was French-Canadian," he told her. "I speak it, too." He lowered his voice. "I know some really sweet words in French."

She flushed.

He laughed. "Sorry. I couldn't resist it."

She laughed, too. "I'm educated, but I'm not worldly."

"And that delights me," he said softly. "It may be a sophisticated world, but innocence has a cachet all its own. I love it that you can still blush."

"I'll bet you can't," she returned.

He chuckled, deep in his throat. "No, I can't. And one day, you may be very happy about that."

She didn't dare reply. She concentrated on her menu instead.

The symphony was delightful. She held hands with JL and soaked up every sweet minute of "Afternoon of a Faun" and *La mer*, two of her Debussy favorites. Afterward, they walked slowly down the sidewalk toward the waiting limousine.

Stars twinkled in the sky above, visible despite all the lights of the city. The faint breeze blew tendrils of her hair around her face.

"It's been a magical night," she said.

"Right out of a fantasy," he replied. "How did you end up writing for a hit television series? Were you really a reporter?"

She nodded. "I loved my job. But Dad mentioned me to a friend, who had a friend, and I submitted some samples of my work. They hired me on the spot. I was terrified. I'd never written scripts, I had no idea what working for a series entailed, and I was scared to death."

"But you adjusted."

"Yes. I adjusted. It's been exciting, maddening, nerve-racking, and horrifying, all at once. But I've loved every minute of it."

"You know, I own a private jet," he remarked, sliding his fingers so that they meshed with hers.

"Do you?" she asked, breathless all over again at the slow, caressing contact.

"So if you lived in Benton," he continued, "it would be easy for you to commute."

She could barely breathe. "Yes, it would."

"We have bitter winters in Colorado, but I have a nice big fireplace and plenty of wood for fires."

"Do you?"

"Not to mention, central heat and air-conditioning as well," he chuckled.

"I see."

He stopped and turned to her, towering over her, even though she was wearing fairly high heels. "I bought you a ring," he said huskily. "I was going to give it to you that night, before Cary came in with Marge and ruined everything."

"I knew."

"How?" he asked, surprised.

"Everybody in town knew. The jeweler told people."

He touched her soft cheek with his fingertips. "I bought one for Marge, but it was different. It was a fever, quickly quenched, even if I did think it was like dying at the time when she left me. But when you left, that was the desert after the oasis. I couldn't eat or sleep. I couldn't rest. I left town, because I couldn't bear to see the places I'd seen you in. So much pain," he added huskily. "And I brought it on myself, because I didn't trust . . ."

She put her fingers over his firm mouth. "We were both at fault. You didn't know me. I didn't try to explain. But that's in the past. That's over."

He turned her hand and kissed the palm hungrily. "I still have the ring."

Her breath caught at the passion in his tone. "Do you?"

"And I got information on getting a marriage license this morning."

She gasped.

"We could go down to the Office of the City Clerk together and get one."

"We could?"

"I've got everything arranged already for next Friday," he added. "Think of the embarrassment if I have to call it off. I mean, I invited total strangers to the event. I'm having Mary and Agatha and your dad's former boss, Bill Clay, flown up here. I'll never live down the shame if you say no."

She just gaped at him. "But, JL, I don't have a wedding gown . . . is it a civil service?"

"It is not. And we can get a wedding gown. I had a couture boutique put several on hold, just for you. I've been shopping." He grinned.

"But . . . but . . ."

He bent and kissed her, very softly. "Just say yes. Everything else will work out. Honest. I have the best wedding planner in the city. She's amazing."

She just shook her head. "Oh . . . okay!" She gave up. It was probably going to be a disaster, but she loved him and she didn't care. She threw her arms around his neck. "I love you," she said huskily. "We can get married by a beachcomber, I don't even care how."

He lifted her and kissed her hungrily, oblivious to passersby and cars and cabs and the whole world.

"Get a room," someone yelled humorously.

"I'm getting a room, after I marry her!" he yelled back.

There was raucous laughter.

Cassie laughed, too, and snuggled close in his arms.

* * *

The wedding planner was truly amazing. She had it all arranged, right down to the wedding gown, the bouquet, the church, the minister, the works. Two little girls who belonged to one of the series' stars of *Warlocks and Warriors* were flower girls. The ring bearer was the son of another. Roger Reed was JL's best man and the show's female star was Cassie's matron of honor. The wedding was covered by the media. And Mary and Agatha and Bill Clay, along with Bessie and her daughter, from Benton, Colorado, sat in the front pew and watched with utter delight and a little bit of shock. They'd had no idea who their new friend actually was. All of them were fans of *Warlocks and Warriors*.

JL lifted the delicate, lacy veil from her face and kissed Cassie with exquisite tenderness. His eyes were full of love. He hadn't said the words, but he didn't need to. She knew. She'd always known.

She smiled up at him with her whole heart in her own eyes.

"My beautiful wife," he said gently. "Mrs. Denton."

She flushed and laughed. "I like the way that sounds."

"Me too."

He shook hands with the minister, took Cassie by the hand, and they walked back down the aisle towards the exit.

The reception was held in the Bull and Bear restaurant at the Waldorf Astoria. There were more people than Cassie could account for. JL mentioned that he'd invited several members of his board of directors and at least one Arab prince. He pointed the man out to Cassie, who would never have guessed his identity because he was wearing an expensive suit, not robes.

"You have some amazing friends," she remarked later.

"Yes, I do. I don't pick them because of their bank accounts, either. They're just plain people. They don't put on airs or equate wealth with character."

"The prince is nice," she remarked.

He chuckled. "He's a big fan of *Warlocks and Warriors*," he informed her. "Never misses an episode. In fact, neither do I. I'll have to show you one of my T-shirts when we get back home. It's black with 'Here Be Dragons' in white across the chest."

She grinned. That phrase was the watchword of the show. Most people recognized it instantly. "I didn't come up with that," she said. "It was Frank's." She sighed. "We all still miss him. He was a great writer, and a sweet man."

He bent and brushed her cheek with his lips. "For years to come, people will murmur that phrase and think of him," he said comfortingly. "He'll have a taste of immortality."

"I didn't think of that. It's nice."

"So am I," he drawled with a grin.

"And now I have a son to go with my daughter," Roger Reed chuckled as he hugged JL and Cassie. "Welcome to the family."

"Thanks," JL said. "I'm happy to be part of it. And very lucky that she has a tender and forgiving heart," he added dryly.

"I didn't think to ask, where are you two going for your honeymoon?" Roger asked.

JL looked down at Cassie with mischievous eyes. "It's a surprise. But we'll send you a postcard eventually," he promised her father.

"I'll have to talk with my bosses. . . ." Cassie began worriedly.

"Already taken care of," her father said easily. "I play poker with your producer. I told him I'd let him win a hand and he said you can have a week off."

She hugged her father. "You're the best father on earth."

"Yes, I am," he chuckled. "Now go have a happy honeymoon and don't worry about things back here. By the way," he added softly, "you were a beautiful bride. Your mother would have been so proud." He had to stop and fight tears.

"She would have," Cassie agreed, and hugged him in a moment of shared sadness.

Before things could deteriorate, the photographer JL had hired interrupted them for a shot of Cassie and JL with her father. They obliged and smiles replaced sad faces.

JL and Cassie posed for pictures and then said their farewells to the Benton natives who'd come so far to see them wed. JL was sending them home in business class on commercial airlines. He apologized but added that he and Cassie would be taking his jet on their honeymoon. Nobody had a problem with that, especially when he added that the guests would be spending the weekend in New York City with prepaid credit cards, prepaid hotel bills—at the Plaza—and all the food and entertainment they could wish for, also prepaid. Cassie was delighted that he was so generous with their friends. But, then, that was the way JL was. Happiness was spilling out all over.

Cassie had thought they might spend the night in New York City, but JL had them driven to the airport after they said their good-byes.

"Not a thing to worry about," he assured her. His eyes twinkled mysteriously. "I have a very special wedding surprise in store for you. We're going to join an exclusive club."

"We are? Which one?" she asked, wondering if it was a restricted area in the airport where members of certain groups got VIP treatment.

"Wait and see, sweetheart," he said softly, and held her hand tightly.

"Oh, my gosh!" she exclaimed just as they reached the airport. "JL, I forgot my suitcase! It's still at Dad's apartment! I won't have anything to wear!"

"Already taken care of," he said easily. "Your dad packed it and I had it picked up. It's already on the jet."

"The jet?"

"My own jet," he said. "Big, roomy, comfortable, with a pilot who's the best in the business. We even have in-flight meal service." His eyes twinkled. "You're going to love it."

She did. She'd been on an executive jet just once, when she was needed urgently for a story conference and the CEO of the company that produced *Warlocks and Warriors* had sent his own jet to pick her up in Atlanta. But even that luxurious jet wasn't a patch on JL's.

"This is absolutely unreal," she said as she looked around. There was TV, a bar, a comfortable sitting area with tables, and a male steward, who greeted them at the door.

"This is Dennis," he introduced her to the pleasant man. "He's been with me for eight years."

"Nice to meet you," she said, shaking hands and smiling.

"Nice to meet you also, Mrs. Denton. Will you be wanting to eat soon?"

JL looked at his watch. "In about two hours, I think. Until then, no phone calls, okay?" he added, and tossed his cell phone to Dennis.

He held out his hand. Cassie got the idea. She handed him her cell phone, which he also tossed to Dennis.

JL took Cassie's hand and led her toward the back of the jet. The engines were just revving up for takeoff.

"Shouldn't we be strapped in or something?" she asked worriedly.

"We're about to be," he assured her.

He opened a door and nudged her inside. He followed her. It was a bedroom, complete with television, stereo, a computer, a desk, and the biggest, cushiest bed she'd seen in a long time.

He picked her up and put her gently on the bed as the jet began to speed up and rise into the air.

"Have you ever heard," he asked her amusedly, "of the 'mile high club'?"

She flushed. "Everybody has," she stammered, referring to those who'd had sex in flight, high above the earth.

"Well, darlin'," he whispered as his hands went to the fastenings on her beautiful wedding gown, "we are about to join the club!"

Chapter Eleven

Cassie had no experience of intimacy. A few kisses and some groping, yes, but nothing really intimate. So what JL did to her came as a shock.

"It's all right," he whispered. He'd removed her gown between soft, tender kisses and put her under the covers while he removed his own clothes. She hadn't watched. It was pretty intimidating already, this initiation into true adulthood. But he hadn't made fun of her shyness. It had delighted him. Now he was touching her in ways and places that embarrassed her, and she caught his wrist worriedly.

"It's really all right," he said again, brushing her mouth with his. "Just relax. There's no reason to be embarrassed. This is part of the process. You have to let me touch you. It's how I can be sure that I won't hurt you, when the time comes."

"I don't understand," she whispered back, and she really didn't. Her few girlfriends had been mostly like her, uninitiated, and what she heard from experienced people was general rather than specific.

He chuckled. "Okay." He whispered it to her, so that she understood what he was doing, and why.

Her faint gasp indicated how new to it she really was. She swallowed, hard, and let go of his wrist.

"That's it. Yes. Shhhhh." His mouth opened on hers, tasting her, arousing her, while his hands were doing the most incredible things to her body.

She began to writhe on the sheets, shivering with each new touch.

"It won't be hard at all," he said huskily. "And by the time we start, you won't be afraid anymore."

She was barely hearing him now. Her body was throbbing with new sensations, new experience. She opened her legs for him without coaxing, gave him back the hungry kisses with new passion, arched up to his hands and then, unbelievably, his mouth!

She wanted to protest, but all at once, she shot up into the sky, exploding, throbbing, dying of pleasure. She cried out helplessly, a sound she'd never heard from her own lips.

"Oh, yes," he murmured just as he went into her.

His mouth covered the faint little cry that was less protest than enticement. She was sensitized now, so that the joining of their bodies was warm and sweet and welcome. She wrapped her long legs around his and held on, shuddering as he moved, feeling him swell in her, feeling her own body respond urgently to the slow, deep movements of his hips.

Then, all at once, it became something else, something primitive and devouring, a throbbing need that ached to be fulfilled, that demanded heat and motion and passion. She bit his shoulder in her ecstasy, crying, sobbing as she begged him not to stop.

His mouth buried itself in her throat as he pushed harder, harder, and then suddenly went rigid above her and cried out. She found her own fulfillment at the same time, riveted to his hard body, shivering and convulsing in a pleasure she'd never known existed. It was almost unbearable at the last, a sweetness so volcanic that she thought she might pass out.

Finally, she was able to relax, to flow into his body as she felt him go heavy against her. He started to pull away, but she held him there, coaxed him back to her mouth so that she could kiss him hungrily, with new and sweet knowledge of him as a man, as her husband.

He lifted his head and looked down into her soft, sated eyes. He smiled at her expression. His big hand brushed back her unruly red-gold hair. "Now you know," he whispered.

She nodded. "Now I know."

He covered her mouth with his and kissed her hungrily. "That exclusive club I mentioned?"

"Umhmm," she murmured lazily.

"We are now members in good standing," he chuckled.

Her eyes laughed as they met his. "Yes, we are. So. Where are we going?"

"Jamaica," he said. "Montego Bay, to be precise. We can be beachcombers for a week."

"Maybe enlist on a pirate ship and raid small villages?" she suggested.

He pinched her bottom and laughed when she flinched and grinned at him.

"Maybe sit around drinking piña coladas and enjoy the swimming pool," he countered.

"Spoilsport."

He smoothed back her damp hair. "My darling, if you wanted a pirate ship for real, I'd go right out and get you one. I'm the happiest man in the world right now."

"I hope to keep you that way," she replied. She touched his hard mouth. "What does JL stand for?"

He smiled. "John Lewis," he said. "But I've gone by JL for so long that it's pretty much my name now."

"I have a better one."

"You do?"

She nodded. "My sweetheart."

He grinned from ear to ear. "I like it."

She tugged him closer. "Me too. And this is where we live happily ever after, right?"

He rolled over, taking her with him. "Happily ever after and after and after."

"Promise?"

"Cross my heart."

She smiled with her whole heart and kissed him again. "I love you," she whispered.

"I love you more."

She beamed. It was the first time he'd really said it. "You do?"

"I loved you when you were standing in the rain holding a protest sign, with your hair all wet," he confessed. "You stole my heart, when I didn't think I had one left. If I'd lost you, I could never have gone home again, you know," he added solemnly. "I'd have been a wanderer for the rest of my life, rootless, useless."

She touched his mouth with her fingertips. "You stole my heart when you took me home and dried my clothes and made me coffee."

He smiled. "And here we are, married."

"Married." She looked at the beautiful diamond, set in gold, with its beautiful wedding band. "Now I feel married," she added with a wicked look.

He chuckled. "So do I." He pursed his lips. "Hungry yet?"

She moved under him. "Yes. But not for food. . . ." she whispered against his mouth. "Suppose we have another go at that exclusive club you mentioned?"

He smoothed his body over hers. "We should have just about enough time before we land," he said with a grin.

And they did. Just.

Nine months to the day later, a little boy was delivered in the community hospital in Benton, Colorado. His name was Cole Reed Denton and he had so many godmothers and godfathers that they couldn't all fit into the waiting room. They spilled out onto the parking lot and some were left sitting in stretch limos until they could get into the building.

It was talked about in Benton for many years to come. The rancher and his famous wife, who were just JL and Cassie locally, no matter how famous she got or how much richer he got. The lovebirds, as they were referred to, were just part of the big family that was Benton. And they did live happily, ever after.

Colorado Cowboy

In Memoriam.
Patricia Gail Dorroh Nash
My Friend
1950–2020

CHAPTER ONE

It was snowing. Esther Marist was cold and frightened walking along the highway. She pulled her blue fox jacket closer around her and nervously pushed back a long strand of platinum blond, curly hair. She was still wearing the gray wool slacks and the purple silk blouse she'd put on that morning. There was a dark stain on the hem of one pants leg. It was blood. Her mother's blood.

Her pale blue eyes stared into the darkness without really seeing it. Her mother, Terry Marist, had just been killed in front of her eyes, from being picked up and literally thrown down the staircase by her latest gigolo boyfriend.

Terry had several homes. This one was in Aspen, Colorado. It was the prettiest of the lot. They'd come here against Terry's wishes, several weeks ago, because her gigolo boyfriend was meeting somebody. Esther hadn't been able to hear all of it, but there had been something said about Terry financing a scheme of his that two partners were involved in. They were going to meet the men here. Darrin had forced the two women into Terry's Mercedes and driven them here from Las Vegas, where Terry had reluctantly financed several days of reckless gambling by her vicious boyfriend.

Terry had finally realized what Esther had known from the beginning, that Darrin was dangerous and money-crazy. But it was too late. Esther's mother had paid the price, and if Esther couldn't get out of Aspen before Darrin Ross found her, she'd be paying it as well.

Her mother had tears in her blue eyes as she shivered and clawed at her daughter's cold fingers. Her leg under her short dress was twisted horribly from the fall. Her blond hair was covered in blood from where her head had collided with one of the banisters. She was gasping for breath and then Terry realized that there was a cut on her mother's throat. Blood was pulsing out of it like a water fountain. Esther knelt beside her mother and frantically tried to stop the flow with her hands, but she couldn't.

"I'll call an ambulance!" she told Terry quickly, glancing up the stairs in fear that Darrin would come. She started to pull her cell phone out of the pocket in her slacks and remembered that she'd left it upstairs in the drawer of her bedside table, charging.

"No," her mother choked. "Too late. I'm . . . dying."

Terry put the huge seven-carat pink diamond ring she always wore into Esther's palm and closed her daughter's fingers around it. "Keep the will I gave you last night. Keep the ring, too. He thinks . . . I put it on the dresser, like he . . . told me to. Run," she whispered frantically. "I'm so sorry . . . ! You can go to . . . your . . . grandfather . . ."

But before she could say anything more, she made an odd little sound and the light left her eyes. Her pretty face was white from the blood loss. Upstairs, the boyfriend was cursing. "Where is it?" he was raging. "Where's that damned ring? I saw her put it . . . right here . . . on the dresser!"

Esther felt for a pulse, but her mother's eyes were open, her pupils were fixed and dilated; darkness was settling in them, just like when one of Esther's pets had died and she'd watched the same thing happen to their eyes. Terry was dead. Darrin had killed her! Tears ran down her cheeks as she took one last look at her only refuge in the world. Her mother was gone and she would be at the mercy of Terry's murderous boyfriend.

Esther knew better than to stay. Darrin Ross was drunk and he was very dangerous when he drank. He'd taken up with her mother weeks ago, despite Esther's pleas. *But he loves me*, her mother had said with a laugh, *and you'll get used to him*. Esther hadn't. And once he started knocking her mother around when she wouldn't give him as much money as he wanted, Terry Marist had realized the mistake she'd made. Darrin was abusive and frightening. Terry was sorry, but she was too afraid to try and leave him.

He'd become obsessed with the enormous diamond ring that Esther's mother had been given on her eighteenth birthday by her father. Even though they were estranged, Terry Marist spoke of her father sometimes and told her how kind he'd been to her when she was a little girl, before Terry married a man he didn't approve of. The ring had sentimental value. But past that, it was worth a king's ransom. Darrin had tried to take it off her finger once, when she was asleep, but Terry's poor hands were arthritic and swelled badly. He'd been sure at the time that all Terry had would be his one day, so he'd found an excuse to give her about what he was doing. He was just massaging her poor fingers because she'd been crying out in her sleep. Esther knew better. Terry hadn't.

Now, Terry had truly left him and Esther was going to be next unless she could get away before he came downstairs. He was still upstairs, searching for the ring. He yelled that he'd seen her take it off and put it on the dresser, because he'd threatened her if she didn't. So where was it?

That explained why Terry had it hidden in her hand. Esther had given her mother one last, anguished look, grabbed her coat and purse off the coat tree, and ran out into the snowy night.

She had only the money in her purse, her unspent allowance. She didn't even have a credit card, having always used her mother's. The money was all in her mother's name as well, and Darrin would have access to it; but not at once. He wouldn't know that Terry had cut up her credit cards so that Darrin wouldn't have access to them, soon after they'd arrived in Aspen. She'd had the premonition then and shared it with her daughter. Terry was truly frightened after the terrifying trip up from Vegas, with Darrin driving the Mercedes, laughing about how much money—Terry's money—he was going to spend on this new venture of his.

Most of Terry's estate was tied up in stocks and bonds and property, not easily liquidated. The ring Esther wore was free and clear and could be hocked or sold for a fortune. Where could she go? She was twenty-three years old and she'd never worked a day in her life. She'd been pampered, taken care of, her every desire fulfilled. Her mother's great wealth had cushioned her, spoiled her. If her mother had only loved her . . .

Well, over the years she'd managed to accept the neglect, while the housekeeper, Agnes, had shared holidays with her and been a wonderful substitute mother. Esther's mother was perpetually in search of the right man, so there was a succession of them in the villas she kept both in the

United States and other countries. Esther had learned quickly to stay out of the way. Her mother didn't like having a grown daughter; it interfered with her vision of herself as a young and beautiful woman. Despite the face-lifts and spas and couture garments, her age was getting hard to hide. When she was at her lowest ebb, cast off by a younger lover, she'd met Darrin Ross. And it had all started to come apart. Even the slight affection Terry had felt for her daughter was suddenly gone, in the passion she shared with Darrin. But so soon, the passion turned to fear. Darrin drank heavily and used drugs, and he had very expensive tastes. Terry became a hostage to his desires. Along with her, Esther, too, became a victim. And now her mother was dead and she was cast adrift in a cold and frightening world, with no family.

Her mother had mentioned a grandfather. But who was he? Her mother spoke once of a falling-out she'd had with her remaining parent over her choice of husbands when she'd married Esther's easygoing, gambling father. Her father was long dead, but the feud apparently remained. Esther knew her grandfather's last name but not where he lived, because she hadn't been told. She couldn't go through family albums or correspondence, because those were in the main house back in Los Angeles, where Terry and Esther had lived. Esther didn't even have her cell phone. It was in the drawer beside her bed, still charging. She'd forgotten to bring it downstairs this evening, having come running when she heard her mother scream.

She could have cried, but it would do no good. She was running for her life. She could call the police, of course, but Darrin would tell them it was a terrible accident. He wouldn't tell them that he'd thrown Terry down the staircase, and when the police left . . . It was too terrible to think about.

There had been at least three 911 calls from the address previously, though, when Darrin had attacked Terry over money. Agnes had called the police despite Terry's pleas. Try as he might, Darrin couldn't intimidate Agnes, who had powerful relatives. He wasn't drunk enough to do that, but he had pushed Terry into firing her. A temporary housekeeper had been engaged to work in her place, and Esther's heart had been broken at the treatment her surrogate mother had suffered. Terry had taken Darrin's side against her daughter for protesting. Darrin had threatened her with a black eye if she interfered with him again or if she dared to call the police. Those 911 calls would be on record. Even though Darrin was sure to swear that Terry's was an accidental death, there would be an investigation, because of Darrin's prior abuses. Surely he'd be found out!

Esther was far too afraid to do anything. She would call the police, she decided, so that at least Darrin wouldn't have the opportunity to hide the body. She'd do it anonymously, however, and from a pay phone. If she could find one. She'd never used a public phone. She wasn't sure where to go. But they recorded those calls, didn't they? And what if Darrin's friend at the police station recognized her voice and traced the call before she could get out of town? What then?

Buses ran. But Darrin would be after that diamond, and even worse, after her mother's will. Esther hadn't understood why her mother had stuffed the legal document into her purse the night before.*You must keep it close*, she'd said, *and never take it out of your purse*. Esther had asked why. Her mother had looked horrified and murmured something about a terrible threat. Darrin was jealous. He thought she was seeing someone else. He wasn't about to give up his luxury bed and board and he'd already started drinking. Her mother had seen an attorney, unknown to Darrin, and changed her will so that Darrin inherited nothing. In one of his rages, Darrin had gone with Terry to an attorney and had her revise her will to leave everything to him. Intimidated, Terry had agreed. But two days before her death, she got up enough courage to go back to the attorney and change the will so that her daughter would inherit everything. She told the lawyer she'd had a premonition. So now Esther stood to inherit the incredible amount of wealth, and she had the new, revised will, naming her beneficiary. She had the diamond, too. But the will and the ring were only useful if she lived.

She had to get out of town and somewhere she could hide, where Darrin couldn't find her. When she was safe, she could decide what to do. Tears stung her eyes. Her poor, sweet mother, who had no sense of self-preservation, who trusted everyone. Esther knew what Darrin was the minute she saw him. Her mother was certain that he was only misunderstood, and he was so manly!

The first time Darrin had struck her mother in the face, Terry had realized with horror what sort of person he really was. But it was too late. He intimidated her to the point of separating her from every friend she had. He watched her, and Esther, like a hawk. The abuse had grown so much worse when he insisted on coming here to Aspen, to the grandest of Terry's many homes. They didn't dare tell anyone. He had a friend on the local police force, he told them, and he'd know if they tried to sell him out. They didn't have the nerve. Agnes, the only one in the household who wasn't afraid of him, had called 911, and been fired.

Poor Agnes, who'd sacrificed so much to take care of the little girl Terry ignored. It broke Esther's heart.

And now her mother was dead, and Esther was running for her own life. She didn't have the price of a plane ticket. But she knew that Darrin had that friend on the police force. He might have someone who knew how to hack credit card companies to find out if a card in Terry's name had been used. So it was just as well that Esther didn't have the card. She couldn't fly, because she didn't have enough for a ticket. She couldn't take a bus because she could be traced that way. Even a train would keep records of its passengers.

But what about a truck? A big rig? She was walking beside a major highway and a huge semi was barreling through the snow that covered the road. Impulsively, she stepped out into the road. If the truck hit her, she wouldn't be any worse off, she thought miserably. At least she'd be with her mother.

The truck driver had good brakes. He stopped, pulled to the side of the road, and got out, leaving the engine idling.

He opened the passenger door and looked down at the pretty little blonde. Her long hair was tangled and she was wearing a fur jacket—probably fake, he thought gently, like that gaudy paste ring she was wearing that sparkled in the headlights. She didn't look like a prostitute. She looked frightened. "Miss, you okay?" he asked in a drawl.

She smiled wanly. "I'm sorry," she said, almost choking on anguish. "I've just lost my mother and I wasn't . . . wasn't thinking. I have to get to my cousin."

He smiled gently. He was an older man. She didn't know why, but she felt that she could trust him. "Where's your cousin live?" he asked.

"Up near the Wyoming border," she blurted out. Her

mother had mentioned a friend who'd lived there once, but she couldn't remember a name. "Benton, Colorado," she added.

He chuckled. "Now that's a hell of a coincidence. Come on." He led her back to the truck and knocked on the sleeper cab. A sleepy, heavyset blond woman opened her eyes. "Jack?" she asked the man. "What's wrong?"

"We've got a passenger. She's headed to Benton, hitch-hiking."

Esther started to deny it, but this was working out better than she'd dreamed. "I have to get to my cousin," she explained in her soft voice. "My mother . . . just died." She choked up.

"Oh, honey." The blond woman, dressed in jeans and flannel, tumbled out of the sleeper and caught Esther up in her arms, hugging her. "There, there, it's okay. We'll get you to your cousin."

Esther bawled. She'd lucked up. At least she had some hope of getting away before Darrin could catch her. And he'd never think that she'd be hitching rides in big rigs.

"You get right in front with Jack. I've been driving for twelve straight hours and I'm burned out." She chuckled. "We're a team. Well, we're married, but we're both truckers, so I'm his relief driver."

"It must be interesting," Esther said.

"Interesting and never dull," the woman said, smiling.

"Thanks so much," Esther began.

"We all have dark times," the driver, Jack, told her. "They pass. Buckle up and let's get going. You had anything to eat?"

"Oh, yes, I'm fine, thanks," she lied.

He saw through that. Her pale blue eyes were full of anguish. "There's a great truck stop a few hours down the road. We'll pull in and have some of the best barbecue in the country. You like barbecue?"

"I do," Esther said, and smiled.

"Okay, then. Let's be off!"

The trucker's wife was Glenda, and they were the nicest couple Esther had ever met. Down-to-earth, simple people, with no wealth or position, but they seemed outrageously happy. They made her feel like family.

She paid for her own supper out of her allowance that she hadn't had time to spend, and theirs, despite their protests. "You're giving me a ride and you won't let me pay for gas, so I'm buying food," she said stubbornly, and smiled.

They both laughed. "Okay, then," Glenda agreed. "Thank you."

"No. Thanks to both of you," she returned.

After supper it was back in the truck again. Four hours down the road, the truck stopped and Glenda got behind the wheel.

Esther was amazed at how the small woman could handle the big truck. "You're amazing," she exclaimed. "How in the world can you manage such a huge vehicle?"

"My daddy taught me to drive when I was only eleven," Glenda said as she pulled out onto the highway and the big truck started to slowly accelerate. "I can drive anything, even those big earthmovers. I love heavy equipment," she added with a flush of embarrassment. "It's why I married Jack. He drove these big rigs, and I loved them. Well, I loved him, too," she confessed. "The big lug. I couldn't do without him."

Esther, who'd never really been in love, just nodded as

if she understood. She really didn't. She'd lived like a hothouse orchid all her life, kept at home because her mother didn't like it if she had friends; they interfered with her boyfriends coming and going from whichever house they were living in. They rarely stayed in one place. Esther had been sent off to school, to a boarding school, and she'd hated every minute of it. When she came home, her mother was curt and unkind to her. Esther got in her way. She was younger and prettier than Terry, and when Terry's boyfriends came to the house, many of them flirted with Esther instead. Terry spent most of her time avoiding her mother and her mother's lovers. She wanted to leave, but she had nothing of her own. Everything belonged to Terry, and she wasn't shy about sharing that tidbit with her daughter if she ever rebelled. Terry could be icy and she was distant most of the time. Sweet Agnes had been Esther's anchor. She still missed the housekeeper.

Now here she was, alone and terrified, out on her own for the first time in her twenty-three years, with her mother lying dead back home. And Darrin no doubt hunting her for that diamond ring that was worth millions of dollars, not to mention that he needed her to be executrix of her mother's estate so he could get to the money. He had the false will, which would give him access to part of the property. He would want it all. But he and her mother weren't legally married, so he had no clear title to her estate. In the will that he thought was the true will, Terry had only made him beneficiary to her bank accounts. He hadn't read it thoroughly enough to realize that, and he certainly didn't know about the revised will in Esther's purse. When he found out, he'd be quite capable of getting one of his underworld friends to go after her.

The thought arose that if Darrin could find her, he could

probably force her to sign something giving him access to Terry's entire estate, no matter what violence it required, and do that without a pang of conscience. But he had to find her first, and she was going to make that very difficult.

They got to the outskirts of Benton before dawn. Esther couldn't afford to go to a motel and have people see her and wonder who she might be, because it was a very small town. Impulsively, she asked the couple to let her out at the end of a long driveway. She saw a small cabin in the distance with lights blazing inside it, through a drift of snow.

It looked like a wonderful refuge, if she could convince whoever lived there to let her stay, just for a day or two, until she could make other arrangements. Surely it was a couple, maybe with kids, and she could work something out.

It was an impulsive move, but she had these rare flashes of insight. Usually they were good ones.

"That's where my cousin lives," she lied brightly. "Thank you so very much for the ride!"

"You're very welcome." Glenda hugged her. So did Jack.

Glenda handed her a piece of paper. "That's my cell phone number. If you need help, you use it," she said firmly. "We'll come, wherever we are."

Tears stung Esther's eyes. "Thanks," she choked.

Glenda hugged her again. "You take care of yourself."

"You do, too."

They climbed back into the truck and waved. They looked very reluctant to leave her. It made her feel warm inside. She forced a smile, turned, and walked down the long trail to the little cabin. She'd memorized the name on the side of the truck. One day, she promised herself, when she had her fortune back, she was going to make sure that the pair had a trucking business of their very own.

As she struggled through the deep snow, her ankle boots already wet, her hands freezing because she didn't have her gloves, she felt as if she were slogging through wet sand. The night had been an anguish of terror. Her mother, dying, apologizing, Darrin raging upstairs, Esther terrified and not knowing what to do or where to go. She shivered. She had no money, no friends because they never stayed in one place long enough for her to make any since she'd left boarding school, she didn't even have a change of clothing. And the fox fur, while warm, wasn't enough in this freezing blizzard. She must have been out of her mind to get out of a safe truck with only the hope of a warm place to stay in the distance. A couple must live there, she told herself. Surely they wouldn't turn away anyone on a night like this!

It was almost daylight by now. She was just a few steps away from the front porch of the cabin when her body finally gave out. She fell into the snowdrift with a faint little cry, lost in the howling wind.

Inside the cabin, Butch Matthews was just turning off the television. It was late. He didn't sleep much. Memories of the war in Iraq, where he'd lost an arm to a mortar attack, still haunted him. He had nightmares. He was all alone here in this cabin on the outskirts of Benton. He'd been engaged once, but she'd gone back to an old boyfriend because, as she put it, she couldn't bear the thought of sleeping with a one-armed man.

He sure could pick them, he thought bitterly. Well, he had a good job with the state wildlife division, and he was a licensed rehabilitator. He looked down at his companion, a three-legged wolf named Two-Toes, who was old and almost blind.

"At least I've got you for company, old man," he sighed, tugging at the neck of his blue-checked flannel shirt. "Damn, it's getting cold in here. I guess I'd better get in a little more wood before it all freezes."

He patted the wolf, ran a hand through his own thick, short black hair. His dark eyes went to the sheepskin coat hanging by the front door. He wasn't a handsome man, but he had regular features at least. He was tall and fit, despite losing part of his arm up until just below the elbow. He had jet-black hair and dark brown eyes, and big hands and feet. He also had an inner strength and an oversized dose of compassion. Everyone liked him, but he didn't mix well, though, and he kept to himself. The loneliness got to him once in a while. It got to him tonight. He was more alone than he'd felt in his life. Both his parents were long dead. His fiancée had bailed on him. There wasn't anybody else. Not even a cousin . . .

He opened the door and his eyes widened. There, in the snow, was a body. It had blond hair and a fur jacket.

"Good God!" he exclaimed. He ran to her, turned her over gently. She was beautiful. Perfect complexion, long blond hair, pretty mouth. And unconscious.

"At least you're a lightweight," he murmured as he shifted her so that he could get her over one shoulder in a fireman's lift.

He carried her quickly into the house and eased her

down on the leather sofa. "Don't eat her," he told Two-Toes firmly.

The old wolf sat on its haunches and panted.

Butch closed the front door and found an afghan that he'd bought at a summer festival in Benton. He eased the woman out of the fur jacket and winced. She was wearing a very thin silk blouse. No wonder she was almost frozen. And what was she doing out in the middle of nowhere, without a suitcase? He noted the hem of her slacks as he wrapped her up. Something dark had stained them. Blood?

He wrapped her in the afghan and went into the kitchen to make coffee. While it perked, he got down an extra mug. Something hot might help. He wondered if he should call an ambulance. Hopefully, she'd only fainted. He'd have to check her pulse and breathing. He'd had basic first aid courses as part of his army training, and later, forest service training, so he knew how to handle emergencies.

He poured coffee, turned off the pot, and carried the mugs to the coffee table.

He sat down beside the woman and shook her gently by the shoulder.

She opened her eyes. They were blue. Pale blue. She looked up at him, disoriented. "I passed out," she said in a soft, sweet voice.

He smiled. "Yes, you did."

She blinked and looked around her. "This is the cabin. I saw it from the road . . ." She'd have to make up some excuse for being here, and she wasn't good at lying. If he tossed her out, she didn't know what she'd do. On the other hand, what if he was like Darrin? Faint fear narrowed her eyes.

There was an odd growling sound nearby. A dog,

maybe? She loved dogs. If this man had pets, he must be nice. But her heart was pounding with mingled fear and worry and grief.

"It's okay," he said, watching the expressions cross her face. She looked very young. "You're safe."

"Safe." She sat up, just in time for Two-Toes to amble over and sit down beside her.

Esther's eyes widened and she held her breath.

"That's just Two-Toes," the man said in a pleasant deep voice. "He's blind. He growls when he doesn't know people, but he's never bitten anyone. Who are you, and what are you doing out here in the middle of the night?"

She recovered her senses and looked at him. The man was tall and well built. One shirtsleeve was empty at the bottom. He wore boots and jeans and a flannel shirt. He had dark hair and eyes. He was smiling.

"Well?" he prompted, but not in a mean way.

"I thought my cousin lived here," she lied. "Barry Crump and his wife, Lettie . . ."

"No Crumps here." He frowned. "In fact, I don't think I've ever known anybody with that name."

"Oh, dear," she said, biting her lower lip.

"I didn't see a car when I found you."

It was a question. She flushed. It made her face brighter, vulnerable. "I don't own one," she said. And she didn't. Not anymore. "I hitched a ride."

"That's dangerous," he pointed out.

She was drawing blood with that tooth in her lower lip.

She sat up, displacing the afghan, and ran a hand through her tangled hair. "Oh, coffee," she exclaimed, and almost fell on it. "I'm so thirsty!"

"Feeling better now?" he asked.

"Oh, yes. I was just so tired. It's been a long night," she

added without elaborating. "I've never fainted before. I guess it was the cold." She smiled shyly. "Thanks for saving me."

"No problem. I'm a licensed rescuer for damsels in distress," he teased.

"What's a damsel?" she wondered.

"Damned if I know, really." He chuckled. "But you were in need of rescue. I slay dragons, too, in case you ever need one taken care of."

She grinned. Her whole face lit up and she was extraordinarily beautiful.

"Who are you?" he asked.

"Esther," she said quietly. "Esther Marist." She cocked her head and studied him. "Who are you?"

He smiled. "Butch Matthews."

"Thanks for bringing me inside," she said softly. "I guess I'd have frozen to death out there." She shivered. "I'm not really dressed for this much snow."

Butch Matthews was no dunce. Something traumatic had happened to her. He could sense it. She was wearing high-ticket items. He knew real fur when he saw it, and that fox jacket was real fox. Her shoulder bag was real leather, like her high-heeled shoes. She didn't have a suitcase, so she'd left somewhere in a hurry. She was wearing a huge pink gaudy ring on one finger. It sure didn't go with the fox jacket. Nobody had a ring that size that was real, he was sure of it. Damned thing covered almost a whole joint of her finger.

He recalled hearing a semi stop out on the highway, a few minutes before this little fragile blond turned up on his doorstep.

He sat down in the armchair across from the sofa with the coffee table between them and sipped his own coffee.

"Now," he said, smiling. "Suppose you tell me what's wrong?"

Wrong . . . ?"

"Come on. Two-Toes and I are mostly harmless."

She laughed. "*The Hitchhiker's Guide to the Galaxy*," she blurted out, because those two words were what were written about Earth in the guide.

He roared. "Truly."

Two-Toes inched toward her, sniffing.

"Friend, Two-Toes," he told the wolf, ruffling his fur. "Friend. Don't eat her."

Esther looked, and felt, horrified.

"I'm kidding," Butch teased.

She looked from him to the big wolf. She'd never seen one in person, and this one was twice the size of any dog she'd seen. He moved closer to her and began to sniff her. Impulsively, because he didn't seem aggressive, she put out a small hand. He took a deep smell, and suddenly laid his head in her lap.

"Oh, goodness," she said softly. She stroked his head, a smile breaking out on her worried face. "My goodness, he's so sweet!"

Butch was speechless. Mostly Two-Toes avoided contact with anyone who came in the door, except Parker, his Crow friend who'd just married.

"Well," Butch said heavily. "That's amazing."

She looked up. "Why?"

"He's not usually that friendly."

She laughed.

"Not to most people," he amended. "Can I get you something to eat?"

"Thank you, but no. The truck drivers were kind enough

to find a truck stop. I got coffee and supper. They were so sweet to me."

"Most truckers are good people," he said.

She drew in a breath. "It hasn't exactly been a night for that." She caught herself and gave him a worried glance.

"Can you talk about what happened?" he asked.

She hugged the wolf and lowered her eyes. "My mother . . . died tonight."

"Good God! Where?"

"Back in"—she hesitated—"where we were staying. Her boyfriend wants all her things. He was drunk. She was all broken up and there was blood everywhere. She told me to run. I didn't think, I just ran!"

He saw a panorama that was disturbing, and this fragile little thing right in the middle of it. "You're afraid of him. The boyfriend."

"Terrified." She drew in a short, sharp breath. "If they find me, they'll make me testify. If I testify, he'll kill me. He has friends in organized crime. He made threats to my poor mother." She closed her eyes and shivered.

"You should go to the police," he said.

"He has a friend in the local department," she replied. "The mob pays him."

"I see." He frowned. "How did your mother die?"

"He threw her down the staircase." She looked at her lap. "I think it broke her spine. Her throat was cut from hitting something on the way down. She only lived a few seconds . . . after . . ."

"Dear God!"

He got up and went to the sofa beside her, pulling her against him with one strong arm. He smelled of soap and aftershave. He was very strong, and warm, and she was aching for comfort. She curled close to him and cried her heart out.

He'd never felt needed in his whole life, not by anybody. And here this beautiful stranger came walking in out of the snow and made him feel ten feet tall with her fragility, her vulnerability.

She drew back after a minute. "I'm sorry, it's just that there's so much . . . !"

He smoothed her hair. "Don't worry about it." He got up. "Come on. This isn't a five-star hotel, but it's got two bedrooms and you're welcome to one of them. The door even locks," he added with a grin.

She smiled. She trusted him implicitly, without even knowing him. "Tomorrow, I'll find someplace to go and see about getting a job."

"What sort of job?" he asked.

She flushed. She'd never worked a day in her young life. But she was strong and she could learn. "Whatever there is," she said finally, and smiled at him.

He admired her spirit. "I'll see if I can help," he said. "But you can stay here for the time being. I'm out a lot. I work for the wildlife service. In my spare time, I'm a rehabilitator."

"Oh, I see! Two-Toes," she began.

"Yes. Two-Toes and other assorted mammals, including a fox. The others live in the outbuilding. It's heated, sort of, and at least sheltered. Two-Toes, though, he's company." He stopped suddenly, close to admitting how lonely he was. He'd been engaged, but when she found out he'd lost his arm, she'd broken the engagement. His parents were long dead. He had nobody, unless you counted his friend, Parker.

"I like animals," she said.

"We noticed," he chuckled, indicating Two-Toes, who was following her.

"He's sweet," she said softly, rubbing her hand over his thick fur.

"Yes, he is. Now if you'd had a big bologna sandwich for lunch . . ." His voice trailed off with amusement.

She just laughed. "You wouldn't eat me, even then, would you, sweet boy?"

The wolf sat down and his tongue lolled out while she petted him.

Butch just shook his head.

The bedroom had a bed, a chest of drawers, and assorted guns.

He made a face. "I guess you hate guns . . ."

"I don't mind them," she said, smiling.

Both eyebrows went up.

"My dad used to take me to the gun range with him, when he was alive. He was a Class A skeet shooter."

He was fascinated. "Can you shoot a shotgun?"

"Just the lightest gauge, the 28," she replied.

"Just," he said, shaking his head. He'd never met a woman who'd even pick up a shotgun, much less risk the noise and recoil of shooting one.

She was looking around the room.

"It's just a spare room," he said. "I had the bed put in because once in a while, somebody comes from one of the agencies and needs a place to stay. But it's not often. It's messy in here," he added.

"I don't mind clutter," she said softly.

"You don't even have a change of clothes," he mused.

"I left in a hurry." Tears stung her eyes.

"Do you want to call anybody?"

"There's nobody to call," she said miserably. "It was just Mama and me. I've got a grandfather, but I don't know where he is. I don't even know who he is. Mama hardly ever talked about him. I can't even call the police. Darrin would find out where I am and come after me."

"Why?" he asked. "Because you saw what he did?"

She opened her purse and took out the will. "Because Mama changed her will and I've got it," she said. "She stuffed it into my purse a day ago and told me to keep it there. She always had premo . . . premonitions." She swallowed tears and grief.

He was noticing the gaudy ring she wore. Costume jewelry, of course. He wondered why she hadn't chosen something less ostentatious, that looked less like a fake. Women were incomprehensible to him most of the time, though. He'd never been able to keep one for long, especially his fiancée. She was hung up on cowboys when they met, and thought that he had a ranch in Wyoming. He'd never lied to her about that. He owned a hundred acres and a few horses, but he was no land baron. Perhaps she'd been wrapped up in daydreams. She hadn't been that crazy about him after a few dates, and to be honest, she'd been pretty drunk when he proposed. He'd thought she was innocent until he took her to bed, where she taught him things he'd never known. Probably it was just as well that she'd left him. Hearing her talk about past lovers made him uncomfortable. It was something he'd never have done.

"Well, I'll leave you to it," he said gently. "Bathroom's down the hall and it has a lock. I hate having people walk in on me when I'm having a shower, even if it's other men." His face hardened for a minute and she wondered if it was because part of his arm was missing, but she didn't say so.

"Thanks for giving me a place to sleep," she said gently. "I'll find something as fast as I can and get out of your hair."

He just smiled and closed the door on her.

She was too tired to take a shower. She took off her slacks and blouse and slid under the covers, nervous and sick and worried. It would be a miracle if she got a wink of sleep after what she'd been through.

But she felt safe. That kind man in the other room had been generous. He didn't know her from a snowball, but he was willing to trust her in his home. It made her feel humble. She had to make sure that she found something soon, so that she didn't have to presume on his hospitality. He wasn't a man who had a lot of material possessions, she could tell, but it didn't matter to her. He had a good heart.

She closed her eyes and, amazingly, went right to sleep.

He tapped on the door around eight. "Breakfast. Hot coffee. Great company!" he called through the door.

She burst out laughing, still half asleep. "I'll be right out."

She got up and put on the clothes she'd been wearing the day before, her eyes wincing at the blood stain still on the hem of her slacks. Maybe she could wash it out later.

They ate in a companionable silence. He'd made scrambled eggs and toast and bacon to go with the coffee. They were great.

"You're a wonderful cook," she said.

"You only think so because you're half starved," he

pointed out good-naturedly. He leaned toward her. "The toast has been scraped. I burned it!"

She giggled.

He grinned and went back to eating.

"Is there a local paper, and does it have want ads?" she asked.

"Yes." He got up and retrieved it from the sofa, handing it to her.

"Thanks." She sipped coffee while she searched through the Help Wanted column. She sighed. "Well, I can't drive an eighteen-wheeler or handle cattle, and I'm pretty sure I'm not cut out to be a shepherd. But there's a waitress job going in town at the Gray Dove." She looked up. "I hate to ask . . ."

"But can I drive you to town," he finished for her, laughing. "Sure. Let me feed Two-Toes and the other critters and I'll drive you in."

"Thanks!"

He shrugged, not even looking back.

His truck wasn't new, but it was well kept and it ran smoothly. She grinned. She'd never been in a pickup in her life. "This is great!" she exclaimed as they went down the road.

"What, the scenery?" he asked, curious.

"This truck!" she said. "It's just awesome!"

He was stunned. She was wearing expensive clothes, he could tell, but she went goo-goo over a truck. He laughed softly.

"What is it?" she asked.

"It's just a truck," he pointed out.

"Yes, I know, but I've never ridden in one. It's just super!"

His eyes widened. "You've never been in a truck?"

"Well, no," she said, hesitating. Her face colored. She shouldn't have admitted that.

He felt guilty when he saw the joy drain out of her. "Listen, don't mind me," he said. "There must be dozens of city people who think cars are the only way to travel. But I'm glad you like the truck." He grinned. "There was this song, about a man who loved his truck."

She laughed, the joy returning.

She was pretty when she laughed. He had to drag his eyes away.

She didn't notice. She was on fire with life, with a new beginning, with a sudden feeling of safety and refuge. She took a deep breath and forced her mother's tragic face to the back of her mind. She had to look ahead. And that meant a job, for the moment.

Chapter Two

The owner of the Gray Dove, Mary Dodd, tried not to gape at the sight of Butch Matthews with a pretty young blond woman. He hadn't dated anyone since he came home from the war and his fiancée threw him over, so it was something of an occasion. But she was quick to hide her surprise.

"I've never done any waitressing," Esther confessed. "But I'll work hard, and never complain, and I'll learn, if you'll teach me. I won't even care about salary . . ."

"You don't have to sell me," the woman said gently. "I read people pretty well. It's not as if we have hordes of people rushing in here trying to get work," she added with a smile. "If you want the job, it's yours."

Esther relaxed. "Thank you!"

The owner went on to tell her about uniforms, which would be provided, and working hours. She'd start the following Monday.

Esther thanked her again, with such enthusiasm that Butch had to hide a smile.

They went out together, onto the sidewalk.

"Are there cabs?" she asked suddenly, worried.

"It's five minutes from the cabin," he pointed out. "I don't mind driving you."

"Are you sure?" she asked, concerned. "I'm causing you a lot of trouble."

"And if I minded, I'd say so," he replied softly. "Okay?"

She let out the breath she'd been holding. "Okay."

"How about riding around with me for a bit?" he asked. "So you get to know the area."

"I'd like that!" she enthused.

"Yeah, right, you're not fooling me. All that enthusiasm, it's just so you can be near the truck," he drawled.

She burst out laughing. So did he.

"Busted," she confessed.

He drove her around town, pointing out the various businesses. There weren't a lot. Benton had a little over fifteen hundred souls. It was like a big family, he explained. People didn't mind each others' business, but they cared about each other.

"That sounds very nice," she commented softly.

"Isn't it like this, where you come from?"

She hesitated. Then she shook her head. She sighed and looked out the window. "We lived a lot of places, but none of them was ever home," she explained. "Mama was, well, adventurous. She was always in love with somebody, and she never chose anybody who was good for her. Darrin was the latest in a long line of horrible men she . . . lived with."

"What about your dad?" he wondered.

"He died years ago. He was a sweet man. I loved him very much. I loved Mama, too, but . . ." She hesitated. She glanced at him. "She did love me, in her way."

"I'm guessing that you had to find ways to avoid some of the men, Esther," he said without meeting her eyes.

She drew in a long breath. She looked out the window again. "Yes."

What a hell of a life, he was thinking. "Was your mother as pretty as you are?"

"Much prettier," she replied, smiling sadly. "She never looked her age. I brought a boy home from school one day and he spent the evening with Mama." She shook her head. "I wasn't much on boys, anyway. Watching Mama with an endless parade of men sort of soured me, I guess."

He felt sorry for her. She had a little material wealth, from the look of her, but without love, it wasn't much.

"How are you going to like waitressing?" he asked quietly. "I'll bet you've never had a job in your young life."

"You'd be right," she said on a long sigh. "But I'm young, like you said, and strong, and I can learn how to do anything I set my mind to."

"I'd bet money on that," he said with a gentle smile.

"I have to find somewhere to live . . ."

"Why can't you stay with me?" he asked simply.

She was shocked. "But, people might talk," she began.

"Sure they might. I don't care. Do you?"

She was thinking about being on her own. She could probably find someplace that she could afford, but she'd be all alone. She grimaced.

"Or does the idea of living with a one-armed man turn you off?" he asked, and there was such bitterness in the remark that she turned her head and gaped at him.

"Is that what happened?" she asked softly. "Your girlfriend turned her back on you when you came home from overseas? What an idiot she must have been!"

Now he was the one gaping, so much so that he had to right the truck back on the highway.

"You took me in and I could have been anybody," she continued. "You live with an injured wolf that you could have had put down instead." She smiled. "You're not a missing arm with a man attached, you know. You're a man who lost his arm."

"Damn!"

Her eyebrows arched. "Excuse me?"

He pulled over onto the grass beside the road and threw the truck out of gear. He looked at her, long and hard, and his lean face was taut with bad memories. "I was engaged to be married," he said quietly. "My reserve unit, army, was called up, so I went to Iraq with a friend of mine, Parker, who lives locally. He carried me through a hail of bullets, after I took a hit from mortar, in Iraq. He saved my life." He stared out the windshield at the distant mountains. "I came home wounded and was mustered out. My girl was waiting for me. I got off the bus and she saw the empty sleeve." He hesitated.

She put out a soft hand and touched his shoulder. "And?"

He grimaced. "She said she was sorry. She couldn't bear the thought of going to bed with a one-armed man. She put the ring in my shirt pocket, smiled, and just walked away. I stayed drunk for two weeks. Parker snapped me out of it and helped me get a job. This job, working as a wildlife rehabilitator for the state of Colorado in this district, and that helps put money in the bank. But I've sort of been off women ever since."

"No wonder," she said quietly. "What a burden she might have been. You had a lucky escape."

He glanced at her, frowning.

"Sorry," she said, grimacing. "I open my mouth and stick my foot in."

The frown went away. "I've never thought of myself as being lucky."

"What sort of wife would she have been, if she didn't love you enough to just be grateful that you came home at all?"

There was a faintly stunned expression in his eyes. It hadn't ever occurred to him that Sadie might not have loved him in the first place. They were good in bed together, but she'd never been emotionally attached to him. He'd almost died with pneumonia the winter they were engaged, and she'd never even come to see about him. Parker had nursed him until he got well.

"Talk about being blind," he murmured. "No. I don't think she loved me at all. We were good in bed together. It was only that. She was on the rebound from another man when I started going with her."

"Does she still live here?" she asked, without knowing why she asked the question.

"No. The old boyfriend turned up and she married him. They moved away."

"When did he turn up?"

"Oh, just before I came home . . ." He stopped in mid-sentence. "Why didn't I remember that?"

"You stayed drunk for two weeks," she pointed out.

He glanced at her again and this time he was smiling. "You're a tonic."

"You mean I taste bad?" she teased.

He pursed his chiseled lips. "I can't comment until I've decided that for myself."

She blushed scarlet. "Oh, gosh!"

He burst out laughing. "Sorry. Couldn't resist it." He put the truck in gear and pulled back out onto the highway. "Are you a witch?" he teased. "You know things you shouldn't."

"We had an ancestor who died in Salem who was accused of witchcraft, so who knows?" she teased.

She was bright and beautiful, and Butch felt as if the sun had just come out in his dreary, cloudy life.

"What about you?" she asked. "Do you have family?"

"Just Parker, and we're not related," he said on a sigh. "My parents were older when they had me, and I was their only child. They've both been dead for years."

"So, you're alone, too," she said in her soft, quiet voice.

She looked out the window, fighting tears again. It was so painful, remembering her mother lying at the foot of the staircase.

"You miss your mother," he said, noting the faint glitter of tears in her averted face.

"She was so trusting," she said, her voice catching, because the loss was very new. "She never saw the evil in people. Especially in men. It was one after the other, most of my life."

"Addiction."

She turned toward him. "What?"

"Addiction," he repeated. "It's not much different than being addicted to alcohol or drugs, or even gambling. It wasn't something she could help."

She was silent for a minute, thinking about what he'd said. "I didn't think of it that way."

"We're all at the mercy of our urges from time to time,"

he said quietly. "But I'm sorry you had to lose her in such a way."

"Me, too." She wiped her eyes with the backs of her hands. "She was all I had left in the world."

"You need to talk to a lawyer," he said. "You can't let your mother's boyfriend get away with murder."

"He's very slick," she muttered. "He could talk people into believing anything."

"You were an eyewitness to what he did," he pointed out.

"Yes, and he has friends who are big-time criminals," she replied. "The minute he knows where I am, he'll come after me. I have Mama's will." She also had Mama's multi-million-dollar ring on her finger, but she wasn't mentioning that. It was gaudy enough to pass for paste, which suited Esther just fine.

Butch was thinking. "There has to be some way you could point a finger at him."

"You think?" she asked on a heavy sigh. She glanced at him. "It would put you in danger as well, and I'm not doing that. Not after you've been so kind to me. They have a good police force in Aspen," she added quietly. "I know, because Mama had to call them, when Darrin hit her . . ."

"So there's a record of it?"

"There is. In fact, there were three incidents while we lived there."

"And that will put him on the suspect list, at least." He glanced at her. "If you want to go back, I'll go with you," he said unexpectedly.

"But you don't know me from a bean," she pointed out. "I could be lying."

He chuckled. "Nope."

"Are you always so trusting?" she wanted to know.

"Not with most people. But you're an open book, sunshine," he teased. "You couldn't hide anything. Your face would give you away." He paused to grin at her. "I'd love to play poker with you."

She burst out laughing. "I guess I'd be pretty lousy at that, anyway. The only gambling I've ever done was at the slot machines in Vegas, and I lost every penny I put into it."

"I used to play poker. I never won, so I gave it up. Now it's checkers or chess, when I have the time."

"I'll bet you . . ."

His phone rang. He pulled off on the side of the road and looked at the screen, then pushed a button and put it to his ear. "Where? When? Sure. I'm on my way. Don't let it out of your sight, okay? Fine."

He hung up. "I have a call to make," he told her. "Do you mind going along?"

"Not at all. What do you have to do?"

"Rescue another wolf, but this one isn't blind or missing a leg," he said. "You'll stay in the truck while I deal with it. Got that?"

"Okay," she said.

He put his foot down on the accelerator. "Two boys with rifles were shooting for sport," he said angrily. "They are not sure they hit it, but they're in custody anyway."

"It's an endangered species?"

"No. They got arrested for animal cruelty. They had a rope around its neck and they were dragging it behind a pickup truck." His face was taut with anger.

"I hope they lock them up for a year," she muttered.

"Me, too."

* * *

It wasn't a long drive. Butch pulled off the main road across from a convenience store and cut off the engine.

"Stay put, okay?" he emphasized.

"I will."

She watched him go over to a pickup truck, which was flanked by a county sheriff's deputy and a state police officer. Butch bent over something, ran a hand over it and stood back up. He glanced at the truck.

One of the deputies picked up the wolf and carried it to the bed of the pickup, where Butch kept a cage.

"Go easy," she heard Butch say as the man slid the injured animal into the cage.

"How will you get him out when you get home?" the deputy asked.

"With a lot of swearing and a little bit of luck," Butch replied with a laugh.

"I'll follow you home and get him out for you," the deputy said.

"Okay. Thanks, Roy."

The other man waved and went back to his vehicle.

"Is he badly injured?" Esther asked.

"A couple of broken ribs, feels like, and a lot of scrapes. I know what to do for them, and there's a wildlife vet I can call to check him over. I'll do that when we get home."

"Those stupid boys," she muttered.

"They're going to be very sorry for what they did, believe me. They won't get away with it."

"I'm glad."

The deputy was waiting at the cabin when they got there. Butch went around to open the passenger door and Esther got out.

It didn't help that the deputy, young and single, stared at Esther as if he was looking at a delicious ice cream sundae.

"Uh, the wolf?" Butch prompted.

Roy cleared his throat, flushed a little, and laughed. "Sure thing. Coming."

He lifted the wolf out and carried him to one of the outbuildings where Butch kept his injured wildlife. The wolf, fortunately, was in too much pain to fight. Several minutes later, the men came out of the building.

"Thanks for the help, Roy," Butch said, and shook his hand.

"That's one beautiful girlfriend you've got there," Roy said. "Is she local?"

"No. And she's not my girlfriend." He hesitated. "She's my fiancée."

"Well! Congratulations, you sly dog, you." Roy chuckled. "No wonder you were giving me the evil eye."

"Can't help it. She's gorgeous and I'm ugly," Butch said.

"Baloney. If you need help anytime, though, you can call me."

"Thanks."

He went into the house to find Esther in the kitchen, looking for a cookbook.

"Hey," Butch said. "What are you up to?"

She turned. "Have you got a cookbook?" she asked.

"Uh, no, not really," he said slowly.

"Well, if I'm going to stay here, I have to earn my keep," she said softly. "So I'm going to learn how to cook."

Anticipating a few weeks of burned meals, he just smiled and said that was a great idea.

"I may have done something bad just now," he added slowly.

"How bad?"

"Well . . ."

She propped her hands on her hips and gave him a mock glare. "How bad?"

"You really are a dish," he murmured, starstruck.

"Butch," she prompted.

"Oh. The bad thing." He snapped out of the daze. "Well, it's like this. Roy, the guy who helped me with the wolf, he's single and woman-crazy and persistent."

Her eyebrows arched. "And?"

"And a real rounder. He was giving you the eye. So I told him something. It may make you angry . . ."

She cocked her head.

He cleared his throat. "I sort of told him we were engaged."

Her eyes glimmered with pleasure. She smiled. "You did? Really?"

"You're not angry?"

"Oh, no," she said softly. "I was already worrying about your reputation. You work for the state government and . . ."

He chuckled. "I don't really think they concern themselves with our private lives," he pointed out. "I was thinking of your reputation. You're sort of green, honey. I don't mean that in a bad way, just that you're not very, well, brassy. And Roy . . ."

"And Roy's a rounder," she finished for him.

"Exactly."

She smiled slowly. "Okay."

His eyebrows went up. "You don't mind?"

She laughed. "No. I don't mind at all."

He studied her quietly. "It's just while you're staying

here," he said. "I mean, you don't have to think of it as binding or anything."

"Oh."

He couldn't quite decipher the look on her face. "Anyway, I've got to go out and see about my new charge."

"I don't guess I could come with you?" she asked.

"He may be dangerous . . ."

"But I'll be with you," she said.

He felt a foot taller. "Okay, then,"

She grinned and followed him out the door.

The wolf had lacerations all down one side, probably the one on which he'd been dragged. Butch had an antibiotic ointment that he smoothed over the cuts after he'd cleaned them, having muzzled the animal first.

"I can't really afford to lose the other arm as well," he teased as he glanced at a spellbound Esther, standing next to him.

"I understand. Any animal can be dangerous, though, even a house cat."

"So true."

He smoothed his hand over the wolf's head. "Poor old man," he said gently. "I'm sorry to belong to a species that could do something so terrible to an animal."

The wolf opened one eye and looked at him, almost as if it understood him.

"I'll get you well and you can go home," he added. "Just rest now. The vet's coming over soon to see about you," he added, having called the vet as they walked into the shed room.

"He's so beautiful," Esther said as Butch closed the cage. "They're losing habitat so fast. Animals have no place to go. Civilization is making them extinct."

"Pretty much," Butch had to agree.

"What else do you have in here?" she wondered.

"Come and see."

She paused by the injured fox and winced. She was wearing a fox coat, although it was blue and this beautiful animal was red and white.

Butch bent down to her ear. "It's a dead fox. What you're wearing," he pointed out.

"Oh." She smiled shyly. "How did you know I was thinking that?"

"I'm taking a mail-order course in how to read minds," he teased.

She chuckled. "Okay." She moved with him to the other cages. One of them held a strange animal. She'd never seen one like it. "What is this one?" she asked.

"A badger," he replied. "Don't get too close. They can be aggressive."

"So can wolves," she returned.

"Yes."

She turned to Butch. "What you do, it's awesome," she said. "All these poor creatures would be dead if it wasn't for you."

He felt warm all over. She made him feel different. Useful. Better than he thought he was. "If I hadn't done it, somebody else would have," he began.

"Yes. But nobody else did. You did." She smiled.

He drew in a breath. "You really are a boost for my ego," he mused. "I won't be able to get my head through the door."

She laughed.

"We should go," he added. He adjusted the thermostat in the building, which controlled the gas heat, and shepherded her out the door and back into the cabin.

* * *

They had mashed potatoes and a small piece of cube steak for supper, with fruit for dessert. Butch had cooked. Esther peeled the potatoes.

"I peeled them too much," she said sadly.

"You did fine," he replied. "Especially for somebody who's never set foot in a kitchen before," he added with a grin.

"Thanks. I'll get better. I just need a cookbook and some practice."

"The cook at the Gray Dove is awesome," he pointed out. "I'll bet she'd be happy to give you some pointers if you just ask her."

"What a great idea! I'll do that."

"You might also mention that we're engaged," he added, because he knew the cook, and she was very conservative.

He was very protective already. She liked that. She smiled to herself.

He saw the smile. "What?" he asked.

She looked up, eyebrows arching.

"You smiled when I said that," he told her.

"Oh." She flushed. "It sounded, well, protective." She shifted. "I've never had anybody who tried to protect me. Mama was always looking for the right man. I know she loved me, but I was sort of an afterthought. And she didn't like having a grown daughter. She went to spas, had face-lifts, all those things really beautiful women do to try and look younger than they are." Her face was bland. She looked up at him. "What use is it?" she asked solemnly. "I mean, you may look younger, but it won't change how old you are, will it? And if you have to do so much work on yourself to deny how old you are, who's going to know or want the person you really are?" She made a face. "I'm making it all muddled . . ."

"You aren't," he replied, and he was serious as well. "I know exactly what you mean. My former fiancée was like that," he added bitterly. "She was always using creams and lotions and dyeing her hair, wearing clothes that were too young for her. She couldn't stand the thought of a new gray hair or a wrinkle in her face."

"That's just sad."

"It is." He studied her. He smiled. "You really are a knockout."

She flushed. "That's all on the outside," she said.

"I like what's on the inside even better," he returned softly.

The flush deepened.

His eyes were probing. "Haven't you ever had a boyfriend?"

She laughed softly. "They couldn't get past Mama," she said. "She was so beautiful . . ." She bit her lip. Tears stung her eyes. "Sorry. It's still so new."

"And so painful," he agreed. He slid his big hand over her small one and held it just for a minute. He let go then. "Don't let that steak go to waste," he said, forcing laughter. "It's one I bought from a local rancher. Filled up half my freezer. Grade A beef, no antibiotics, no hormones, just good beefsteak!"

She grinned. "I like steak," she said. "But just once in a while. I mostly eat fish and vegetables."

"Desserts?"

She paused and then shook her head. "I don't like sweets."

"Neither do I. Well, I like a chocolate pie once in a blue

moon. The cook at the Gray Dove makes them. I eat there about once a week."

She beamed. "So I'll see you at work one day a week?"

He chuckled. "Yes, you will."

She finished her meal and her coffee. "Want more coffee?" she asked, getting up.

"One more cup. It keeps me awake at night if I have more than that," he said.

She sighed. "I don't sleep, whether I drink coffee or not," she said. "Mama was always wanting to go somewhere. California, Nevada, Idaho, New York City, overseas. I don't think we ever spent more than a month at home. I don't like traveling."

"That makes two of us," he said. "I got moved around a lot in the military. Up until then, I'd never been out of Benton in my whole life."

"Honest?" she asked, surprised. She put his coffee mug down in front of him.

"Honest. My folks were ranchers." He chuckled. "Hard to go off and leave the cattle while you party in some other country. One guy I know went to Tahiti for a month. When he came back, his cattle were gone. He went to ask his foreman what happened to them, and his foreman was gone as well. The guy forged his boss's name on a bill of sale and sold the lot. Took the rancher two weeks to track him down. He hadn't had time to spend much of the money, so he got it back and recovered his cattle. Foreman went to prison."

"Good enough for him," she said.

"It also taught the rancher a valuable lesson," he added with twinkling eyes. "Not to be too trusting."

She chuckled. "I can see the point."

* * *

After they finished supper, Butch got Esther's fox fur and helped her into it.

"Where are we going?" she asked.

"Walmart," he replied. "You can't wear the same clothes to work every day."

She flushed. "I didn't think about that."

"We'll get you some slacks and shirts and a coat that won't attract attention," he said.

She sighed. "I guess it does look a bit out of place. But maybe people will think it's fake fur," she added.

"Not in this part of the country, they won't." He laughed.

"At least I still have some money," she said, and gave him a long, hard look that indicated he wasn't paying for anything for her.

"What an expression," he mused. "Have you ever knocked anybody out with those dagger-eyes?"

She relaxed and laughed softly. "Just making the point that I pay my own way," she replied. "And you'll get rent as soon as I get my first paycheck. I won't argue," she added softly. "You've been kinder to me than anybody ever was, except my parents."

Now he was flushing, high on his cheekbones. "Okay, then," he said, remembering that his former fiancée had begged for pretty things and never offered to do a thing for him. "Let's go."

Chapter Three

The store was crowded, and the first people Butch met were his friend Parker and Parker's new wife, Katy, and his stepdaughter, Teddie. They were an interesting combination, because Parker was Crow—and had the jet-black hair and dark eyes and olive skin to prove it—and Katy was blond and blue eyed.

"Hey, buddy, how's it going?" Butch asked.

Parker grinned at him, his arm around his wife. "Things are great. How're you doing, Sarge?" he asked, and his eyes went curiously to the pretty blonde in the fox jacket standing so close to his friend.

Butch slid his one good arm around her and pulled her gently close. "She's my fiancée. Esther, this is my friend Parker, and his wife and daughter."

"Nice to meet you," Parker said. "Fiancée, huh? And you didn't say a word to me about it?" he teased.

"We haven't known each other long," Butch said, smiling down at a worried Esther, "but we both . . . just knew," he said, shrugging.

"I know how that feels." Parker chuckled. He looked down at Katy. "I knew, too."

Katy laughed up at him. "Me, too."

"How's Two-Toes?" Teddie asked excitedly.

"He's doing great. He likes to watch game shows." Butch chuckled.

"How does Esther like living with a wolf?" Parker teased.

"He follows her around like a puppy," Butch said, amused.

"He's so sweet," Esther said gently. "We've got a new wolf, too." Her face clouded. "He had a vicious introduction to people."

"Indeed he did," Butch muttered. "There were arrests. And there will be prosecutions. Poor old wolf. He'll live, but he may not be able to go back out into the wild either." He shook his head. "We live in strange times."

"How's Bartholomew?" Butch asked the little girl.

She grinned. "I can make him trot without falling off now!"

"Good for you!"

Esther looked puzzled. "Bartholomew?" she asked.

"He's my horse," Teddie said, smiling at her. "He was a rescue. Dad's teaching me how to ride him!"

"Mom's also teaching you," Katy said with pretended annoyance.

Teddie hugged her. "Sure you are. But Dad's at home when you're teaching. Well, when he's not breaking horses for Mr. Denton, anyway."

"It must be nice," Butch said to Parker, indicating Katy. "Your very own daughter. I'm so jealous!"

"You need a couple of your own," Parker told him with a grin at Esther's high color.

"We just got engaged, give us time." Butch laughed out loud.

"We have to get going," Parker said. "It's *Warriors and Warlocks* tonight, and this is a special one. The bad guy's going to get his. At least, the previews almost promised that he was."

"Don't you believe it," Butch drawled. "I have it on good authority that J. L.'s wife, Cassie, likes that bad guy a lot, and she's resisting any attempt to kill him off."

"Spoilsport," Parker teased.

Butch grinned. "I like him, too."

Parker glanced at Esther. "Do you watch the show, too?"

She shook her head. "My mother didn't even own a television," she said, and her face went taut again.

"She just lost her mother," Butch said, pulling her closer. "It's fresh."

"I'm truly sorry," Katy said gently. "I've lost both my parents. I know how it hurts."

"Thanks," Esther said in her soft voice, and her blue eyes were warm as they met Katy's.

"It gets easier," she added.

"It does," Parker agreed. "Okay, female troops, let's head out."

Katy made a face, but Teddie laughed.

"It's sort of like being in the military." Katy laughed.

"Oh, I can certainly identify with that," Butch said, and smiled as he waved them goodbye.

"Your friends are nice," Esther said as they walked down the aisle that contained women's clothing.

"They are," he agreed. "Parker's a special case. He saved my life overseas. Damned interesting guy, too," he added. "He has a degree in theoretical physics."

"What?" she exclaimed, her eyes wide.

"No kidding. He goes off to the nation's capital from time to time to work with one of the letter agencies, deciphering code. He's got a mind like a steel trap."

"He's Native American, isn't he?" she asked.

"Crow," he replied. "He has cousins on the reservation up in Montana."

"He seems to really love the little girl."

"He does. I expect he and Katy will have some of their own. Parker's been on his own for a long time. A family is just what he needed." He hesitated. "It's what I need as well. Being alone is for the birds."

She grinned.

He grinned back. "Do you like kids?"

"I love them," she replied. "I haven't been around them much. We had a housekeeper who had two little granddaughters who would come to see her in the summer. She had to bring them to work a couple of times. Mama was mad about it, but I loved it. Children are special, Agnes was the best grandmother." She sighed. "I really missed her after Darrin made Mama fire her. See, Darrin didn't like her." She made a face. "Children make the world a magical place," she said with dreamy eyes.

"I've always thought so myself. Parker brought Katy and Teddie over to see Two-Toes when I first brought him home. He loved Teddie at once."

"She seems like a sweet child."

"Her dad was in the military, a doctor. He died while he was completing a tour of duty in Iraq." His face closed up.

"That's where you were, isn't it?" she asked.

He drew in a breath. "There sure are a lot of pretty sweaters over here," he said instead of answering her.

She didn't push. She knew he'd had a hard time in the military. "Yes, these are lovely," she agreed, not mentioning that it was the first time in her life that she'd been in a store that didn't sell couture garments. She was actually enjoying herself.

Finally, she ended up with two pairs of slacks and four

colorful pullover sweaters, two gowns, a sweatpants set and some serviceable underwear. It amused her that Butch went to look over the electronics when she went into the lingerie section of the store. He was a conundrum, she thought. But she liked him very much.

Her first day on the job was grueling. She wasn't used to standing for long periods of time, and she was amazed at how hard it was. At the same time, she was fascinated with the fact of earning a living for herself. She'd never had to worry about money. In fact, she'd always been able to buy anything she liked. This was different. It was exciting. Everything about it was new, and her enthusiasm was visible.

The owner of the café, Mrs. Dodd, chuckled when Esther was taught how to take toast out of the toaster and butter one side, then put both pieces of bread together so that the heat melted the butter on the slices.

"Imagine, getting excited about toast!" she chuckled.

Esther just laughed. "It's all new and exciting," she said. "I've never had to work a day in my life."

The owner's eyebrows arched.

Esther flushed. "I lost my mother . . . recently," she said gently, not going into details. "She took care of me. Now I'm learning to take care of myself."

"And doing nicely," the older woman said, smiling kindly. "The standing will get easier. But you need tennis shoes to work in, honey, not hard-soled ones," she added gently, indicating the high heels Esther was wearing with her slacks. "Standing is hard enough in comfortable shoes."

"I'll get Butch to take me back to Walmart after work and I'll buy a pair," Esther assured her. "Thanks for the advice, too."

"So few people ever take any. You're a breath of spring," came the reply. "Okay, ready to move on to taking orders?"

"I wish my memory was better." Esther groaned.

"That's why we have pads and pencils." The other woman chuckled. "You can practice on me before the lunch rush. Ready . . . ?"

By the end of the first month, Esther was dashing back and forth between the tables and the kitchen with a light step in her new tennis shoes and making a small fortune in tips. She put her long hair in a ponytail at work. Her waitress uniform fit in all the right places, which was causing her some problems. She was pretty, and men noticed.

She'd never had to work at discouraging men, because her mother had been around to absorb any interest she was likely to get. But one of the deputy sheriffs, and a couple of cowboys, were growing more insistent about wanting to take her out, either to dinner or a movie. And Esther didn't want to go. She had more reason than many women to distrust men, especially after Darrin. Besides, she wasn't interested in other men. Just in Butch, who became more important to her by the day. She was careful to remind other men that she was engaged. She only wished she had a ring, to prove it. Butch hadn't mentioned the ring at all.

She dumped her tips out on the kitchen table before they started supper. They shared cooking, which Butch was teaching her. She'd already produced several very edible meals under his tutelage. She and Butch sat down to roll her loose change into coin envelopes. This was one of their nightly rituals. It was something they could do together, and Esther loved the companionship. They had their respective jobs, and Butch was out of the house a lot. Sometimes, he had to go out of town overnight, but he left her with Two-Toes and she felt safe. Besides, there was that 28-gauge shotgun he'd loaded for her. It was locked in the gun safe, but she knew where the key was. If she could bring herself to shoot somebody. Hopefully, Two-Toes would be a deterrent if she was ever really threatened.

There had been no news of Darrin, although Esther had secretly looked online, on Butch's laptop, and found an account of her mother's death. It was brief, just mentioning that it was an accident, citing her monied background, and mentioning that there had been only a memorial service. Nothing about homicide. So Darrin was still out, obviously, and probably looking for Esther. It made her nervous, but she was careful to conceal her worries from Butch.

"Quite a haul," he teased as they separated the various denominations of coins.

She laughed. "Yes, it is. We should buy you a new coat."

His high cheekbones flushed. "You need a raincoat," he protested. "I can't wear nice coats doing the work I do. It gets messy when you work with animals."

She smiled at him, liking the way his eyes crinkled at the corners when he smiled back. "I have a raincoat," she protested.

"One you bought at that thrift shop," he muttered.

"Hey, don't knock thrift shops," she returned. "Most of the stuff they have is barely worn at all. It's got a hood and it's warm." She searched his dark eyes. "Butch, I don't need fancy things anymore. I like it here, just being a normal woman."

"Truly?" he asked. "I haven't said much about it, but that fur jacket you wear is real, and the clothes you were wearing that first night didn't come off a rack." He didn't add that he'd been suspicious of her. She could have been a thief, for all he knew. In fact, that was still a possibility. She didn't act like a rich woman might. And, too, there was that gaudy fake diamond ring she wore. Maybe she thought it would give her the appearance of wealth, even more than her clothes.

"No, they didn't," she confessed. She thought about what she wanted to tell him. He wasn't wealthy. She didn't want him to be intimidated by the life she'd left. "I had a small savings account that my father left me," she prevaricated. "It was my birthday, so I splurged."

"Your mother had money, though." He was probing. Curious.

She sighed. "Well, not really," she lied. "She had a nice little nest egg that my father left, some stocks and bonds and certificates of deposit. Too, there was the house in Aspen." She didn't mention the others her mother owned. "It was free and clear. Plus she owned a good amount of land that she inherited. But it was all tied up, you know, and it wasn't easy to get to any of it. Darrin wanted it all. He'd have sold it to buy drugs. I'm sure he still does want it, but I have her will. He can't get to it unless he finds me." She shivered delicately. "I'd honestly rather be locked up than have to face him." Her eyes were troubled. "He's very dangerous. In fact, he served time for assault. But Mama didn't find that out until it was too late to do her any good."

"We should get a daily paper, one from Aspen, just to see if there's any news about her death," he added.

She almost panicked. She didn't want him to know how wealthy her mother had been, what her estate was worth. It would change things, between her and Butch. He was a proud man. He wouldn't even let her buy him a cup of coffee. It would be a disaster if he learned anything about her real background.

She'd tell him someday, she thought, but not right away. She was having fun, learning about him, being with him, having a real relationship with another human being. Her mother had been distant, barely affectionate. There hadn't been anyone else in her young life who was affectionate, except her father, and Agnes, who had truly been a surrogate mother. But that was long ago. She'd become standoffish like her mother, she'd become used to never touching or being touched. Well, except for unwanted touches from various men her mother brought home.

"I'm sorry," he said after a minute. "I know you're missing your mother."

"It's okay," she said. "It's getting easier, as time goes by. But I don't know what I'd have done if you hadn't taken me in, Butch," she added with a warm, affectionate smile.

He shrugged. "I didn't mind. It gets lonely here. Not so much, now," he added, and he returned the smile. "I have somebody to share the chores," he teased.

She laughed. "True."

"You weren't really looking for a cousin, were you, that night?" he asked abruptly.

She shook her head. "I was afraid to go into town. I looked on a map. Benton is really small. I didn't want to just show up there, a stranger that people might ask questions about. I was traumatized to boot." She sighed. "I saw the cabin from the road and it looked, well, welcoming. I guess that sounds odd. But I knew it would be safe here." She met his dark eyes, curious about the look in them. "I don't know how."

"I'm just glad you showed up," he said quietly. "I don't

mix well with people, and I had a rough experience with my ex-fiancée. I guess I'd turned into a hermit."

"A very nice hermit," she said softly. "You're easy to get along with."

"So are you, honey," he replied. "You make a house a home, however trite that sounds."

She smiled from ear to ear. "What a nice thing to say!"

He drew in a long breath, watching her pretty hands working on the coins. He picked up some and started separating them. "They have a machine that does this. I need to get you one."

"It wouldn't be nearly as much fun," she replied. "This is something we do together." She flushed. "I mean . . ."

His big, lean hand slid over hers. "I like doing this with you, too. There's no need to feel embarrassed."

She laughed self-consciously. "Thanks. I don't think I've learned discretion yet. I just blurt things out."

"That's not bad at all. I speak my mind, too."

"I guess people at least know where they stand with us, don't they?"

"What did you do, when you lived at home?" he asked.

She hesitated while she tried to think up something. "Well, not much, really. Mama didn't want me to get a job, and I'd already gone away to school for several years."

"A boarding school?" he asked, thinking of someplace with uniforms and firm rules. "I'll bet you were picked on a lot."

"Yes, I was," she exclaimed. "How did you know?"

"Because you're beautiful and shy, a combination that provokes people who aren't," he said. His face hardened. "Hell would freeze over before I'd send a child of mine away to any sort of boarding school."

"That's how I feel," she replied. "It was miserable.

Mama sent me presents for Christmas and my birthday, but she never came to see me." Her voice was bitter. "It was worse when I came back home, at eighteen." Her face tautened. "It was a constant parade of men, and sometimes she didn't bother to close the bedroom door . . ." Her face flamed and her expression was horrified as she met his eyes.

"You can tell me anything," he said in a gentle tone. "I don't gossip, and you won't shock me. Okay?"

She bit her lip and went on sorting change. "I've never, well, done stuff like that. She screamed a lot . . ."

"Women do, when they're enjoying a man," he said very softly. "It's natural. It doesn't mean they're being hurt."

"Oh." She took a deep breath. "I tried to ask her, but she changed the subject. I never had any close friends. I was too ashamed of my home life to take anybody home with me. Mama would walk around in see-through negligees when she had men living with us."

He was getting a sad, painful look at her life. No wonder she was so naïve. He liked it. He had little experience with innocent women. She was a new experience.

He smiled.

She looked at him, her blue eyes wide and curious.

"I like it, that you don't know much about men," he explained. He grimaced. "I guess that sounds Neanderthal."

"Oh, no," she said at once, and her cheeks flushed. "It sounds, well, protective."

He cocked his head. "That's how I feel when I'm with you. Protective." He scowled. "You need some assertiveness training. I'll teach you."

"You will?" She smiled at him. "What's assertiveness training?"

"Telling people to go to hell when they start annoying

you," he replied tongue in cheek. "I was a natural, but you'll need some educating."

She burst out laughing. "I do like you," she said huskily. "You're so much fun."

Something no other woman had ever said about him. He felt ten feet tall. When he was with her, he forgot about his injuries and limitations. She made him . . . whole.

"So you never had a job?" he persisted.

"Not really. Mostly I stayed in my room and listened to music. Or I painted." She sighed. "I had a sketch pad and canvases and acrylic paint. I really loved doing still life portraits of flowers." She frowned. "I suppose Darrin trashed them all."

"You never know." He was smiling. There was an art supply store in town. He'd have to take her over there one day and get her some paints. She had spare time when she wasn't working. It would give her something to do when he was out of the house.

"Cook taught me how to make that chocolate pie you like so much!" she said abruptly. "If we can afford the ingredients, I'll make one for the weekend!"

He laughed. "She did, huh? I think we can afford to splurge a little on food." He searched her eyes. "You are one of a kind," he said softly.

"So are you, Butch," she replied, flushing a little.

He just looked at her, aware of feelings that were slowly getting the better of him. He would have liked nothing better than to take her to the nearest minister and marry her out of hand. But it was early days yet. He had to take his time. And meanwhile, the man who'd killed her mother needed to be found out and brought to justice. He was working on that, without telling Esther.

He felt it was necessary, but he wasn't comfortable with

the idea. Once she was over her grief and out of danger, she'd probably go back to Aspen, where she'd inherit the house her mother owned and those stocks and bonds. Once she had her life back, this time with him might be just a forgotten episode in it. He'd be relegated to a memory that she might take out from time to time. She liked him, but it was unrealistic to think that a woman so pretty and sophisticated would want to settle down in the wilds of Colorado with a crippled man who had nothing except his paycheck to offer.

"Goodness, you look morose!" she exclaimed, studying him. "Was it something I said?"

"Not at all," he said smoothly. "I've got a visiting dignitary to take around tomorrow. I was thinking about where to take him." It was the truth, but he stretched it a little.

She hesitated. "You're sure you don't mind letting me stay here with you? I mean, I could probably afford an apartment . . ."

"Do you want to go?" he asked abruptly.

"No!" She took a deep breath, oblivious to the joy that washed over his features before he contained it. "I mean, it's nice here, with you and Two-Toes. But I'm a strain on your budget."

"Some strain," he muttered. "You keep the house as neat as a pin, you do half the cooking, you cheer me up when life sits on me too hard. I'd . . . miss you, if you left."

She brightened. "Okay, then."

He felt his own heart lift.

"Something I've been meaning to ask," she began slowly. She flushed. "Maybe I shouldn't, though."

"Spill it, chicken."

"Well, are we really engaged?" she asked without lifting her eyes.

His eyebrows arched. "Why the question?"

She shifted restlessly. "There are these guys who eat at the restaurant every day," she said worriedly. "They're nice, I mean. But they keep asking me to go places with them and I don't want to. It's, well, it's bothering me."

"Why don't you want to go out with them?" he wondered aloud.

She drew in a breath. "I just don't. I'm nervous around most men. It's hard to trust when you've been through what I have, with Mama's lovers."

His heart jumped. "You're not nervous with me."

"No, I'm not." She smiled at him warmly. "I love being with you."

The flush on his cheekbones grew more ruddy.

"Gosh, I'm sorry," she bit off, wincing. "I just open my mouth and words fall out. I shouldn't have said . . ."

"I love being with you, too," he said curtly.

Her expression lightened. "Really?" she asked.

He laughed. "Really."

She sighed. "Okay, then."

"So you don't like being bothered by other men. I could offer a suggestion."

"A suit of armor?" she asked.

He pursed his chiseled lips. "An engagement ring?"

Her lips fell apart. "A ring! You mean it? Honest?"

It wasn't the reception he'd expected. She was excited. Happy. Enthusiastic. He felt warm all over. "Honest."

She grinned. "That would be lovely." She hesitated, and her happy expression turned morose. "Oh. You mean, like a prop, so they'd leave me alone?"

He smoothed his big hand over her small one. "I mean, like a real engagement ring that would lead to a real marriage. Well, someday," he amended, so she wouldn't feel threatened or obliged to him. It would certainly keep gossip down. He didn't want her reputation to suffer, here in this conservative small community.

She stared at him, her eyes bright with feeling. "Wow."

He chuckled.

She grinned. "But you don't know me very well," she began.

"Same here. We could get to know each other. For a few weeks, I mean." He grimaced. "I'm not putting it well."

She sighed. "I would love to be engaged to you, Butch."

"You . . . you would?" he stammered.

"Oh, yes. You've been kinder to me than anybody in my whole life, except my dad and Agnes. I could . . . take care of you, you know? I mean if you got sick or hurt, I'd be there."

A confusion of emotions turned him inside out. She wanted to take care of him. Damn! He'd never had anybody of his own. Not really. And this beautiful little blonde looked at him and didn't see a haunted man with a missing arm. She saw someone she cared for.

"I'd do the same for you," he replied.

"You already have," she teased. "You rescued me from freezing to death in the snow."

"I'd forgotten."

"I didn't. I never will."

He drew in a long breath. "What happens when you end up with your mother's house and those stocks? You've still got the will, and her lover won't be able to get away with it forever. What then? When you have your old life back?"

"I don't want my old life back," she said simply.

He was still hesitant. His eyebrows drew together. "Esther, how old are you?"

"Twenty-three."

His face hardened. He averted his eyes.

"What's wrong?" she wanted to know.

"Honey, I'm thirty-six . . ."

"Oh, yes, you're definitely over the hill, I can tell."

His eyes widened as he looked at her. She was grinning. He burst out laughing.

"Thirteen years isn't so much," she said gently. "I think you're gorgeous."

He cleared his throat, embarrassed. "Well!"

"So, are you going to buy me a ring?" she asked. "Something inexpensive." Her eyes twinkled. "I like turquoise."

"It should be a diamond."

"I don't like diamonds," she returned, and didn't mention that she was wearing a real seven-carat one on her hand, and that she had a safety deposit box back in LA full of expensive jewelry. "I'd rather have something elemental, something natural. Something down-to-earth."

"Okay, then. Suppose we go into town tomorrow while you're on your lunch break and look in the jewelry store?"

She smiled from ear to ear. "That would be great!"

And it was. They avoided the diamond counter because she insisted, and they went to the gemstone section. But she fell in love with a blue topaz ring instead of the turquoise she'd originally wanted.

"Oh, that one," she said, indicating it. "It's Caribbean blue. I love it!"

"Could we see that one?" Butch asked Mr. Granger, who'd owned the jewelry store for thirty years.

The older man chuckled. “Yes, you may. Is it for a birthday?”

“No,” Esther said softly. “It’s going to be an engagement ring. I don’t really like diamonds,” she added.

Mr. Granger glanced at the huge seven-carat diamond on her right hand and saw at once that it was a real stone, with a clarity and brilliance that he’d rarely ever seen. But he didn’t remark on it. He pulled out the tray of rings and let Esther try on the blue topaz one.

“It fits!” she exclaimed, her eyes on Butch’s amused face.

“It looks good on that pretty little hand,” he replied with a warm smile.

She laughed. “I love it. Can I have it?” she asked, looking up at him with soft, shimmering blue eyes.

She could have had the store if she’d asked for it when she looked at him like that. He’d rob a bank, he thought amusedly. “Sure you can,” he said.

He gave Mr. Granger his credit card and waited while the owner ran it. He signed the ticket, they thanked the older man and walked out of the store.

“We are now officially engaged,” Butch told her.

“Not yet,” she said. She pulled off the ring, there on the sidewalk, and handed it to him.

“We’re not engaged?” he asked, and felt his heart sink.

“We’re not, until you put it on for me,” she said softly, searching his eyes. “Then it’s official.” She held up her left hand.

Heart hammering at his ribs, he slid the ring onto her finger. It was poignant, he thought. A moment that would live in his heart forever, no matter how old he got, no matter what happened down the road.

"Thanks," she said in a soft whisper.

His fingers brushed her flushed cheek. He didn't smile. The dark eyes piercing hers were full of some deep emotion.

She reached up and touched her fingers to his chin. "I'll try not to embarrass you," she said quietly. "I'll never do anything to make you ashamed, and I'll take care of you if you need me to."

His lips compressed hard. He averted his eyes, because the emotions she was kindling in him were new and vaguely frightening.

Now she was embarrassed. She'd said too much. "Oh, look, isn't that Parker?" she asked abruptly, indicating a truck that stopped just a few parking spots down from theirs.

He got himself together, with an effort. He felt ashamed of himself for the way he'd reacted, but it was getting harder and harder not to reach for her and kiss her half to death. He had to fight his impulses in a way he'd never had to before. She was very young, and very green, and he didn't want to scare her off. If he made a dead set at her, he might ruin everything. Time enough to lead up to that. He had to go slow. Slow! The engagement, he reminded himself, was just the first step. It would take time.

"Yes," he said after a minute, following her gaze. "I think it is."

"Oh, gosh, I've got to get back to work," she exclaimed, looking at the cheap watch she'd bought along with her new clothes. "I'll see you about six, yes?"

He nodded. "I'll pick you up at the restaurant. Have a good day."

"You, too." She forced a smile that she didn't feel and went across the street and back to work. She couldn't understand why Butch had suddenly become so distant. Was he regretting the engagement? Had she pushed him into something he really didn't want? Tonight, she told herself, they'd sit down and she'd find out. She was so fond of him. He'd been kind to her. She didn't want to make him unhappy.

Chapter Four

Esther was doing well at her job. She enjoyed the local patrons, whom she was getting to know, and the infrequent out-of-town people who showed up at the restaurant. There were occasionally people from New York who came to Benton to see Mrs. Denton about the television show she wrote for. In fact, she learned that Cassie Denton had worked as a waitress at the Gray Dove before she married J. L.

Not that Esther asked the New York people questions, but she listened raptly when they talked about changes that would show up in the series later on.

"It's so exciting!" she told Butch that night. "They say the bad guy is going to turn over a new leaf!"

He knew who the bad guy was. He had a wide-screen television, and he and Esther and Two-Toes never missed an episode of *Warriors and Warlocks*. "I like him, even if he is the bad guy," he confessed while they were sipping second cups of coffee in the living room after a nice supper.

"So do I. It's a great series. Well, it would be, if I could stop blushing," she added, because there was bad language and nudity, a lot of nudity, in it.

"Think of it as free sex education," he teased.

She averted her eyes. "It's not, really, you know. Most of the women get used. The ones who don't aren't interested in having a home and a family, they just sort of sleep around." Her blue eyes met his. "Is that really what it's like, in modern society? I never mixed in it. I had a girlfriend once, my last year in boarding school. She'd slept with a lot of men and had an abortion. She thought having children was stupid. It would get in the way of her happiness." She sighed wistfully. "I love children. I could never think of them as a liability. And if I got pregnant, I just couldn't . . ." She stopped, shocked at what she was saying to him.

He just smiled. "I told you. I'm unshockable."

"Oh." She smiled shyly. "Okay."

"All too often, an accident causes real issues between a man and a woman, especially if he wants a child and she doesn't. It would be hard to shame a woman into giving up eighteen years of her life to raise a child she didn't even want," he added, but his eyes were suddenly sad.

She just looked at him. She knew there was something he wasn't telling her. She could feel it.

He glanced at her and sighed. "My ex-fiancée and I had a few spontaneous episodes," he said delicately. "She got pregnant."

"She didn't want it?" she asked delicately.

"No. She went to a clinic the minute she knew and told me afterwards." His face was harder than stone.

She got up out of her chair and crawled into his lap, laying her blond head on his chest with one soft arm wrapped around him.

He was stiff at first, it was so unexpected. Then he realized that she was comforting him. It shocked him, how much he liked it. His good arm curled around her shoulders, lightly, so that he didn't make her uncomfortable.

"I'm so sorry," she said. She knew that he was a man who'd love a child.

His chest rose and fell against her. His heartbeat was oddly fast and strong. "I couldn't have forced her to have it," he said. "And under the circumstances, I suppose it was the right thing to do." He idly smoothed her long blond hair in its ponytail. "I didn't even know I wanted a child until she told me that. I grieved for it. She said it wasn't the first time she had it done, and it was like having an abscessed tooth pulled."

She made a gruff sound in her throat.

He didn't have to be told that she'd never have made that choice if it had been his child in her body. She'd have fought to keep it, even fought him to keep it. He was surprised at how well he knew her already. It had only been a few weeks since she'd shown up at his door, and it felt as if he'd known her forever.

They were both so lost in thought that they didn't hear the truck drive up. They didn't hear the perfunctory knock at the door, which suddenly opened to admit Parker. He stood in the doorway, grinning at the picture they made—the delicate little blond, still in her waitress's uniform, and the taciturn wildlife officer, curled up together in a big easy chair.

"Oh!" Esther exclaimed, embarrassed, and started to get up.

"Stay put," Butch told her, his arm tightening as he chuckled. "Parker's family. And we're engaged," he reminded her.

She was still. She smiled shyly at Parker. "So we are," she said, and tried to sound sophisticated. Which she wasn't, despite her wealthy upbringing.

"What's up?" Butch asked the other man.

"Are you guys doing anything special on Sunday?" Parker asked.

Butch and Esther looked at each other. "Nothing much," Butch said.

"I don't work Sundays," Esther added.

"Why?" Butch wanted to know.

"Teddie wants to go ice skating. There's a rink nearby and it's open all year. You guys want to come along?"

Butch made a face. "Not sure I can get on skates." He looked at Esther, who grimaced.

"I never learned how," she confessed. "I'd fall and break something and what would my boss say?" she asked plaintively.

Parker just chuckled. "Okay. When we find something a little less reckless, we'll invite you again. Rodeo maybe, later in the year."

"I love rodeo!" Esther exclaimed.

"Me, too," Butch seconded.

They were both beaming.

Parker just shook his head. "Hey, there, Two-Toes," he said, greeting the wolf, who'd been out in the kitchen drinking water. He knelt down and ruffled the animal's fur affectionately.

"He's so sweet," Esther remarked.

"He took to her right off," Butch added with a warm smile at the pretty woman in his lap. "I always knew he was a great judge of character," he added with a chuckle.

"I'll say. He loves my girls, too," Parker said, referring

to his wife and stepdaughter. He stood up. "Well, I'll be off."

"Thanks for the invitation," Esther said. "I'm sorry I'm such a stick-in-the-mud."

"Not at all." Parker returned at once. "Variety really is the spice of life. How boring if we all liked the same things all the time!"

"True," Butch said. "See you."

"Night, Sarge. Esther." He went out, closing the door behind him.

Butch gave Esther a long, penetrating stare. "You lied."

She went red as a beet. "You don't know," she retorted.

He laughed and hugged her close. "Yes, I do. You can skate like a fairy, can't you? I'll bet you float on the ice."

"I took lessons from the time I was three," she confessed. "Mama wanted me to be a contender, but I wasn't crazy about being on the ice all the time. I quit when I was in my mid-teens. I don't think she ever forgave me." She pulled back. "See, that was what she wanted to be, a star on the ice in women's single competition. She didn't have the gift, but I did, and she pushed and kept pushing. Dad didn't like the way she nagged me, but he died and I was left with her." She sighed. "It was the only time she really cared about me, I think, when she was trying to use me to fulfill her own dreams."

He smoothed over her back. "My dad was the same," he confessed. "He wanted me to be a pro football player." He made a face. "I hated football. I was a soccer freak. I still am. I never miss a game."

"I like soccer, too," she said.

"Who's your team?" he asked.

She grinned. "Real Madrid."

His eyebrows arched. "Not the US team?"

She flushed. "Well, I used to know a guy who played for Madrid. He was a friend of my dad's."

His eyebrows arched.

"He was much older than me," she said. "I liked him because Dad did. He was married and had two kids, anyway," she added with a pert smile.

He laughed. "I guess you don't like older men." He sighed.

"I like you," she replied. "But you're only older in your mind," she said solemnly. "You don't look as old as you feel. I'm muddling that . . ."

He drew in a breath and coaxed her back down against his chest. "War makes men old," he said. "I'm still older than you, though, by a good bit."

She smiled against his shirt. He smelled of soap and cologne, good smells. "Why do you think that matters?"

He stiffened for a minute. "Well . . . people talk, you know."

"Butch," she murmured, "like you care what people say."

"I don't. But it might get back to you."

"Oh, I don't care what people say, either. Friends won't mind, and nobody else matters."

He chuckled. "You're a breath of spring."

"Awww. You're just saying that because I finally can make a biscuit that wouldn't kill a man if it fell on him."

He grinned. "You're a natural born cook. I'm amazed that you don't strike envy in the heart of the cook at the Gray Dove."

"She likes me."

"Everybody likes you," he replied. "So do I. A lot."

She sighed. "I like you, too."

They sat like that for several minutes, during which Butch became a little uncomfortable. It had been a few years since his erstwhile fiancée had thrown him over, and Esther was beautiful. He didn't want to make her feel unwelcome, but he did want to get up before she noticed anything she shouldn't about the way his body was reacting to her.

"Men's room," he murmured. "Sorry."

She laughed and got up. "No problem. We all function, at some time or the other," she said with a pert glance.

He just stared at her and sighed and shook his head. "You gorgeous blonde. You'd shame a flower," he mused prosaically.

Both eyebrows went up. "What have you been drinking?" she asked sharply.

He threw up his hands and turned toward the bathroom. "That's what you get for trying to share poetic thoughts with peasants," he called over his shoulder.

"I am not a peasant, and just for that, I'll burn the coffee!"

He laughed as he closed the door behind him.

Esther had worried that Darrin might have tracked her to Benton. But as the days passed without any contact, she began to relax. Well, she began to relax a little. The memory of her mother's death still haunted her. It wasn't right, to let Darrin get away with it, but she'd burned her bridges. She hadn't said anything about the murder. Wouldn't that make her an accessory after the fact? Because she had knowledge of a crime after it was committed, and she didn't report it to the authorities?

It was one more thing to worry her. She'd have talked about it to Butch, but she was still hiding her real background from him. He thought she came from just well-to-do parents; but her mother had been a multimillionaire, and all that wealth would one day come to Esther, whether she wanted it to or not. She couldn't hide for the rest of her life.

She supposed that she needed to get a good attorney and start trying to make up for having been so cowardly. She'd run away, but in all honesty, it hadn't been much of a choice. If she'd stayed, Darrin might have killed her as well, to get rid of the only eyewitness to his crime.

Butch had a computer, and she'd asked to use it to check her email. Instead, she'd pulled up a search engine and looked for any further indication of her mother's death. There had been a big updated notice about it in the Aspen paper, only a fraction of which was available online without paying a fee to subscribe to the newspaper. It said that a well-known socialite had been found dead in her home by her boyfriend. It was thought that her daughter, now missing, might have pushed her to her death. There had been a violent argument, Darrin had told authorities, so the police were asking for anybody with information of the whereabouts of Esther Marist to come forward.

Esther's hands had jumped off the computer keys as if they'd been burned. Now she didn't dare go back! She had no money and no way to get any, other than her salary and tips at the restaurant. She couldn't even afford an attorney. What if they believed Darrin and she went to prison? It had happened to innocent people before this. Oh, why had she run? she wailed mentally. Why hadn't she gone straight to the police and told them exactly what had happened! She'd only complicated her life by running away. Now she was as much a fugitive as Darrin would be if she'd told on him. And had he managed to get access to her mother's fortune by now? If he had, he could afford the best attorneys in the world to represent him. And the best private detectives to find Esther.

She worried for days about what she'd read. She hadn't known how to erase her search history on Butch's computer, but she noticed that he almost never used it except to send emails back and forth and log on to the web page he kept to discuss wildlife rehabilitation. Hopefully he wouldn't bother to check what Esther had done. And she had sent an email to an old friend whose email had been changed, so that it would come back as not forwarded. So she wasn't totally lying, anyway.

Two weeks went by, during which Esther went to work, came home, counted her tips, made supper with Butch, and generally worried herself sick.

She had a little money now, so she'd had Butch take her back to the local Walmart to get a few more items of clothing. It wasn't what she'd been used to, but there was great satisfaction in earning her living, paying for her own clothes. No more pampered little rich girl getting anything she asked for. Terry had been generous. Of course, Terry had also substituted money for love and hugs and understanding. It had been the housekeeper, Agnes, who had kissed away the little girl's tears and bandaged the cuts and made Christmas special for her. It had never been Terry, who was constantly on the road with some new boyfriend to exotic and luxurious places.

If she ever had a child, Esther told herself, the baby would never be left with a housekeeper, not even for a day. Her child would go where she went, and she'd love the little one so much! She thought about children a lot. She and

Butch spent time with Parker and his wife, Katy, and Katy's daughter, Teddie. Esther loved Teddie. The little girl was sweet and smart and loved horses. So did Esther. When they'd lived in California, when her father was still alive, her father had owned a ranch and they rode horses together. Her mother had no use for animals of any sort. Sometimes, even through the sadness of loss, Esther thought about her mother's reaction to her daughter living with a wildlife specialist and rehabilitator, who had a wolf in the house. It amused her no end.

"What are you cackling about?" Butch teased, joining her in front of the television with a refilled cup of fresh-brewed coffee. It was well after supper and they were watching an episode of *Warriors and Warlocks*.

"I was thinking about my mother," she said, smiling as he sat down beside her. "She wouldn't let me have pets. She thought all animals were filthy. I was imagining her reaction to us living with a wolf in the house." She chuckled. "It was funny."

He leaned forward, the cup held in his one hand. "It's getting easier for you to talk about her, isn't it?" he asked.

She nodded. "Still stings a little," she confessed, smiling at him. "But I can remember some of the fun times now."

"Was she a good mother?"

She rolled her eyes. "She was in love with love. There was a new boyfriend every other month and she loved to travel. She was mostly gone after Daddy died. I lived with our housekeeper. I never saw much of Mama until I was in my last year of high school. Even then, she made sure I was out of the way when she brought people home." She laughed softly. "It bothered her to have a grown daughter. She didn't want her friends to see me and conjecture about her age."

He sighed. "Pity."

"Yes. You can't change how old you are. You can only disguise it."

"I could always color my hair . . . ?"

She laughed and punched him playfully, almost upending his coffee mug. "Oh, you! Anyway, you're in your prime of life right now. Why would you want to be younger?" She leaned toward him. "I don't like men my own age," she said in a conspiratorial tone. "So if you start looking younger, I'll have to move out!"

He chuckled. "Never. I'd send out search parties and bribe you to come home."

"Bribe me with what?" she asked, and arched her eyebrows several times.

"Chocolate," he said with twinkling dark eyes. "It's your greatest weakness."

She drew in a long breath. "I guess it is. I never met anything chocolate that I didn't like."

He sipped coffee and put the mug down. "We need to talk about what happened to your mother," he said abruptly.

She bit her lower lip. She hadn't told him about Darrin's accusations. She probably should . . .

"There was a investigator in town this morning, at the police department. I'd stopped in to check with them about Darrin."

Her face went white. She wasn't even breathing.

He saw the terror in her eyes. "He was looking for you. Honey, I don't know how to tell you this. They think you pushed your mother down the staircase."

Tears stung her eyes. She had to react as if it were a surprise; she didn't want Butch to know that she'd read that in the Aspen newspaper. She hadn't even planned to tell him about it, because she didn't want to worry him.

"Oh, don't do that," he said tenderly, and pulled her close. He wrapped her up against him, kissing her soft blond hair. "Don't! I won't let them hurt you!"

She clung to him, shivering a little. "Darrin's good at telling lies, when he's sober," she said. "I thought he'd say it was an accident," she added miserably.

"Apparently, the coroner lodged some doubts about her injuries not aligning exactly with an accidental fall."

"I'll bet that put a stick in Darrin's spokes," she muttered.

"I don't doubt it. But it puts you in a dangerous position," he added. "I know you're not capable of murder, certainly not of killing your own mother. But he could claim to have seen you push her down the stairs."

She nodded. "I worried about that." She closed her eyes. "I can't even afford a lawyer. And if Darrin has access to Mama's bank account, he can afford the best. Even if he can't, he can sell stuff she had, for money to help keep him out of prison. It's not right."

His lean hand smoothed up and down her spine. "We'll come up with something."

"Is the investigator still in town?"

"I don't know."

"I guess Darrin could afford to hire him, too."

"He wasn't hired by your mother's boyfriend. He was an investigator with the district attorney in Aspen."

"Oh, dear," she moaned.

"Honey, you've got your mother's will in your pocketbook," he pointed out. "That being the case, do you think Darrin's anxious to find you?"

She grimaced and drew back. "That would give me a motive for murder."

"Yes, but it would be bad for him, wouldn't it, because

it would prove that you inherited your mother's estate. He'd be left with nothing."

"Oh." That hadn't occurred to her. She stared at Butch. "It would put you in danger, if that investigator finds me." She sat up. "I need to find a place to go . . . !"

"No, you don't," he said shortly. "I lived through hell in the Middle East. I'm not afraid of some two-a-penny bad guy who has to get drunk to beat up a woman to make himself feel big!"

Her expression softened as she looked at him. She smiled gently. "Do you know, your ex-fiancée was a total idiot?" she mused.

He chuckled. "What brought that on?"

"You're very protective of people you like," she said simply. "I'm glad I'm one of them."

He smiled at her. "I can't lose you," he said. "I can't make a biscuit," he added, tongue in cheek.

"You beast!" she accused.

He leaned forward and kissed her pert nose. "I thought I might talk to that investigator, if I can find him."

She felt her whole body shake with nerves. "I don't know, Butch."

"You can't live your life in fear," he pointed out. "At some point, you have to stand up to him. I'll be right there with you."

"You could be right there in jail alongside me, too," she said abruptly. "Accessory after the fact? I saw a man commit a murder and I didn't report it."

His chiseled lips fell apart. He hadn't considered that.

"Now do you see why I didn't go after Darrin to begin with? If I'd had the sense God gave a billy goat, I'd have gone to the police that same night and they'd have protected me. But I was afraid that Darrin had a contact in the

Department. Instead I made myself a fugitive, and the only person who's going to benefit by that is Darrin. It was a colossal mistake." She sighed. "I was so scared of him, so traumatized by what I'd seen." Her hands clenched on her jeans. She looked up at Butch. "I don't know what to do. I don't want to go to jail. I don't want you to go to jail, for protecting me."

He caught her hand in his and held it tight. "We're a matched set. I'm not turning my back on you."

"I know," she said, and a glimmer of humor escaped her. "You can't make a biscuit."

"Damned straight," he replied. But his dark eyes were saying a lot more than that. "Now, suppose we watch the series and forget about Darrin and the investigator and the rest of the world for a few minutes?"

She snuggled up closer to him with a contented sound. "Okay."

He slid his arm around her and rested his cheek on her hair as the commercials ended and the program came back on.

Esther went back to work the next morning, still perturbed about the changes in her life. One of her first customers was a casually dressed man in slacks and a sports shirt with a leather jacket over it. He sat down at a table where he could put his back to the wall and started looking around.

She went with her pad and pen, her uniform spotless, and smiled at him as she put down utensils wrapped in a napkin and handed him a menu. "What would you like to drink?" she asked. "And do you need a few minutes to look at the menu before you order?"

"Not really." He had a nice voice, friendly and calm. "Black coffee, scrambled eggs, biscuits and sausage."

She nodded, writing it on the pad. "How would you like your eggs?"

"Over easy."

"Okay. Be right back."

She was aware of his eyes watching her as she went to the counter to give the order to the cook. It wasn't unusual. She drew attention because she was pretty. She didn't think much about it.

He was served and she went to wait on other customers. She noticed that the man had finished his meal and she went back to hand him the check, smiling.

"Esther Marist?" he asked quietly.

The smile faded, to be replaced by a look of sheer horror.

"Don't panic," he said quietly. "And don't run. I know you didn't push your mother down a staircase. Please, sit down for a minute."

She sat, too frightened to think that it might cost her her job to be familiar with a customer.

"I've already spoken to the owner," he said. "She knows why I'm here." He indicated Sadie, another waitress, who was suddenly waiting tables, filling in for Esther.

"I didn't even think about that," Esther said. She met his pale eyes. "I ran. I'm so sorry. I was terrified. He was drunk and making threats . . . !"

"It's all right," he said gently. "I've interviewed a dozen people who know you. Not one considered you a suspect. Neither do I. Darrin, on the other hand, has a rap sheet as long as my arm, and priors for assault. He was arrested on suspicion of murder a few years ago, but the charges couldn't be proven beyond the shadow of a doubt. There's not much guesswork involved in how your mother died."

She let out the breath she'd been holding. "She was so trusting," she said. "I knew what Darrin was, the day I met him."

"Your mother had a history of choosing the wrong sort of partners, I'm afraid," he replied. "This time, it ended badly."

"Darrin was furious because she wouldn't buy him a sports car," Esther said quietly, staring at the table. "She argued, and he just . . . hit her. She staggered and he hit her again, then he picked her up and hurled her down the staircase." Her eyes clouded. "She'd given me her will the night before, shoved it into my purse and told me to hold on to it, in case something bad should happen. I didn't realize why, not until she was gasping for breath. She told me to run. I did. I was so afraid . . . !"

"It's all right," he said gently, calming her. "Nobody will blame you for that. Certainly not the authorities back in Aspen. But you will need to come back and testify."

"Darrin has friends in organized crime. He also has somebody in the police department," she added solemnly.

His eyebrows arched. "He does?"

"Yes. So the minute I go back, I'll have an accident, and Darrin will go free. I'm the only eyewitness. Isn't that how it works? If I don't testify, he can't be convicted."

The man looked thoughtful. "I suppose so."

"Then what can I do?" she asked. She noticed that he was giving her diamond ring a long, careful scrutiny, and that there was the faintest smile on his face.

"Where's the will?" he wanted to know.

She thought it an odd question. She was about to tell him, however, when the bell on the front door rang and Butch walked in, tall and handsome in jeans and chambray shirt, boots, wide-brimmed Stetson and a shepherd's coat.

He looked around, spotted Esther, and made a beeline for her.

"Butch," she exclaimed, with some relief, and smiled at him. "This is Mr. . . ." She paused. "I'm sorry, I don't know your name," she said.

"Cameron," the other man replied, and shook hands with Butch, who pulled up a chair.

"Butch Matthews," came the answering greeting. "You're the investigator."

Cameron nodded. "I've just been going over the case with Miss Marist here."

"I wonder if you could put it off until the morning?" Butch asked with a smile. "I'm sorry, but I've got an emergency and I need her to help me with it. It's Two-Toes," he told Esther.

"Oh, no!" she exclaimed. "What happened?"

"He got out into the road," he said heavily. "A truck hit him . . ."

"He's not dead!" she exclaimed, almost in tears.

"No!" he replied at once. "But he's bruised and I'm pretty sure his hind leg is broken. I need you to help me get him inside." He looked at the investigator and indicated his empty sleeve. "She's handy. I can't manage a lot of things on my own."

"Well . . ." The investigator hesitated. "I could go with you, I guess . . ."

"Two-Toes would eat you. He's a wolf," he added, his dark eyes meeting the other man's. "I'm a wildlife rehabilitator, and he lives with Esther and me. She's the only other person he'll allow to touch him," he informed the other man, with a quick warning glance at Esther, who read it at once and didn't blurt out that Parker was familiar to Two-Toes and would certainly help if asked.

"I'll come with you right now." She turned after she got to her feet. "I'll be working in the morning, if you could come back then?" she asked. "If it's not too much trouble?"

"No trouble at all," Cameron said with a forced smile.

"Okay, then. Butch, let's go. I'll stop by and tell them why I'm leaving . . ."

She headed to the counter, with Butch right behind her.

Chapter Five

"Okay, what's going on?" Esther asked Butch when they were in the truck and headed home. "Parker would have been glad to help you get Two-Toes inside."

"Sure he would, if I needed help. Two-Toes is watching television. Sorry I had to scare you, but I had to get you away from Cameron in a hurry and that was the best way. You looked upset when I walked in. Why?"

"He asked me where the will was. Mama's will." She frowned. "Isn't that an odd question for an investigator to ask?"

"It would be, if he was one," Butch said curtly. "One of the sheriff's deputies called Aspen to ask if an investigator had been sent out here. They said no."

Her lips parted on a breath. "Oh, my gosh, Darrin's found me, hasn't he? You're in danger!" she exclaimed, looking at Butch with sheer horror in her eyes.

His heart jumped. Her life was in danger and she was worried about his safety. It was enlightening. Flattering. He felt like dancing. Except that the situation was dire and getting more dire by the minute.

"Yes, I'm afraid the man knows your mother's boyfriend.

Aspen authorities told the deputy that the coroner actually did find your mother's death suspicious, but they aren't looking at you. They're looking at Darrin. The way she was tossed down the staircase isn't something a woman your size would be capable of. They're fairly certain they can prove Darrin did it, so he's after ready cash for a quick getaway."

"Oh, dear." She wasn't remembering just Cameron's question about the will, she was remembering the way he was studying the diamond ring on her finger. Quick cash. Yes, that ring could be pawned for a small fortune, certainly enough to get Darrin out of Aspen, even out of the country in a hurry, before murder charges could be filed against him.

"Even if he got the will, it would have to go through probate," Butch was saying, although she was only half listening.

"Well, yes, but Mama had things he could pawn," she replied. She didn't mention the ring.

"You don't have any of her stuff with you, except that fox fur," he said. "So you're safe if we can get that will in a secure place."

She hadn't told him about the ring. Why hadn't she taken it off and left it at home? It was going to put a target on her back!

"Esther, did you hear me?" he asked.

She looked up. "Yes. Sorry. I was thinking about Mama." She fought tears. Even though her mother had been a trial to her, she was the last parent Esther had, and now she was alone in the world.

"Don't cry," Butch said gently. "I'll take care of you," he added. "Nobody is going to hurt you here. Benton is a very small town. Everybody knows everybody else's business. If any strangers come looking for you, nobody's going to tell them anything," he told her.

She grimaced. "Butch, somebody told Cameron where I was."

He frowned. "I guess so. He must have been very convincing."

"Darrin knows people everywhere, people who do bad things," she told him. "I was always afraid of him, even from the first. Mama had no judgment about men, ever."

"There are women who look for dangerous men," he said. "I always thought of it as like an addiction. You know, people go nuts over gambling and have to go into rehab? Stuff like that."

She nodded. "That was Mama. She had a different man in tow every few months."

"What a hell of a home life that would have been for you," he said, imagining it. "You're shy and pretty." His lips flattened as he considered that, and added her sad expression to his collection of facts about her past. "How many times did you have to find ways to get out of the house?"

"A lot," she said. "I had places I could go, even schoolmates who would hide me out for a few days. It made Mama furious, but sometimes it was the only way out. Some of her men liked threesomes," she added with evident distaste.

"Good Lord," he said reverently. "You've had some hard times."

"Well, they do say that steel has to be tempered." She smiled at him. "I guess I'm really tempered."

"Tempered," he agreed. His eyes dropped to her soft mouth. "And sweeter than honey," he added in a husky tone.

She sighed and smiled up at him. "We don't know each other very well," she said out of the blue.

"Don't you think we should?" he asked seriously. "After all, we are engaged. We could, you know, get married. If you wanted to, that is."

Her heart flew up over the world. "You want to marry me?" she asked, and the pleasure she felt was as clear as a sunny day.

Butch saw that and it amazed him. "Yes," he replied. He hesitated. "I mean, it wouldn't be a bad idea, since you're living with me." He grimaced. "I'm sort of old-fashioned. My former fiancée was a wild girl and I was younger. But now, I guess I'm getting more conventional. It doesn't look good, you living here without us being married."

She smiled with her whole face. "I love it that you're sort of old-fashioned," she said gently.

He smiled back. He'd done more smiling with her than he had since his fiancée departed. She made him feel strong, courageous, all the things he hoped he really was.

They got out of the truck and walked into the house.

"I'd love to marry you, Butch," she said huskily, as they walked through the door and into the living room

His high cheekbones flushed. "You would?"

She nodded, moving closer. One soft little hand smoothed up the front of his shirt. "You want a real marriage, don't you? I mean, we wouldn't have separate bedrooms and live like friends, or . . . anything like that?" she faltered.

"Yes, we'd sleep together," he said, his body already tautening just at the thought of this beautiful little blonde in his arms all night. But he gritted his teeth. "It won't bother you?" he added roughly. "I mean, I only have one arm . . ."

"That's okay," she said softly, lifting her face. "I have two. I'd give you one of mine, if I could . . . !"

She stopped because his mouth covered hers, fierce and hungry and tender, all at once.

"I think I dreamed you," he said gruffly, and he kissed her again.

She loved being in his arms. She loved the feel of his hard, hungry mouth on her lips. She loved it that he wanted her. She wasn't so naïve that she couldn't feel that. But he might think she was experienced, and she had to tell him.

She pulled back just a little, her mouth swollen, her body singing as she looked up into turbulent dark eyes. "Butch," she began shyly, "you know that I've never . . . I mean, I don't know how . . ." She groaned.

"You've never had sex?" he asked, and despite his earlier suspicions that she was innocent, he was shocked. She was so beautiful!

She shook her head. "Seeing Mama with all those men," she replied. "It soured things for me. I mean, it was like just animals, she went from one man to the next, constantly. Some of them wanted me." She shook her head. "I was afraid of most of them, especially Darrin." She looked up. "But I'm not at all afraid of you," she confessed, studying his hard face. "I love being with you, talking to you, going places with you. I love kissing you . . ."

She stopped as he bent and kissed her again, but this time with exquisite tenderness, holding her against him from head to toe, letting her feel his own hunger.

She started to jerk away, but he held her, without pressure, and smiled down at her. "This is something you'll have to get used to," he explained gently. "Men get aroused when they kiss women. Doesn't mean I'm going to jump on you all at once. Okay?"

She laughed away the embarrassment. "Okay."

He drew in a long, slow breath. "Well, our first time is going to be an experience," he commented.

"Because I don't know anything?" she asked.

He shrugged. "Because I haven't been with a woman since I lost my arm. I guess I'll wobble all over the place and make a mess of the whole business."

"No, you won't," she said gently and nuzzled her face into his throat. "We'll manage. People come home from wars in all sorts of conditions," she added quietly. "I don't think most women care what condition that is, when they love their husbands."

His hand smoothed over her soft, fine hair, almost to her waist in back when she let it loose, as she had earlier. "I was so busy thinking about my men that it never occurred to me that I'd end up half dead. If it hadn't been for Parker, I wouldn't be here. He's got several wounds that he sustained because he carried me off the battlefield. He's a hell of a guy. My best friend."

"He likes you, too. It shows."

"Men form bonds in war," he said solemnly, nuzzling the top of her head with his cheek. "You go through so much horror. It makes for lasting friendships, especially when you get out and have to deal with the aftermath. I was in the hospital for a while, and then they started trying to talk me into a prosthesis. I tried one or two, but the things just don't have what they need to have, to replace an arm. I mean, you can't lift with them. You can't feel through them. They're only good to pick up stuff, and I can even do that with my teeth if I have to."

She smiled. "I knew a man in college who had an artificial arm. He was one of the adjunct instructors. He'd been in the Middle East, too. His prosthesis was high-tech.

He actually had sensation in it, and it was linked to his muscles and even his brain so that he could control it."

"Must be nice," he sighed. "On my paycheck, I might afford one if I could save up for about thirty years." He laughed. "By then, I'd be so old, I wouldn't care, you know?"

She grinned. But inside she was thinking that she'd have all the wealth she needed to do that for him, when her mother's estate was settled. She didn't dare tell Butch that. He thought she was an ordinary girl with a well-to-do mother, down on her luck. Even with their brief relationship she knew that he wouldn't react well to being married to a millionaire. It would kill his pride, even in the modern world, to have a rich wife who had more money than he'd ever make.

But she pushed that thought to the back of her mind. It was a problem for another day. On this day, Butch had proposed, and something much better than a pretend engagement to save her reputation and keep people from asking too many questions.

She smiled as she drank in the clean, manly scent of him. "I never want to leave here," she murmured absently. "I want to take care of you. I've never really had anybody, not since my father died. Now I'll have you."

His arm tightened. "And I'll have you, honey girl," he whispered. "I'll take care of you all my life."

She snuggled closer. "When?"

"When what?" he murmured.

"When are we getting married?"

He drew in a breath. "Spring weddings are nice . . ."

She lifted her head and looked up at him with something like horror. "You want to wait?"

That blatant disappointment could have made him strut.

"No. I don't. But I thought you might . . . you know, so that we could save up for a fancy wedding gown and a reception," he began.

She reached up and kissed him softly. "I don't want a fancy wedding gown and a reception," she said. "I just want you."

"Oh, baby, that's not something you should say to me right now," he ground out.

"Don't you want me, too?"

He was almost shivering with need, and trying to deny it. "We have to drink some coffee," he told her, moving her aside. "Right now. I'll make it."

She sat on the sofa where he'd all but dumped her, staring after him with wide, stunned eyes. It took her a minute to get her breath and realize that he was at it again. Protecting her. From himself. She grinned from ear to ear and walked into the kitchen.

"You're a sweet man," she said gently, and went to get the sugar dish and some cream from the refrigerator.

"Just looking out for my own," he said, and winked at her.

They sat together on the sofa, but a little apart, going over plans for the wedding.

"I just want the two of us and maybe Parker and his wife and stepdaughter," she said. "Unless you have somebody you want to invite, too. Do you?"

"Yes. J. L. Denton and his wife," he replied. "I used to work for J. L. until I lost my arm. He's been good to me over the years."

"I'd love to have them there. And I'd really love to have her there, so I could pump her for information about that bad guy in her TV series and see if he's really going to turn out to be a decent person!"

He just laughed. "She never talks about scripts, so give it up. But she'll be happy to meet you. She doesn't look like a famous person, you know. She's thin and red-headed and shy."

"Really?!" she exclaimed.

"You lived in Aspen, didn't you? Don't all those movie stars come up there, and millionaires and such?" he teased.

She had to fight to control her reaction. "I guess so, but we were mostly on the ski slopes," she improvised. "Mama loved to ski."

"Can you?" he asked.

"Oh, yes. I love it. Mama was dating a ski instructor before Darrin," she said. "We stayed with him until Darrin came along."

She was clouding the explanation. Butch realized it but he didn't understand why. "Your mother had money, didn't she?" he asked.

"Yes, in investments," she returned. "Not much except that, though," she lied with a smile. "You know, you can't just pull money out of an investment brokerage. And Darrin will never get his hands on that, because I'm the beneficiary on all her investments." She gave him a sly glance. "So we'll have stocks and bonds and our kids will end up with them, because they're long-term investments."

He let out a whistle. "Thank God!"

"Excuse me?"

"I really don't want to be Mr. Esther Marist," he said dryly.

She burst out laughing, a little too enthusiastically, because his reply was close to the bone and he didn't even know it. "So we'll have rich kids and they can worry about the stock market. Right?"

"Kids." He was looking at her with an odd expression.

"Kids," she replied, and the look she gave him was both shy and excited. "Do you like kids?"

"I love them," he said huskily.

She recalled that his fiancée had gotten rid of his. She reached over and slid her hand into his big one. "I'm an only child. I'd love to have several children, if we could afford them."

"Nobody can afford children," he teased, "but they have them anyway. So will we." His dark eyes held her blue ones. "Our daughters will be beautiful if they take after you."

She flushed and laughed. "You're very good-looking, too, Butch," she said, sighing. "Our boys will have to look like you."

"We'll put in an order for one, right after we're married," he said with a big grin. "You do know that the stork brings them, right? There's bound to be some sort of store where you can order the kid you truly want."

She grinned. "You nut," she accused, and hit him playfully. "We'll take what we get and be grateful."

"Works for me," he said, and grinned back.

They were married at the local Methodist church on a Sunday after church in the chapel, with most of Benton in the pews. J. L. Denton and his wife, and Parker and his wife, stood up with them as best men and matrons of honor, and Teddie, Parker and Katy's daughter, was the flower girl.

The church was full of roses. They were a present from the Dentons. The smell was awesome. Standing up with

Butch in a pretty white dress off the rack at a department store, with a veil that she found at a thrift shop, with Butch in his only good suit, they were married by the church's minister.

When Esther came to the vows, she looked up at Butch and spoke them with her heart in her eyes. She hadn't planned on getting involved with anybody when she ran away, but it seemed as if fate had pushed her into Butch's cabin and given them both a second chance at happiness. Esther had come to adore him in the weeks they'd been together. Butch was happier than he'd ever been. It was a marriage that would succeed. They were both sure of it.

They exchanged the simple yellow gold rings they'd purchased, and when they were pronounced man and wife, Butch lifted her veil and looked at her for a few seconds with an expression she couldn't puzzle out before he bent his head and kissed her with breathless tenderness. Seconds later, before she even had time to enjoy it, they were running down the aisle and out the front of the church.

The girls in the Gray Dove with whom she worked had produced a beautiful wedding cake and they'd organized the reception, which drew most everybody in town.

Esther in her lacy white dress felt like Cinderella, and Butch was definitely her idea of Prince Charming. He'd certainly charmed her. The only shadow on her happiness was the threat of Darrin, somewhere out there, waiting for a chance to pounce. He'd get what money was available, most likely, because Esther couldn't be found. But that investigator, Cameron, had found her and Darrin knew where she was. Cameron had seen the diamond ring on her finger, the one that Butch thought was paste. It sent cold chills down her spine. She was worried for Butch, who had been so kind to her.

"Hey, this is a wedding, not a wake," Butch teased at her ear. "Why so sad? Are you having second thoughts?" he added, and looked suddenly worried.

She bumped her hip against him. "I am not having second thoughts," she murmured. She peered up at him with mischievous eyes. "And you'd better eat lots of cake. You're going to need all the energy you can get, later."

It took him a few seconds to puzzle that out and he actually flushed.

She laughed softly, flushing a little, too, at her own boldness. "Sorry," she said.

"Don't be. I love it." He grinned down at her. "You'd better eat a lot, too, honey girl."

She sighed. Let Darrin do his worst. This was her wedding day, and she was married to a man she could love and respect. In fact, she thought, as she looked up at him while he accepted congratulations from the Dentons, she already loved him. It was like a jolt of lightning. She loved him! And what a time to find it out. He was marrying her to protect her. Maybe he wanted her, too, but men could want without loving, hadn't she learned that from watching her mother flit from man to man?

She wiped the consternation from her face and clung to Butch's hand while she teased Mrs. Denton about the series and the bad guy who might turn out to be a hero.

"Give it up," Cassie Denton told Esther with a sly laugh. "You'll never find out until they actually air the last episode of the season. But," she added, "you're going to love it. Honest."

"Okay!" Esther said, and grinned from ear to ear.

* * *

She'd been full of joy and laughter until they got back to the cabin and went inside together. Everything was different, now. She wasn't a house guest, or even a fiancée. She was a wife.

She looked up at Butch with all her worries in her blue eyes.

He smiled. "Nothing's changed except we're married," he said softly. "So suppose you change into some comfortable clothes and we'll go out to eat? Then we can go riding, if you like. J. L. said we could go around the bridle path at his place, and he's got plenty of horses."

"Oh, that's so nice of him! We haven't been riding together," she added. She hesitated, worried again that she'd put her foot in her mouth.

"I can ride, tenderfoot," he teased, reading her expression. "I'm not graceful getting on or off, but I know my way around horses. You sweet little woman. Were you worried?"

She nodded. "I wouldn't do anything to hurt you, even with words."

His chest felt twice its size. He smiled at her. "Lord, Esther, every time I look at you, I feel like I've won the lottery. You're beautiful and sweet and kind." He shook his head. "I don't know what I've done in my life to deserve a wife like you."

"Awww," she said. She went close and hugged him. "I feel like that, too. You're such a sweet man, Butch. I'll be the best wife in the world, honest. I just need to, well, I need . . ." She searched for the words and flushed.

He chuckled, deep in his throat. "You need a dark room."

She let out the breath she'd been holding. "Well, yes," she faltered, and looked up at him. "How did you know?"

He leaned down. "I wasn't always experienced," he told her. "My first time, I got my zipper caught in my underwear and fell over a chair."

She gaped at him. "What did you do?" she exclaimed.

He laughed. "I ran for my life, of course. She told everybody she knew, so it was really bad for a while. I was in the service before I had my first real experience. Fortunately, the zipper didn't get stuck that time."

She was laughing. "I can't believe it."

"She was a very sophisticated girl," he recalled. "The one where I had the zipper issue." He made a face. He studied her. "You'd have laughed, but not at me. You'd have laughed with me, and I wouldn't have been embarrassed."

She smiled. He knew her very well already. Her eyes were bright with joy as they met his. "I'd never laugh at you," she said softly.

He bent and kissed her lightly. "You look very pretty in that dress," he said.

"It's off the rack," she replied, "but I thought it looked bridal."

"It does. Very. Okay, go get changed and let's find something nice to eat on our wedding day."

"We could go to the little Scottish place," she called over her shoulder.

He scowled. "What little Scottish place?"

She poked her head out of her bedroom door. "McDonald's," she teased, and closed the door. She could hear him laughing, even through the wood.

* * *

They had hamburgers and fries and then drove over to J. L.'s place, where one of the cowboys was waiting to saddle horses for them.

"This one is nice and tame," the cowboy said as he led it out.

Butch's face hardened. Did the man think he needed a rocking horse because he was disabled?

"This horse is for Miss . . . Mrs. Matthews," the cowboy said quickly, wincing at Butch's offended expression. He tipped his hat to her and returned her smile. "I thought you might like an easy horse at first, ma'am."

She laughed. "I would. I haven't been riding for a while. Thank you."

"This one's for you, Mr. Matthews," the cowboy said as he went to retrieve a gelding. "Rudolph. He's not quite as tame as the other," he added dryly.

Butch chuckled. "I can ride anything that has a mane and a tail," he said.

"That's what the boss told me."

"Why Rudolph?" he asked as he sprung into the saddle, unhampered by the lack of his left arm.

"If you aren't careful, he'll toss you into a tree and you'll have a red nose," the cowboy replied, tongue in cheek.

Butch burst out laughing. "Enough said." He looked back at Esther, sitting comfortably in the Western saddle. "Ready?" he asked.

She grinned. "Ready!"

They went off on the bridle path that led around the ranch. And if the cowboy thought it was an odd way to celebrate a wedding, he didn't voice his thoughts.

* * *

"It's so peaceful here," Esther said on a sigh as they rode, with only the creak of saddle leather and birdsong around them to break the silence of the woods.

"I like peaceful," he teased.

"Me, too. We had a house in Los Angeles when my dad was alive." They still had it, she just wasn't ready to share that with her new husband. Not yet. "It was noisy and polluted. I hated every minute we spent there, although I loved my dad."

"Did he look like you?" he asked, curious.

She shook her head. "He had dark hair and gray eyes. I look like my mother."

"She must have been beautiful," he remarked, his eyes warm on Esther's face.

She smiled. "She was. But it was all she thought about." She frowned, staring down at the pommel of the saddle. "She was terrified of wrinkles and even one gray hair." She looked up at him. "It's not a bad thing, getting older."

"We, the aged population of Benton, applaud your consideration."

She chuckled. "Stop that. You're not old."

"Older than you, cupcake," he said softly. "Maybe too old."

"You are not, and stop talking like that or I'll get off this sweet rocking horse and throw something at you."

He felt lighter than air. "Okay."

"Age has nothing to do with how people feel about each other," she continued.

"You're very young, even for your age," he mused.

She met his eyes. "I'll grow three gray hairs and soak

my face in water so it wrinkles, just for you," she said with a twinkle in her blue eyes.

He made a face. She made one back.

"As long as you're happy, honey girl," he said gently. "That's all that matters."

"I've never been so happy in my life, Butch," she replied, and it was the truth. "I love being with you."

"I love being with you, too."

They came to a crossroads. "Right is back to the ranch, left is off to J. L.'s lake, where he likes to fish," Butch told her.

"I'd love to see the lake," she said.

"Okay, then." He hesitated, frowning. "It's starting to snow."

She knew already how quickly snow could turn to ice. "You want to go back, don't you?"

"I think we'd better," he said reluctantly. "Neither of us needs to take a toss on our wedding day, and it gets icy here when the temperature drops and snow hits the ground."

She smiled. "Okay."

He shook his head as they turned back. "And that's what I like most about you."

"What?"

"You never complain. You never fuss. Life with you is . . . easy," he said after a minute. "But that's not the word I want, either. You make everything seem simple, even when it's not. You're the best companion I've ever had."

She smiled. "I'm glad. Because you're my best friend, Butch."

"Best friend." He said the words as if they bothered him.

She realized belatedly that they did, and why. She reined in her horse gently, and Butch paused beside her.

"I don't mean that the way you're probably thinking,"

she said, flushing a little. "I mean, you don't get excited just being with a friend, do you?"

His eyebrows arched and his eyes, so sad a moment before, were now twinkling. "You get excited with me?" he asked softly.

She cleared her throat. "We, um, we should move along, don't you think? Snow's coming down faster."

Chapter Six

The snow was deep by the time they got back to Butch's cabin. Esther's ankle-high boots were going to get full of snow on the way to the front door.

Butch solved that problem very easily by hefting her over his broad shoulder, catching her behind the knees with his good arm.

He chuckled at her surprise as he bumped the truck's door shut with his hip. "We learn coping skills when we lose limbs," he teased.

She laughed, too. "Yes, we do. Thanks! My feet would have frozen. The snow's halfway to my knees already."

"We're most likely going to get snowed in for a day or two," he remarked as he put her gently down on the porch. "That being the case, I'd better get out back and make sure my furry house guests have enough to eat and that their water bowls are plugged in so the water doesn't freeze." He sighed. "Then we hope we don't lose power, or I have to go out and water them two or three times a day."

"How do you get water when there's no power?" she asked, and was honestly curious.

"Melt snow, if it's the only way. But we have an

emergency generator. I can connect it to the well head if I have to."

"Wow. Science!" she teased.

He grinned. "All the comforts of home, regardless of the weather. And it's the weekend, so I don't have to work—except for feeding our furry guests. I won't be long."

"I'll start supper."

"Damn," he muttered. "I should have stopped somewhere and gotten us takeout, so you wouldn't have to be in the kitchen cooking on our wedding day!"

"I love to cook, since you taught me," she protested. "Really. It's not even like work."

"You sure?"

She smiled. "I'm sure."

"Okay, then. I'll go see to the animals."

She went into the kitchen and started looking through the meat in the freezer.

She cooked a beef casserole and made biscuits to go with it. Dessert was vanilla pudding from a mix, with some Cool Whip and peaches mixed in.

Butch just shook his head as he savored the dessert. "Honey, you have a way with food," he said. "You can take the simplest things and make them uptown."

She grinned. "Thanks. It's better if you have yellow cake or shortcake and put peaches and ice cream over it and then add the Cool Whip, but I didn't have ice cream or cake."

"We had cake at the fellowship hall." He groaned. "They told me to bring the rest of the cake home with us. I forgot!"

"They'll save it for us," she said with certainty. "I'll

phone the Gray Dove later, to make sure. It's not a problem, you know. We're eating dessert!"

He sighed. "You're the easiest person to live with," he said.

"So are you."

He looked up. "I'm really not," he told her. "I'm impatient, bad-tempered from time to time, unreasonable . . ."

"You're just you," she interrupted. "We all have times when we're irritable. I get that way, too."

"I've never seen you irritable."

"Well, I don't get that way often. Never with you," she added, her eyes soft with affection.

He finished his dessert and sat back to enjoy his second cup of coffee. His eyes slid over her with pure appreciation. She was wearing jeans and a long-sleeved yellow sweater that brought out the highlights in her blond hair.

"Why do you wear your hair up like that?" he asked curiously.

She laughed, touching the high topknot held up with a yellow scrunchy. "It gets in my way when I'm cooking," she explained.

He pursed his lips. "But you're not cooking right now."

She rolled her eyes, but not with irritation. "Men," she laughed. She took the scrunchy out and shook her head, so that her long blond hair settled around her shoulders.

"You take my breath away," he said, and he wasn't smiling.

She met that intent stare and couldn't look away. The tension in the room was suddenly so thick it could be felt. Even old Two-Toes, asleep on his rug in the corner, lifted his blind eyes momentarily before he curled up again and went back to sleep by the fireplace.

"What we need right now," Butch said in a husky tone, "is a nice, warm, dark place."

Her heart raced. "I think I know the very one," she replied breathlessly.

He stood up and curled her fingers into his. "I'll be slow, and careful," he said softly. "I promise, I won't hurt you."

"I know you won't."

She followed him into his bedroom. The light was already off. He closed the door, leaving them in total darkness. Esther could hear her own heart beating. She felt the heat of him as he moved closer, felt his breath on her forehead, her nose, and then on her mouth as he bent and kissed her with exquisite tenderness.

He sighed. It was like drowning in velvet. He murmured that and she smiled under his mouth, because it felt like that to her, too. She slid her arms around his neck and waited for whatever came next.

She was unprepared for the sudden flash of desire that sparked between them when his hand slid under her sweater and up to the catch behind her back. He loosened it, feeling her stiffen, just a little.

"Nothing to be nervous about," he whispered against her lips as his fingers moved around, just under her soft, firm little breast and teased it.

She'd never felt such sensations. She jerked a little, surprised that such a light tracing could produce such an explosion of pleasure.

"Am I going too fast?" he asked at her lips.

"No. Oh, no. It feels . . ." She swallowed. "It's like falling into fire," she choked.

He let out the breath he'd been holding. "It feels just like that," he agreed.

His fingers moved up, up, teasing the nipple into sudden hardness, causing sensations in her untried body that she'd never felt in her life. She moaned softly.

"I can use something," he managed. "If you want me to."

Her arm tightened around his neck. "You said . . . you liked children," she whispered.

"You said you did, too," he ground out.

"Then why are you talking about using things . . . ! Oh, do that again! Please . . . !"

She was arching backwards, moaning even more harshly as he fumbled the sweater up under her chin and put his mouth squarely over her hard nipple. He suckled it, feeling the shudder that went through her, hearing the soft cry of anguished desire.

"Yes," he said, as if she'd spoken.

He propelled her to the bed and eased her down onto the coverlet, his own body shuddering with need. It had been so damned long . . . !

She was a little embarrassed when he coaxed her out of her clothing and stood up to get rid of his own, but she was on fire for him, so that the embarrassment was quickly gone.

When she felt his nude body over her own, she hesitated, uncertain.

"It's part of being together," he whispered, bridling his own desire to kindle hers. "Trust me, honey girl. I'll make it good for you, however long it takes."

That relaxed her. He wasn't in a hurry, and he wasn't rough. Her fingers slid up and down the muscles of his back as he balanced on what was left of his arm and moved his mouth tenderly all over her body.

She moved involuntarily, so caught up in pleasure that it felt as if her body was on fire. Everything he did was new and exciting and wonderful.

"Still okay?" he whispered.

"Better . . . than . . . okay," she choked, arching and shivering as he touched her in a new place, an embarrassing place, but it felt so good that she didn't even protest. "Oh, my goodness . . . !" she cried out as pleasure shot through her like an arrow.

His mouth pressed down hard on her soft belly. He thought of her having his babies with real hunger. She was writhing under him now, so lost to passion that she wouldn't have protested anything he did.

He took her from one level of pleasure to the next as he slowly eased over her, parting her legs with his own. He moved down into stark intimacy, but she was blind with need, arching up toward him, not protesting as he slowly, surely, invaded her.

"Oh!" she whispered with wonder. "Oh, is that what it feels like? It's . . . !" She lifted off the bed as his hand moved between them, arousing her so that the tiny barrier he could feel now wouldn't interrupt her pleasure. At least, thank God, he knew what he was doing. He wouldn't have hurt her for the world.

He moved down against her, each thrust going deeper, slower, as his mouth finally found hers in the darkness.

She was whimpering. But her body was arching rhythmically, shivering with pleasure, her nails biting into his back. Whatever she was feeling, it was definitely not pain. He felt a sense of pride he couldn't remember ever experiencing with any other woman, not even the fiancée with whom he'd thought himself in love.

Her long legs wrapped suddenly around his and she pleaded with him. He could taste her tears in his mouth as he gave her what she wanted, driving into her with such passion and strength that he very quickly brought her to ecstasy.

She hung there, in thrall to a pleasure she hadn't known existed, shivering, sobbing. Then she felt him driving for his own satisfaction, felt his muscles coil as he pushed down one last time, with all his strength, and cried out with the force of the pleasure her body gave him.

"It's good, isn't it?" she whimpered at his ear, shivering again and again as he moved helplessly inside her. "It's so good, so good . . . please don't . . . don't stop, please, please . . . !"

Incredibly, those soft pleas hardened his body, an experience that was a first in his life. He groaned as he grew even more potent than he'd been before. He drove into her, hard and fast, as hungry as she was. It took longer, but the culmination, when it came, lifted them both off the bed and they cried out helplessly in unison as the world slowly came back into focus in the heated, dark room.

"You okay?" he asked as they lay damp and shivering in each other's arms.

"Okay is too mild a word," she whispered, and laughed wickedly. "Incredibly satisfied is much better."

"I have to agree," he replied, holding her closer. "I should tell you that most men can't go at it twice in a row without a few minutes in between to recover."

"I always knew you were one of a kind," she teased, sliding her long leg against his hairy one.

"You inspired me to unimaginable skill." He laughed. "God, what an experience!"

She arched with pleasure, sighing. "Oh, yes."

He was chuckling to himself.

She rolled over, close, and snuggled against him. "Why are you laughing?"

"I'm feeling very smug."

"You are?"

"You were a virgin, and I satisfied you the first time."

She smiled against his chest. "Abundantly." She smoothed

her hand over his hairy chest. "And your arm didn't cause you to fumble, did it?" she teased.

He sighed. "Apparently not." He laughed.

"I told you. People cope."

"What will you do if I turn on the light?" he asked.

"Not notice," she said. "I think I'm boneless now."

While she was wondering what he meant, the soft light of a lamp spread over the bed. He turned back to her and caught his breath. She was pink and cream. Flawless skin, firm, pretty little breasts with their dusky crowns relaxed in the aftermath. Slim waist, flaring hips, long legs. He whistled, obviously spellbound.

She was more inhibited. She glanced down and then back up and colored.

"You'll get used to me," he said softly. "Men aren't as pretty as women without their clothes."

"It's hard," she managed.

He laughed. "It gets easier." He smoothed back her long blond hair, damp with sweat. "I think I dreamed you," he whispered. "You're the most beautiful woman I've ever seen."

She smiled. It wasn't possible to be embarrassed when he was looking at her as if she was the very mystery of life. She stretched, watching his eyes follow the movement up and down her body.

"I thought it would hurt," she said.

He grinned. "I knew a couple of ways around that," he replied, and tried not to look as smug as he felt.

She nuzzled her face against his chest. "And now I'm sleepy," she said, apologetic.

"Me, too."

He reached up and turned out the light. "It's been a long day, Mrs. Matthews."

The sound of her married name made her feel warm all over. "Yes, it has, Mr. Matthews."

"No regrets?"

"Oh, no. Not even one," she replied.

He kissed her forehead and then pulled the sheet over them.

"I need my gown," she began.

"No, you don't," he said easily. "If we have to run out of the house, I'll wrap you up in the sheet first. Okay?"

She just laughed. "Okay."

She didn't mean to go to sleep, but she did.

The light coming in the window woke her. She opened her eyes and her new husband was sitting on the side of the bed, dressed in jeans and boots and a blue flannel shirt, a coffee cup in his hand, just looking at her with pure male appreciation.

She felt the faint chill and realized before she looked that he'd tugged the sheet away.

"Couldn't help myself," he murmured with a smile. "It's like having my own private art gallery. Beautiful."

The soft words eased away any embarrassment or indignation she might have felt. She just smiled. She was getting used to those dark eyes caressing her. And she didn't really mind. It was new, to love, to be intimate, to be married. All those things. With any luck at all, one day his affection for her might suddenly turn to love, just as hers had, for him.

"I'll get older and gain weight and have wrinkles eventually," she said with a teasing expression.

"I won't mind at all. I won't even mind if you get as big around as a pumpkin. I thought about it, somewhere in the middle of our first time."

Her heart jumped. "Did you?" she asked, breathless. "So did I."

He put down the coffee cup and his big hand smoothed over her creamy, flat stomach. "You're still very young," he murmured, and the smile faded.

She put her hand over his. "My mother was eighteen when she had me," she pointed out, smiling.

He drew in a long breath and laughed. "You have a way of chasing my concerns right out the window."

"This one isn't even a concern. I'd love a baby. We could share him."

His heart jumped up into his throat. A little boy who'd follow him around the forest. A little girl who'd look like her beautiful mother. "Wow." The way he said the word made her toes curl.

She smiled up at him. He smiled back.

They went to the feed store to get grain for the wild animals that couldn't forage in several feet of snow. While they were there, they stocked up on dog food.

"Do you feed it to all the creatures in the outbuilding?" she asked, noting the cases of dog food.

"I do," he replied. He grinned. "It beats sitting out in the woods with a hunting rifle trying to get fresh game for them every day."

She laughed. "I guess it does." She didn't add that she wasn't sure he could manage a rifle anymore. It would have dented his pride, and she couldn't have that. She was so much in love that she felt as if she glowed, just walking beside him around the feed store.

She drew attention. She was pretty, and even wrapped

up in the inexpensive shepherd's coat he'd bought her, men looked.

Butch was annoyed a little, but he was proud that she belonged to him. His hand slid into hers as they waited at the counter for the bill to be tallied.

"Here you go, Butch," the clerk said with a grin. "How many critters you got right now?"

"Several," Butch chuckled. "They come and go."

"You got that poor wolf those kids dragged behind a truck?" he asked, and his face went hard. "Hell of a thing to do to even a wild animal."

"They're facing charges for it," Butch assured him. "And the wolf is mending. It never ceases to amaze me how resilient wild things are."

"Truly. I forgot to congratulate you two," he added, looking from Butch to Esther with a smile. "You look good together."

"Thank you," Esther said with a shy smile.

Butch chuckled. "She's turned me into a happily married man," he commented, smiling at her. "I like having somebody who can help with the cooking."

"Only because you taught me how." She glanced at the clerk. "I couldn't boil water at first."

"Neither can I," the clerk confided. "But my wife, now, she's one of the best cooks in Benton. I guess I'd starve on my own."

They all laughed.

"You really do draw men's eyes," Butch mused as they cooked supper together. "I thought I was going to have to punch one of those cowboys who were buying feed for Ren Colter's ranch and gaping at you."

"You did?" she asked, surprised.

He looked down at her and frowned. "Honey, don't you know how beautiful you are?"

She just sighed and smiled at him. "Not really. I'm glad you think I am, though. You aren't bad-looking yourself," she teased.

He chuckled as he took the biscuits out of the oven and set them carefully on an oven mitt in their cast-iron container. "You make me feel like a man with two arms," he murmured.

She moved close to him. "You worry about that too much," she said, and she was serious. "I don't mind it, not at all. You're just perfect to me, the way you are."

He sighed and smiled. "Blind little woman."

She laid her cheek against his chest, smiling as she felt his heartbeat. "Love does make people blind to imperfections." She sighed.

He went very still. "What?"

She looked up at him. He seemed all at sea.

"You . . . love me?" he got out.

"Of course I love you, you big idiot," she muttered, searching his dark eyes. "Why in the world do you think I married you?"

"For my abundant worldly goods?" he asked, recovering his poise with humor.

"Absolutely," she teased. "I mean, you have so many!"

He smoothed his hand over her soft blond hair. "I wish I had millions," he said huskily. "I'd deck you out in real diamonds, one as big as that paste one you wear," he added with a chuckle.

She felt those words to the soles of her feet. What would she do? She had millions. One day, her life would get sorted out, Darrin would get what was coming to him, and

Esther would inherit her late mother's estate. It was so extensive that even she didn't know exactly how much money was involved. How would her husband react to that? Surely, it wouldn't matter so much . . .

"I know what you're thinking," he teased. "But don't worry about it. We'll have rich kids, but what you inherit won't affect us. Not a bit."

She recalled what he'd said, that he didn't want to be Mr. Esther Marist. She ground her teeth together and forced a smile so that he wouldn't realize she'd lied to him about her background.

"Not a bit," she agreed, and turned suddenly back to the potatoes she'd been cooking, to test them.

They ate lunch quietly. Butch was still recovering from the fact that a woman as beautiful as Esther could love him, when he had few possessions worth anything and he was missing an arm. She was young and gorgeous. She could have had any man she wanted, but she wanted him, imperfections and all, because she loved him. He felt like floating. Except there was the guilt. She was so young. She'd run away from a frightening man and apparently she'd had no experience of men, young men. She clung to Butch because he was the first man who'd been kind to her. But that wasn't love. It was gratitude. He wondered if she knew the difference. He felt guilty, as if he'd pushed her into a relationship before she had time to experience life without the burden of her mother and her mother's lovers. And he'd failed to protect her. They both wanted a child, that was true, but what if she came to her senses too late, after she was pregnant, and she didn't want Butch or a baby anymore? His own worries tormented him.

Esther saw that he was worried. She wondered why. He'd seemed so happy the night before. She flushed, remembering their shared passion. It had been a revelation to her. Butch hadn't said that he loved her, although she'd certainly said it to him. Could he still be grieving for the fiancée who'd thrown him over, who'd had his child in her body but refused to bear it? Men were strange to her, even at her age. Often they seemed to love women who mistreated them. Was he missing his fiancée and regretting his hasty marriage to Esther?

She withdrew into herself, talking as naturally as she could and smiling, but the tension was growing as Butch, too, succumbed to his own tormented thoughts. It moved them apart at a time when they should have been growing closer together.

After that day, Butch went to bed only after Esther was asleep, and got up before she was awake. She felt inadequate. He didn't seem to even want her anymore, which reinforced her fears that he regretted marrying her.

She went to work every day, and they carried on impersonal conversations, talking about everything under the sun—except themselves.

They were starting to cook supper one night a couple of weeks later when there was a knock on the door.

The sheriff's deputy she knew from the restaurant came in past Butch and tipped his hat to Esther.

"I'm afraid I have some bad news," he said quietly.

They both stared at him.

He drew in a breath. "We did a search on Cameron and found that he had an outstanding warrant, so we arrested him. I should have told you sooner, but we've been busier than usual." He paused. "So Cameron made a phone call this morning, and two well-dressed attorneys from Aspen came and bailed him out of jail."

Esther's heart tried to jump out of her chest. "Oh, dear."

"The attorneys mentioned that they were also representing a Mr. Darrin Ross and that he was planning to have Miss . . . excuse me, Mrs. Matthews here, arrested for pushing her mother down a staircase."

"I didn't," Esther said quietly. "What about the coroner? He said that my mother was thrown down the staircase. I can hardly lift a ten pound bag of dog food, much less a grown woman!"

"I mentioned that. The attorneys said that the coroner had a change of heart and amended his autopsy report." The deputy smiled gently. She did look so frightened.

Esther's eyes closed. "If he can have me charged with murder and sent to jail, he'll get Mama's estate, won't he, Deputy?" she asked, her blue eyes wide with pain. "If I remember the law, a felon can't inherit, is that right?"

The deputy felt terrible. He hesitated. "Yes."

"Well, that's just lovely," she said, feeling strangely isolated from the world.

"We'll get you the best lawyer we can find," Butch said curtly. "J. L. Denton has a whole firm of them, and he'll help if I ask him to."

She looked up at Butch. He'd been so remote lately that she wondered if he didn't want to see the last of her. But he seemed to care about her fate. "Do you think so?" she asked.

"I know so." He turned back to the lawman. "Pressure was put on the coroner, I'm betting. He's just one man, and if he has a family, they could be threatened."

"Exactly what I thought. I hate to see a man get away

with murder, much less try to blame it on an innocent woman," he said shortly. "Not going to happen. I know the chief up in Aspen. I'll talk to him."

"Policemen have families, too," Esther said sadly.

He chuckled. "This one doesn't. He has a mean temper and most people are afraid of him."

Esther felt more hopeful. "Okay. Thanks. What do I do in the meantime?"

"You talk to J. L.'s attorneys," Butch said.

"Good idea. I'll be in touch when I know more."

"Thanks, Deputy," Esther said.

He smiled. "No problem. See you."

Butch walked him out. When he came back inside, his jaw was taut and his dark eyes were flashing. He pulled out his cell phone and pressed a number.

"Hello, J. L.? It's Butch. I have a small problem and I need some help." He went on to outline briefly what was going on. He listened, his eyes on Esther's worried face. He smiled. "Yes, that's what I thought. You will? I'll owe you one. Sure thing. Thanks."

He hung up. "J. L.'s going to contact his attorneys. One of them will be over in the morning to talk to you."

Esther went close. He stiffened a little, but he didn't touch her. She felt a brush of sorrow. They'd been so good together. Now it all seemed lost. "Thanks," she said.

"Thank J. L.," he said, and he forced a smile. "Let's finish lunch, okay?"

She nodded. "Okay, Butch."

CHAPTER SEVEN

The attorney, Barton Frazier, arrived promptly at eight o'clock the next morning. Esther had arranged to come in an hour later at the Gray Dove so that she could talk to him at home. Her boss had been understanding and very kind.

Mr. Frazier accepted a mug of coffee and sat down at the kitchen table with her. Butch had already left for work, so there were just the two of them in the house.

"I want you to tell me exactly what happened the night your mother died," Mr. Frazier said quietly. He was a tall man, dark headed and dark eyed, older than Butch. He inspired confidence.

She sighed. "My mother had lived with Darrin for several weeks. She had no judgment about men at all. He was brutal to her, demanding things all the time, expensive things. She'd refused to give him money to buy an expensive sports car the night she . . . died. He was drunk. She mouthed off at him and he picked her up and threw her down the staircase. She was barely conscious. She pulled off her ring . . . this ring." She showed it to him. "She gave it to me. She'd already pushed her revised will into my purse the day before and told me to hold on to it. She was afraid. She always had some sort of premonition that she'd die violently. I think she knew, the day before, that Darrin was going to do something bad."

He was taking notes. "You have the will?"

"Yes. Darrin sent some man, a Mr. Cameron, down here pretending to be an investigator for the Aspen authorities. Except he wasn't. He saw the ring. He'd have told Darrin that I have it." She looked up. "It's worth millions of dollars."

"And your mother's estate?"

"Probably close to two hundred million dollars." She sighed. "It's mostly tied up in stocks and bonds and land. She owned several houses, many high-ticket cars, a closetful of fur coats . . ." She hesitated. "I suppose Darrin has hocked the furs and other easy-to-find antiques to get money for lawyers. He does have some mob ties to minor gangsters. Maybe they're funding him, in hopes of some easy money."

"That's always possible. Did your mother have any living relatives besides you?"

"I have a grandfather, if he's still alive. Mama seldom talked about him. He disapproved of my father." She smiled sadly. "My dad was a wonderful person. Mama ran around on him. He was so sad. He really loved her."

"What was your mother's maiden name?"

"Cranston," she said. "But she never talked about her past, where she was from, even her parents. She didn't like her father at all, though she did tell me of some good times with him, and her mother died when she was small, I think." She smiled. "It's amazing, how much I don't know about my own background."

"We can find your grandfather, if he's still alive."

"That would make him a target, Mr. Frazier," she said sadly. "I've made Butch one, by marrying him. I'd die to keep him safe from harm. I don't want him hurt, because of me. I love him more than anything."

He smiled. "We'll do our best to keep both of you safe. And your grandfather, if we find him. Was he well-to-do?"

"Mama said he was very rich," she replied. "He lived in some remote place." She frowned, trying to remember. "I think it was Jamaica. She mentioned it once. He left the States when his wife died and his daughter married who he considered the wrong man. Mama said he stopped caring about anything after that."

"What did your father do?"

"He flew airplanes," she said, smiling. "He was a test pilot." The smile faded. "That's how he died, testing a new plane. Mama was off with one of her lovers. Our lawyers had to take care of the funeral, because I was too little to know how to do any of that. When Mama came back and they told her about Daddy, she just shrugged and said there was a big party coming up in Europe and she was taking her new lover there."

"What a life you've had," he remarked, still taking notes.

"We had a wonderful housekeeper. She took care of me all those years." She grimaced. "Darrin made Mama fire her the day he moved in. And Mama didn't say a word, she just did it. I don't think Agnes even got severance pay." She looked up. "Her full name is Agnes Meriwether, and she lived in Billings, Montana, before she came to work for Mama. While you're trying to find my grandfather, do you think you could look for Agnes, too? If we can get my inheritance back from Darrin, I'll have more than enough money to give her a pension and pay your fees so Mr. Denton won't have to."

"We can worry about all that later," he said kindly. "I'm going to get right on it."

He had a few more questions. Esther answered them all. "Just one more thing," she said to Mr. Frazier as he was leaving. "I don't want my husband to know any of the particulars, especially how much I'm worth."

He nodded. "I won't tell."

"Thanks. I told him that Mama had some minor investments that were long-term, and I laughed and said they'd belong to our kids. He said he didn't want to be Mr. Esther Marist." Her eyes saddened. "His pride wouldn't take it. I should have told him the truth up front, but I was so afraid. I'm still afraid."

"You don't need to be. We'll manage this. Trust me."

She looked up into warm dark eyes. "I will," she said.

Butch wanted to know what the attorney had said when they were both home from work later that day.

"He's going after Darrin," she said simply. "I hope he gets what's coming to him."

"So do I," Butch agreed. "When will you know something?"

"Very soon," she assured him.

He made a face and sighed. "I don't like having you in danger," he said abruptly.

"I don't like having you in danger either, Butch," she said softly, and her eyes adored him. "I wish we could go off to some island somewhere and never have to come back again."

He smiled sadly. "That's a pipe dream, honey girl," he told her. "We all have bad times. Best way to handle them is to face them right away."

"Yes, and I didn't do that," she said sadly. "If I'd only gone to the police right then . . ."

His hand slid over hers on the table. "And you might have been lying dead in the snow and I'd never have met you."

"But I'm such a burden," she protested, her blue eyes wide and sad.

"Some burden," he said huskily. "You take my breath away. I can't even believe that you're married to me."

She smiled. "Really? You don't act like you want me around lately."

"I want you around all the time, that's the problem," he said through his teeth. "You're new to marriage, and intimacy. I thought it would be better to give you a little breathing space."

"Silly man," she said, with her heart in her eyes. "I don't need any breathing space."

He drew in a breath. "You don't? Really?"

"Really." She hugged him close. "After supper, I could convince you of that. I mean, if you wanted me to." She looked up at him intently. "You can tell me if there are times when you'd rather not be with me. I can handle it."

"That's the problem."

"What is?"

He cleared his throat. "I want to be with you all the time. Too much."

"Awwww," she whispered, kissing his warm throat. "I want to be with you all the time, too, Butch."

His breath caught. His arm contracted hungrily around her. He felt his body start swelling at once.

"That's really nice," she whispered, and moved closer.

"Esther . . ." he choked.

She reached up and whispered in his ear, shameful things, intimate things that would make her squirm in the aftermath, but all she wanted right now was Butch.

He caught her hand and drew her down the hall, into the bedroom, and locked the door. She went into his arms at once and started kissing him.

A couple of hours later, lying in a tangled, damp mass, Esther looked up at the ceiling and she laughed.

"What's funny?" he asked drowsily.

"You thought I wanted breathing space," she teased. "But I can't even breathe away from you. I was afraid you were having second thoughts, that you might want me to leave."

"I'd do anything to keep you here," he confessed quietly. "You make everything good and sweet. If I lost you, it would take all the color out of my world. I wouldn't even want to go on living."

It was a powerful thing to say. She could literally feel the words. She moved closer to hug him close. "I'm so glad I married you," she whispered. "Even if you weren't the best lover in Colorado, I'd still be glad."

His heart ran wild. She loved him in bed. That meant so much. At the last, his fiancée had noted that he wasn't very good at satisfying a woman. But here was Esther, who had been innocent, and he knew without words that she achieved satisfaction with him every time they were together. Of course, so did he.

"It makes me proud, that you feel that way about me," he said softly.

She smiled, sighing against his hair-roughed, muscular chest. "I'll never leave you," she said gently. "Unless you throw me out," she added, and felt sick to the soles of her feet.

He just laughed. "Fat chance."

He didn't know how rich she was. It was going to be a hard thing to have to tell him. Maybe she should do it now.

"Butch, there's something I need to tell you, something about Mama, and about me," she began reluctantly.

The only answer she got was a mild snoring sound. She lifted up so that she could see his face. He'd gone to sleep. She sighed and sank back down against him. "Well, maybe I can tell you later," she murmured softly to herself. And she drifted off into sleep as well.

J. L. Denton's attorneys lived up to their excellent reputation. They arrived in Benton two days later, loaded for bear. Esther already knew the attorney she'd spoken to, Mr. Frazier. But this time there was another attorney with him, one belonging to the same law firm, and he made Esther uncomfortable. Not that Edward Thornton was unkind. He was simply taciturn, and his pale silver eyes made her nervous.

"Don't let Thorn intimidate you," Mr. Frazier chuckled. "He's hell in a courtroom, but he's mostly kind when he isn't doing a summation."

"Nice to meet you, Mr. Thornton," Esther said gently, and lifted a hand.

He shook it gently and gave it back. "Where can we sit to discuss our findings?" he asked at once. "And do you want to call your husband so that he can share the news?"

"Mr. Thornton," she said in a low tone of voice, "my husband thinks I'm the daughter of a wealthy woman and I'm hiding from my mother's boyfriend. He doesn't know how wealthy my family is." Her face went hard. "He won't take it well, I can tell you that. So it's better if you just talk to me."

"Very well," Mr. Frazier returned gently. "Now. On to Darrin Ross. A friend of his fenced four very valuable fur coats through a shady acquaintance. The guy who fenced them is known to the Aspen police, and they arrested him for theft. Afraid of going back to jail again, he gave them Darrin's name. So Mr. Ross is sitting in the Aspen jail biding his time until his attorneys can find some way to get him out."

"He'll need money for those attorneys," she said quietly. "And he knows about the ring I wear. Most people think it's paste." She held it out for them to see. "It was valued at several million dollars by the jewelry firm where my mother bought it. Darrin knows about its worth. Mr. Cameron gave it a great deal of scrutiny." She looked up at them. "I should have taken it off and put it in a safe deposit box, but it was the last thing my mother gave me, before she died . . ." She choked up and had to take a minute to get the pain out of her voice.

"If he saw it, someone may try to come and get it for him," Mr. Thornton said quietly. "It would easily pay all his legal fees."

Esther's blue eyes sparked. "He's not getting it. Not if I have to take it out in the woods and bury it somewhere!" She looked worried. "I've put my husband in the line of fire. I couldn't bear it if he got hurt because of me. I love him so much!"

"We won't tell him," Mr. Frazier promised. "But you have to keep the doors locked all the time, even during the day. And be careful where you go. Take your husband with you when you go to work or come home."

"Butch takes me to work and comes to get me," she assured them. "And he's always armed. Poachers and such people can be very dangerous. Butch is a cautious man."

"So he is. Now. Let's go over the case again," Mr. Frazier said, changing the subject.

He wanted to know about the will, how Darrin had behaved just before and just after Terry died. She told them in a choked little voice, about Darrin picking up Terry and hurling her headfirst down the long winding staircase at the Aspen house. She told them of her wild flight, and how she'd ended up in Benton and later married the man who'd saved her life.

"He's such a good man," she told the attorneys, and she was beaming with happiness. "I'd go crazy if I ever lost him." She gave them a sad look from big blue eyes. "He'll have to know what's going on sooner or later. When he finds out what I'm worth, he'll leave me."

"Why? I know I asked you before, but please repeat the reason you think that," Mr. Frazier asked gently.

She sighed and smiled. "I told him there were a few stocks and bonds that we could give to our children. He said that was great because he didn't want to be Mr. Esther Marist," she told them flatly.

Mr. Frazier sighed as well. "There are ways around that, Mrs. Matthews," he replied. "In fact, you could leave what you inherit in a trust for your children, when they come along, and just let the stocks and bonds remain in the hands of your investment broker."

"That would be a fine solution. But what about my mother's bank accounts, and the jewelry she had in the safe deposit box?"

"Your mother's lover might already have that."

She shook her head. "Mama never told him about it. I've carried around a key to it for the past few years. It was something Mama never shared with any of her lovers. She didn't want to be taken advantage of, you see."

"That was wise," Mr. Thornton agreed.

"So Darrin couldn't get to the jewelry and our statements from the broker and the amount of cash she stowed there for emergencies. He doesn't even know which bank the safe deposit box is in," she added with a quiet smile.

"Well, it will keep him busy looking for it, I imagine," Mr. Thornton said, "but I think he has bigger problems than that. He's just about to be charged with first degree murder. One of our criminal attorneys is handling the case for us. He's already out with an investigator—a real one," he added with a twinkle in his eyes, "looking for the witnesses that he swears will point to you as the murderer. This should be very interesting. We're also interviewing people." He smiled smugly. He didn't share why.

"What if they come and arrest me?" Esther asked, frightened.

"They won't arrest you," he promised. "You have to trust us, Mrs. Matthews. This isn't our first walk around the courtroom."

"You sound very certain of that," she replied warily.

He smiled. "I am."

She drew in a breath. "Okay, then. You'll keep me posted, about what's going on?" she added as they started to leave.

"You may count on that," Mr. Thornton told her.

Later, when they were curled up in bed together, Esther hinted about her mother's estate and what Darrin was actually after.

"You said that your mother just had a few stocks and bonds," Butch began.

She drew in a breath. "Yes," she said, retreating. He didn't sound encouraging. "A few minor ones, here and there."

“Then why are the lawyers worried that your mother’s boyfriend might send someone down here after you?”

She thought fast. “The will,” she said.

“Oh. I see.”

She felt him relax. She moved closer with a sigh, resting her cheek on his chest. “That was all I was worried . . . about . . . oh, dear . . . !”

She was on her feet and running for the bathroom. She barely made it. She lost her supper, her lunch—even, apparently, her breakfast.

Butch was right there with her the whole time, a wet washcloth held in his hand to mop her up afterwards.

He kept a strong arm around her, back to the bedroom and eased her onto the bed, dropping down beside her.

He looked very sexy in the soft light of the lamp. Even when she felt nauseated, he was deliciously attractive to her.

She laughed softly. “Even when I’m sick, you’re soooo sexy, Mr. Matthews,” she teased weakly.

He wasn’t laughing. She had the wet cloth over her eyes when she felt his big hand rest lightly above her flat stomach.

She moved the cloth away, her eyes suddenly glued to his pale face. He looked . . . she couldn’t decide how he looked.

Her breath drew in sharply. “Do you think . . . ?” she faltered.

“My God.” He wasn’t swearing. His voice held an odd reverence. His big hand smoothed so tenderly over her stomach. He looked up at her, and there was wonder in his eyes, in his face.

She relaxed. She smiled. She beamed. She laughed with pure joy.

He slid down next to her and cradled her tenderly

against him. “Oh, glory,” he whispered into her hair. “Daddy Matthews.”

She laughed again. “Mommy Matthews.”

He nuzzled his face against hers. “We’ll have to start thinking about names and a good college, and when she’ll get married,” he began.

“When he’ll get married. I want a boy,” she said. “And he has to look just like you!”

He fought tears. His life had been empty, cold, almost savage. Now, suddenly, he was part of a family. He loved it. He wished he could put it into words. He didn’t know how.

“Life takes things away from you. Then God gives them back, in the sweetest way,” he whispered.

Her arms tightened around his neck. “I’m glad you aren’t angry.”

“Angry!” He lifted his head and looked down at her. “I’ve just won the lottery. Hit the jackpot. Climbed Mt. Everest.” He looked down at her stomach, concealed by the pretty, thin, blue lacy nightgown she was wearing. “Glimpsed heaven,” he added reverently.

She sighed, lying back on the pillow. “It might be a false alarm,” she said, and looked worried.

He pursed his lips. “When was your last period?” he asked.

She started, because she hadn’t been keeping track at all. She counted. Her eyes widened. “Six weeks!” she exclaimed.

“Almost to the day we married,” he chuckled.

“Wow.”

“Double wow,” he murmured. “You don’t mind? We haven’t been married long.”

“I don’t mind at all,” she said dreamily. “I never wanted to travel the world or become famous in a profession. I just wanted a man to love, who was a good man, and children, and a real home where I wasn't moved around every month to someplace else." She looked up at him with wonder. "And I found it all, right here, almost overnight."

He bent and kissed her eyelids shut. "So did I. You're my whole life. If I lost you, I couldn't go on," he said huskily.

Her arms tightened around his neck. "You'll never lose me," she said fervently. "No matter what! I promise!"

But life has twists and turns, and fate isn't always kind. Or so it seemed. A few days after Esther had been to the doctor for a blood test and had her pregnancy confirmed, a tall, dignified man in a very expensive suit, with a silver-topped cane, walked into the Gray Dove and asked if a woman named Esther Marist worked there.

Esther was called out of the kitchen, where she'd been helping the cook clean up a minor disaster on the grill.

She stared at the old man, frowning curiously. He seemed to be doing the same, his face bland and his blue eyes blazing. For a few seconds, she was afraid he was one of Darrin's friends.

"I'm Esther," she said hesitantly.

The old man let out a sigh. He moved closer. "Yes, you look like your mother." His blue eyes filmed for just a few seconds and he looked away, clearing his throat. "I don't suppose she spoke of me."

"I'm sorry, sir, but who are you?" Esther asked.

He turned back to her. "I'm Blalock Cranston. Your mother's father. Your grandfather."

She bit her lower lip. She'd thought her whole family was dead, that she had nobody left. And here was the grandfather she'd never known. Tears bled from her eyes.

The old man moved closer, hesitantly, just as Esther flung herself into his arms and bawled.

Luckily, it was midmorning, and only a couple of cowboys were in the restaurant. But Esther wouldn't have cared if it had been full. She'd never been so happy, not since she'd married Butch.

"My girl," the old man choked. "I'm so happy . . . to have found you, at last. Some attorney from here called me. I was on my estate in Jamaica. I had my pilot fly me right over. Damned hard, finding this little town on any map, but the driver I hired seemed to know right where it was." He drew away. "I'm so sorry. I had no idea what sort of trouble your mother was in. We lost touch many years ago." He grimaced. "I didn't know your father, Esther. If I had, well, a lot of misery could have been avoided. I found out many things about his life, after he was gone. He must have been a fine man. The fact that he didn't come from a founding family shouldn't have mattered. Not at all."

She managed a smile. "He was a wonderful father. I mourned him. I still do." She looked up at the old man. "I'm married, you know. He isn't from a founding family, either, but he's a good and kind man and he loves animals."

He smiled back. "And that's not a bad reference."

"He loves children, too, which is a good thing." Her hand flattened against her stomach. "Because we're pregnant. We only found out for certain a couple of days ago." She laughed. "So you'll be a great-grandfather!"

He didn't look displeased at all. He patted her on the shoulder. "I'll try to be a better grandfather than I was a father," he promised. "I'd love to meet your husband."

"He comes in for lunch," she said, "every day."

"Then I'll be back for lunch. We have many things to talk about." He leaned down so that they couldn't be overheard.

"Your mother's murderer is in a passel of trouble, and his friends have all deserted him. So the lawyers think he's without means to pursue that will your mother left you."

"Oh, I hope so," she said fervently. "If they came after me, they might hurt Butch. He's a war veteran," she added quietly. "He lost an arm overseas, but it doesn't even slow him down. He's a licensed wildlife rehabilitator."

"A brave man," he replied. "I served in Vietnam. Seems like a hundred years ago," he added, and there was a bleakness about his expression. "So. I'll see you both at lunchtime!"

She grinned. "That's a date!"

The owner of the café and the cook and the other waitress gathered around her excitedly when the old man left to climb into a stretch limousine that was parked at the curb.

"Who is he?!" they exclaimed.

"My grandfather!" Esther told them. "I thought he was dead. I didn't even know who he was! It's just so exciting!"

They all laughed. "Well, he seems to be a gentleman of property, if that's the right phrase," the owner teased.

Esther hesitated. "He has an estate in Jamaica, and I believe he's very wealthy. Oh, dear, what am I going to tell Butch?" she wailed.

"Listen, he loves you. He's not going to say anything," the cook said.

"Absolutely," the waitress agreed.

The owner just smiled gently.

Butch was full of news when he came in to sit at his normal booth right near the door of the restaurant.

"I'm getting a raise," he said. "And just in time! Now

we can go shopping for baby furniture . . . what's wrong, honey?" he asked abruptly, because she looked forlorn.

She moved closer, with her pad out, but nobody was close enough to hear. "My grandfather's in town."

"He is?" Butch smiled. "So you do have a little family left, don't you, honey girl?" He caught her other hand and squeezed it gently. His dark eyes were bright with joy. "He'll be our baby's great-grandfather. Did you tell him?"

She nodded.

"Is he nice? Do you like him?"

She took a deep breath. "About that . . ."

"Well, would you look at that?" one of the cowboys remarked loudly as a big black limousine pulled up at the curb. "Must be some rock star in town to film a video. Or maybe a Mafia don." He chuckled.

Esther ground her teeth together.

"What's wrong, honey?" Butch asked, worried when he saw her expression. He looked toward the door, where a tall, silver-haired gentleman walking with a cane came into the restaurant, looked at Esther, and smiled as he approached them.

"Esther, who is that?" Butch whispered.

She drew in a deep breath as the old man joined them. "Butch, this is my grandfather, Blalock Cranston. Grandad, this is my husband, Butch Matthews."

Then she waited for the explosion.

Chapter Eight

To say that Butch was dumbfounded was an understatement. It didn't take psychic abilities to figure out that the man who'd climbed out of the stretch limo was loaded. The fancy suit, silk shirt, expensive shoes said it all.

Butch looked blankly at his wife.

"So you're my new grandson-in-law," the old man said, smiling as he held out a hand that Butch shook. "Glad to meet you. Very glad. And I hear I'm to be a great-grandfather! Congratulations!"

Butch shifted his shocked eyes to Esther's taut face and moved them back to the old man's. He felt as if he'd been clubbed. "Sure. Nice to meet you, too. Won't you sit down?" he asked, remembering his manners.

"Thanks." The old man grimaced, leaning the cane in the booth beside him as he sat. "Damned leg still gives me fits. I got caught by one of those miserable bamboo traps they laid in Vietnam. Damned near lost the leg, but I told them I'd live with it or die with it, but they weren't taking it off." He sighed. "They didn't listen. But the artificial one works fine. The joint kills me in cold weather, though, which is why I live in Jamaica."

Butch lost the shock and looked at the other man with new eyes. "Where were you stationed?"

"Da Nang," came the quiet reply. "I was there during the Tet Offensive, if you read history. My unit was sent out on a scouting mission and we ran into booby traps. I was the only survivor. Got sent home. I yelled the whole way, cursed everybody I could think of, but they wouldn't let me go back." His eyes were sad. "I lost my best friend, and two guys who'd been in the same boot camp with me. War is hell. Truly hell."

"Yes, it is," Butch agreed solemnly. "I got hit by mortar fire. My best friend ran through gunfire and carried me to safety. He came home with me. A lot of other guys didn't."

"At least we lived, yes?" The old man chuckled. "And that's not a bad thing."

Butch smiled. "Not a bad thing at all."

"Well, I'm here with news," the old man said. "The attorneys who tracked me down are the ones working to put your mother's so-called boyfriend in the jailhouse for the next lifetime or two. Which brings to mind a technical detail. Do you have your mother's will?"

"Oh, yes," Esther said.

"And you've still got that damned ring I gave her," he added, his eyes on her slender fingers. His eyes teared up and he averted them. "She never took it off."

"I haven't, either. I suppose I shouldn't have been wearing it all this time. Darrin's cohort saw it, when he was here posing as an investigator."

"Why is the ring a concern?" Butch asked curiously. "It's just paste . . ."

"Paste?" the old man asked, astounded. "It's worth millions."

The blood drained out of Butch's face.

Esther tried to stop her grandfather, but he was like a car with the accelerator stuck. "Terry owned property and stocks worth almost two hundred million," he continued. "We can't find Darrin, but there's a rumor that he found somebody to forge a new will."

"Why would he do that?" Esther asked. "Oh," she said after a few seconds. "He doesn't know I've got Mama's, unless Mr. Cameron told him."

"Exactly. Hopefully, Cameron didn't have a chance to tell him," the old man said. He sighed. "My poor little girl. She never had much sense about men. Except for your father. I'm sorry I never gave him a chance, girl, sorry I fouled everything up for him."

"You didn't know him," Esther said, her eyes worried as they were riveted to Butch's hard, blank features.

"You have to understand. Your mother was wild even as a teenager. Her mother tried so hard." He sighed. "She was a good woman. She never knew how to handle Terry. Neither did I. I suppose we didn't want to face the fact that she had psychological issues, not until it was far too late. By then, we couldn't convince her that she needed a psychologist."

Esther stared at him. "Psychologist," she echoed.

"Yes. She had an addiction to men. We didn't realize that such things existed. I suppose my wife and I were stuck in the Dark Ages. We moved to Jamaica and lived out in the sticks, where we didn't have much contact with the modern world."

"Isn't it dangerous over there?"

"No more so than here," he said simply. "My family has owned the house there for four generations. We have bananas and cashew nuts and all sorts of tropical fruit. You and your husband should come over and stay with me for a while. You'd love it."

"That would be hard. Butch works for the wildlife service," she said.

"I'd forgotten. Well, he won't need to work once the will's through probate. Speaking of which, you have to come with me to Aspen," her grandfather added. "And don't worry about Darrin. I brought two bodyguards with me. One drives, the other rides shotgun." His eyes, so like her mother's, were like blue flames. "Nobody's hurting my granddaughter."

"Darrin had a contact on the police force . . ."

"Not anymore," her grandfather said. "And most of his cronies are facing prosecution for various and sundry crimes. I've had two investigators on the job. One of them's like a shark. He never quits."

Esther was unsettled. Butch still hadn't said a word. And customers were starting to come in.

"I have to go back to work," Esther said. "I'll talk to my boss about getting off. When do you want me to go with you?"

"Tomorrow. Let's get this thing settled. Are you coming with us?" he asked Butch.

Butch just stared at him blankly.

"We'll talk about that tonight," Esther said quickly. "Are you staying in town?"

"Yes, at the motel." He named it. "I'll give you my cell phone number before I leave here. Now. Since you're working here, I assume that the food must be excellent." He smiled at her. "So what do you recommend?"

* * *

Butch excused himself to go back to work after a meal with stilted conversation. He'd had the shock of his life. He didn't know what to do. He'd expected to live with Esther and have their child grow up in his cabin, the two of them making ends meet, but frugally. And she was wearing a ring that was worth more than every penny he'd make for the rest of his life. He was shellshocked.

"Try not to let this ruin your marriage," the old man said to Butch before he left. "I know it's a shock. But it's not Esther's fault. She can't help the circumstances of her birth. She loves you. She's carrying your child. Don't turn your back on her over money, son," he said gently. "It's so unimportant in the scheme of things."

"Unimportant if you have it," Butch said.

"My wife's parents were caretakers," the old man said. "We had our own hard time when she found out what I was worth. It took me months, but I finally convinced her that she'd be happier with me and the money than she would all by herself."

Butch couldn't find the words. He just looked at the other man.

"Give it time," he advised. "It's like a fresh wound right now. Let it heal for a day or two and then take another look at your situation. It really boils down to this. Is your pride worth more to you than Esther?" He got up, patting the younger man on the shoulder. "And don't worry about her. I won't let anything happen to her. But we can't let Darrin take away everything her mother had without fighting back. The man killed my daughter," he added, and his blue eyes glittered. "He'll pay for it."

"I'm sorry about your daughter," Butch said, finally finding his voice.

"I'm sorry that I had to disrupt your life," the old man

replied. "Things happen. But it's how we react to them that matters. Esther will keep in touch with you while we're away."

Butch managed a smile and nodded as he got up. The old man noted that he took his own slip to the counter to pay for his meal. Esther's grandfather wouldn't have tried to pick up the tab. Butch and his pride were going to have some conflicts before this was over, but he was certain that the man loved his granddaughter enough to overcome the obstacles. What Esther felt was more than obvious. They'd manage.

Esther waited on the curb for Butch to pick her up. He was late—a first, because he'd never been late before. He got out of the truck and helped her into the passenger seat before he got back in and drove them away.

He didn't say a word all the way home. Esther tried to make conversation, but it was so difficult that she finally just gave up and sat quietly beside him until they reached the cabin. He helped her out and went ahead to unlock the door.

"I'll get supper," she said.

He glanced at her. "I'll need to feed the animals out back."

He went out. She changed out of her uniform into slacks and a loose blouse and went into the kitchen to find something to cook.

By the time he came back, she had a nice omelet and fresh biscuits on the table, along with perfectly cooked bacon.

"Please notice that the biscuits don't bounce," she said, trying to lighten the atmosphere at the table.

He didn't seem to notice. He finished his meal and turned on the television set, intent on the news.

Esther cleared the table and washed dishes. One of their future purchases was going to be a dishwasher. She didn't dare mention it now.

She sat and worked on a crossword puzzle, watching him covertly while he settled down with a documentary program after the news went off.

He still hadn't said a word.

When he turned off the television, she just looked up at him with sad eyes. "Do you want me to leave?" she asked.

"If you like," he said. His voice was flat. He looked around. "You're used to crystal and silver and probably half a dozen people to keep up the houses your mother owned. What a hell of a comedown this must have been."

"Actually, I spent most of my life avoiding my mother's boyfriends. I had our housekeeper, Agnes, to make my birthdays special and fix presents for me at Christmas. I don't remember my mother ever being home for any holiday at all." She averted her eyes. "It isn't where you live, Butch. It's how you live, the people you live with, that make it a home. I'm happier here in Benton than I've been anywhere in my life. I don't expect you to believe that." She shook her head. "I should have told you the truth at the very beginning. But you were so kind." Her blue eyes lifted to his cold, dark ones. "I'd never had kindness from a man, or real affection. It was . . . like magic."

He felt guilty. But only for a few seconds. She was rich and he was poor. His pride couldn't get past that. How could any man live with it?

"I'm sorry," he said. He shrugged. "Sometimes relationships just don't work out."

"I'm pregnant," she pointed out.

He swallowed. Hard. "Well, it's early days yet," he said, biting down hard on the agony it cost him to say that. "If you want to do something about it . . ."

She got up from her chair, walked past him into the bedroom, and started filling a duffel bag with her few items of clothing.

He watched her, his mind on fire with doubts and aching loneliness. She was going away, and he'd forced her into that decision. Him, with his pride and his insecurities.

"Your grandfather said to give it a few days," he said curtly.

"Sure. We'll give it a few days." She was furious and trying not to show it. She put the last of her few possessions into the bag and walked back into the dining room. She had her grandfather's phone number. She pushed it in on her cell phone. When he answered, she asked if his car had GPS and when he said it did, she gave him the address. "Can you come get me right now?" she asked, fighting tears.

There was a long sigh. "I can. I'm so sorry, honey."

She lifted her face and looked at Butch, who was quiet and solemn. "Fortunes of war," she said into the receiver, and hung up.

Her grandfather got her a room of her own, next to his, and introduced her to his two bodyguards. They weren't big, brutish guys. One was slender with blond hair and pale eyes, the other was dark with broad shoulders and a cowboy's lankiness. They shook hands with polite smiles and promised to keep her out of harm's way.

"Your husband couldn't face it, I gather?" her grandfather asked quietly.

She didn't speak. She just shook her head.

"Well, we'll manage," he said after a minute.

She almost strangled on her next words. "He said it was all right if I wanted to do something about the baby."

The older man put his arms around her and let her cry. "Men say terrible things when they're upset," he said. "I'm sure he didn't mean it."

She wasn't sure. But it didn't matter. "I'm not giving up my baby," she said shortly. "He doesn't even have to see it. I'll . . . I'll go someplace and live where he won't ever see me again."

"Oh, that's easy," he said gently. "You'll come home with me."

She smiled weakly. "Okay."

He sighed. He'd lost his daughter years ago, but it was almost like having her back. He'd take care of Esther and her child, and maybe it would make up, just a little, for the misery he'd caused Terry by shutting her out of his life when she married Esther's father. He'd failed Terry. He wasn't about to fail Esther.

Darrin had hired a man to get to Esther and kill her, if possible. He had a brand-new will that was forged but looked legitimate.

When the old man showed up with Esther in Aspen, and with the legitimate will, everything was quickly over for the murderer of Terry Marist. It made all the best news shows. It was a big story, a celebrity murder, an estranged wealthy father, a daughter who was press-shy and kept well away from reporters.

Back in Benton, Butch watched the story play out in the news. His heart ached. He was alone again. He missed Esther. He was furious with himself for what he'd said to her, the way he'd treated her. He'd invited her to get rid of their child. Probably she had, thinking her idiot husband didn't love her or want her because she had more money than he did.

He really hated himself. How much became apparent when he didn't show up for work three days in a row and his best friend, Parker, came looking for him.

Parker found Butch so drunk that he couldn't even get words out of him. He set to work, cleaning up the cabin and then cleaning up, and sobering up, Butch.

After a pot of coffee, Butch was a little more lucid. "She's in Aspen, facing that trial all alone, and I'm up here feeling sorry for myself. She'll never speak to me again, and I deserve it. We were going to have a baby . . ." He almost choked on the coffee. His voice broke and he had to fight to steady it. "I told her it was okay with me if she didn't want it . . ."

"My God," Parker said heavily. "No wonder you got drunk."

"She's worth millions," Butch said through his teeth. "I work for wages."

"If she loves you, and you love her, what's the problem?"

"I just told you," Butch said belligerently. "She's worth millions and I work for wages."

"So have her put all the money into a trust for the kids and go back to work at the Gray Dove restaurant."

"I can't ask an heiress to wait tables!"

"You never asked her to in the first place," Parker pointed out. "She offered." He smiled. "She loves you."

"She did."

"Trust me, love doesn't wear out just because you have a fight. And I'd know," he added tongue in cheek.

Butch chuckled. "Yeah. I guess so."

"If they haven't fired you for laying off work, why don't you take some of that vacation time you never use and go to Aspen?"

"Oh, sure. Go hat in hand to the door of a mansion dressed like this." He indicated his jeans and flannel shirt.

Parker sighed. "You could call her, you know."

Butch stared at the floor. "She blocked my number." His shoulders moved. "That's why I got drunk."

Parker didn't know what to say. He felt bad for his friend. He wished he knew a way to help him. "I could use some more coffee," he said after a minute.

"I'll go make some," Butch volunteered.

While he was out of the room, Parker took Butch's cell phone and copied Esther's phone number off it. By the time Butch came back, with more coffee, the phone was right where he'd left it, with Butch none the wiser.

"Oh. Hi, Parker," Esther stammered when her unexpected caller identified himself. She didn't usually answer unknown numbers, but she was expecting a call from one of her mother's attorneys.

"Hi, yourself. How's it going?" he asked.

"Well, they've got Darrin in jail, along with that Cameron man, and he's been arraigned. The trial won't come up for several months. In the meanwhile, I've got lawyers trying to straighten out the mess Mother left. I never knew finances could be so complicated." She hesitated. "How's Butch?"

"Drunk."

The single word was shocking. "But he doesn't drink," she said. "He doesn't even keep liquor in the cabin."

"Oh, he bought some," Parker replied pleasantly. "About four fifths of whiskey, actually. He spent several hours throwing up after I found him. He's almost sober now."

"Almost."

"Yeah. His butt's real sore."

"Why?"

"He's been kicking it. Well, metaphorically," he added. "He hates himself for the things he said to you."

"He might have said so," she muttered.

"He said you blocked his number."

She took a sharp breath. "That was just after I left," she said sadly. "I unblocked it . . . He tried to call me?"

"Yeah. That's why he started drinking."

She winced. "He said I didn't have to have the baby," she choked.

"That's why he's kicking himself."

"Oh."

"You might call him. He's pretty broken up. Pride's a damned silly thing, you know. I told him you could just put all the money in trust for your kids and grandkids and go back to work at the Gray Dove."

"What did he say to that?"

"That you probably wouldn't want to wait tables anymore, or ever see him again."

"Idiot."

"Yeah. That's what I called him, too."

She hesitated. "You know, I could really put it in a trust. I could give away a lot of it, too. My grandfather's absolutely loaded. He doesn't need it. And I like waitressing."

"You could tell Butch that. He might stop drinking."

She smiled to herself. It was the first time she had, since the turmoil had started.

"Think about it," he told her. "And don't tell him I called you, okay? He's my best friend, but he might not like it that I stole your number out of his phone without telling him."

"I won't say a word," she promised. "Thanks, Parker."

"You're welcome!"

It took a little time to get the will through probate. The first thing Esther did was to track down Agnes and give her a pension. Their reunion was sweet, especially when Agnes was told about the baby. Esther promised that she'd be invited to the christening, and she'd send a private jet and a limo to transport her. Agnes was sad about Terry, but she adored Esther and was only happy to have her back again in her lonely life, at least.

Esther's second discovery was the whereabouts of Jack and Glenda Johnson. She found them outside Aspen, where they worked for a trucking concern. She promptly bought them their own private trucking business.

"But you don't need to do this," they both protested when she found them and promised to set them up with their own trucks and a handful of truckers to help haul cargo. They were shellshocked to learn who their mysterious passenger was that night in the past. They were more shocked at the way she repaid them.

She just laughed. "I owe you two so much. I'm married. And pregnant. And so happy. I would never have made it out of Aspen without you two. So just hush. I'm not doing it solely for gratitude." Her face pulled into a mischievous smile. "I have a favor to ask!"

Butch was miserable. He'd been on his own far too long. He'd tried to call Esther, but he'd only gotten a message that her phone wasn't available and after one try, he'd assumed the number was still blocked and he'd given up.

Life was a misery. He was too proud to go to Aspen begging, and too miserable to do much else. He and Two-Toes had the cabin to themselves. Even the wolf looked sad.

It was snowing again. It was the weekend and he was by himself. Parker, the fink, had taken away his last bottle of whiskey, so he didn't even have a way to drown his sorrows.

He listened idly to the weather report while his ears picked up the sound of traffic on the highway. He heard the sound of airbrakes, like on a big rig, and then gears shifting as the truck went along. Probably hit a slick spot, he thought to himself, and went back to the weather.

There was a knock on the door. Probably Parker, keeping an eye on him, he thought absently. He'd been a good friend. Well, except for taking away his liquor.

He opened the door and his heart dropped into his boots. She was wearing a blue fox jacket and dark slacks and a silk blouse, almost the exact things she'd had on when they first met, when he found her outside his cabin.

"I'm all alone and I have no place to go," Esther said, her heart racing. "I'm looking for some cousins of mine that live here; the Crump family."

"No Crumps here, I'm afraid," he said huskily. "Would you settle for a miserable husband and a handicapped wolf?"

She smiled.

He smiled.

He held out his arms and she ran into them, bawling as he closed the door and shut them into the pleasant warmth of the cabin.

"I'm sorry. I'm so damned sorry," he murmured into her hair as he held her. "I've been a fool!"

"I'm sorry, too. I should have told you the truth, but I thought you wouldn't want me."

"I want you," he whispered. "For the rest of my life!" He drew back and he looked agonized. "The baby . . . ?"

She gave him a sardonic look. "Am I the sort of woman who would do that?"

He relaxed. "No."

She linked her arms around his neck. "My mother's attorneys are working on a trust. The money will go to our children and grandchildren—and probably our great-grandchildren," she added with a laugh. "Meanwhile, I'll go hat in hand and beg for my job back. After all, every penny counts."

"God, I love you," he murmured against her mouth.

She smiled under the devouring kiss. "I love you, too," she whispered.

On the floor beside them, a contented old wolf lay down with his head on his paws and closed his eyes.

* * *

Darrin Ross went to prison, for such a nice number of years that the Matthews' firstborn would have gray hair before he got out. Esther's grandfather came to visit from time to time and coaxed them into coming to Jamaica on gift tickets so he could see his great-grandson and two great-granddaughters more often.

When he passed away, and was mourned by his family, his bequest was a shock to his attorneys and his granddaughter. Because he left his entire estate to Butch.

"Well, darn it," Esther said after the will was read.

"What?" Butch asked, still poleaxed, and deeply touched

"Honey, everybody will think I married you for your money," she said.

He laughed. "Your grandfather would laugh himself sick."

"I'll bet you that he's already doing that, and having a wonderful reunion with my grandmother and my mother," she added.

He drew her close. "I won't take that bet. What a hell of a sweet thing to do."

"He was a sweet man," she replied. "And he was very fond of you."

"Daddy's rich," their son, John, said when they told him.

His sisters were just a little too young to understand that.

"Daddy's sort of rich," Butch said, picking up the little boy with a chuckle. "But that's only with money. Daddy's much richer in love."

"Love is worth more than money," Esther agreed, hugging her husband. "Far, far more."

Butch just kissed her. And that was enough.

Please turn the page for an exciting peek at:

THE SNOW MAN

by
Diana Palmer

Meadow Dawson just stared at the slim, older cowboy who was standing on her front porch with his hat held against his chest. His name was Ted. He was her father's ranch foreman. And he was speaking Greek, she decided, or perhaps some form of archaic language that she couldn't understand.

"The culls," he persisted. "Mr. Jake wanted us to go ahead and ship them out to that rancher we bought the replacement heifers from."

She blinked. She knew three stances that she could use to shoot a .40 caliber Glock from. She was experienced in interrogation techniques. She'd once participated in a drug raid with other agents from the St. Louis, Missouri, office where she'd been stationed during her brief tenure with the FBI as a special agent.

Sadly, none of those experiences had taught her what a cull was, or what to do with it. She pushed back her long, golden blond hair, and her pale green eyes narrowed on his elderly face.

She blinked. "Are culls some form of wildlife?" she asked blankly.

The cowboy doubled up laughing.

She grimaced. Her father and mother had divorced when she was six. She'd gone to live with her mother in Greenwood, Mississippi, while her father stayed here on this enormous Colorado ranch, just outside Raven Springs. Later, she'd spent some holidays with her dad, but only after she was in her senior year of high school and she could out-argue her bitter mother, who hated her ex-husband. What she remembered about cattle was that they were loud and dusty. She really hadn't paid much attention to the cattle on the ranch or her father's infrequent references to ranching problems. She hadn't been there often enough to learn the ropes.

"I worked for the FBI," she said with faint belligerence. "I don't know anything about cattle."

He straightened up. "Sorry, ma'am," he said, still fighting laughter. "Culls are cows that didn't drop calves this spring. Nonproductive cattle are removed from the herd, or culled. We sell them either as beef or surrogate mothers for purebred cattle."

She nodded and tried to look intelligent. "I see." She hesitated. "So we're punishing poor female cattle for not being able to have calves repeatedly over a period of years."

The cowboy's face hardened. "Ma'am, can I give you some friendly advice about ranch management?"

She shrugged. "Okay."

"I think you'd be doing yourself a favor if you sold this ranch," he said bluntly. "It's hard to make a living at ranching, even if you've done it for years. It would be a sin and a shame to let all your father's hard work go to pot. Begging your pardon, ma'am," he added respectfully. "Dal Blake was friends with your father, and he owns the biggest ranch around Raven Springs. Might be worthwhile to talk to him."

Meadow managed a smile through homicidal rage. "Dariell Blake and I don't speak," she informed him.

"Ma'am?" The cowboy sounded surprised.

"He told my father that I'd turned into a manly woman who probably didn't even have . . ." She bit down hard on the word she couldn't bring herself to voice. "Anyway," she added tersely, "he can keep his outdated opinions to himself."

The cowboy grimaced. "Sorry."

"Not your fault," she said, and managed a smile. "Thanks for the advice, though. I think I'll go online and watch a few YouTube videos on cattle management. I might call one of those men, or women, for advice."

The cowboy opened his mouth to speak, thought about how scarce jobs were, and closed it again. "Whatever you say, ma'am." He put his hat back on. "I'll just get back to work. It's, uh, okay to ship out the culls?"

"Of course it's all right," she said, frowning. "Why wouldn't it be?"

"You said it oppressed the cows . . ."

She rolled her eyes. "I was kidding!"

"Oh." Ted brightened a little. He tilted his hat respectfully and went away.

Meadow went back into the house and felt empty. She and her father had been close. He loved his ranch and his daughter. Getting to know her as an adult had been great fun for both of them. Her mother had kept the tension going as long as she lived. She never would believe that Meadow could love her and her ex-husband equally. But Meadow did. They were both wonderful people. They just couldn't live together without arguing.

She ran her fingers over the back of the cane-bottomed rocking chair where her father always sat, near the big stone fireplace. It was November, and Colorado was cold. Heavy snow was already falling. Meadow remembered Colorado winters from her childhood, before her parents divorced. It was going to be difficult to manage payroll, much less all the little added extras she'd need, like food and electricity . . .

She shook herself mentally. She'd manage, somehow. And she'd do it without Dariell Blake's help. She could only imagine the smug, self-righteous expression that would come into those chiseled features if she asked him to teach her cattle ranching. She'd rather starve. Well, not really.

She considered her options, and there weren't many. Her father owned this ranch outright. He owed for farm equipment, like combines to harvest grain crops and tractors to help with planting. He owed for feed and branding supplies and things like that. But the land was hers now, free and clear. There was a lot of land. It was worth millions.

She could have sold it and started over. But he'd made her promise not to. He'd known her very well by then. She never made a promise she didn't keep. Her own sense of ethics locked her into a position she hated. She didn't know anything about ranching!

Her father mentioned Dariell, whom everyone locally called Dal, all the time. Fine young man, he commented. Full of pepper, good disposition, loves animals.

The loving animals part was becoming a problem. She had a beautiful white Siberian husky, a rescue, with just a hint of red-tipped fur in her ears and tail. She was named Snow, and Meadow had fought the authorities to keep her in her small apartment. She was immaculate, and Meadow brushed her and bathed her faithfully. Finally the apartment manager had given in, reluctantly, after Meadow offered a sizable deposit for the apartment, which was close to her work. She made friends with a lab tech in the next-door apartment, who kept Snow when Meadow had to travel for work. It was a nice arrangement, except that the lab tech really liked Meadow, who didn't return the admiration. While kind and sweet, the tech did absolutely nothing for Meadow physically or emotionally.

She wondered sometimes if she was really cold. Men were nice. She dated. She'd even indulged in light petting with one of them. But she didn't feel the sense of need that made women marry and settle and have kids with a man. Most of the ones she'd dated were career oriented and didn't want marriage in the first place. Meadow's mother had been devout. Meadow grew up with deep religious beliefs that were in constant conflict with society's norms.

She kept to herself mostly. She'd loved her job when she started as an investigator for the Bureau. But there had been a minor slipup.

Meadow was clumsy. There was no other way to put it. She had two left feet, and she was always falling down or doing things the wrong way. It was a curse. Her mother had named her Meadow because she was reading a novel at the time and the heroine had that name. The heroine had been gentle and sweet and a credit to the community where she lived, in 1900s Fort Worth, Texas. Meadow, sadly, was nothing like her namesake.

There had been a stakeout. Meadow had been assigned, with another special agent, to keep tabs on a criminal who'd shot a police officer. The officer lived, but the man responsible was facing felony charges, and he ran.

A CI, or Confidential Informant, had told them where the man was likely to be on a Friday night. It was a local club, frequented by people who were out of the mainstream of society.

Meadow had been assigned to watch the back door while the other special agent went through the front of the club and tried to spot him.

Sure enough, the man was there. The other agent was recognized by a patron, who warned the perpetrator. The criminal took off out the back door.

While Meadow was trying to get her gun out of the holster, the fugitive ran into her and they both tumbled onto the ground.

"Clumsy cow!" he exclaimed. He turned her over and pushed her face hard into the asphalt of the parking lot, and then jumped up and ran.

Bruised and bleeding, Meadow managed to get to her feet and pull her service revolver. "FBI! Stop or I'll shoot!"

"You couldn't hit a barn from the inside!" came the sarcastic reply from the running man.

"I'll show . . . you!" As she spoke, she stepped back onto a big rock, her feet went out from under her, and the gun discharged right into the windshield of the SUV she and the special agent arrived in.

The criminal was long gone by the time Meadow was recovering from the fall.

"Did you get him?" the other agent panted as he joined her. He frowned. "What the hell happened to you?"

"He fell over me and pushed my face into the asphalt," she muttered, feeling the blood on her nose. "I ordered him to halt and tried to fire when I tripped over a rock . . ."

The other agent's face told a story that he was too kind to voice.

She swallowed, hard. "Sorry about the windshield," she added.

He glanced at the Bureau SUV and shook his head. "Maybe we could tell them it was a vulture. You know, they sometimes fly into car windshields."

"No," she replied grimly. "It's always better to tell them the truth. Even when it's painful."

"Guess you're right." He grimaced. "Sorry."

"Hey. We all have talents. I think mine is to trip over my own feet at any given dangerous moment."

"The SAC is going to be upset," he remarked.

"I don't doubt it," she replied.

In fact, the Special Agent in Charge was eloquent about her failure to secure the fugitive. He also wondered aloud, rhetorically, how any firearms instructor ever got drunk enough to pass her in the academy. She kept quiet, figuring that anything she said would only make matters worse.

He didn't take her badge. He did, however, assign her as an aide to another agent who was redoing files in the basement of the building. It was clerical work, for which she wasn't even trained. And from that point, her career as an FBI agent started going drastically downhill.

She'd always had problems with balance. She thought that her training would help her compensate for it, but she'd been wrong. She seemed to be a complete failure as an FBI agent. Her superior obviously thought so.

He did give her a second chance, months later. He sent her to interrogate a man who'd confessed to kidnapping an underage girl for immoral purposes. Meadow's questions, which she'd formulated beforehand, irritated him to the point of physical violence. He'd attacked Meadow, who was totally unprepared for what amounted to a beating. She'd fought, and screamed, to no avail. It had taken a jailer to extricate the man's hands from her throat. Of course, that added another charge to the bevy he was already facing: assault on a federal officer.

But Meadow reacted very badly to the incident. It had never occurred to her that a perpetrator might attack her physically. She'd learned to shoot a gun, she'd learned self-defense, hand-to-hand, all the ways in the world to protect herself. But when she'd come up against an unarmed but violent criminal, she'd almost been killed. Her training wasn't enough. She'd felt such fear that she couldn't function. That had been the beginning of the end. Both she and the Bureau had decided that she was in the wrong profession. They'd been very nice about it, but she'd lost her job.

And Dal Blake thought she was a manly woman, a real hell-raiser. It was funny. She was the exact opposite. Half the time she couldn't even remember to do up the buttons on her coat right.

She sighed as she thought about Dal. She'd had a crush on him in high school. He was almost ten years older than she was and considered her a child. Her one attempt to catch his eye had ended in disaster . . .

She'd come to visit her father during Christmas holidays—much against her mother's wishes. It was her senior year of high school. She'd graduate in the spring. She knew that she was too young to appeal to a man Dal's age, but she was infatuated with him, fascinated by him.

He came by to see her father often because they were

both active members in the local cattlemen's association. So one night when she knew he was coming over, Meadow dressed to the hilt in her Sunday best. It was a low-cut red sheath dress, very Christmassy and festive. It had long sleeves and side slits. It was much too old for Meadow, but her father loved her, so he let her pick it out and he paid for it.

Meadow walked into the room while Dal and her father were talking and sat down in a chair nearby, with a book in her hands. She tried to look sexy and appealing. She had on too much makeup, but she hadn't noticed that. The magazines all said that makeup emphasized your best features. Meadow didn't have many best features. Her straight nose and bow mouth were sort of appealing, and she had pretty light green eyes. She used masses of eyeliner and mascara and way too much rouge. Her best feature was her long, thick, beautiful blond hair. She wore it down that night.

Her father gave her a pleading look, which she ignored. She smiled at Dal with what she hoped was sophistication.

He gave her a dark-eyed glare.

The expression on his face washed away all her self-confidence. She flushed and pretended to read her book, but she was shaky inside. He didn't look interested. In fact, he looked very repulsed.

When her father went out of the room to get some paperwork he wanted to show to Dal, Meadow forced herself to look at him and smile.

"It's almost Christmas," she began, trying to find a subject for conversation.

He didn't reply. He did get to his feet and come toward her. That flustered her even more. She fumbled with the book and dropped it on the floor.

Dal pulled her up out of the chair and took her by the shoulders firmly. "I'm ten years older than you," he said bluntly. "You're a high school kid. I don't rob cradles and I don't appreciate attempts to seduce me in your father's living room. Got that?"

Her breath caught. "I never . . . !" she stammered.

His chiseled mouth curled expressively as he looked down into her shocked face. "You're painted up like a carnival fortune-teller. Too much makeup entirely. Does your mother know you wear clothes like that and come on to men?" he added icily. "I thought she was religious."

"She . . . is," Meadow stammered, and felt her age. Too young. She was too young. Her eyes fell away from his. "So am I. I'm sorry."

"You should be," he returned. His strong fingers contracted on her shoulders. "When do you leave for home?"

"Next Friday," she managed to say. She was dying inside. She'd never been so embarrassed in her life.

"Good. You get on the plane and don't come back. Your father has enough problems without trying to keep you out of trouble. And next time I come over here, I don't want to find you setting up shop in the living room, like a spider hunting flies."

"You're a very big fly," she blurted out, and flushed some more.

His lip curled. "You're out of your league, kid." He let go of her shoulders and moved her away from him, as if she had something contagious. His eyes went to the low-cut neckline. "If you went out on the street like that, in Raven Springs, you'd get offers."

She frowned. "Offers?"

"Prostitutes mostly do get offers," he said with distaste.

Tears threatened, but she pulled herself up to her maximum height, far short of his, and glared up at him. "I am not a prostitute!"

"Sorry. Prostitute in training?" he added thoughtfully.

She wanted to hit him. She'd never wanted anything so much. In fact, she raised her hand to slap that arrogant look off his face.

He caught her arm and pushed her hand away.

Even then, at that young age, her balance hadn't been what it should be. Her father had a big, elegant stove in the living room to heat the house. It used coal instead of wood, and it was very efficient behind its tight glass casing. There was a coal bin right next to it.

Meadow lost her balance and went down right into the coal bin. Coal spilled out onto the wood floor and all over her. Now there were black splotches all over her pretty red dress, not to mention her face and hair and hands.

She sat up in the middle of the mess, and angry tears ran down her soot-covered cheeks as she glared at Dal.

He was laughing so hard that he was almost doubled over.

"That's right, laugh," she muttered. "Santa's going to stop by here on his way to your house to get enough coal to fill up your stocking, Dariell Blake!"

He laughed even harder.

Her father came back into the room with a file folder in one hand, stopped, did a double take, and stared at his daughter, sitting on the floor in a pile of coal.

"What the hell happened to you?" he burst out.

"He happened to me!" she cried, pointing at Dal Blake. "He said I looked like a streetwalker!"

"You're the one in the tight red dress, honey." Dal chuckled. "I just made an observation."

"Your mother would have a fit if she saw you in that

dress," her father said heavily. "I should never have let you talk me into buying it."

"Well, it doesn't matter anymore, it's ruined!" She got to her feet, swiping at tears in her eyes. "I'm going to bed!"

"Might as well," Dal remarked, shoving his hands into his jeans pockets and looking at her with an arrogant smile. "Go flirt with men your own age, kid."

She looked to her father for aid, but he just stared at her and sighed.

She scrambled to her feet, displacing more coal. "I'll get this swept up before I go to bed," she said.

"I'll do that. Get yourself cleaned up, Meda," her father said gently, using his pet name for her. "Go on."

She left the room muttering. She didn't even look at Dal Blake.

That had been several years ago, before she worked in law enforcement in Missouri and finally hooked up with the FBI. Now she was without a job, running a ranch about which she knew absolutely nothing, and whole families who depended on the ranch for a living were depending on her. The responsibility was tremendous.

She honestly didn't know what she was going to do. She did watch a couple of YouTube videos, but they were less than helpful. Most of them were self-portraits of small ranchers and their methods of dealing with livestock. It was interesting, but they assumed that their audience knew something about ranching. Meadow didn't.

She started to call the local cattlemen's association for help, until someone told her who the president of the chapter was. Dal Blake. Why hadn't she guessed?

While she was drowning in self-doubt, there was a

knock on the front door. She opened it to find a handsome man, dark-eyed, with thick blond hair, standing on her porch. He was wearing a sheriff's uniform, complete with badge.

"Miss Dawson?" he said politely.

She smiled. "Yes?"

"I'm Sheriff Jeff Ralston."

"Nice to meet you," she said. She shook hands with him. She liked his handshake. It was firm without being aggressive.

"Nice to meet you, too," he replied. He shifted his weight.

She realized that it was snowing again and he must be freezing. "Won't you come in?" she said as an afterthought, moving back.

"Thanks," he replied. He smiled. "Getting colder out here."

She laughed. "I don't mind snow."

"You will when you're losing cattle to it," he said with a sigh as he followed her into the small kitchen, where she motioned him into a chair.

"I don't know much about cattle," she confessed. "Coffee?"

"I'd love a cup," he said heavily. "I had to get out of bed before daylight and check out a robbery at a local home. Someone came in through the window and took off with a valuable antique lamp."

She frowned. "Just the lamp?"

He nodded. "Odd robbery, that. Usually the perps carry off anything they can get their hands on."

"I know." She smiled sheepishly. "I was with the FBI for two years."

"I heard about that. In fact," he added while she started coffee brewing, "that's why I'm here."

"You need help with the robbery investigation?" she asked, pulling two mugs out of the cabinet.

"I need help, period," he replied. "My investigator just quit to go live in California with his new wife. She's from there. Left me shorthanded. We're on a tight budget, like most small law enforcement agencies. I only have the one investigator. Had, that is." He eyed her. "I thought you might be interested in the job," he added with a warm smile.

She almost dropped the mugs. "Me?"

"Yes. Your father said you had experience in law enforcement before you went with the Bureau and that you were noted for your investigative abilities."

"Noted wasn't quite the word they used," she said, remembering the rage her boss had unleashed when she blew the interrogation of a witness. That also brought back memories of the brutality the man had used against her in the physical attack. To be fair to her boss, he didn't know the prisoner had attacked her until after he'd read her the riot act. He'd apologized handsomely, but the damage was already done.

"Well, the FBI has its own way of doing things. So do I." He accepted the hot mug of coffee with a smile. "Thanks. I live on black coffee."

She laughed, sitting down at the table with him to put cream and sugar in her own. She noticed that he took his straight up. He had nice hands. Very masculine and strong-looking. No wedding band. No telltale tan line where one had been, either. She guessed that he'd never been married, but it was too personal a question to ask a relative stranger.

"I need an investigator and you're out of work. What do you say?"

She thought about the possibilities. She smiled. Here it

was, like fate, a chance to prove to the world that she could be a good investigator. It was like the answer to a prayer.

She grinned. "I'll take it, and thank you."

He let out the breath he'd been holding. "No. Thank you. I can't handle the load alone. When can you start?"

"It's Friday. How about first thing Monday morning?" she asked.

"That would be fine. I'll put you on the day shift to begin. You'll need to report to my office by seven a.m. Too early?"

"Oh, no. I'm usually in bed by eight and up by five in the morning."

His eyebrows raised.

"It's my dog," she sighed. "She sleeps on the bed with me, and she wakes up at five. She wants to eat and play. So I can't go back to sleep or she'll eat the carpet."

He laughed. "What breed is she?"

"She's a white Siberian husky with red highlights. Beautiful."

"Where is she?"

She caught her breath as she realized that she'd let Snow out to go to the bathroom an hour earlier, and she hadn't scratched at the door. "Oh, dear," she muttered as she realized where the dog was likely to be.

Along with that thought came a very angry knock at the back door, near where she was sitting with the sheriff.

Apprehensively, she got up and opened the door. And there he was. Dal Blake, with Snow on a makeshift lead. He wasn't smiling.

"Your dog invited herself to breakfast. Again. She came right into my damned house through the dog door!"

She knew that Dal didn't have a dog anymore. His old Labrador had died a few weeks ago, her foreman had told her, and the man had mourned the old dog. He'd had it for almost fourteen years, he'd added.

"I'm sorry," Meadow said with a grimace. "Snow. Bad girl!" she muttered.

The husky with her laughing blue eyes came bounding over to her mistress and started licking her.

"Stop that." Meadow laughed, fending her off. "How about a treat, Snow?"

She went to get one from the cupboard.

"Hey, Jeff," Dal greeted the other man, shaking hands as Jeff got to his feet.

"How's it going?" Jeff asked Dal.

"Slow," came the reply. "We're renovating the calving sheds. It's slow work in this weather."

"Tell me about it," Jeff said. "We had two fences go down. Cows broke through and started down the highway."

"Maybe there was a dress sale," Dal said, tongue-in-cheek as he watched a flustered Meadow give a chewy treat to her dog.

"I'd love to see a cow wearing a dress," she muttered.

"Would you?" Dal replied. "One of your men thinks that's your ultimate aim, to put cows in school and teach them to read."

"Which man?" she asked, her eyes flashing fire at him.

"Oh, no, I'm not telling," Dal returned. "You get on some boots and jeans and go find out for yourself. If you can ride a horse, that is."

That brought back another sad memory. She'd gone riding on one of her father's feistier horses, confident that she could control it. She was in her second year of college, bristling with confidence as she breezed through her core curriculum.

She thought she could handle the horse. But it sensed

her fear of heights and speed and took her on a racing tour up the side of a small mountain and down again so quickly that Meadow lost her balance and ended up face-first in a snowbank.

To add to her humiliation—because the stupid horse went running back to the barn, probably laughing all the way—Dal Blake was helping move cattle on his own ranch, and he saw the whole thing.

He came trotting up just as she was wiping the last of the snow from her face and parka. "You know, Spirit isn't a great choice of horses for an inexperienced rider."

"My father told me that," she muttered.

"Pity you didn't listen. And lucky that you ended up in a snowbank instead of down a ravine," he said solemnly. "If you can't control a horse, don't ride him."

"Thanks for the helpful advice," she returned icily.

"City tenderfoot," he mused. "I'm amazed that you haven't killed yourself already. I hear your father had to put a rail on the back steps after you fell down them."

She flushed. "I tripped over his cat."

"You could benefit from some martial arts training."

"I've already had that," she said. "I work for my local police department."

"As what?" he asked politely.

"As a patrol officer!" she shot back.

"Well," he remarked, turning his horse, "if you drive a car like you ride a horse, you're going to end badly one day."

"I can drive!" she shot after him. "I drive all the time!"

"God help other motorists."

"You . . . you . . . you . . . !" She gathered steam with each repetition of the word until she was almost screaming, and still she couldn't think of an insult bad enough to throw at him. It wouldn't have done any good. He kept riding. He didn't even look back.

She snapped back to the present. "Yes, I can ride a horse!" she shot at Dal Blake. "Just because I fell off once . . ."

"You fell off several times. This is mountainous country. If you go riding, carry a cell phone and make sure it's charged," he said seriously.

"I'd salaam, but I haven't had my second cup of coffee yet," she drawled, alluding to an old custom of subjects salaaming royalty.

"You heard me."

"You don't give orders to me in my own house," she returned hotly.

Jeff cleared his throat.

They both looked at him.

"I have to get back to work," he said as he pushed his chair back in. "Thanks for the coffee, Meadow. I'll expect you early Monday morning."

"Expect her?" Dal asked.

"She's coming to work for me as my new investigator," Jeff said with a bland smile.

Dal's dark eyes narrowed. He saw through the man, whom he'd known since grammar school. Jeff was a good sheriff, but he wanted to add to his ranch. He owned property that adjoined Meadow's. So did Dal. That acreage had abundant water, and right now water was the most important asset any rancher had. Meadow was obviously out of her depth trying to run a ranch. Her best bet was to sell it, so Jeff was getting in on the ground floor by offering her a job that would keep her close to him.

He saw all that, but he just smiled. “Good luck,” he told Jeff, with a dry glance at a fuming Meadow. “You’ll need it.”

“She’ll do fine,” Jeff said confidently.

Dal just smiled.

Meadow remembered that smile from years past. She’d had so many accidents when she was visiting her father. Dal was always somewhere nearby when they happened.

He didn’t like Meadow. He’d made his distaste for her apparent on every possible occasion. There had been a Christmas party thrown by the local cattlemen’s association when Meadow first started college. She’d come to spend Christmas with her father, and when he asked her to go to the party with him, she agreed.

She knew Dal would be there. So she wore an outrageous dress, even more revealing than the one he’d been so disparaging about when she was a senior in high school.

Sadly, the dress caught the wrong pair of eyes. A local cattleman who’d had five drinks too many had propositioned Meadow by the punch bowl. His reaction to her dress had flustered her and she tripped over her high-heeled shoes and knocked the punch bowl over.

The linen tablecloth was soaked. So was poor Meadow, in her outrageous dress. Dal Blake had laughed until his face turned red. So had most other people. Meadow had asked her father to drive her home. It was the last Christmas party she ever attended in Raven Springs.

But just before the punch bowl incident, there had been another. Dal had been caught with her under the mistletoe . . .

She shook herself mentally and glared at Dal.